A STRAWBERRY SPRINGS NOVEL

AS THEY ARE

ELLE RIVERS

This book is a work of fiction. Any similarities to real individuals are purely coincidental. All events are from the author's imagination and are not to be taken as realistic.

Cover Design by Summer Grove

Developmental editing by Mae Peredo, Wildwood Author Services

Copyediting by Kasey Kubica, Basic Behemoth Edits

Proofreading by Mae Peredo, Wildwood Author Services

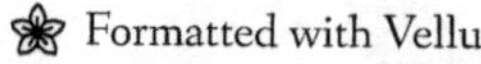 Formatted with Vellum

A NOTE FROM ELLE

As They Are contains mature and potentially triggering content that some people might find upsetting. Please be advised that the following content can be found on-page unless otherwise noted.

- Emotional/verbal abuse
- Explicit, open-door sexual content
- Parental Abandonment
- Pregnancy of a side character
- References to cheating in fake relationships (not between the main characters)

None of the harmful behavior is committed by the main characters. Please take care of yourself and your mental health while reading any novel.

PLAYLIST

Chasing Pavements—Adele
Happier Than Ever – edit—Billie Eilish
I Look in People's Windows—Taylor Swift
The Prophecy—Taylor Swift
Secrets—OneRepublic
Counting Stars—OneRepublic
New Rules—Dua Lipa
Cruel Summer—Taylor Swift
Bed Chem—Sabrina Carpenter
Lose Control—Teddy Swims
Part of Me—Katy Perry
Watermelon Sugar—Harry Styles
Feels Like—Gracie Abrams
Riptide—Vance Joy
Adore You—Harry Styles

STRAWBERRY SPRINGS COMMUNITY GUIDE

Jackie Anne Tyler—Owner of Hair Haven salon
Kerry Winsor—Stay-at-home mom, resident gossip
Nicole Rudder—Teacher at Strawberry Springs Elementary School
Cain Smith—Farm Manager at Bennie Grove Farm
Tammy Jane and Ron*—Married owners of Center Point Diner
Hugh Jeffries—Retiree, resident grump
Marjorie and Henrietta Brown—Married retirees
Dr. Atticus Thompson, DVM—Veterinarian
Jade Clark—Owner of Jade's Goodies gift shop
Grace Day—Owner of Treasure Trove clothing store
Dale Garrett—Owner of Food 'n' Things grocery store
Mike Finch—Sheriff of Strawberry Springs
Dr. Henry Connor, MD—Clinic doctor
Mark Bell—Owner of Bell's Brews bar
Theo Murf—Town handyman
Brooke Day—Aspiring singer
Mollie Wilson—Owner of Bennie Grove Farm

*Tammy and Ron have not consented to the inclusion of their last name in this guide at this time.

WREN

Fifteen Years Ago

THE WORST SOUND in the whole world was that of a crying four-year-old. Or maybe it was just Ginnie's cries.

When she fell onto the concrete walkway next to the playground, Mom rushed over and doted on her, checking on every inch of her skin.

The scars on my knees panged. Years ago, she'd told me falling was no big deal.

I was playing chase with Ginnie, even though Mom had just been ordering me to slow down. My half sister had fallen before Mom finished her sentence. I immediately knew I was in trouble.

I'd been getting in trouble the second I'd arrived two weeks ago to stay for summer. Dad was out of state working on a new apartment complex, and it was either I come to stay with Mom or I be in our tiny trailer by myself.

As Ginnie's cries turned into soft whimpers, I started to think that being by myself would have been better.

"Say you're sorry," Mom said as she looked up at me.

"I'm sorry," I replied. "I was about to slow down."

"You're way too big to play with her like that."

"But she wanted to—"

"I don't care! You're the older sister here. Be responsible. She's fragile."

Ginnie whimpered once more, burrowing into Mom. My eyes narrowed. She'd bugged me all day, begging me to play with her. She'd suggested chasing and nagged at me until I'd obliged.

I felt bad that she fell, but I hated that I was the bad guy in the situation—the one who should always know better. Was I not allowed to have lapses in judgment? To make mistakes?

Apparently not.

Mom told me I needed to be nice to Ginnie all summer. I was trying my best to, even if I had to fight with the annoyance that she had *everything*.

"Do you want me to go get some Band-Aids?" I asked.

"Go find something else to do. She needs to be away from you."

"But—"

"Go," Mom said before turning back to Ginnie.

I bit my tongue and walked away. In the hot summer sun, the only place that was bearable was under the playground.

It was an old wooden structure that had seen better days. Most kids didn't go on it. I'd heard parents telling their kids to play in the field instead. Underneath it was a touch cooler than out in the sun, and I found a support plank to sit on and stay out of the way until Mom remembered I existed.

I plopped down as my irritation rose.

The plank fell out from under me.

I yelped as I dropped straight onto my back. My head hit the ground, aggravating the building headache in my temples.

Now my shame made my face impossibly hotter. Was I too

big for the playground? The summer before my freshman year had given me an unwanted growth spurt. I towered over most kids my age and a few of my old classmates had whispered about it behind my back, calling me a giraffe, or whatever other animal they could compare me to.

"You better not be getting in trouble over there!" Mom called.

"I—"

"I don't wanna hear it, Wren!"

My back ached. Now *I* was hurt.

And she didn't care. *At all.*

"Fuck this shit," I said under my breath, not caring if Mom heard me curse. She was too busy to do anything anyway.

I sprang up and glared at the piece of wood. One of the nails had failed, leaving it dangling. I grabbed it and yanked it out of its spot before looking at the other ones. They were *all* hanging on by their last nails, all ready to break on someone.

This was supposed to be a nice neighborhood. Mom always wanted the fanciest of things. And her new, perfect husband could provide it. Obviously, it wasn't *that* perfect if the playground was falling apart.

If one broke, more would too. I grabbed another board with both hands, pulling it with all of my might. It came loose, and the feeling pushed away my anger for a second.

In fact, it felt *good*.

I moved to another and did the same thing. It put up more of a fight, but I didn't mind. Taking it apart distracted me.

When I was done, there was a stack of boards. Nails stuck out at odd angles and I had more splinters than I could count. My chest heaved, but I felt like I was finally doing exactly what I was supposed to be.

"Wren Harper Hackett!" Mom screeched. "What do you think you're doing?"

My tenseness returned.

Suddenly, the pile of destruction was another one of my mistakes.

"I . . . It was broken!"

"Yes, because *you* broke it! Why would you ever—"

"I fell!"

"That doesn't mean you can ruin my neighborhood playground! What's *wrong* with you?"

She'd asked that before too. More so than ever since I came to stay with her.

"I'm sorry."

"Sorry doesn't cut it. I'm calling your father so he can deal with this."

She never called Dad unless I'd done something wrong. He'd begged me to make this work with Mom. I told him I would.

"No, wait! I can fix it."

"Oh, really? You can fix all of this?"

I looked back at it. Dad had let me watch him when he fixed our old porch. I'd been fascinated by how he was able to hit a nail and make it go clean through the wood in one go.

"Yeah, I can."

"You have until the end of the day," she said as she hoisted Ginnie on her hip. "Go see if one of the neighbors has a hammer and some nails."

"I don't know anyone here."

She rolled her eyes. "Then knock on doors."

"Don't you have—"

"I'm busy with Ginnie. I'm not fixing *your* problems too." She turned and walked away, leaving me in the heat. I wondered if she would use her soft voice while dressing Ginnie's wounds and give her the apple juice that she never gave me when I was her age.

It made me feel worse. I took a walk of shame on the hot sidewalk, knocking on two doors with no answer.

I was going to give up after the third one, but then a girl with brown hair answered. She was shorter than me, coming up to my collarbone like most kids my age did.

"Uh, hi. Do you have any hammers or nails?"

"Me? I don't." She shook her head. "But I think my papa gave us some to use a while ago. They're in the garage. Why do you need them?"

"The playground is busted and I need to fix it."

She perked up. "Finally someone's taking it seriously! I've been saying that it needs work, but the HOA always tells my mom it's fine."

I had a feeling she wouldn't be very thrilled if she knew *I* broke it. "So, can I borrow the stuff to fix it?"

She nodded and led me to the garage. She grabbed nails, a hammer, and a saw.

"I don't know if you'll need this," she said as she handed it to me. "But the wood is so old, I figured it would help."

The girl was right. Even if I used new nails, the wood was gray with age and sagging.

"Do you know anyone who has the wood for it?"

She nodded, rocking onto the balls of her feet. "My neighbor two doors down does woodworking for fun! Come with me."

She ran out the front door. I followed her, but she was already halfway across the street. She was *fast*.

"Wait!" I called out after her. "I can do it by myself!"

"You said you had to fix it!" she answered. "And I wanna help!"

"But we don't even know each other!"

She stopped, lips pursed as she considered it. "You're right." She jogged back over to me. "I'm Mollie. What's your name?"

"Wren."

"Cool. Now we know each other."

I jerked back. Was it that simple?

To Mollie it was. She was back on her mission of going to the neighbor's house.

If anyone questioned why a fourteen-year-old girl needed wood and a saw, they didn't say anything. I had a feeling it was because they didn't think I was young at all.

Soon, we were back at the playground, everything spread out on the ground.

I followed what Dad did when he worked on things. I measured the wood twice, cut it slowly, and then nailed it in place. Mollie watched it all with wide, hazel eyes and kept asking if she could help. I wasn't sure what to do with the attention.

With each swing of the hammer, I felt better. Mollie cheered me on, even when the first nail bent at a bad angle.

I finished as the sun set. I wiped sweat from my brow and let out a sigh of relief as I saw new wood mixed with the old.

"You are *so* cool," Mollie said. "I wanna be like you when I go to high school in a few weeks."

"You're about to be a freshman?" I asked. "Me too."

Mollie's jaw dropped and she gasped. "No way! Where are you going?"

Mom had told Dad to enroll me in a school near her. Not so she could watch me, but just so I could go to a school that was better than any of the ones in the outer city. She said that she was terrified I would ruin my life if I got a second-rate education.

I hadn't been excited about it until I said the name to Mollie. Her entire face lit up. "We'll be at the same school! Yes!"

My hand went to the back of my neck. "Um, I don't think

I'm as cool as you think I am." I gestured to the old boards. "I . . . kinda got in trouble for taking this thing apart myself. I broke it."

Mollie blinked. "You got *all* of those boards off with *just your hands?*"

"The first one broke when I sat on it, but the rest were because I was mad."

"Holy *shit*—I mean, wow! You're so strong."

"But I broke the playground that you love."

"Technically, time made it super weak. If it wasn't you, it could have been some little kid. Plus, you fixed it. Now it's as good as new."

I looked over at my work. "Yeah, maybe you're right."

"You're good at fixing things."

I slowly nodded, realizing that for the first time since I came to stay with Mom, I felt . . . okay. Like I wasn't miserable.

"Is there anything else that's broken?" I asked.

Mollie thought about it. "I think the tennis court net is messed up. Wanna go see?"

"Yeah, I do. Lead the way."

I followed Mollie and stayed out until way past sunset, trying to figure out how to fix the net. Mom didn't come and check on me until after nine when Ginnie was in bed.

"So, you fixed it." Her hands were on her hips. "At least I won't get fined for it."

"Did I do a good job?"

"It looks about like what a fourteen-year-old can do."

"Hi!" Mollie said. "Are you Wren's mom? I'm her friend."

"You're the Wilsons' daughter, aren't you?" Mom tapped her chin. "You're a good kid. Did she ask you for help?"

"No, she did it all and I watched."

Mom looked in between us as if sniffing out a lie. I twisted my hands. I let Mollie carry some stuff. Did that count?

"Anyway, you need to take your little friend home and clean up. Your dad is on his way."

"He's on his way? But you said you wouldn't call him if I fixed it."

"I can't have a destructive teenager near my daughter. You went way too far today, so I called him the second I was finished patching Ginnie up." She shook her head. "I hope you learned your lesson."

"But I—" I didn't get to reply. Mom turned and walked off without another word.

"Whoa, she's kinda mean." Mollie's voice was quiet.

"Yeah, a little. Sorry we won't get to hang out more."

"I'll find you at school, don't worry. We'll be besties there."

"Are you sure you wanna hang out with me?"

"Um, *duh*." She rolled her eyes. "I'm so nervous for my first day. But now I can go in and know I have a friend."

Despite everything, I smiled. Normally, I didn't believe someone when they made a promise, but I hoped that this time it was true.

"Me too." I looked down at my mess. "I should clean up, though."

"I'll help you!" she replied. "I know where it all goes anyway!"

Mollie carried half of the things we needed to give back, completely unfazed by the fact that she was covered in wood dust. I hugged her before saying goodbye and heading to Mom's.

When I returned to the house, Dad was waiting for me and silently opened the car door while Mom came out with my duffel bag.

"I told you this wouldn't work out," she said.

"I guess you did," he replied, not meeting her eyes. "What do I need to fix?"

"Nothing," I muttered. "I did it."

His thick eyebrows raised. "*You* did it?"

"Hopefully no one notices," Mom said, crossing her arms. "You need to watch her. She gets mad."

"Only because of you," I snapped.

Her eyes narrowed. "Don't you even start with me. I can't do anything right with you anyway." She threw her hands up in the air and walked off without saying goodbye.

"She's never like this with Ginnie," I muttered as I slammed the door.

"Ginnie's her perfect kid," Dad said.

"I'm sorry. I shouldn't have snapped. I wanted to fix it so she wouldn't call you."

"She's lookin' for a reason, Wren. Don't worry about it. You can call her in a few days after she cools off."

I stared out the window as we drove away, trying to think of what Mom wanted to hear when I called. Eventually, we passed by Mollie's house, and my gaze locked on it, even as we drove by.

At least I'd made a friend throughout all of this.

That was the only thing that made it easier when Mom didn't pick up when I called three days later.

HENRY

Strawberry Springs Neighborhood Watch

Hu Gh: I do NOT give Facebook permission to use my personal information. Everything we've ever posted becomes public tomorrow!!! Share to spread the word.

Comments:
Jade Clark: You can't really believe this will do anything, right?
Marjorie Brown: I've gotta hide my nudes!
Tammy Jane: Trust me, Marj. Those were taken down years ago for violating people's eyes.
Marjorie Brown: I was hot once!!!!

"Do you really have to go?" Mom's grip was tight on my shoulders as she pulled away from our hug.

My temples pounded and everything felt like I was being

repeatedly hit with a sledgehammer. "A patient called. I need to be back in Strawberry Springs as soon as possible."

That was a lie. While I could probably find something to do, what I truly needed was to be *home*. Since I'd visited this morning, I'd listened to Mom tell me her stories about her job as a nurse, ignoring the way her loud voice made me wince over time. She couldn't help it, especially since her hearing wasn't what it used to be, so I smiled and dealt with it, counting down the minutes until I could leave.

To her, I was her perfect, smart doctor that she was proud of. Though she didn't get why I chose small-town life over a higher-paying gig in the city, she loved me. And I loved her.

But she didn't *get* me. There was a look she would wear whenever I was overwhelmed. Her head would tilt to the side and she would frown. She'd never understood it and I didn't blame her. She was from a different time when traits like mine were hidden. Hell, I didn't understand it until I was an adult.

Sometimes, I was grateful for her lack of understanding, for the way she'd push me to be better. I'd learned how to pretend to be normal for everyone else.

At least for a while.

My battery was low, though. And I knew better than to tell her that her loud speech about Nurse Janice had sent me over the edge.

"Work calls. I understand." She pulled me into another hug, and my smile dropped for all of one second before she pulled away. "I'll call you soon."

"I look forward to it." And I did. At least on the phone, I could turn down the volume. The picturesque city street would be charming to some, but a siren a few roads over nearly sent me over the edge. It was always like that here. More people meant more noise. It was never quiet, even in a smaller city like this.

When I'd lived here, I found the little pockets of nature, hoping to find a quiet place.

Anywhere I'd found was temporary.

Thankfully, I was only a visitor. I was able to leave in the end, and once I had, my GPS couldn't count down to zero fast enough.

As noise gave way to silence, my exhaustion fully hit me. My dress shirt was too tight and the ambient sounds of the highway were grating. I didn't have the radio on, and not even my health and wellness podcast could pull me out of the mood I was in.

It didn't help that I had to drive past the house where I had once spent a lot of my free time. Ace's house hadn't changed much, even though he posted that he'd bought it from his parents. The car in the driveway belonged to his wife Norah. I knew that car because she had had it since high school, when *I* taught her how to drive it.

I'd been a different person then. I pushed myself more, desperate to keep up with all the things Ace did. I ignored it when things were too hectic and loud. And when I finally started to lose my cool and looked like a complete ass, it had pushed them away, toward each other.

With a sigh, I unbuttoned my shirt to give me room to breathe. The irritation I tried to hide waned. Silence continued on, feeling like a salve on my emotions as I got out of the city and returned home.

I checked the GPS some time later. I was twenty minutes out. Instead of buildings and other people surrounding me, there were fields of green. If not that, it was a tree-lined hillside. This was one of my favorite parts of the drive, where everyone else vanished and I was enveloped by the country.

It also meant I was close to home.

Then, in the distance, there was a red truck on the side of

the road. One of the tires was flat, and the owner was kneeling, staring at it.

I slowed immediately. Was I too tired for this? Yes. Did I know how to change a tire? No. But if there was one thing I'd learned about small-town life, it was that you offered whatever help you could give. And if it meant I Googled how to change a tire, then that was what I did.

I pulled over behind the truck, trying to think of who in town owned that kind of vehicle. Most people here still believed the myth that red cars got pulled over the most, even though the sheriff didn't even do traffic stops anymore unless there was a major infraction.

"Hey!" I called as I got out of my Honda. The sun was hot on my skin. Summer was going to be brutal this year. "Need some help?"

The person looked over at me and my heart stopped. This was *not* someone from Strawberry Springs.

The truck's owner was a woman with strawberry-blonde hair tied back into a ponytail that glistened in the sun. Her green eyes were framed with light lashes and a smattering of freckles painted her face.

She eyed me up and down, and I resisted the urge to run and hide. I always tried not to appear imposing to women, but I wasn't sure that was possible with her. She stood, and I realized she was almost my height. Maybe an inch or two shorter.

She was the prettiest woman I'd ever seen—I knew that without a shadow of a doubt. Though it was nearly impossible, the entire earth warmed up in her presence, and I was sure I was about to get burned if I stood too close to her.

"You from around here?"

Even her voice was incredible. Melodic.

"Y-yeah."

She looked at her tire and at me. "I guess I got one heck of a welcome. I don't think I'm lucky enough for this tiny town to have a tire shop."

"Unfortunately, no. But there are a few people who can fix it if you ask nicely."

She huffed out a laugh. "I'm not the biggest fan of asking for help. I've got this." She walked around to the back of her truck and pulled down the tailgate. She cranked something, sending a spare down for her to grab.

"You know how to change a tire." I said it like a fact.

She hummed. "It's one of the best things anyone can know. You never know when you'll need it. My dad taught me."

"Do you at least need a ride somewhere?"

She sighed. "The only place I need to go is my friend's house and then a tire shop. The spare'll work for the first thing, but the second is a little too far for friendly help from a stranger." Her hand ran over the treads of the flat tire before she leaned back down. "Found it. I must've hit a nail. That's ironic."

"Why's it ironic?"

She stood and lifted the spare tire onto her shoulder like it was nothing. "I work in construction. It's probably a miracle that I haven't had this happen before, but it gives me a chance to figure out how to plug a tire."

That was when I realized she was not only fucking gorgeous but also smart. Practical. Could fix all of her own problems.

And she was way, *way* out of my league.

In the time that I spent staring at her, she had loosened the lug nuts enough to get to the next step. She looked up at me from her crouched position.

"Need something?"

"Uh, no," I said. "I was just . . . Sorry. I just didn't want you to be alone while fixing this."

"I'm sure no one else will come by, but thanks."

It was a clear dismissal, even to me. I shifted on my feet. I wanted to stay to make sure she was able to get back on the road, but I also wanted more time to talk to her. A woman like her didn't show up in a town like this that often. I wondered if I would ever even see her again.

"Still. Moral support and all that."

She raised an eyebrow. "Are you sure you're not watching to see if I mess this up?"

My eyes widened. "What? Why would I do that?"

"I'm changing a tire. I'm a woman."

"Clearly you're a woman . . . I still don't understand what the implication is."

Her lips pursed and she got onto her stomach in order to position the portable jack under the truck. "It's not a typical job a woman does. And a lot of guys like to make sure it's done right or whatever."

Horror dawned on me. "N-no, absolutely not! You obviously know more than I do. I'm just here because . . ." I trailed off. If I were being honest, I didn't want to leave. But a woman who was alone changing a tire being watched by a man who didn't want to leave? Yeah, that didn't seem the best.

"Because what?" She got back onto her feet and removed all of the lug nuts with ease and finesse.

"We take care of people here," I finished. "It's pretty rude to leave someone stranded on the side of the road before making sure they can get somewhere. It's like driving off before the person gets into their house."

She paused to look up at me and then back down to the tire. "Been a while since I've been around people who do that."

I put my hands in my pockets to keep myself from fiddling with the sleeve of my shirt. "Let me be the first to say welcome."

She huffed out a laugh and pulled off the popped tire. "Thanks. Mind being useful and holding this?"

She rolled it to me. I grabbed it and held it still. "See? I have a use other than just standing here."

"You're right. I'm sorry I doubted you." She put the spare in place. It took her barely any time at all to get it on the truck. Then she lowered the vehicle.

The *muscles* on this woman. Construction had done a lot for her.

"I think I've got it now. Thanks for hanging out with me."

"Need to go far to see your friend?"

"Thankfully, no. I should be good now."

I wanted to ask where she was going, but she was already hopping in her truck before I could even open my mouth.

"Have a nice day!" I managed to say before she shut the door.

She peered out, hair glowing in the late afternoon sun. "My day was pretty bad, but it got better for just a little bit." Her eyes met mine and she smiled. "I appreciate you stopping, kind stranger. And being my bodyguard."

I was pretty sure my heart stopped at the sight alone, so I stood there like a fool and watched as she drove off.

I adjusted my glasses. That . . . could have gone better. I was usually so much better at socializing, but I was way too tired to get words right.

My mind still circled back to her as I pulled into town. I could see her so clearly in my mind's eye, and I wondered if I'd seen her somewhere before.

Finally, I pulled into my driveway. I lived near downtown Strawberry Springs in a two-story home with a decent-sized backyard, only a few streets away from the square. It was nothing compared to some of the land the other people in town owned, but it was close enough to the clinic that I could walk on nice days, and had enough land for me to enjoy one of my favorite pastimes.

The city center here was nothing like I was used to. There were hardly ever visitors, save for the farmers market when it came through on Saturdays, and usually, people took the direct route in. There were hardly any sirens and most of the residents respected each other enough not to rev engines or be loud while on the streets. The longer I stayed, the more I loved it.

The spring air was warm. I'd enjoyed it more than usual since Bennie Grove Farm had opened back up. I still had frozen strawberries from Mollie that I could use in smoothies. I always liked to grow plants, but seeing her work pay off made me want to plant even more.

My thing was with flowers, though. Ever since I bought my house, I'd added more and more to my yard. I loved to find the meaning of each bloom. When I first moved here, I'd go for a plant that corresponded with some other part of my life. I'd gotten white lilies to symbolize new beginnings, potted lavender for serenity, and bluebells after I made a mistake at the office for humility. Over the years, I'd gotten more that didn't have a connection to my life, though I knew each and every one of their meanings.

No matter how tired I was, checking in on all of my plants was a part of my routine. I eyed the few remaining tulips, and then went to the back to ensure there were no weeds in the other plants. I had already gone to a greenhouse out of town to get everything I needed, and all I had to do was wait for them to fully bloom.

I loved taking care of things. So much so that it had even expanded to the rest of the town. The pots and the fairy lights were my work, and it kept me busy.

After I made sure everything was in order, I took off my shoes at the door and checked on the seedlings I'd been bringing up. Then I showered, changed my clothes, and finally flopped on my bed.

Tomorrow, it would all start again when I woke up. I would make a smoothie, water the plants that needed it, and go into the office to keep the people in town healthy. Everything was exactly as I expected. Nothing more. Nothing less.

It was a comfort zone, one that I held on to tighter than anything else.

The last bit of tension left my body as I took a deep breath.

Being alone might have been boring at the end of the day, but it made sure that everything went exactly as expected.

And if I wanted to be the kind doctor who everyone knew, who everyone *liked*, it needed to stay that way.

RWL Superfan Discussion Central

Carly Ware: Season two is INCOMING! Where do you think Wren and Jude will go next?

Comments:

Jamie McCullough: There's the old school! Ooh, or the prison?

Neve Bullock: Why would she renovate a prison?

Jamie McCullough: She could make it a community center!

Neve Bullock: I'm all for reusing spaces, but that one should be left alone.

Jamie McCollough: As the person who called Wren and Jude before the show even started, I can tell you that I see what others don't.

Neve Bullock: They were obvious from the START.

Kerry Winsor: I know someone who knows Wren! I should ask if she knows anything!!!

"Wow," I muttered to myself as I pulled into the gravel driveway. I wasn't sure what I expected, but most of my day had been *unexpected*. From the second I woke up, I knew I needed to get away. Then my tire blew and I was sure I'd made the wrong choice. Then a cute stranger stopped and kept me company while I put the spare on my truck.

I was sure the small-town charm was only a thing in Hallmark movies.

Maybe I was wrong.

But then Mollie's new home was different from what I had pictured. She'd told me that it was massive, but I didn't expect . . . *this*.

The driveway had a newer-looking addition of a gravel parking lot. The farm was closed, but there were still a few strawberries out in the fields. The house sat farther back, standing tall with white siding and a beautiful porch.

I'd told Mollie to keep this place from the second I knew she'd inherited it, but it was even better in person. Like a dream come to life.

The air smelled sweet as I shut the door, a stark difference from the fresh wood I was used to and the slightly burnt brake smell my truck had given off when I changed the tire.

It was nice. The perfect place for me to find something to do.

As the season finished wrapping, I was only given a week off, but even that felt like too much. After the way things were left with Jude, I needed the distraction, and I figured Mollie's old farmhouse would need some help. If she would have me, that is.

I'd been bad about keeping up with her. As time went on and I grew busier and busier, our text chain had mostly been her telling me about the show and asking for updates about Jude.

I'd been having a hard time responding.

If she were mad, I would understand. I would have been if I were in her situation. Hell, I *had* been when she would go quiet while she was with her asshole ex, Trevor. I was so determined to keep her in my life, and I hated the man who had tried to take her from me.

Now, I'd fallen into bad habits. It was too easy to.

I took a deep breath before walking up to the door and knocking.

The man who opened it was my height, with brown hair and a hulking frame.

Hot farmer, my brain instantly said. When Mollie first met him, that was all I knew him as. Over time, she had started calling him by his name. *Cain*.

I missed the version of me who screamed over text with Mollie about this man. I was determined to get that version of me back.

"Uh, hi." His voice was uncertain. "You must be Wren."

"You know me?"

"Mollie makes me watch your TV show."

Had I become that famous? The thought made me nauseous. The show had been a fun way to do bigger projects, but now I realized it came with more strings than I could deal with. Strings like fame. And Jude.

"Right . . ." *Come on. Get it together.* This had been easier when it was a stranger on the side of the road. I'd probably never see that man again, even if I wanted to. But this was Mollie's boyfriend. She really liked him. I needed to try to be my usual self. "It's nice to meet you, by the way. Hopefully you're treating her right."

"I'm trying to."

Cain looked me over and I tensed. There was no way he could know I was off. I needed to get this in check before Mollie saw me.

"Hey, Mollie!" he called. "Come here a sec."

Never mind.

"Is it pie-tasting time?"

Mollie smiled when she saw me and the tightness in my chest loosened. She'd cut her hair. I'd only ever seen her with it longer, but it looked incredible. "Oh my *God*! You're here." She pulled me into a hug and I could have *cried*. She didn't hate me. "I was worried about you!"

"No need to be worried," I explained. "Just needed some time to get affairs in order."

Technically, I needed to get affairs in order now. I'd be going back to Nashville soon to film season two of *Renovating with Love*, immediately followed by a complete remodel of an old house, both of which would keep me away from my best friend for months on end. So, I was making time to catch up.

Mollie immediately narrowed her eyes. "You're sad."

Dammit. Curse my beautiful, kind, smart best friend.

"No, I'm not."

"Come on. I know you. What happened?"

"Nothing."

"Wren . . ."

"I'm done with filming," I said. "And that's what's important. I wanted to see the town you moved to and . . . get away for a bit."

"Get away from what?"

I thought of Jude. Of the cameras. Of the way my chest ached any time I thought of anything to do with *Renovating with Love*.

"Everything." My voice came out dark. Mollie raised an eyebrow, expecting me to elaborate.

But this had broken open a part of me I'd buried a long time ago. Something that no one, not even my best friend, knew about.

"Okay," Mollie said. "You're welcome to stay with us. Right, Cain?"

"Yep. I can get the guest room ready."

I gave them both a grateful smile and stepped inside. Cain disappeared up the stairs to get to the guest room, and I finally looked around. I'd been so focused on the two of them that I hadn't seen the house.

It was just as incredible inside as it was on the outside. The floors were old hardwood, stained in the original warm-toned yellow. The walls were blue and welcoming and coupled with original wood trim. It was a little outdated, but very homey. Just the way I liked to start with projects.

This part of the house was more than likely exactly how it was built. I could imagine what it would look like with some work.

"Wow. This is so spacious."

It would be even more so without a few of the walls.

"Thank you. I can't take credit for the furniture. That was all Papa Bennie's and Cain's doing."

My gaze traveled over the small couch and the different storage baskets. When I'd worked with Jude, he expected me to do all of the decorating. I wasn't sure why men either refused to look at design or chose the most industrial, soulless things, but it infuriated me.

As did even the thought of him.

"You're thinking pretty hard about something," Mollie said. "Wanna talk about it?"

"Is the kitchen this way?" I asked, walking toward the back of the house. I was greeted with an old tile floor. It was white and worn with age, as were the countertops, the tiles decorated with hand-painted leaves. That would definitely be staying. "Wow. All original. Both here and the living room."

"Yep. Just as Papa Bennie left it."

"You know, this has room to put in an island. And I bet butcher block would look great with the original tile." I could see it now. Modern comforts and space with the classics that Bennie left her. I could easily pull all-nighters to get it done.

But then I looked at Mollie, her arms crossed. "Aren't you supposed to be on a break?"

I blinked. "Yes, but that doesn't mean I can't help my best friend make the house of her dreams."

Her gaze was downright calculating. "But I *have* the house of my dreams."

"What? You don't wanna change anything?"

She shook her head.

"Seriously?"

"I know it's not perfect, but I can't think of a single thing I'd change. This place is how he left it. And while it might not be magazine perfect, it feels like home. Isn't that the most important thing?"

I blinked. I'd known she loved this place and wouldn't want to change much, but surely there had to be something I could do. When I walked in, I'd seen a bunch of things I would have done if it were mine.

But it wasn't mine. It was Mollie's. Of course she'd want to keep the inside exactly as it was.

"Are you sure there's *nothing*? Not even outside? What about a fence? A new house for the animals?" I'd never tried anything like that before. I bet it would be a ton of work.

Exactly what I wanted.

"Wren." Her voice was gentle. "You just got done renovating a whole *mansion*. Relax and take your break. You'll need it for when you work on season two."

"But—"

"Cain and I have a good handle on the farm. You need to take your break."

Fuck. If she didn't have anything for me to fix, then I'd have to do what I was *supposed* to be doing.

The director, Madison, had told me to use my break to find a new place to renovate in Nashville for the upcoming season. We'd found a few options, but none were bigger and better than the mansion we'd just finished. When time kept passing without us deciding on something, she'd grown more and more annoyed. Now she wanted all hands on deck to get this figured out. Even I had to chip in, despite everyone knowing I needed this week off. So I came here anyway. It was petty, but the slight rebellion after letting her tell me what to do felt nice.

And what felt nice was catching up with Mollie and finding something to swing a hammer at.

"I'll try to relax," I said. "But you know me."

"You love working," she replied. "But you have a second season that'll be keeping you busy soon, right?"

Too soon.

"*That* can wait."

"Really? They're waiting? It's so popular, even here. I bet half of the town has seen it by now, and they started it before I told them I knew you."

My stomach rolled again. Seriously? Half the town knew me as Wren from *Renovating with Love?* Fuck. They'd see me as the Wren who was with Jude. The one who flirted so hard it nearly killed her.

And who was I now? Just Wren. Just a woman looking for something to fix.

"Wren, what happened on the show?" Mollie asked. "Was it not what you expected?"

"The show was great," I said. "And I loved where the mansion ended up."

"But?"

"There's no but. It was just great."

Mollie squinted at me. She knew I was hiding something, and I wouldn't blame her for being mad at me for keeping it from her.

I couldn't talk about it. At least not when I had to go back in a week and do it all over again.

"Fine," she said. "I get what it's like to have some bad things happen. Things you're not ready to talk about."

"Do you mean Trevor?"

"Yes," she said. "And, you know, it took a while for me to open up about it. And it wasn't easy, but when I did, I felt so much better."

"Really?"

"Yeah," she said. "It was kinda like magic."

"Guest room's ready!" a voice called, and both of us turned to see a short kid with dark hair and wide eyes.

"Hey, Eric. Meet my friend, Wren."

Eric waved so hard that he almost fell over.

This was a very cute kid. But I had no idea why he was here.

"Oh!" Mollie said. "Did I tell you Cain was a dad?"

"You did not," I said, turning back to Eric. "It's nice to meet you."

I thanked every god that my voice sounded somewhat normal. Because inside, I felt like melting into a puddle on the floor. I'd played off how much I'd missed Mollie, but the fact that she had been living with a *kid* this whole time and I didn't know? Yeah, it stung.

I wasn't angry with her. She couldn't help that she'd had the adventure of a lifetime, that she'd gone out on a limb and found love and family out here. I'd never ask her to hold off for me to be free.

But I *missed* it. I missed all of this for a show that I wasn't even thrilled with. For the opportunity that tried to break me.

"Are you okay?" Eric asked, tilting his head to the side.

Oh God. The *kid* noticed I was sad? Fuck. I had to get it together.

"Just a little tired." I laughed and shook my head. "But once I'm over it, I have to get to know you."

"I'm sorry," Mollie said. "I should have mentioned it in my texts."

"No, don't be. You had a lot going on."

"We both did. And trust me, you'll know *everything* that happened here."

Sure, I'd know. But I didn't get to see it.

"Eric, did you tell Wren what I told you to?" Cain asked.

"Yes," Eric said. "We were all having a moment."

Cain walked into the room, took one look at me, and raised his hands innocently. "Sorry. Didn't mean to interrupt."

"You're being way more considerate of her than you were me." Mollie crossed her arms. *"Rude."*

"I'm trying this new thing where I don't look like an a—" He stopped. "Butt."

Eric snickered.

"That was you that almost let a curse word slip this time," Mollie said.

"You're a bad influence."

"I'm a *great* influence. What about when I taught Eric how to hold a ladder?"

"That's gonna be great until he climbs it and falls off a roof like you did."

"At least you rescued me."

I looked between them, jaw agape. Mollie had *never* been like this with Trevor. Here she was comfortable and happy.

And apparently fell off a roof.

I swallowed the cotton in my throat. "You guys will definitely have to tell me that story soon, but I think I need to go to bed."

"Okay!" Mollie said. "Take all the time you need."

Cain looked at the window, where sunlight was still streaming in, and then at me.

Mollie elbowed him.

"Yeah! Yep! You do that."

"It's still dayli—" Eric went to say, but both Mollie and Cain shushed him.

They were *so* cute. God, it was making things worse. I walked past them and up the stairs. I went to the only room with an open door. The room had a bed and a dresser. The walls were green and the lighting was low. I opened the closet to put my bags away and spotted a pile of scrapbooks on a shelf.

Pulling one down, a lot of them had Mollie as a kid, younger than even I knew her. I opened the rest of them, stopping when I got to a scrapbook that was brand new and hadn't been filled yet.

I didn't ever meet Papa Bennie, but I could feel his love even now. Mollie was incredibly lucky, even though he was gone.

Images of Mollie's smile at Cain, this new side of her that I'd been absent for, filled my mind, making my sadness even worse.

I squeezed my eyes shut. I needed to find something to do in my week off. I needed to catch up with Mollie. Then I needed to go back to Jude and the show.

But how did I do that when I didn't feel like myself?

HENRY

Strawberry Springs Neighborhood Watch

Tammy Jane: Watch out, folks! Raccoons spotted in the trash behind the diner.

Comments:
Kerry Winsor: Omg! We need some pest control!
Jackie Anne: Do we really? They're kinda cute. Like little trash pandas . . .
Hu Gh: I could take care of 'em. You'll never hear from them again!
Jackie Anne: NO.

THE SUN STREAMED through my curtains, waking me up before my alarm could go off. I blinked awake and slowly got up, heading to the bathroom to start my morning routine.

My messy hair and the shadow of a beard caught my attention in the mirror. I yawned and shook myself awake before styling my hair in its usual pushed-back position and shaving.

Doctor Henry stared back at me when I was done, and I felt far more prepared for the day.

The next step in my routine was to put on my dress shirt and slacks as well as a sweater, just in case it was cold in the clinic. Then I watered all of my plants, made a smoothie, and walked out the door.

It was a comfortable morning in Strawberry Springs, though the sun promised heat later in the day. I might regret walking when I left work this afternoon, but for now, I wanted to be outside to make sure my mood was good for the long day ahead.

I passed by Jade, who was out walking with earbuds in, and gave her a polite wave. Then I saw Hugh hobbling into Center Point Diner for breakfast. And I ran across Jackie, who was getting the salon ready for opening.

This was the kind of life I could deal with. It was quiet and peaceful, and everyone here knew me as the friendly doctor. And I *was* the friendly doctor. It was easy enough to be the best version of myself here.

I entered the clinic and was about to prep the water and coffee for the waiting room until I realized I was completely out. I usually bought in bulk to keep my purchases to a minimum, making this situation so rare that the unexpected deviation from my routine—especially after seeing Mom yesterday—hit me harder than usual. It shouldn't have been a big deal, but it felt like it.

After taping a note to the door, I walked to Dale's.

He was at the register talking with Marjorie as he scanned things for her.

"How mad was Henrietta this time?" he asked. Marjorie huffed out a laugh as I grabbed the largest bag of a generic coffee brand. Marjorie loved annoying people in the local Facebook group, but it also drove her wife, Henrietta, up the wall. She was always apologizing for Marjorie's comments; though if I were being honest, Marjorie was far less annoying than Hugh, who constantly put ridiculous things in the group. But he wasn't trolling. He was always very serious.

"The usual amount. I know we said we would relax when we retired, but I'm so *bored*." She let out a sigh. "At least the Neighborhood Watch is entertaining."

"You always give me a chuckle. Though, I think Kerry's one comment away from banning you."

"I know how to make a new profile. She can't keep me out for long."

I joined the line, coffee in hand, right as Marjorie finished. She turned around and her eyes met mine.

"Oh, hey, Doc."

"Hi," I replied. "Everything okay?"

"Right as rain," she said. "Staying active always helps. Just like you told me."

I nodded. "It's a good day for a walk."

"Hen has my phone again." She let out a sigh. "So, I might as well find something to do."

"Has reading not been enough?"

She shrugged. "Hard to read and not miss the days when I was surrounded by books."

"Understandable."

"This is why I read Facebook and ruin people's days. Though it might break my marriage." She sighed. "I'll figure something out. Thanks, Doc."

Marjorie walked off, and I turned to Dale, only to see him looking at someone else.

I followed his gaze to strawberry-blonde hair pulled together into braids.

It was *her*.

The coffee fell out of my hands, something I would usually never let happen, and I raced to catch it before it hit the ground. But now she was looking at *me*.

"It's you!" she said. "My bodyguard."

"Henry?" Dale laughed. "A bodyguard? Didn't know you had a job on the side."

My brain ground to a halt. I was used to constantly remembering how to be normal. Confident. Dr. Henry Connor. "I . . . uh, she's kidding. Of course."

"Not really." She crossed her arms. "You were so sweet about making sure no one bothered me while I had a tire issue. He could make it a full-time job."

"Unfortunately, I'm a little busy being the town doctor." I managed to get my thoughts back online and held out my hand. "Henry Connor. Nice to meet you."

"Wren Hackett." She gave me one hell of a handshake. My dad always said he could learn a lot of things about people from the way they shook.

"I'm Dale. Not that anyone asked."

Wren turned to him. "Sorry, nice to meet you too."

"You look familiar," he said, narrowing his eyes.

For a moment, Wren's mouth pressed into a thin line. "Do you know where the light bulbs are?"

"Third aisle on the right," I replied. She walked away with only a glance at Dale, and it finally hit me that maybe she didn't want to be recognized for some reason.

"Damn. Was I rude?" Dale asked. "I can't take being compared to Hugh again."

It had happened once when he was tired and didn't answer Kerry while she talked to him. He'd been mortified.

"I don't think so."

He hummed and gestured for me to hand over my coffee. I

forced myself to keep my eyes on him. I felt like I'd been knocked off of my game and I didn't know how to recover.

What were the odds that a woman like that was *here* of all places?

Nonchalantly glancing over my shoulder, the top of Wren's head peeked over the aisle.

"She's pretty," Dale said under his breath.

"She looks like she's Jade's age," I reminded. I wanted it to be gentle, but it came out harsher than I intended.

"Not for me." Dale rolled his eyes. "You can stand down, Mr. Bodyguard. I mean for *you*."

"What? Me?"

"You keep looking at her. I'm not blind."

"Oh, absolutely not. I'm busy with work. I don't . . . I can't . . ." I couldn't do a relationship, no matter how attractive the person was. Not after I'd screwed things up so badly with Norah and pushed her to my best friend. I couldn't be the version of myself that everyone liked, not when someone was in my space at all times.

"You know, for a small town, you have a great selection of light bulbs." Wren's voice got louder as she walked to the front.

"Gotta compete with Walmart. It's why I put the 'Things' in the name." Dale turned to me and I was terrified that he would hint at me and Wren being *anything* once more. Instead, he told me my total.

I paid and was planning on getting back to the clinic as soon as possible.

Instead, I turned to find Wren looking at me.

"Do you know Cain and Mollie?"

"What?" I asked. "Of course I do. Cain a little more than Mollie, but that's because I'm Eric's doctor."

"So, hypothetically, if I were to build something for them, you might know what they want?"

"You want to build something for them?"

She sighed. "It needs to be good, especially since Mollie told me to relax and I'm definitely not doing that. I already ordered a tire plug, and now I'm fixing the lights in the bathroom, so—"

"Is there a reason you're not relaxing?" I asked. "It's good for the mind."

"Not *my* mind," she said. "I like to stay moving, and what better way to do that than to help my best friend?"

"If there *is* something about Mollie I know, it's that she's stubborn. Very much so. If she told you to relax, then she won't be thrilled if you don't listen."

Wren rolled her eyes. "Yeah, but—"

I put my hands in my pockets, determined to stay calm even as I pushed back a little.

"You said you like to move, right?"

"I do."

"And you're new in town. Do you wanna see more of it?"

"Of course. I wanna know why Mollie likes it so much."

Now I had it. "The square is old. It's been here for generations. Right now, the irises are blooming in multiple colors. Yellow, pink, light purple, and dark purple. You could find each one and learn a little about the people who live here while you do it."

It was perfect timing that they were blooming too. Irises could mean a lot of things, like hope, wisdom, or valor. She wouldn't know the meaning, and I wasn't sure if she would care to know the explanation.

"That sounds cute, but I work with my hands."

"They need weeding." I planned to do it myself, but I'd hand it off to someone if it would help them. A small deviation, but worth it.

"It's been years since I even *looked* at a garden. I usually hire landscapers because I'm so exhausted."

"Exhausted from what? Your construction job?"

The door to the store slammed open, causing both of us to jump.

"Oh my *God*!" Kerry raced inside, running up to Wren. "You're Wren Hackett!"

"That's me." Wren's voice was quiet.

"That's it!" Dale called. "You're from that show."

I turned to Wren, eyebrows raised. Her lips were pressed together once again, every inch of her body tight. "Yep. I am."

"I just finished the first season!" Kerry said. "I'm a superfan. You and Jude are so adorable together."

"Yeah. We are." Her voice lowered. She was with someone? I didn't know that, but it made sense. A woman like that didn't stay single. I took another look at her. She stood straighter and smiled at Kerry as if putting on a mask. There was a tiny crack in it, though. One of her hands didn't sit still, and she was picking at one of her cuticles. "I'd heard some people in town had seen it."

"Oh, I *love* watching home renovation shows! But yours was incredible! And then I find out Mollie knows you?" Kerry fanned herself. "It might be the best thing that's ever happened to me. Second to actually getting to *meet* you, of course. I'm Kerry, by the way."

"Wren," she replied. "But you already know that."

"Have you had breakfast yet? The diner makes incredible food."

"I haven't. Maybe I could head there next."

"You could come with me! My husband is finally in town and can watch my son. I'm free as a bird."

"I . . . suppose I should get to know people." Wren's eyes cut to me. I'd just given her the same advice, but I meant for her to *relax*. Kerry didn't seem to be relaxing her.

I stepped forward to . . . what, save her? Invite her to the clinic for a checkup? I had no idea what to say. Yet I felt the need to do *something*.

"Yes!" Kerry said, linking her arm through Wren's. "Wow, you're *strong*. I thought all of that lifting was show business, but obviously not."

"Nope. I did all of this before."

Kerry began walking, taking Wren with her.

"Wait, you forgot your light bulbs!" Dale called.

"Oh, I'll come back." Wren's eyes met mine again. "I suppose I've found something else to do."

She smiled at me, and my gaze followed her as she and Kerry walked outside. Her smile didn't waver and she looked happy.

But her hand never stilled.

"I've never won a bet before," Dale said. "But I think this time I might."

I blinked back into myself. "Gambling can be addictive."

"Chill out, Dr. Connor. I'm not gonna go to the slot machines. I just finally have inside info." He leaned forward with a smile on his face. "And when you make a move on Wren, I'll be *rich*."

"No," I said. "Absolutely not. I'm not gonna make a move on anyone. For many reasons."

He hummed. "So, I'll need to say it'll take a while. That's fine. I'm patient."

"I'm very busy with the clinic. I'm fine just being a doctor."

"It's a big world out there, Henry. You can be more than just a doctor."

4

WREN

Strawberry Springs Neighborhood Watch

Atticus Thompson: Whose cow is this?

Comments:
Kerry Winsor: @Mollie Wilson, is it one of y'all's?
Mollie Wilson: Oh SHIT. THAT'S MOOSLEY.
Atticus Thompson: Your Moosley pooped on my porch.
Mollie Wilson: Use it for whoever pisses you off next. Trust me, it works.
Kerry Winsor: Are you speaking from experience?? How did that happen?
Mollie Wilson: It was Cain's doing, you'll have to ask him about it.
Kerry Winsor: We're just now getting along!!! Do you really think I can text him about POOP?

THERE ARE THE YELLOW IRISES.

Kerry was still talking in my ear, but I was too busy trying to find the flowers. The first one was near a plaque that had information on the town. And now I wanted to read it.

But she was dragging me to the diner and I had to focus on looking as normal as possible. Thankfully, Kerry seemed to be as deep as a puddle of water. All she could talk about was the show, and she hadn't looked twice at me to parse out how I was feeling.

The diner was a short walk from the store, and I let my eyes take in more of the town square. I'd come here to fix the flickering light bulb in Mollie's bathroom. She'd been busy working in the fields, and I tore off to town before she could get on my case about relaxing. I thought I could figure out something to bide my time, but Henry was right. Mollie would kill me if I kept at it.

I just needed something else to do.

Once I finished this meal with Kerry, I would find the rest of the irises. That would keep me busy for maybe an hour.

Kerry opened the door to the diner, pulling me inside. I was met with pink walls and checkered tile—a pinnacle small-town diner. Madison had wanted us to find a place like this in Nashville to do some of our filming. We'd made it work, but most of the old-time establishments had closed down in favor of newer, flashier restaurants. Places in the city were forced to grow or close.

It was nice seeing something stay the same.

A woman with dyed blonde hair and a name tag that read *Dakota* turned around. She took a look at Kerry and me and put her hands on her hips.

"Now who did you find?" she asked. "Please tell me you haven't started kidnapping people to fill your time."

Kerry scoffed. "I only need to because you're so rude. This is Wren. You've heard of her."

Dakota hummed and looked at me. Then she paused, eyes widening when she realized who I was.

"Here I am," I said, hoping my laugh didn't sound awkward.

"Can you believe we have a *star* here?" Kerry asked. I resisted the urge to run again. "I can't believe Mollie knew her the entire time."

A *star*? Is that what I wanted to be? Sure, being a Nashville local legend had its perks, but stardom?

"Don't put the poor woman on a pedestal before you even get to know her." Dakota rolled her eyes. "Nice to meet you, kid. I'm Tammy."

"Tammy?" I asked, blinking. "But your name tag says Dakota."

She laughed. "Gotcha! I always wear the wrong one. Keeps things fresh."

"Her last name isn't even on the Facebook group," Kerry added. "It's all her husband. He's secretive."

"Ron likes his privacy, and I do too. Though I like watching Kerry freak out about deer too."

"Hey! My Brussels sprouts deserved better!"

Tammy let out a full-bellied laugh before looking at me. "You want a table by yourself?"

"What?" Kerry asked. "I invited her here!"

"And if you make her feel weird, she'll never like it here either."

Tammy had just met me, but the fact that she was so determined to make me feel welcome was so sweet. Just like Henry had been when he made sure I could get into town okay.

Slowly, a little of the ice in my chest melted. Minutes ago, I'd thought it was a good thing Kerry hadn't looked twice at me to figure out how I was feeling. I'd been wrong.

"I'm okay, but thank you. A kind doctor told me to get to know the people here, so I will."

"A kind doctor? You mean Henry?" Tammy asked.

"She was talking to him in Food 'n' Things when I walked in," Kerry said. "He's a sweet guy. Keeps to himself, though."

"Mostly," Tammy added. "He does warn us about *health hazards*."

They both turned to look at an old man who was sipping coffee in the corner. Kerry shuddered and leaned over to me. "*Don't* shake his hand."

"Why not?"

"Just trust me on this one."

Tammy grabbed menus and led us to a booth. I sat across from Kerry, but then Tammy sat right beside me.

"Don't mind me joining you. I'm here to make sure Kerry doesn't run you off."

"Hey, I'm *very* nice."

"And so am I. But I know when to close my mouth."

"My big mouth has done things for this town. You just want to get to know Wren too."

"I do." Tammy turned to me and my stomach flipped.

"I'm not as interesting as I appear on TV," I warned.

"I don't care about who you are on TV. I know everyone's order in town, and now I can't say that I do. I wanna know what you *like*."

"And if it's French toast, you're boring," Kerry said.

"Cain will hate you again if he hears you say that," Tammy scolded.

"Mollie loves French toast too," I added.

"They're two peas in a pod," Tammy replied. "But don't dodge the question. My life's easier when I know everyone."

I glanced down at the menu. "Probably an omelet with some toast."

"Protein heavy," Tammy said. "Is that how you got so tall?"

"That was all genetics, I'm afraid. My dad was six foot five."

"Was?" Kerry asked. *"Ow!"*

"'Was' hints at something you don't ask a near stranger about," Tammy hissed.

"Did you just *kick* me?"

"It got your attention, didn't it? Should've done that a lot sooner."

"It's fine," I said. "My dad passed a few years ago because of a heart attack. I miss him, but I can talk about it."

"I'm so sorry, though," Kerry said. "If it makes you feel any better, we're all like a family here."

"One big, gross, dysfunctional family," Tammy added, looking at Hugh.

"Don't make me think about Hugh while I'm also thinking of food. I'll never be able to look at him the same way after what he posted in the Facebook group."

"I'd show you, but you'd leave and never come back," Tammy said to me. "Now, what's gonna be your usual? First meal is on the house."

"Are you sure about that?" I asked.

"You didn't do that for me," Kerry protested with a frown.

"You were a kid when you first came here. And I was a teenager."

Kerry sniffed. "You could have pulled some strings."

"Well, you weren't as cute as she is. I mean, look at her! She and Mollie could break hearts!"

"Ooh, I bet they did."

Both women giggled.

I looked down at my outfit. My long hair was braided and I wore overalls. Most of the time, when people looked at me, they told me I could be cuter if I dressed up.

Madison had. I was sure she was going to angle to give me some glow-up in season two.

A warmth spread through me, making me feel a little more like myself.

"Thanks," I said quietly. "I needed to hear that."

"Any time, kid." Tammy patted my shoulder and stood. "Now, tell me what you're drinking and what to put on that omelet, and then I'll come back and chat some more."

I told her my toppings and drink just before a loud voice interrupted us.

"Tammy!" Hugh called. "I need a refill."

Her smile fell in the blink of an eye.

She turned to Hugh. "That's the fourth one! I'm cutting you off!"

"Don't make me leave a goggle review!"

"Once again, it's called Google!" Tammy yelled over her shoulder before disappearing into the kitchen.

I'd left the diner with a full belly and a good mood much later than I intended. Talking to both Kerry and Tammy took up most of the morning, and I spent the afternoon exploring the town square. I thought finding all of the irises would take me a few minutes at most, but as I circled the whole square and then the surrounding roads, I was getting frustrated.

Henry seemed like a kind guy, but he'd sent me on a wild-goose chase, and I was pretty sure it was a damn prank. It was nice to slow down and see the history of Strawberry Springs, but I was on a mission. I'd found every one of the irises except for the dark purple ones, though he might have misspoken about those. However, to be missing a color made my little scavenger hunt feel unsatisfying.

A lot of things had felt that way lately.

I figured the clinic closed at five, so I busied myself with weeding until late afternoon in hopes I could run into him and ask about the last irises.

"Wow," a voice said. "You took what I said seriously."

I pulled the last weed out of the ground next to the playground and turned to Henry. He had his hands behind his back and watched me with a small smile on his face. In the light of the late afternoon sun, he was cute.

Really cute.

I'd thought it the first time I'd met him too.

Ever since pursuing Jude, I'd put all of my attention on him. I hadn't noticed a man ever since. At least I *could* notice someone else.

"All colors, you said. And yet, there are no dark purple irises." I sat back on my heels. "Am I a joke to you?"

He rubbed the back of his neck. "To be fair, I didn't know you'd get to work so quickly."

"You gave me a task. I got it done. Up until you tricked me." I pointed at him. "You seem to be a nice, friendly doctor. But you have another side of you, don't you?"

His shoulders tensed for a second, and I wondered if I'd stuck my foot in my mouth. But then he was back to normal.

"The last one *was* a bit of a trick," he replied. "But they *are* here."

"If you tell me they're in my soul, I might throw a dandelion at you."

"Those are medicinal, you know."

"Please tell me more about medicinal weeds *after* I find this dark purple iris." I brushed off my hands after tossing the weed. I made to stand and he held out a hand. "You don't have to treat me like I'm fragile."

"I'm not offering you a hand because I think you're fragile. I'm offering it to be polite."

"My hands are a mess."

"I can wash them. I'm no stranger to dirty hands."

That made me blink. Just what did the buttoned-up doctor of Strawberry Springs get into? I took his offered hand, letting him pull me up.

This town was so . . . *friendly*. And it was in a genuine way, not the fake smiles Madison would give me when she would catch me covered in dust after working overnight on the mansion.

"Follow me," he said.

We crossed the street, and I quickly realized where we were heading.

"Are you taking me to that massive abandoned building that people seem to avoid? Is this where you tell me you've had a plan to kill me this entire time?"

"That would go against the Hippocratic oath," he said. "And no. This is where I show you where those irises are, but if you're uncomfortable—"

"Me? Uncomfortable by being near a huge abandoned building?" I laughed. "This is my *shit*." I ran ahead of him, taking in the tallest building in Strawberry Springs. Unlike the rest of the buildings, its paint was peeling, and I could barely see the word "library" on one of the signs.

"Oh, the stories you could tell." I put my hand against a spot of peeling paint where I could see the original large bricks. Sometimes I wished walls could talk so I could hear about what they saw.

"Strawberry Springs is lucky in a lot of ways," Henry said, hands in his pockets as he looked up. "We've stayed stable in some places, but when the economy went downhill a little over a decade ago, the state stopped funding the library."

"Of course. Why would a small town need to read?" I asked sarcastically.

He sighed. "It went under before I moved here. It looked a

lot like this, actually. But I bet it was the center of town when it was open."

I let my eyes wander, trying to imagine what the paint would have looked like before age got to it. What the doors and windows would look like if they weren't boarded up. Even in ruin, it was still beautiful, but I'm certain it was showstopping before. "I bet the people loved it."

"Follow me." He waved his hand and walked toward the side.

The building extended farther than I expected, but there was a small patch of green halfway down the massive building.

We approached an old iron fence. I turned to look inside. At first, all I saw was weeds. Then, near one of the corners, a hint of dark purple.

I latched onto the bars. "There it is! And it's in the coolest spot in town!"

"Most people would consider it the *former* coolest spot in town."

"I *live* for abandoned places."

"For the show, you mean?"

I resisted the urge to groan. The last thing I wanted to be thinking of while looking at this beautiful place was *Renovating with Love*.

"So you *did* see it?"

"Still haven't. I didn't even have time to Google it today. Being a doctor keeps me busy."

"There's hardly anyone in this town. How many times could they be sick?"

"I branched out a few years ago to provide care out of town. You'd be surprised at how little competition there is for competent doctors this far away from the city."

"Smart," I replied and turned back to the library. For the longest time, life felt like it had been drifting around me. Every decision was made. And if it wasn't, I had strict things I could and couldn't do. But now, I had something in front of me that *I* wanted to see. Without cameras around to stop me. "And . . . if you wanna continue being smart, you should probably walk away right about now."

His brow pinched. "Why?"

My eyes traced every part of the fence. "Because I'm about to do something very illegal, and I'm giving you an out."

"Do *not* deface this place."

"What kind of woman do you take me for?" I finally turned to him, putting a hand on my heart.

"Sorry," he said. "I'm just a little protective of something with this much history."

"Understandable. I promise I'll be very respectful here in a few minutes when I do what I have to."

Now Henry's eyes narrowed. "And what are you planning on doing?"

"I'm gonna break in and see the inside of it."

5

HENRY

Strawberry Springs Neighborhood Watch

Jade Clark: Just found this spider. What kind do you think it is?

Comments:
Dale Garrett: A dead one, that's for sure!!!
Kerry Winsor: It was smaller in person, right? Where did you find it?
Jade Clark: It was crawling on my back. Hopefully it didn't bite me.
Kerry Winsor: @Henry Connor help??? Should she come into the clinic?
Kerry Winsor: @Henry Connor HELLO
Marjorie Brown: Do you think he's a damn spider collector in his free time? How would he know?!
Kerry Winsor: I don't know what kind of hobbies he has!!!

WREN HAULED herself to the top of the iron fence before I could register what she was saying.

"*Wren!*" I hissed. Thankfully, it was close to dinnertime and most of the townspeople were either in the diner or at home, but I still checked to be sure Mike wasn't lurking around the corner. "What are you doing?"

She paused as she straddled the fence. "I told you I'm going in."

"Breaking and entering? Really?" I didn't know much about her, yet this seemed like a thing she would do. She had this air of capability and determination around her. If she wanted to see something, she would find a way to see it. Even if it was boarded up and left to rot.

"Just turn and walk the other way," she said. "I won't break or mess with anything. I just wanna see the inside."

"It's been abandoned for more than a decade."

She smiled. "Exactly."

Then she cleared the fence, landing on the grass. I could only gape at her as I quickly went over all of the things she could get herself into that would send her right to the clinic. Dust. Sharp edges. A floor could fall in and she could break her leg.

There was a reason none of us had ever tried to go in there. We had no idea what age had done to it, and none of us knew how to make a library as massive as this usable again, even if the mysterious STM grant covered costs.

Before I realized what I was doing, my foot was on the fence, and I followed her movements. When I landed on my feet, her green eyes were wide. "You're following me? Why?"

"I'm making sure you don't get hurt in there."

"But you don't—"

I crossed my arms. "I wouldn't let you sit on the side of the road by yourself. What makes you think I'm letting you go into an abandoned library alone?"

She blinked, mouth falling open for a second, but then she shook herself out of it. "This is *not* gonna be a thing you enjoy."

"And how do you know what I enjoy?"

She let out a bark of laughter. "All right, you have me there. But seriously, old buildings like this are gross. Dusty. Dirty."

"Possibly filled with things to fall and get hurt on," I added. "I'm ready for all of those things."

She raised an eyebrow. "You are?"

"I'm a doctor. My first priority is making sure people stay healthy. You're gonna do this whether I approve or not." I took in a lungful of air. "So, I might as well go with you."

"I didn't think politeness in this town went as far as breaking and entering," she said. "But I won't complain if I have company. Though, you might once I get in here."

"I can handle more than you think."

Wren's cheeks grew pink. She turned to the building and made a path through the tall grass and weeds until we were at what used to be the back door. It was boarded up, but I could picture this courtyard being something beautiful. A stone path used to lead to a few tables and chairs where readers would sit.

Wren tried to move the door, but it didn't budge. I wondered if it was game over, but then her eyes moved upward. "There! One of the windows is broken."

"That's a second-story window," I said.

"And I never leave home without my ladder in my truck."

She was gone before I could process the fact that she always had a ladder and intended on using it.

There was a *clang* as she launched it over the fence and then followed.

"Wait a minute," I said as she leaned it against the brick. "How do you know it's safe in there?"

"I don't."

"Wren—" Before I could talk some sense into her, she'd gotten the ladder to where she needed it and was scrambling up to the window.

Wren was an explorer.

And a danger to herself.

"There's no shame if this is where you stop." She peered down at me as she was halfway up. "If anyone asks, you saw nothing. And if I disappear . . ." She shrugged. "Well, tell everyone I died doing what I loved."

Correction: She was a danger to *me*. Just listening to her had my heart racing.

There was no way I was letting her do this alone.

That was the only logical reason I had for climbing up onto the ladder behind her. I didn't love heights, but at least I could make sure she didn't get hurt in there.

"Wren, slow down," I said. "At least make sure it's safe."

She turned with wide eyes. "You're coming with me?"

"You're determined to do this. I'm determined to make sure you don't fall through something."

"You could call the cops to stop me, you know."

"You're overestimating how much the local sheriff here can do. If anything, he'd wait outside."

"So, you're telling me you're braver than the sheriff?"

"I don't know about *that*—"

She tilted her head to one side. "You wanna see inside of here too, don't you?"

The second she said it, I knew she was right. I'd stared at this place since I first moved here. Instead of giving her an answer, I turned to make sure no one was walking down the sidewalks. "We need to get moving before someone catches us."

She laughed. "You are *not* what I expected."

Neither was she.

Wren barely fit through the window. I had a bit more trouble, but made it inside too.

The air was musty, and the old carpeted floors were probably the culprit. Wren used her phone as a flashlight to illuminate rows of metal shelves. This was a massive space, and the shelving stretched as far as the eye could see.

I'd never been in a building that had sat empty as long as this. I thought I knew what to expect, but this was still so much darker than I assumed.

"This was *huge*," she said.

"People said it was." Still, it didn't do it justice. How much information had been in here? What all had been lost?

"This is in incredible shape for how long it's stood empty." Her voice was quiet as she walked, but I could barely make out her words. She was in awe, just like I was. "It's got good bones."

Wren walked along the empty hallway, shining her phone's flashlight down each pathway. I followed and pulled mine out, doing the same. This was once a bustling library. Who had walked these floors? What books were here?

It was empty. Forgotten to time.

The opposite of haunted.

Eventually, the shelves ended, leaving an open space that looked down onto the first floor.

"What are the odds that I fall if I get close to that?" she asked.

"It's an overhang that was abandoned for ten years."

"I'm willing to risk it." She walked forward. My gaze followed the old wood and saw the way it leaned. Even the stairs buckled.

I grabbed her arm and pulled her back to me before I could stop myself. "Bad idea. That can't support you."

She was silent, and I regretted how firm I'd been. "I think

you're right. I should've caught that. I'm too distracted by everything in here."

Wren walked off and I shook my hand. It tingled from where I'd touched her.

I didn't do this. I didn't touch women without their permission. I didn't tell them what to do.

Then again, I didn't break into abandoned buildings either.

Still. It needed to be a fluke. A single mistake.

"There has to be another way down, right? A back staircase?"

"You're asking the wrong guy," I said. She headed back to where we came from and I followed her.

"I'm gonna hunt for it."

"I'll go with you."

The surprise from me following her must have faded, because she turned with a smile. "That's what I was hoping for."

We came to another clearing where there was a wooden desk taking up a corner.

"Cool," she said. "I wonder if anything was left behind."

We walked around it. Nothing physical remained, but there were markings in the wood.

"M and H," I said to myself. "Marjorie and Henrietta."

"What?" Wren asked.

"Two of the ladies that live here. They used to run the library. Marjorie and Henrietta. They left a mark."

I could practically *see* them here. Marjorie would have been the one to do it while Henrietta scolded her.

"Wow," she said. "I've seen a lot of things like this, but I never get to hear about the people who did it. What's left behind is usually a mystery."

"It's still here." I looked out over the empty space. "I wish more was."

Wren took everything in and an eerie silence settled over

both of us. "We haven't seen it all yet. Come on, there has to be another staircase somewhere."

It took a bit of exploring to find another way down. The stairs were tucked into a corner that was darker than everything else. Dust specks drifted in the air as we slowly headed toward them.

Most everything was in good shape, but these steps were wobbly at best. They appeared to be wood underneath the old carpet, and time hadn't been kind to them.

Wren was quiet as we moved, but I kept an eye on her. She had started descending in front of me, and I assumed she was taking it all in.

Then, a step collapsed underneath her.

My hands wrapped around her waist before she could fall, and I pulled her flush to my front.

"Careful," I said in a low voice.

"Jesus. It's been a long time since that's happened to me. I'm off today. Thanks for catching me."

Her body was warm against mine, and it took me a second longer than it should have to let her go.

Something pressed into the back of my mind. It had been bothering me since I grabbed her upstairs. A detail from today that I needed to remember.

Wren wasn't single.

Horror climbed onto my cheeks, shame making them hot.

Wren didn't seem to take note of it. She continued her trek downstairs, stepping far more carefully this time.

"Are you still coming? Or do you sense more danger?"

I blinked out of my thoughts. Wren had gotten to the bottom of the steps and had turned to look at me with a raised eyebrow.

"I'm still following." I caught up with her. "But about the stair . . ."

She'd opened the door at the bottom, eyes going wide. "Hold that thought."

She waved me forward, and suddenly, I was too busy marveling over the first floor to finish my thought. It was much more open, with meeting spaces and a colorful kids' section. The tiles were faded, but we could tell they matched all the colors of the paint on the buildings in the square.

"Holy shit," Wren whispered. Her eyes were on the wall behind us.

I turned and saw the remnants of a mural of the entire town. Bennie Grove Farm was on it, as well as every single building in the square. Things had changed over the years, like store names, but this was a snapshot of the town from years ago.

"All of this," she said as she walked up to it, "it's just standing here *empty*."

"Like an eyesore," I added.

"God, I bet the people here miss it."

"*I* miss it and I wasn't even here for it. I've heard it was more than a library. The town hall was connected to the back. People had parties. The government offices were here, but it all closed when the library did. I wish there was something to be done, but even if we had the funding, a project like this would be massive."

"Way bigger than a mansion," she muttered.

I would have let her stay as long as she wanted, but my lungs were already burning from the musty air, and I knew hers had to be too.

"We should go," I said. "It can't be good for us to stay in here too long."

"You're right. I have a few calls to make anyway."

We made it back up the stairs, but my thoughts were no longer with the library. They were on Wren. If she was going to be calling people, I wondered if her costar boyfriend was one of them.

After we were in fresh air and on solid ground, I knew I couldn't leave it.

"Hey, about what happened in there . . . I'm sorry."

She turned. "What are you talking about?"

"The stair breaking. Me grabbing you. *Twice.* After what Kerry said, about you and . . . Jude, was it? I didn't mean anything by that. I don't make moves on women in relationships."

Wren raised an eyebrow. "But you just saved me from falling."

"Still," I said. "It matters to me."

Wren huffed out a laugh. "That's very sweet of you, but . . . you don't have to worry about apologizing."

"But Kerry said you and Jude are—"

"Jude and I aren't . . . anything."

My brow pinched. "Did Kerry misunderstand something?"

She shuffled her feet. "No, the show says we're together. But it's show business. They want a couple for people to root for. And that's all it is."

"You're not really . . ."

"Nope."

Was that a thing people did? Pretended to be together?

"I see," I replied. "But if there are rules about this thing, or I ever cross a line, let me know."

Despite her newfound rigid posture, she smiled. "I will. But I don't think we'll have an issue with that. You're probably one of the most polite people I've met. Thank you for exploring the abandoned library with me."

She thought of me as polite. Good. I hadn't messed this up that badly, then.

"You're welcome," I said, giving her one last smile before she walked off.

It then hit me that it was way past my usual dinnertime, and I needed to get home or else my whole night would be off. Messing with the routines that kept me together wasn't something I did easily.

After I made dinner, I hopped in the shower to scrub off all the dust. Then I checked social media to see if anything was happening in town. I answered something Kerry tagged me in before going through my feed.

That was when I saw it was Norah's and Ace's two-year anniversary. She'd reposted the picture of their wedding where they were surrounded by family and friends. Both of them had always been like that. They loved being the center of attention. I tried to like it, once upon a time . . .

And then I couldn't anymore.

Mom had been at the wedding, though I wasn't invited. With how things had been left, I wasn't surprised. I was shocked they'd even sent me friend requests on Facebook.

With a sigh, I liked the post and shut off the phone for the night. I hadn't followed my routine closely since Wren's arrival, and I knew I would regret it if I didn't get back to my usual. I'd done well in Strawberry Springs. People saw me as a dependable doctor.

If that facade shattered, I wasn't sure if they could get past it.

Ace and Norah sure hadn't.

Strawberry Springs Neighborhood Watch

Jade Clark: Does anyone have a mattress that vibrates? I need info.

Comments:
Kerry Winsor: WHAT kind of info could you possibly NEED?
Mollie Wilson: Jade, you don't need the whole mattress. Let me send you a website.
Jade Clark: Not for THAT, for sleeping! Get your minds out of the gutter. No one else would think that!
Atticus Thompson: I did.
Theo Murf: I did too.
Marjorie Brown: Now, for anyone who needs recommendations on other vibrating things, let me know.

I BURST into the farmhouse with the perfect plan to make my producer work on the library. I was ready to call her up and send her my proposal to get her here, but I forgot that my best friend also lived in this house and she would have a lot of questions for me.

"Well, you certainly had a fun day." Mollie's hands were on her hips, but she didn't look angry. "How was your *relaxation?*"

"It's safe to say that I did *some* relaxing," I began. "I was gonna fix the lights in the bathroom—"

"You don't have to do that."

"I know. I wound up hanging out at the square. I may have been invited out by Kerry."

Mollie gasped, putting a hand on her chest. "Please tell me you didn't go to Center Point Diner without me."

I winced. I probably should have thought this through more than I had. "I'm sorry. When she met me, she immediately invited me out, and I didn't know how to say no."

"With Kerry, you don't," Cain interjected. "I really hope she wasn't your first impression of the town."

I thought of Henry. "No, she wasn't. And even if she was, it wasn't that bad."

"It kept you distracted," Mollie added, "which I appreciate. I was half worried you were planning to come back with a pile of wood to build something."

I laughed awkwardly. That was exactly what I had been planning until Henry talked me out of it. "I should go wash my hands and make a few calls."

"You'll join us for dinner, right?" Mollie asked. "We eat together every night, and everyone, even guests, join."

"What are you having?"

"Chicken and rice."

My eyes went to the back of the farm. "Like fresh chickens?"

"God, no." Cain shook his head. "Those are egg-laying hens. Some farmers sell them for meat, but I try to give them good lives."

"And then you eat ones from other farms?"

He grimaced. "I try not to think too hard about it. Otherwise, I might never eat meat again."

Mollie laughed and rubbed his shoulder. I had to look away. I thought I'd have this with Jude.

And that didn't work out.

"I need to go make those calls," I repeated. "I'll be back down in a few."

Mollie nodded, though she had that suspicious look on her face that meant nothing good for me. I took the stairs two at a time to get to the bathroom. Once my hands were free of all dirt, I opened my phone.

> Got an idea for the season two location. Call me ASAP.

I'd only been gone for two days, but Madison had hounded me on it despite the fact that I was supposed to be on a break. They were moving lightning fast on the second season since they wanted to finish filming before I started my other scheduled project. When they'd decided that they could make it work, we hadn't planned for a massive bump in the road with the mansion. Now, we were on borrowed time.

I was used to moving fast on things. Usually, I liked it. But the endless tasks of being on a show weren't as fun as I'd hoped they would be.

Madison wasted no time. Minutes later, she called.

"Hey," I answered.

"I hope you're calling with good news," she said. "Like you've found a location instead of going on vacation like I'd heard you'd done."

I sighed. Only the contractors I knew were aware that I was visiting Mollie. They must have told her while she was on the hunt for me.

"It isn't a vacation. I'm visiting a close friend."

"Sounds like a vacation to me."

"It turned out to be something good. I know where we're filming season two."

"Okay, I'm listening."

"Strawberry Springs."

"Where?"

"It's a small town a few hours outside of Nashville."

"*Hours?* Wren, our show is based *in* Nashville."

"Our show is based in *history*, and trust me, this place has a lot of it."

I could still see the ghosts of years past in those hallways and the memories of what once was. God, I wanted to bring it back to life.

"I told you to find another place in the city."

"Yes, but this is unlike anything else I've ever seen. This is inspiring, Madison. It's the center of a small town run down by a lack of funding. We could change lives with this!"

She sighed. "I mean this in the kindest of ways, Wren. But the network isn't interested in changing lives in a small town. They're interested in changing lives through *TV*."

"Don't people love an underdog story?"

"They do, but you have to consider what kind of under-taking restoring a library would be. It needs books, employees, and long-term funding that the show can't provide. Unfortu-nately, libraries in small towns like that close for a reason."

"But what if I funded some of it?" I was growing desperate. I wanted this *so* badly. Working on the show here was the only way I could stomach doing it. At least I wouldn't be alone with

Jude while he flirted with me on camera and avoided me off of it. At least I wouldn't miss any more of Mollie's life.

"Then we could consider it, but you'd have to fund it long term. We can't renovate a library and have it close in a year for the same reasons."

"Still—"

"Wren, I understand that this is important to you. And I applaud you for finding it. But unless something changes, I don't think this is a project worth your time. I'll send you a few options I've found on my own. Pick from those. We need to move fast on this."

I squeezed my eyes shut. I regretted signing a contract for season two when I still thought I had a chance with Jude. When I didn't feel like . . . this. It was ironclad. I couldn't get out of it.

"I'll look at them," I muttered.

"Thank you for listening to reason." She hung up without another word and I flopped onto the bed.

Between all the work I had finished and planned to do in Nashville, plus the income from both seasons of *Renovating with Love*, I had money. But was it enough to fund a library?

A place like this deserved to be showered with income. They deserved the ability to buy new books and host things without worrying about how they'd pay for it.

I could keep it running for a year. Maybe two, if I took consistent flips and houses and upped my rates. But I couldn't give it what it deserved by myself.

I stared at the ceiling, my emotions crashing over me. It had been a long time since I'd felt this much disappointment. Usually, I could find a project to work on to make it better.

And I thought I had.

A knock at the door pulled me from my thoughts. "Hey," Mollie said. "Ready for dinner?"

I wasn't. I wanted to be miserable for a little longer. But I also didn't want to be a rude guest.

"Yeah, I am."

"Did your calls go well?" she asked.

I bit my lip and shook my head.

"Do you wanna talk about it?"

"I had hoped for something and it's not gonna happen." I shrugged.

"Two heads are better than one. And you'd have four if we were all downstairs."

"I'm not trying to hijack your dinner with work talk."

"You're not hijacking anything. We all talk about our days at dinner. And something tells me you have a lot going on."

"I'm not hiding it as well as I could be, huh?"

"You look a little bit like I did when I first came here," she said. "And we still have that spot where we can bury the body of any man who hurts you. Although the farm has some good ones too."

Despite everything, I laughed. "There are certainly more options now."

"Let's go eat. And then we can talk about everything."

Cain and Eric were already at the dining room table. Cain was locked in a long conversation about a kids' show.

I sat with them, trying to resist the urge to feel out of place among their little family. When I was a kid and I went to Mollie's house for dinner, I felt the same way. Her parents weren't perfect, like many weren't. But they cared—and that felt alien to me. Sure, Dad had tried, but he was too busy putting food on the table. He didn't have time to sit and enjoy it.

It was obvious that Cain was busy too, yet he still had time for Eric. So far, it had been a struggle not to be jealous. Especially when I was the outsider. But I shoved it all into a box and smiled at the scene.

Even if it fought me every step of the way.

"What's your favorite show, Wren?" Eric asked.

I blinked. "I don't really watch TV."

"And you're *on* TV?" Cain asked.

Mollie glared at him. "Seriously?"

"Sorry. That came out ruder than I meant it to. I'll keep my thoughts to myself."

"It's fine," I said, trying to keep my voice level. "The TV show was never the official plan, but they could offer funding that I couldn't. For certain things, apparently. It comes with restrictions."

"Like what?" Mollie asked.

I stabbed at the chicken on the plate, still feeling raw from Madison's no. "They'll fund the things *they* believe in. Not what's actually good for a community."

"Is that the call you made?" she asked.

"Yeah. I had an idea for a project. It won't work out."

"What was it?"

"It was something you would've loved. No need to get your hopes up only to crush them like mine were, though."

"You don't need to protect me," she said. "I'll be fine. I'm more worried about you right now."

I sighed. I wasn't used to being told no after years of being my own boss. It was tempting to hide and lick my wounds, but Mollie wouldn't let this go. "You know the library on the square? I wanted to work on that."

Mollie's fork clattered. "Seriously? Here?"

"Yeah. I could work on it and then stay for a while. It would give me a few months here to catch up with you guys before I have to get back for some other projects. But they said it would need long-term funding, and they weren't willing to do that for a small town, because God forbid they do something charitable."

Bitterness rose in me. It had been growing ever since I was

halfway through season one. Now it felt like it was taking over completely.

"Having a library would be cool," Eric said. "I'm sorry they said no."

"Thanks," I said softly. "Anyway, that's why I didn't want to get your hopes up. Or anyone's, really."

I looked up at Mollie, only to find her staring at Cain. "Are you thinking what I'm thinking?" she asked him.

"Yep."

"Would it cover that?"

"No idea, but there's not much it *doesn't* cover."

Mollie bit her lip, eyes lost in thought.

"What are you guys talking about?" I asked.

"There's a grant here," Mollie said. "Just for this town. It might cover the funding."

"What, like a government one?" I shook my head. "If they were gonna cover that, they would have."

"No," she said. "It's private."

I blinked in shock. "What kind of private grant cares about small towns?"

"Not many, but this one is called the STM grant. It covers Strawberry Springs."

"Only here?"

"Yep."

"Why?"

Mollie shrugged.

"It's helped a lot of us," Cain said.

"Did you use it for the farm?"

"No, the eggs and milk keep that afloat. It was for my personal life, actually. It paid me back for the custody battle I was in with Eric."

My eyebrows raised. That sounded too good to be true.

"I know," Mollie said, catching my disbelieving expression.

"I thought the same thing, but the money is real. And it pays out every time."

"How long has it been around?"

"Five years," Cain said.

"And the end date?"

"There isn't one."

"I'm sorry, but money coming from nowhere? That seems fishy."

"I agree," Mollie replied. "But you can ask around. Get some firsthand accounts from people who've received it. If you really want this, then it's worth a shot."

I bit my lip again. Maybe Tammy knew something about it. Henry too. "Okay, I'll do that."

"And Wren?" Mollie started. "I think it's really sweet that you wanna work on the library. Most people would see it and walk right past."

"You know I love bringing things back to life."

"It always seems to be what you need to make yourself feel better," she said. "So I'll help in any way I can."

"You're back already! And this time, you brought Mollie!" Tammy seemed genuinely excited to see us.

"She owes me a diner breakfast," Mollie said, linking her arm through mine. "And we can chat while we're at it."

This morning, Mollie caught me as I was coming down the stairs, declaring that Cain was working on the farm and she would be helping me get information on the STM grant. She wouldn't take no for an answer, even when I wanted her to focus on her work, and drove me here herself.

This was the Mollie I knew. The spunky girl from high school who'd broken past everyone else's words and became my best friend. I hadn't realized how much of her I'd lost while she was with Trevor.

"Chat? You know I love that." Tammy walked us over to our table. "Coffee for Mollie and water for Wren, right?" she asked.

"That's right," Mollie said with a smile. "Then, we have a question for you."

"I'll get your drinks, but then you'll have to scoot over. If I'm getting questioned, I'll at least sit with you."

Mollie nodded as she chuckled. Tammy went to get our drinks.

"She's awesome," Mollie said. "Most people here are."

"It's different," I mused. "Everyone knows each other."

"For the good and the bad. But I like it. After being lost in the anonymity of the city, it feels good to be known."

The idea sounded great. To be liked no matter who you were. To be a part of something. I was good at being a part of things, but there was always something people didn't like. Something that excluded me.

Now more than ever.

"We're gonna have to talk about whatever gave you that look on your face," Mollie said. "Because I know it wasn't the library."

"I'm—"

"If you say you're fine, I'm gonna start throwing sugar packets at you."

My shoulders slumped. "You know me too well."

"What did Jude do?"

"How do you also know it was him?"

"All we talked about was you and him, and now you won't mention his name. It's a process of elimination."

"It really wasn't that bad in the end," I said.

"Somehow, I doubt that. But you can have a few more minutes of denial if that makes you feel any better."

"I'm back!" Tammy announced. "Coffee and water. Now, what were you gonna ask?"

She sat next to Mollie, facing me. Mollie gave me one last pointed look before fully turning to Tammy.

"You know the STM grant, right?" Mollie asked.

"Of course I do."

"How much do you trust it?" I asked.

"At first? Not at all. Small towns are used to being forgotten, but nowadays? It keeps the town afloat. It fixed rent prices. Makes sure all the businesses can stay open. We would be hurting without it."

"And it regularly pays out? It's never missed anything?"

"No. Why?"

"Wren wants to work on the library." Mollie said it before I could stop her.

"*Maybe* work on it," I rushed to add. "I don't know if I can make it happen."

But Tammy's eyes were wide. "You want to bring it back? Oh, kid, that would be incredible."

"Yes, but I can't afford it on my own. I wanted to do it on the show I'm on—"

"You want to bring a *show* here too?" Tammy laughed. "Are you trying to save the whole town while you're at it?"

I blushed at the praise but shook it off. "I wouldn't get excited. They're saying no. Not only is it not Nashville based, but it needs long-term funding."

"And that's where the STM grant comes in," Mollie said.

"It would cover it," Tammy replied. "A few of us have talked about wanting to apply for the library ourselves, but we had no one who could do the work." She looked at me. "Until you."

"She should do it, right?"

"She should. One hundred percent."

Mollie and Tammy seemed so close. I wondered if Mollie had added her to a part of her support system.

And if I'd fallen out of it.

It only made me need to be here more than ever. I wanted to be part of her life, and even though I'd be going back to Nashville at the end of this, at least I would know everything about my best friend once again.

But the idea of depending on money from something I didn't understand was still hard.

I didn't know a lot of people here, but the one person who had the most logic was Henry. "Hey, um, is Henry working at the clinic today?"

Tammy raised an eyebrow. "You need to see a doctor? Don't tell me we've driven you to question your mental health *this* quickly."

"No," I said. "I just want his advice too."

Both Mollie and Tammy glanced at each other.

"How do you know Henry?" Mollie asked.

"I've met him a few times." *And broke into a library with him.* "He's sweet."

"He is." Tammy nodded. "But you're taken, right?"

"For now," Mollie said.

"For now? What's goin' on there?"

"Nothing." I waved them off. Madison would kill me if too many people knew. "And there's nothing with Henry either. He's sweet in general. And he seems smart."

"He is," Tammy replied. "He should have the clinic open by now."

"Then that's our next stop."

"He's also single, by the way." Tammy smiled and leaned in. "In case you think he's a better choice."

Mollie laughed but covered her mouth. I could only gape at Tammy. "I . . . Well, no. That won't happen."

"Sure. Definitely not. But if it helps, Henry's a good guy. If Jude screwed up, you have options."

"Maybe it wasn't Jude who did it. I could be terrible at relationships."

Mollie huffed. "Now, hang on a second. We're *not* blaming ourselves for shitty men."

"I'm not saying it's *not* him. I'm just saying that I could have been part of the problem."

Tammy hummed. "I'll let you in on a secret. When I meet a woman with a great personality and she's having relationship problems, it's usually not her that's the issue."

I rubbed my chest, feeling warmth growing at her comment. She was just being nice to a newcomer. It didn't mean anything. "All right, fine. You'd . . . mostly be right. Kinda." I thought of the fake relationship. It made everything so complicated.

Tammy narrowed her eyes as she appraised me. I thought she was going to question me, but someone called her to the table. I watched her go, but when I turned, Mollie was staring at me.

"So, are you finally gonna tell me what Jude did?"

"It was just one comment."

"And it was enough to break the two of you up?"

"We were never together."

Mollie blinked. "I'm sorry, what?"

"We were fake dating. For the show."

"Hang on. But you flirted."

"Yep."

"And *kissed*. It was all fake?"

"I wanted it to be real." I shrugged. "He didn't."

Her jaw dropped. "You have to be *kidding me*. How dare he! You're a catch!"

I messed with my straw. "Not to him. I thought I could get him to change his mind, but obviously not."

"Fuck, Wren. I'm sorry."

"It's fine."

She looked at me as if I were a stranger. And she was right to. I *was* a stranger. Both to myself and to her. "It's not fine."

"Mollie, it has to be. I have a second season to do with him and it's in my contract."

Her eyebrows furrowed. "Seriously? They're making you do it?"

"Our romance is a part of the show. And I signed on for the second season before he turned me down." I sighed and sat back. "It's why I wanna work on the library. At least if I'm working on something I care about and hanging out with you, I can feel like I'm not losing it."

"Are you sure there's no way to get out of this?"

"Not that I can find. And if I keep working with them, they'll invest in more and more. Imagine what I could do."

Madison had already offered the idea of many seasons beyond the second once I was finished with my projects. If I took it, I could give that back to the library too.

"Yeah, but only within their limits. Sounds like this isn't what they told you it would be."

Her words brought back that bitterness I'd been feeling earlier. I closed my eyes for a long moment to try and wrestle it back into place.

"I'm trying to get them to see reason. And if I do, I can do more."

"I get it," she said. "But I don't like the idea of you being miserable."

"I don't like being miserable either, but it won't last for long." I forced my lips upward. "Once I'm in that library, everything will feel better."

"And you're sure about this?"

No. But I could pretend. "Yes."

I wasn't sure if she believed me. Her eyes were narrowed in my direction. "Okay, fine. But that means you need to apply for this grant."

"If it's real," I said.

"Tammy said it was."

"I know, but I want Henry's opinion first."

"Yeah, about that . . . Why him?"

"You heard what I said earlier. He's smart."

"And no other reasons?"

I could have said he was cute. Really cute, in a nerdy way. He considered others, but stepped in when he needed to.

But that would open up a whole other slew of questions I wasn't ready for. So, I shook my head. "Nope. No other reasons."

HENRY

Strawberry Springs Neighborhood Watch

Hu Gh: In search of a sewer!!!!!

Comments:
Kerry Winsor: A sewer???? A SEWER???
Atticus Thompson: Hugh, Strawberry Springs is an old town. We don't do sewers here. You probably have a septic tank and need a plumber.
Marjorie Brown: @Theo Murf
Theo Murf: Absolutely not. Not again.
Hu Gh: What are all of you on about now? I need someone to sew the crotch of my pants up.
Kerry Winsor: Oh! A sew-er. You must mean a seamstress.
Hu Gh: Seamstress. Sewer. Who cares? I just need someone to fix my crotch asap.
Jade Clark: Hugh, no one wants to fix your CROTCH.

"I CAN'T BELIEVE I burned myself with a curling iron. What am I, a rookie?"

I was wrapping Jackie's hand with gauze. The hairstylist came in teary-eyed with reddened skin, and I immediately got her back in a room. "It happens. Don't worry about it."

"Still. Sorry to take you away from what you were doing."

I hadn't been doing much, other than planning out which flowers were going in my garden this year. Hugh had canceled his checkup, saying he was fine and didn't need me. He wasn't, and had a list of health concerns longer than my textbooks in medical school, but he was incredibly stubborn.

"Your comfort is important. I'd trade time for that."

"How are you single, Henry?" Jackie asked with a laugh. "Women should be fawning over you!"

That was the second time today someone had brought that up. "Please tell me there isn't a bet already in the Facebook group."

"No. Why would you think there is?"

My cheeks heated. "No reason."

"*Is* there a woman?" Jackie's eyes were wide. "Is it Jade?"

"No. She's only a friend."

"Grace?"

"Also a friend."

"Who else could it be?" She gasped. "Brooke?"

"Not my type," I said with a shake of my head. I didn't have a thing for women who stirred up drama, but especially ones who did it purely because they were bored.

"Oh, you have to give me something. I'm injured!" She weakly waved her bandaged hand in my face.

I gave her a flat look. "I think you'll survive."

The front door of the office opened, jingling the overhead bell to announce any new arrivals. I didn't have a nurse and preferred to do my work myself, so it gave me the perfect out.

"Just keep that covered and clean. You should be good by tomorrow."

"You're lucky that there's a distraction."

I gestured for her to follow me. I *had* gotten lucky.

Or at least I thought I had.

But when we entered the lobby, I once again saw the woman who had been on my mind this entire time.

"Wren?" I asked. "What are you doing here?"

Jackie gasped. "It's her! I heard there was a new girl in town!"

"Am I invisible?" Mollie asked. I blinked and realized that I hadn't even noticed she was next to Wren.

"Oh, honey. No." Jackie smiled and brought her in for a hug. They were close since Jackie was like a mother to Cain. "I was just admiring your friend here."

"You know me from *Renovating with Love*, don't you?" Wren asked.

"Yes! It's so cute." She put her good hand on her cheek and then turned to me. "When did you two meet?"

"A few days ago." My eyes lingered on her. Her hair was down today.

"I like to call him my bodyguard," Wren added. She had no idea how that sounded.

"Oh, *interesting*."

I sighed and pushed my glasses up on my nose. "Nothing is interesting here."

"Sure it's not." Jackie looked in between us again. "Have fun, Henry!"

Once upon a time, Jackie was only halfway into the drama in town. But things had changed after Mollie stuck around, and now she was far more open. I'd seen her post more in the Facebook group too.

Normally, I didn't mind talking with the town. But there

was something about Wren that made it hard for me to be normal. And if the town started pushing me with her? I was doomed. If they sniffed out a crush, they would never let me live it down.

"What can I help you ladies with?"

"I need a gynecological exam." Wren's voice was deadpan, and I thought the floor fell out from under me.

"W-what?" I was *way* too into her to handle that professionally.

"Just kidding. Your reaction was good, though."

My face could now fry an egg. "So what do you actually need?"

"Advice. And depending on the answer, it could be as fun as a gyno exam."

"You're gonna give him a stroke if you keep that up," Mollie said. "What happened to Sad Wren?"

"She's on vacation. Now I'm Annoying Wren."

"You're not annoying," I said. "Just shocking. It's too early in the morning for me to be thinking about a gynecological exam."

"It's one in the afternoon."

"What if we *pretended* it was still the morning?"

Wren laughed.

"Okay," Mollie said. "I hate to interrupt this because she really needs to laugh, but we did come here for a reason."

Wren's smile faded and she stood up straighter. "Right. The STM grant."

I gathered myself before I could answer. "What about it?"

"Is it legitimate?"

"As far as I know, yes." I put my hands in my pockets and I forced myself to focus on what she'd asked. I found it much easier not to embarrass myself when talking business with Wren rather than . . . whatever had happened at the library yesterday.

"I've used it some. Most small businesses have. Why do you ask?"

"I wanna use it to fund the library."

I blinked. "You want to *what*? But that would mean renovating it."

She smiled. "I know. I do have a show about that. They have reservations, but the long-term funding was the major issue. If the grant covers that, then I think it could work."

"You went in there *once* and you want to remodel it?"

"Hang on," Mollie said. "You went inside?"

"Yeah." Wren rubbed her neck. "We both did, actually."

"*What?*"

"Are you trying to get us in trouble for that?"

Wren waved her hand. "The statute of limitations has expired."

"It most certainly has not."

"I thought you said the sheriff wouldn't do anything. Besides, this is Mollie. She can keep secrets."

I glanced at Mollie, whose eyes fell to her feet. I'd been a witness to Facebook drama that was caused by her letting a secret slip.

"I can keep secrets *now*," she eventually said. "Just not when I've had things to drink."

"Isn't that why you usually don't drink in public?" Wren asked.

"I went back on that once and might have spilled a secret of Cain's to the town gossip. I learned my lesson, though."

Wren crossed her arms. "I thought you learned it when you got drunk and told a bouncer that your thong was up your ass."

"*Wren!*" Mollie hissed. "That stays in the *vault*. Where no one hears about it!"

"I didn't hear a thing," I said, putting up my hands. "In fact, I have no idea what we're talking about."

Mollie glanced at me and then back at Wren. "I see why you committed a crime with him now. But next time, you're taking me."

"Done." Wren nodded.

"So, what was it like in there?" Mollie asked.

"Spooky," Wren replied. "Dusty. But it has a lot of potential. It's honestly the first time I've been inspired in a while."

"Were any of the books left?"

"Unfortunately, no."

"There was a desk that Marjorie carved M and H into," I added. "But that and the mur—"

Wren shook her head, and I snapped my mouth shut.

"The what?" Mollie asked.

"The mur . . . dered body." Wren tried to cover it up.

"There was *not* a murdered body in the library."

"Well, *no*, there wasn't." She turned to Mollie. "But we're going with that because you can't know what it is yet."

"Rude," Mollie muttered. "But okay, I'll let it go purely so Wren can win something. She's been sad lately, unless she's with you. I guess you're the exception."

"I-I'm just—"

Mollie stopped my stuttering in its tracks. "You have the final say about the STM grant. Wren trusts you."

There was a lot to unpack there, but if I tried to do any of it in front of Mollie and Wren, I might explode.

So, I focused on the grant. Back to business talk for me.

"I think it's worth a shot. They're usually willing to provide funding promises in writing. The only downside is not knowing why it's so willing to help but . . . I think we can both agree the library is worth a little risk, right?"

"We can," Wren said. "You'll have to wish me luck."

An idea popped into my head. "I can give you more than just a wish. Come outside with me."

I took them both to the back of the clinic where I'd set up a table and chairs for eating outside. There was a small patch of greenery, most of it clover.

I bent down and picked one. "Here. A four-leaf clover. For luck."

I handed it over to Wren. "You knew this was here?"

"Every spring, I look for them. I don't have a patch of clover in my yard, so I do it here. I found one a few weeks back and saved it. Probably for this moment."

Her cheeks turned pink. "Thank you."

I looked behind her, remembering we weren't alone. Mollie stared at us, her eyes wide. "I could try to find you one if you want."

"Oh, no. I'm good. Just watching. And definitely *not* having thoughts."

"You shouldn't be," Wren warned. "Not about anything here."

Her voice was firm, and I wondered if Wren knew how people were taking our interactions. Admittedly, they weren't all innocent. But who could look at a woman like Wren and *not* flirt?

But her rigidity on the subject was a needed reminder. Just because I thought she was pretty meant nothing. Just because she seemed happy with me didn't mean anything either. She technically wasn't single. And I didn't need to get entangled with anyone.

It wouldn't end well with her.

"I hope it gets approved," I said, trying to sound as normal as possible.

Wren twirled the clover in her fingers. "I'll try my best. Thanks, Henry."

She left soon after, but the buzz of having talked with her remained long after she was gone. I checked the Facebook group, thankfully seeing no bets, but still couldn't shake the feeling.

In the end, I wound up closing the clinic early to go home. My routine would help, just like it always did. I could water my plants, eat dinner, and then finish my list of gardening chores. And decidedly not think about the gorgeous woman who might just throw everything off the rails.

RWL Superfan Discussion Central

Bethany Perry: [Link: Jude Putman spotted kissing Alana Barnes, heiress to hotel fortune.]

Comments:
Alicia Parrish: OMG! The second season is gonna be so GOOD.
Kerry Winsor: I'm so sad!!! How could he do this to her?
Jamie McCullough: I'm ready for draaaamaaaa. Do you think Wren will finally cry on camera? Ooh, or wear a dress? She'd look so good in one.
Neve Bullock: I have a feeling she'll get her glow-up. FINALLY!

I TWIRLED the four-leaf clover in my fingers, staring down at it. It was just a plant, yet it made me feel like I was luckier than usual. Like I could do anything.

"I could dry this, right?" I asked Mollie.

"I'm sure you could. Why?"

"It's cute. And I might always need luck."

There was a crease in between Mollie's eyebrows. "You're usually not so . . . sentimental."

She was right, but it also felt wrong to throw something like this away. "Is it bad?"

"No!" She shook her head. "Absolutely not. You should definitely save it. Being sentimental is a good thing sometimes."

"There were some scrapbooks in the closet of the guest room. Can I save this in one of those?"

"Yes, of course. And maybe when I get flowers back in the fields, we could add some there too."

When I went back to Nashville, I would need that. "Yeah, I'll save all the memories from here. I wonder if Henry has any more things to give me." Mollie went silent, and I realized how it sounded. "Like, in a friendly way," I added.

"You sure are *friendly* with him."

"So?"

"Tammy said he was single. And he's cute."

I gasped. "You're a taken woman."

"I am, but I have eyes. He's sweet and dependable. Though . . . you've never dated a hot nerd, but there's a first time for everything."

"Yeah, because my normal type has gotten me a lot of places lately," I muttered. "Henry would be . . ." I shook my head. "Why are we even talking about this? It's not even like I could do anything. Whether this grant goes through or not, in a few days, I'll be dating Jude again."

Mollie rolled her eyes. "You already know how I feel about that. We're bringing out the body hiding spots if he says anything else to upset you again."

"You'd have to take Madison, the director, with you. She's the one who wanted the romance."

"The spots can be for more than just men. I'm an equal opportunity murderer when it comes to you."

I laughed. "It's so good to hear you sound like yourself again."

"That's what happens when you start to take your needs seriously."

"I *am*, which is why I'm pushing for this season to be filmed here."

"But if you find an out, use it." Her voice was firm. "There's always something you can do to make things work."

I thought about it but hit a wall the second I remembered the contract. A renovation show with a side of love. That was what had been promised.

"Let me get this grant figured out," I said. "Then we plan the rest out."

She nodded, and we lapsed into silence as we got closer to the farmhouse. I tried not to let my thoughts slip to Henry as she drove.

By the time we were at the farm, my thoughts turned to the grant. I went inside and looked up everything I could on it, and only found an email address to send my inquiry to. I shot that off, asking for at least ten years of funding, just to see what they would say. It was more than they'd give, but I would work with five. Then I went outside to install the patch on my truck's tire.

Mollie was busy working with Cain, catching up on all that she'd missed. Apparently, she was hard at work diversifying the crops at the farm and hoped to join the vendors at the local Saturday farmers market soon.

I tried to only feel joy at Mollie's new life, but it was tinged with the regret that I had missed it. Hopefully, the season gave me enough time to catch up with her. I was so happy she had a life and home out here, but I had no idea what life would be like once I went back to Nashville and she remained here.

"Hey," a young voice said, and I turned to find Eric. "Mollie said you build things."

A distraction? Perfect. "I do. Need something?"

"Only the greatest marble run of all time. Can you do that?"

"A marble run?" I was hoping to work with wood, but I would take anything I could get. "Sure, lead the way."

Eric took me upstairs to his room where he had more toys than I could count. He showed me the pieces of the plastic marble run and described the massive setup he wanted.

"I might need a few more if I'm gonna make something this big."

Just as I said that, he pulled out a huge container of parts.

I wasn't sure who was more excited, him or me.

As I worked, I realized it was easier to build things with plastic. I didn't have the worry of it having to hold up to the test of time. As the pieces came together, Eric grew more and more excited.

I did too.

"All right, I think I've got it."

This thing was massive. It was as tall as he was, with multiple places for the marbles to go.

"Do you think they'll fall out?"

"They shouldn't," I said. "But let's test it."

They didn't fall out, not even when they went around the sharp turns and down the drops. Eric watched every second of it like it was his favorite show on TV.

"This is *awesome!*" He jumped up and down before adding more marbles to the top. "Mollie didn't tell me you were a genius."

My cheeks heated. "I don't know about *genius.*"

"When she helps me with this, the marbles fall out a *lot*. And for Dad too."

"Engineering's not everyone's thing."

"I'm glad it's yours. I could use a bunk bed soon."

Now *there* was an idea. I was getting too close to my deadline for the show to start it now, but I was more than happy to add it to the list to get done either after I did the library or whatever else Madison dragged me to do.

Out of habit, I looked around his room, trying to figure out where to put it. Most people wanted a bunk bed either because they were cool or because they needed to save space, but with a room like Eric's, I doubted it was the second one.

"Are you at the age where you think bunk beds are super cool?"

"Kinda. But also, Dad and Mollie are talking about things, and I think I'll have a sibling soon."

A marble fell out of my hands. "R-really?"

"Yeah. I want them to sleep in my room!"

Mollie would be a great mom, but some days it felt like we were still teenagers. Nowhere near the age of having kids.

Dear God. We were actually almost thirty. How had I never thought about this?

When she'd been with Trevor, the topic of kids never came up, at least not with me. But from what I knew about him, I was worried he'd try to push her before she was ready. Now, seeing how Cain and Mollie functioned with Eric as a family, I could see it.

But would I miss it?

Eric was watching me closely and I didn't want him running to tell Mollie about any more meltdowns. I took a shaky breath and put on my brightest smile.

"I would be an aunt! Again!"

"Again?"

I gestured to him. "I kinda already am."

Eric perked up. "With me?"

"Um, *duh*. But this time, I get to buy them things from the get-go. I'm *so* excited."

Eric seemed to believe me and laughed. I was glad I could fool at least one person.

"Wren!" someone yelled as the front door opened.

"Mollie? What's wrong?"

"Oh, *whew*. I haven't run the full field before." She doubled over. "This is really humbling."

"Is everything okay? Do you need something?"

"Me? No, I'm good. This is more for you."

She turned her phone around and showed me a Google search.

It was of Jude.

I gasped. He was making headlines for kissing another woman.

"You've gotta be fucking kidding me!"

"Curse word!" Eric said.

"Sorry." I winced. "But the sentiment still stands. How big is the news?"

She bit her lip. "Pretty big. It's only a matter of time before the Facebook group sees this."

"What Facebook group?"

"The town one. Sometimes it's used for useful things. Most of the time it's for gossip. And this is definitely that."

Horror dawned on me, making my cheeks hot. "They'll all think I got cheated on?"

"At least they'll be on your side."

"Oh my *God*. Of all the things he could do, he did *this*? And then got caught?"

"Is it time to murder? We can make what you said you found in the library true."

"Isn't that illegal?" Eric asked. Mollie shushed him.

I groaned, wondering how I was going to look anyone in the eye for the next few days after they all thought Jude was seeing someone else.

Then my phone rang.

"It's Madison," I muttered. "Probably calling to tell me the news."

"Glad I got to you first." She let out a long breath. "Good luck."

I was walking into the guest room and shutting the door as I heard Mollie exclaim, "Whoa, look at this marble run! This is so cool!"

I wished I was out there with them, not hitting answer on my phone.

"Glad I caught you." Madison sounded harried. "I'm sorry to tell you this, but—"

"Jude was pictured kissing"—I looked at my phone—"a hotel heiress."

The pinnacle of femininity. Just what he wanted.

"So you saw."

"I did."

"We'll have to launch a campaign to fix this. Wherever you are, you need to come back to Nashville right now. We have work to do on your relationship."

I jerked back, glad she couldn't see me. "Our relationship? Do you really think I would stay with him if he cheated on me?"

"It's not real. We can spin this to—"

"I don't want to *spin* anything. He should have done his job to lay low. I would never get back with him, and doing anything but breaking it off would be disingenuous."

"This whole thing is disingenuous, Wren. It has been the whole time."

But back then I thought I had a chance of being with him earnestly.

"Still," I said. "There have to be consequences for this."

"*Ugh*, if you insist, fine. You can be having a rough patch at the beginning of the season. It'll make the viewers interested anyway."

"I'm supposed to forgive him for cheating on me?"

"We're signed on for another season. You have to."

"*No,*" I hissed.

She let out a long sigh and the line went silent for a while. The two of us were brick walls. I wondered who would give first.

"What can I do to get you fully on board?" Madison asked.

I heard an email notification from my phone and I pulled it away for a second to check. My eyes widened when I saw the exact email I needed to see.

Application for STM Grant. Approved. I quickly opened it and saw they'd agreed to the whole ten years of funding.

I had to read it twice. They'd agreed to my massive request? In less than an hour?

There was no way.

But there it was. In writing. And they were asking where to send the money.

Both Tammy and Henry had said it was real, and now I had exactly what I needed to get the library done.

"Hello?" Madison asked in the distance. I put the phone back to my ear.

"I'm here."

"Did you hear my question?"

"I did," I said. "And I have an answer."

"What is it?"

"You come to Strawberry Springs and work on this library."

She let out another sigh, harsher this time. "But the long-term funding—"

"I took care of that. The library has ten years of funding."

"How?"

"A local grant. It's legit." Or so I thought it was. "I can send you the approval. And you can look it up too. But this is what I want. The library. I'm not taking no for an answer."

She was silent for a long time again. "Send me the details. If this is real, then you get the library. And I get to make sure the romance happens exactly as I want it to."

My stomach churned at her words, but I agreed. If I got to work on the library, I would have to force myself to deal with the rest.

HENRY

Strawberry Springs Neighborhood Watch

Kerry Winsor: I'm heartbroken! Crushed! Jude from *Renovating with Love* was spotted with another woman.

Jade Clark: Men are TRASH.
Marjorie Brown: There's a reason I married a woman.
Jackie Anne: Poor thing. I bet Wren is heartbroken. Is there anything we can do to help?
Mollie Wilson: I'm doing my best friend duties and saying to treat her as usual. She'd hate attention because of this.
Tammy Jane: Damn cheating bastard. Let me at him!
Dale Garrett: So, she's single now?
Jade Clark: Dale, EW.
Dale Garrett: NO, NOT FOR ME. For someone else. I swear!
Tammy Jane: Not the time! We need to give her time to heal.
Dale Garrett: Then can we place bets?

"Absolutely not!" I could hear Jade's voice from down the road. She was facing Kerry, arms crossed tightly. I had to walk past them to get to the clinic, and I hoped whatever thing they were arguing about didn't involve me. "I don't care how cute they were in the show, if he cheated, she better not get back with him!"

Now I knew what they were talking about. The Facebook group had been alight ever since Jude was caught in LA kissing someone else. Since everyone thought he and Wren were together, it had started a massive debate.

One that I should *not* be involved in.

"Henry!" Kerry said, stepping in front of me. "You heard the news, right?"

"Don't you even try," Jade said, shaking her head. "He's *so* gonna be on my side about this."

"All I'm saying is that time can heal this wound. Especially if they work together. Right, Henry?"

I shook my head. "This isn't . . . really my area of expertise."

Fake dating wasn't, at least. I was curious about how Wren was doing with the news, but how she would handle the social issues of the news was beyond me.

Jade, of course, took it the wrong way.

"Really?" She raised an eyebrow. "You've never dated anyone?"

"I've dated. It just . . . didn't end well."

That was an understatement.

"A guy like you could get anyone," Kerry said.

"Then maybe *he* should date Wren. I have a feeling Henry wouldn't cheat on her."

Kerry turned her appraising eyes on me.

"Wait, no!" I said, holding up my hands. "I've only talked to her a few times."

"A *few*?" Kerry said. "That's more than me."

"I haven't even been able to say hello," Jade added.

"Is there something you wanna tell us?" Kerry asked.

"Nope!" I needed to stop this and *fast*. "Nothing!"

"This is your chance to swoop in and save her!" Kerry said.

"Wren does *not* need saving," I said. "And what she's told me about Jude stays between me and her."

Kerry's eyes went wide, and I knew I'd made a mistake. "She's told you things?"

"Now you've done it," Jade said with a smile.

"No, it's nothing like that. And she's way out of my league anyway."

"What?" Kerry rolled her eyes. "You can't really think that."

Jade counted on her fingers as she spoke. "One, you have a good job. Two, you care about others. Three, you're emotionally available. Do you know how hot that is for most women? She would be a fool not to go for you."

"You're so sweet, Jade," Kerry cooed. "It's too bad you stopped dating people in town after Gabriel."

Jade rolled her eyes. "Really?"

"Is it still a sore subject?"

Jade shook her head. "Why are we talking about this? We're trying to convince Henry to make a move."

"I'm not making a move. There's *nothing* going on."

There was the sound of a rumbling truck, and I turned to see a red one pulling up.

Wren's hair was visible through the windshield. She parked and leaned out the window.

"Henry!" she called. "I need to talk to you!"

"Look at the *timing*." Jade snickered.

"It's like it was meant to be."

I gave them a flat look. I liked it better when they were arguing.

"Wren," I greeted as she jogged up to me. I tried to think of something normal and definitely not flirty to say. "You're in a good mood."

"You're gonna be in one too when you hear what I have to say." She winked at me.

That . . . didn't help.

"Sorry to interrupt this cute moment," Jade said, clearing her throat. "But I at least have to introduce myself. I'm Jade."

Wren finally realized we weren't alone and she looked behind me. "Oh! Sorry. I didn't even notice Henry was talking to someone. I'm Wren."

"It's so nice to finally meet Mollie's best friend. I've heard so much about you since she and I started hanging out."

Wren blinked. "You guys hang out?"

"Yeah. A lot actually. I'm kind of the backup friend for when you're busy. I took Mollie to the bar, got way too drunk with her, and had to be carted home."

Wren's smile slowly faded but she replaced it quickly. "I'm glad Mollie has someone here to spend time with."

"You're welcome to come too," Jade said. "Though, you might have a lower opinion of me after."

"I'll be too busy with . . . a thing." Wren grabbed my arm. "Henry, time to talk."

I gave both women what I hoped was a normal smile before I let Wren drag me to the clinic.

Yeah, that looked suspicious.

"Back to what has me in a good mood," Wren began. "The library was selected for *Renovating with Love*."

"It was? Really?"

"Yep. The grant came through, and the showrunners owe me, considering it looks like I got cheated on." She muttered the last part. "But I'm not gonna worry about that because I have *plans* and once those are in place, no one will be thinking about Jude."

She still looked better than when she'd first come to town, but Wren had that look in her eye. She was avoiding something.

"I'm really excited for the library, Wren. But a lot has happened in the past twenty-four hours for you, with the news and then the town's reaction. Are you okay?"

"I'm *so* okay," she replied. "I have a project to work on."

"I'm not in the business of being too harsh. But you're smart enough to know you're not okay. And whether or not you wanna talk about it is one thing, but don't lie. Not to me."

For a second, she stared. Then she slowly shook her head. "Being cheated on isn't the end of the world."

"But it doesn't feel great." My mind flashed to nearly a decade ago and the horror I'd felt seeing Ace and Norah together. "I would know."

She paused. "You would?"

I nodded, and at her raised eyebrow, I knew questions were coming. "Long story short, I tried to run from it for a while. It didn't work."

Wren's face fell. "I'm not *running*. I'm digging my heels in, actually. On the library here."

"So, it's not a distraction?"

"Maybe you have me there." She said it slowly, as if she wanted to be able to say no.

"It's Jude, isn't it?"

She sighed and her shoulders slumped. And I knew I was right.

"Did you know whole *Reddit subs* are talking about his little affair? Hell, the Facebook group here is in on it, but it's not the only one. It's huge news. If I did something like this, I'd be sued for breach of contract! But not him, I guess."

"Does fake dating usually have a contract?"

"This one does," she said with a sigh. "It said we couldn't be seen with anyone else. And now he has, and I look like the fool."

"You're not a fool for being cheated on."

"Is that what you told yourself when it happened?" she asked.

"That was different. It was my fault."

"The cheating was *your* fault?"

"It wasn't cheating. It was . . ." Bad timing. Norah going to Ace right after dumping me. "She found someone better for her. Quickly."

"So, you blame yourself?"

"Sometimes."

"Can I blame myself?"

"Wren, what could you have possibly done?"

She pressed her lips together. "Yeah, I know. I just hoped that . . . Never mind. It doesn't matter. Obviously, he's busy. Typical Hollywood guy. Nice for the cameras, a selfish dick when they're off. I doubt he's thought twice about me."

I let out a laugh without realizing. "What an idiot, then."

"Why is he an idiot?"

"Anyone who doesn't think twice about you obviously doesn't have eyes." Her cheeks turned dusty pink and I realized the enormity of what I'd said. "I . . . mean in a friendly way, of course."

"Of course." She tucked a piece of her hair behind her ear. "You know, you're being nicer than he was. And I'll still have to date him when they tell me to. I put my foot down that I wouldn't ignore him kissing someone else if it were real, but I know they're aiming to have us back together in the show."

Instantly, I knew I hated the idea of her being forced to even interact with a man who didn't give her the time of day. Usually, I was good at separating myself from others' problems, but not with her.

"If he is as you say he is, then it isn't worth it."

"I know," she replied. "But this was my chance to do bigger

and better things. I should have realized it came with strings attached."

"When do they get here?"

"Next week," she replied. "And while having him here isn't gonna be fun, I'm so excited to spend more time with Mollie. I didn't realize how much I'd missed . . ." She trailed off as she looked back over at Jade.

"Is that why you were shocked by what Jade said?"

She blinked. "Nothing gets past you, does it?"

"Half of this town avoids telling me what's going on with them. Usually it's about health things, but sometimes mental health too. I've learned to look."

"It's not like it's a big deal," she said. "I'm happy that she came here and made new friends."

"But you're worried about it."

"Yeah." She sighed. "It's a bad habit of mine."

"She talked about you all the time when you weren't here. She was so happy about the show."

"She's the best. I wonder how the distance will feel once this is all over."

"When you go back to Nashville, you mean?"

She nodded. "I have a lot of jobs there. Even if I don't continue the show. It's a huge market. I always thought Mollie would be there too. Not that I'm complaining that she found all of . . . *this*."

"Feelings are complicated. And she's your best friend."

"She's my only friend."

"That's not true. You have me now."

"You're right," she said with a laugh. "How could I forget? Anyway, I should let you get back to whatever you were doing."

"I was just walking to work from my house."

"A *house*?" she asked. "Wow, you have it all together. Is it in need of work?"

"Keep your eyes on the library," I replied, shaking my head. "It's perfect for just me."

"Come on. You have a house. A good job. What don't you have?"

Confidence. The ability to be the center of the room and not know it. Things she had. She was a powerhouse, and so out of my league that it hurt.

"I could probably use more sweaters."

She eyed me. "Something tells me that's a lie."

She was right.

After an awkward pause, she said, "Well, I have to go figure out all the legal stuff, but I wanted you to be one of the first to know."

"Because I broke in with you."

"Yes, but also because you love it." She gripped my shoulders tightly. "I can't wait to see your *face* when you get in there. You're the only one who'll get to see it from beginning to end."

"It's an honor."

"So, you're glad you broke the law with me?"

"I am. And I'd do it again."

Her eyes widened and I realized she was still touching me. She must have realized it too, but she didn't let go.

I needed to move away, but I couldn't. We were far too close for friends, yet neither of us made a move to step back into the place we belonged.

"One hundred bucks on this happening in a week!" a male voice yelled. Wren and I sprung apart, only to see Dale had stepped outside of Food 'n' Things.

"Two hundred on it already being a thing!" Jade yelled back.

"A hundred bucks on this being a slow burn!" Kerry added. "We can't forget about Jude!"

"What're they doing?" Wren asked.

I scrubbed a hand across my face. "Betting on when we'll get together."

Her eyes bugged out. "What? But that's . . . not happening. For many reasons."

"You can't stop them once they start."

More people came outside to join the bet. I'd never seen them do all of this in person, and I wasn't sure whether to be honored or mortified.

"Should I have Mollie say it'll never happen and become rich?"

I thought of the way Mollie looked between us. "Do you think she'd take that bet?"

"Probably not. What if I created a secret identity and did it?"

"Split the winnings with me, and I'll add fake-you to the clinic roster to give you believability."

WREN

RWL Superfan Discussion Central

Neve Bullock: Does anyone have any info on Wren? No one's spotted her recently and she hasn't been active on her socials.

Comments:

Carly Ware: This is all so dramatic when Jude probably kissed that other girl for a publicity stunt.

Jamie McCullough: She'll have to say something soon. They should be announcing the reno project for season two any day now.

Kerry Winsor: I happen to know that she's not in Nashville. We're supporting her through this difficult time.

Alicia Parrish: Who is WE???? What do you know??

Bethany Perry: I don't believe you. The show is set in Nashville, and they're gonna start filming soon. You're just clout chasing for likes.

Madison climbed out of her blacked-out SUV. She faced the library, taking it in, but didn't bother removing her sunglasses.

"Well. This is certainly something."

"It's massive. Way bigger than the mansion."

"And not where the show should be set." A hand landed on her hip. "Still don't love that."

"Look at the rest of the town. People will love the charm."

She slowly turned, lips pursed as she looked at everything else. The potted plants were sprouting new flowers in all kinds of bright colors for the incoming summer season. Most of the buildings looked great, as long as they were open.

"It's cute, but most of our sponsors are Nashville locals. I made it work, but they're not thrilled about this."

Sponsors. Money. I hated to even think about it. But it was the reason I'd signed up to do the show in the first place.

That, and Jude.

"Give me the pitch," she said. "I wanna know what you'll tell the cameras about why you like this town and library."

I nodded, trying to get into character. I explained the history, how it had been here for generations but stayed small, how the library was not only the cornerstone of the town, but the whole county, and everyone here missed it.

When I was done, Madison appraised me.

"Not bad," she said. "You have that excitement people love. I just wish it wasn't *here*."

"Hey," I said, crossing my arms. "This is someone's home. They really like their town."

"And I'm sure it's great for them, but I also have a business to think about. We need this season to do well. Better than the first, even." Her gaze was back on the library. "Though I'll admit, this would be a massive transformation. And it would look good to fix something so defunct."

While Madison inspected every brick of the town library again, I let my gaze roam over the rest of the square. Quickly, I realized that people were watching. Kerry was at the diner, looking at us through the window. Jackie was in her shop doing the same thing.

My spine straightened. I needed to remember who this was for and why I was doing this.

"Can we agree that this is the project for season two?"

"Fine." She let out a harsh sigh. "If you're insisting, then we'll make it work. Even if the inside is completely trashed."

"It's not. A . . . few people have been in. It's in need of work, but it's as solid as the mansion was."

"All right, but I want your full cooperation. If we're not in Nashville, then we need everything else to be perfect."

"Yes. I'll be present and ready to make this place incredible." That was what I could promise. The stuff with Jude was something I'd have to make myself do. And I was never good at forcing anything.

Thankfully, she didn't press for clarification.

"Fine. I'll track down the owner."

"I did that. And they're willing to sell. I'll cover it like I did the mansion. The network just pays the reno cost. And . . . travel for employees."

Her eyes cut to me. "You should cover that, considering this was all your idea."

"I'll cover it for *my* guys," I answered. "The ones I work with regularly. Whoever you bring, you need to cover."

Last season, they'd doubled my team. It wasn't just contractors. It was personal assistants, a filming crew, and even actors who were designed to pretend they were working on the mansion.

Madison narrowed her eyes at me. I was pushing her, and I knew that, but the show itself was *her* thing.

"We'll split it," she said slowly. "But this better be the best season yet."

"Once people see this place, they'll love it. I know they will."

Her lips pressed into a thin line and she nodded. "Send me the offer once you have it. And tell me who you're bringing. *Not* the one from season one."

Last summer, Madison had a tryst with one of the best men I worked with. He was a notorious ladies' man and was very clear upfront that he didn't want a relationship with her.

Madison had hoped for one anyway.

Not having him here would suck. He was great to work with professionally.

"Will do."

"I'll get Jude and we'll film your reunion first thing."

"R-reunion?" I asked.

"Yes."

"Do I need to remind you that it looked like he *cheated* on me?"

"Even if he did, you still miss him. You'll hug and kiss before doing an interview about how you're angry but are willing to work on it."

"Once again, I'm not kissing someone who cheated on me," I said slowly through clenched teeth.

"You said you would cooperate. This is what that means. I know what will sell, and you two are it."

She was gone before I could say anything else, and I had to ignore the rising panic. *Fuck.* I should have known she wouldn't let sleeping dogs lie with this thing with Jude.

Luckily, I didn't have to worry about it long, because someone was running up to me.

"Oh my God!" Kerry looked like she'd just won the lottery. "Who was that? Why was she looking at the old library?"

I blinked back into focus. "I don't know if I can share yet."

"*Please!* Is this about the show? She looked so official!"

"It . . . might be, but we're still working stuff out on that."

"Kerry, I swear!" Tammy had followed her. "Not only did you make me run, but now you're hounding the poor woman!"

"It's okay," I said. "I'm sure it's big news."

"If you're gonna be fixing that old thing up, you'll be under a lot of stress. And Kerry here wants to know too much."

"This isn't a bad topic this time," Kerry said with her hands on her hips.

"You and the rest of the town are on thin ice after starting a betting pool in the town square." Tammy narrowed her eyes.

"It's how we welcome people. And you joined the bet later."

"You joined?" I asked. "What did you bet?"

If she'd said it would never happen, then she was going to be a rich woman. I was still considering making a fake identity to get the winnings, but something was stopping me. I knew Henry and I wouldn't happen, but if hell froze over and we did, it would be mortifying to lose a bet with myself.

"She bet that you two would be in denial and be together by late summer."

Tammy went red in the face. "Kerry, I swear to *God*—"

"It's fine," I said. "It's your money to lose."

"Lose?" Tammy asked. "What, do you know something we don't?"

"I'm not single, guys."

"You're still with that little twerp?" Tammy nearly yelled. I realized my mistake.

"No, not really. I mean, it's just complicated. I'm not ready to move on."

Kerry and Tammy looked at each other, seemingly silently exchanging words between them.

Then Kerry spoke. "I think you had something on the denial thing."

"I'm not dumb."

"Can we get back to whatever we were talking about before?" I begged. There was something about the idea of me and Henry that made my entire body hot. In the early summer heat, it wasn't good for me.

"Oh, right!" Kerry said with a laugh. "I have information to get." She suddenly turned serious. "The library. What's happening with that?"

"*Kerry*," Tammy warned.

"She's on a major show, Tammy! We could be featured! Do you know what tourism does to economies? Good things. This could be great for us."

"Mollie's gonna kill me for saying this, but we all know she's going through something because of the twerp she was with. Can you give her a break?"

Suddenly, I wished we were talking about the bet again. Thinking about whatever post must have gone up about me was my worst nightmare. I hated that they even knew about Jude, but what I hated more was that they would all see me cave and go back.

"I'll get over it," I ground out. I had to. "I'll have plenty to focus on if the show comes here."

"So it's a possibility?" Kerry asked.

"It's getting more and more real by the second."

"Can I post this on the Facebook group? *Please?* I'll do whatever you want!"

"Let me finalize the sale. It would be worse if this didn't happen and everyone was excited."

"Okay. So don't post. But I can draft it!" She ran back to the diner, obviously thrilled by the idea of drafting a post.

Tammy sighed. "She never stops."

"It's sweet. Definitely different than Nashville." I looked at Tammy and bit my lip.

She caught it immediately. "Got a question for me?"

"What did they say in the Facebook group?"

"You really wanna know?"

"No. Yes. I'm not sure."

She pulled out her phone and handed it over. "I'm only doing this because it's nothing bad. And because you have a good friend."

I scrolled through everything. Just like Mollie said, they were on my side. Tammy, inexplicably, seemed the angriest.

"Hypothetically," I said slowly, "if I were to . . . forgive him, what would they say then?"

Her voice was low. "If you were to *what?*"

"Move on. Move forward." My skin crawled just saying it. "With him."

"Once a cheater, always a cheater." Tammy shook her head. "You deserve better."

I did. "Still . . ."

"I'll tell you what I tell my daughter when she's considering something dumb. It doesn't matter what I think or what anyone else does. If you do this, in the end, *you* have to live with it. Is that something you can do?"

"I think I *have* to. For the show."

"You know"—Tammy walked close and put a hand on my shoulder—"things might seem like they have to go a certain way, but nothing is ever set in stone. You're a smart woman, Wren. Whatever you don't wanna do, I bet you can find a way out of it."

"I don't know if I can this time. And I keep trying to figure out some way to move forward and get work done—"

Her hand tightened. "You just got done fixing up a whole

mansion. You keep busy. What you need is to fill up your cup and *relax*."

"I'm terrible at that."

"Step one. Come inside the diner and get a drink and some food. I'll make sure you get well fed. Step two. We figure it out."

"I'm sure you're busy. I'll be—"

"None of that." Her hand squeezed again and she started pushing me toward the diner. "I'm not above giving you a coloring page if it means you sit still for a bit."

"Does that ever work?"

"It does. I gave one to Jade until she was twenty. What a relief that was."

The cool air of the diner hit me as we walked in, and Tammy gave me a table and a coloring page. I planned on working on the design for the library, but every time she caught me, she took away my crayons.

"What, am I in time-out?"

"That's what you get when you don't listen. Now you just have to sit and talk to me."

"About what?"

"Oh, there are a lot of things. Let me tell you about the time Ron figured out about those internet trackers and tried to throw out my phone. That always gets people to laugh."

She launched into a story about her husband. At first, I wasn't sure if I would enjoy hearing about a man I'd never met, but Tammy was a good storyteller. I was laughing by the time she was done with her tale, and she immediately launched into another one about Kerry.

I didn't get a chance to think about the show or the library the entire time.

And honestly, it was nice to be free of it for a bit. It felt like I was a part of something for once.

Even if it wouldn't last forever.

11

HENRY

Strawberry Springs Neighborhood Watch

Kerry Winsor: IT'S OFFICIAL! *Renovating with Love* is coming to Strawberry Springs for season two to renovate the library!

Comments:
Marjorie Brown: Listen, I know I've been a pain in your ass, but this is just mean. The library is closed. It always will be.
Kerry Winsor: It's not a joke!!! I happen to know firsthand that it's real!
Jade Clark: HOLY SHIT! SHE'S NOT LYING!
Marjorie Brown: NO FUCKING WAY.
Jade Clark: I'm finally gonna read again!
Nicole Rudder: When will it be done? By the next school year or so? I need to see if I can take the kids there for more books. The school one has an awful selection!
Dale Garrett: @Henry Connor Did you see this?
Kerry Winsor: Oh, we know he knows. He knows EVERYTHING.

Henry Connor: Guys, please. Whatever you're thinking, it's NOT gonna happen.
Kerry Winsor: But you've known all along, right?
Henry Connor: . . . Yes.

***

I HAD JUST FINISHED PLANTING marigolds in the garden when four cars drove by. One of them was a sports car with a rumbling engine that I could hear coming from miles away. If I were anywhere else, I wouldn't think much of it. But this was not normal for Strawberry Springs.

Filming would be happening soon, though I had no idea when it would start. Since I'd been outed as the one who knew this was coming, people had been incessantly asking me to tell them what I knew, which was next to nothing. Wren had all but disappeared in the last few days, and I assumed she was getting the final details worked out. I wasn't sure when I would be ready for the chaos of a show to start, but I was happy the town was getting the library back.

The cars returned as I watered the rose bushes in the front of my house, and I found myself growing annoyed.

"Hey, you!" a male voice called.

I slowly turned and saw a man with dark hair leaning out of the sports car. Of course he would talk to *me* of all people.

For living so close to town, it was always quiet here.

Not anymore, apparently.

"Yes?" I asked. I put on my polite face, ignoring the churning in my gut.

"Can you tell me where the square is? This little town has terrible signage."

That was because they'd faded a long time ago. "Most people don't need them. Are you visiting?"

He laughed. "Did you not hear? We're filming *Renovating with Love* here."

"I did, but I didn't think it would be starting so soon."

"We're too popular. Gotta strike while the iron is hot. Now, where's the town square?"

"Go two roads that way and turn right."

"Cool. Thanks, man. Tell your wife I said those are some nice flowers."

He drove off, the loud engine of his car rattling every single one of my brain cells. My grip on the watering can grew tight. He'd said *we're popular*.

Please tell me that's not Jude.

I'd planned on avoiding anything related to filming. I needed my weekends to rest my mind for the week ahead. Usually, I spent the time either reading or catching up on medical journals and podcasts.

But now I was curious. If he were Wren's costar, then I could see why things had ended as they had. Sure, from the outside, he was conventionally attractive. I usually didn't let my first impressions of people mean much, but the loud car and the way he'd spoken to me meant nothing good for Wren.

And before I realized it, I was going inside to wash up and head into town.

The square was as busy as a farmers market day. The area near the library had been blocked off. People were concentrated on one side, all facing the filming that was taking place. I froze. How fast was the show moving? Wren had mentioned some time off, but had she even gotten that?

I could see the woman who was on my mind in the distance. Her hair was wavy and down today, falling over one shoulder. Her arms were tightly crossed as she talked to a woman with glossy black hair.

Her eyes met mine. I gave her a polite wave, planning to go ask what the hell was going on. Kerry would know.

But Wren was jogging over to me.

She had light makeup on, her lashes darker than usual. She looked good.

But not like the Wren I knew.

"Henry! Hi."

"Hey," I replied. "Weren't you in the middle of something?"

"It can wait," she replied. "I didn't know you'd be here today."

"I didn't know this was happening today."

She blew out a breath. "Yeah. They move fast. The second the location was figured out, they wanted to start. Why wait?"

"Did you get your full break?"

"Like I was relaxing anyway." She crossed her arms again and looked at the whole crew. "The sooner I do this, the sooner it's over with." Her body was tense. Every inch of her was coiled tight.

"You don't seem thrilled about that."

"I'll be fine. Today is a reunion with Jude and talking about the library."

"And what does that reunion entail?"

"Nothing great," she muttered.

"Is he here?"

"Yep." She pointed to a man walking over to the front of the library. His dark hair was visible from a mile away. It was the same man who'd asked me where the square was. "That's him."

His eyes flicked to Wren and then right back to the woman he was talking to. There was no second look. No moment to admire how beautiful she was.

Inexplicably, my hands tightened and I shoved them in my pockets.

Her hands gripped the barrier. "I don't even wanna *look* at him."

"Then don't."

"What, just, say hello and nothing else?"

"Exactly. You're in control here."

She took a breath. "I don't think the director agrees with you."

"She might run the show, but you're still a person. Which means some level of control."

She nodded. "You're right. Or at least you should be." Her lips curved upward. "Thank you. I needed that reminder. How long are you staying?"

I thought about it. I could only mentally handle a few minutes. I was used to my schedule of being alone on the weekend.

But it was *Wren*.

"Let's get this started!" Jude called. He pumped his arms at the crowd watching.

Only Kerry clapped. Silence then followed.

Jude's smile fell and he loudly grumbled, "Tough crowd."

"How long do you want me to stay?" I asked.

"I'm sure you're busy."

"I can make time."

She bit her lip before answering. "Four hours. Can we talk after it? I'll buy you dinner."

"Yeah. Of course."

"Thank you. You're a lifesaver."

She rejoined the director and Jude, only giving him a shallow wave. I stood there like a fool before walking over with everyone else.

"She's not even giving him the time of day," Marjorie said. "Good for her."

"I hate that she has to do this at all," I muttered.

"Ooooh, protective."

"Not you too."

"I can't help that I have eyes and live for annoying people. But if it makes you feel any better, I didn't get in on the bet."

"Oh, please." Henrietta rolled her eyes. "You were in the bathroom when everyone was talking about it. Otherwise you would have joined in too."

Marjorie shushed her and I shook my head. I was glad the town was having fun, but they would be proven wrong when Wren made it look like she was dating Jude.

My fists clenched again at the mere thought. I hadn't realized it at the time, but I'd avoided the topic of filming not only because of the chaos, but because I wasn't sure I could watch her be with him.

But she'd asked me to stay. And I would.

Wren didn't smile or even hug him the first time they interacted. She was focused solely on the camera. I heard Madison bark something about Wren running to Jude, but she only shook her head in response.

Good. She deserved to be able to say no.

They did multiple versions of the reunion before the woman behind the camera threw her hands up and told them to go inside, presumably to film the tours.

I couldn't help but smile.

"It's been a long time since I've seen those doors open," Marjorie said. "Oh, I can't wait to run that place again."

I turned to her. "You'd be coming out of retirement?"

"Me and Henrietta both. We started our life in that building. We might as well be back there."

It was rare to see her so serious, but everyone knew both of them had been crushed when the funding was cut.

"I bet you'll both be happy."

"It'll be like old times. Maybe I can sneak her to the back like before we told everyone we were together."

"Gonna carve more desks while you're at it?"

"She'd kill me if—" Marjorie paused. "How did you know about the desk? That was before you moved here."

"There's no chance you'd forget you heard that?"

"Nope. I'm always gonna need an answer. Just ask Theo. He knows I don't let things go."

"Wren and I . . . snuck in a while ago."

Marjorie gasped. "You *what*?"

Now people were turning to us. "Keep it down. I don't want Mike hearing about it."

"That's the final straw. Where's Dale?" She turned and hobbled away. "I have a bet to enter!"

I winced and looked at Henrietta. "Sorry."

"Oh, don't be. It keeps her entertained." She shrugged. "Oh, and I'll be entering it too. You sneaking in somewhere? You have it *bad*."

I sighed. "You people never let stuff go."

"Watching you young people fall in love is all we have." Her eyes traced the crowd. "Oh, Marjorie's handing money over. I better place mine too."

She was gone before I could tell her not to waste her money. People were gonna be pretty mad when they lost it all. Maybe Hugh would finally win something. He was known for being negative.

Eventually, Wren came back out. When she finally did, her shoulders were tense, and I stepped away in case she needed me.

She walked over the second she saw me.

"How's it going?" I asked.

"We're about to refilm the reunion scene." She took a long drink of water. "I'm sticking to my guns and focusing on what really matters." Her eyes moved to the people behind us. Kerry, who had been recording the whole thing, waved. Wren waved back, which turned into nearly everyone in town waving at her, grins on their faces.

"Good."

"I don't know if it'll change anything in the end, though. It seems like it's pushing back the inevitable. The show needs its *love*." She said the word as if it were a curse.

"You can make it about any love. It could be for the town or . . . someone else."

She raised her brow. "Someone else?"

This was treading near something I couldn't follow through on. "I meant some*thing* else. Work with anything you have."

She considered the words, looking between the town and me. "You're still staying, right?"

"I will."

The director called her back over. I watched closely as she was instructed on what to do. From here, I could barely make out the conversation.

"You'll run and hug him," the director said. I could hear her far better from my new spot. "He'll apologize, and then you'll say you're happy to see him. And then you'll kiss."

"I already said no to kissing him. I don't want to."

"Rude," Jude said. His voice was louder, and the town all heard him. "Come on. What I did wasn't that big of a deal."

Someone in the crowd scoffed. I was pretty sure it was Jade.

Wren glared over at him, and I had to resist the urge to step in.

"We're filming this *now*," the director said. "No more putting this off. Go down the road and run to us."

My chest tightened when she did what they said. I didn't want to see this, but she'd asked me to stay. The director yelled *action* and Wren started to jog. I watched every movement she made as she got close to both of us.

I expected her to run to Jude and pull him into her embrace. And at first, she was. But then her eyes cut to me and she hesitated. The entire square was silent.

When she finally got moving again, she didn't go to Jude.

Instead, she came to *me*.

As she got close, I opened my mouth, expecting her to ask for advice. I was going to tell her to end it for the day. Everyone was frustrated and she needed to figure out some common ground to get her out of what she didn't want to do.

All of those words vanished in a puff of smoke when she got to me.

Because she grabbed the nape of my neck and pulled me into a searing kiss.

12

WREN

Strawberry Springs Neighborhood Watch

Kerry Winsor: HENRY? KISSING WREN AT THE LIBRARY? THIS IS NOT A DRILL!!

Comments:
Dale Garrett: I SAW IT TOO! AND I CALLED IT!!! GIVE ME MY MONEY!!!
Jade Clark: I WAS A DAY OFF!
Hu Gh: All this filming ruined my coffee time!
Tammy Jane: Chill it, Hugh. We're all talking about the cutest couple in town.
Mollie Wilson: HANG ON, WHAT?
Kerry Winsor: WAIT DID YOU NOT KNOW? YOU SAW THE BETTING POOL, RIGHT?
Mollie Wilson: I THOUGHT YOU ALL WERE ABOUT TO LOSE MONEY! Cain told me to join and I DIDN'T!

MY FIRST THOUGHT WAS, *I can't do this with Jude.*

My second was, *Henry is gonna be so mad.*

And the third? *It's unfair that he's a good kisser.*

For a second, we both stood still, making for what could have been the most awkward camera kiss ever. I moved my lips against his, preparing to pull away if this last-second change didn't work.

But then he kissed me back. One hand cupped my cheek and his lips slotted over mine. He smelled like fresh linen and oranges, and I was having a hard time remembering why I'd done this in the first place.

All I could think about was him.

"Cut!" Madison bellowed, her voice echoing off everything.

Everyone around us whispered among each other, and I could feel eyes all on us.

I pulled away, cheeks as warm as the sun, looking Henry in the eye.

"What—" he began.

"Can you please go with it?"

"Go with what? Are we dating? Did I completely miss us agreeing to that?"

"No, of course not. This is just—"

"What the *hell*, Wren?" Madison yelled as she stalked over to us. "You were supposed to go kiss Jude, not some random guy on the side of the street."

I really hoped he'd back me up here, or else I was in for a lifetime of embarrassment.

"He's not some random guy. This is my boyfriend. Otherwise known as the reason I can't fake a relationship with Jude."

I reached for Henry's hand, hoping that he wouldn't pull away and run for the hills.

Luckily, he let me latch onto him.

"That's . . . right," he said. "I'm Wren's boyfriend."

Henry glanced over at the crowd of the town. They'd gone deathly silent, which probably wasn't a good sign. I followed his gaze and everyone had some version of shock on their faces.

This didn't look good.

Madison let out a long breath, narrow eyes darting in between us. "I'm not falling for this."

"I am!" Dale yelled. "They've been two peas in a pod since he saw her!"

"They're so cute!" Jade added.

My cheeks were on fire. Henry and I were so sure this would never happen, and now, it was getting me out of being with Jude. Everyone's nosy nature was literally saving us.

"It's . . . new!" I defended. "And I just couldn't even touch someone else knowing my boyfriend's standing right here. You said that the show needed to be about love, so it can be about love with someone else."

Henry's hand went rigid in mine. One look at him told me that his entire body was the same way. *Fuck.* I wish I'd had this idea *before* the lie had started. At least I could have talked to him about it. Or figured something else out when he said no.

This whole time, I'd been thinking about myself. Did *he* want to date me? The town thought so. Maybe they had it wrong.

"Are we almost done here?" Jude yelled. "I wanna head back to Nashville to hit up a bar tonight."

I rolled my eyes. In the first season, he spent all of his extra time with me. He'd said he wanted me to be his guide. But when we'd go to the bars, he would vanish and I would be alone, forcing me to call a car to come get me. Then he got involved in the Nashville scene, becoming a well-known figure at events. That was around the time he told me he wasn't interested.

"Jude!" Madison said. "Did you not see her kiss someone else?"

He only shrugged. "I thought it was revenge. An eye for an eye or something."

Madison groaned, letting out her frustrations at the blue sky. "I can't do this today! We're done. We'll figure this out tomorrow."

"I have a shoot tomorrow," Jude said. "Bud Light's sponsoring me."

"Dammit! Then Monday." She pointed at me. "This is not the end of this."

She stormed off. Jude shrugged and walked over. I didn't think it was possible for Henry to tense even more, but he did.

"So, was that just revenge?" Jude asked. It was the first thing he'd said to me all day.

"No. I'm really dating someone else."

He looked between me and Henry. "Interesting. You know, I'll let this happen. The whole fake dating thing was really limiting anyway. Good luck dealing with Madison, though." He waved and walked off, completely unbothered.

"Nice people," Henry remarked, his voice tight.

I took my hand out of his. "We should talk."

"Yes, we should."

He didn't sound thrilled with me, and I didn't blame him. I should have figured out a way to deal with my problems without dragging him into it.

"I'm rich!" Dale yelled. "Finally, I won a bet!"

"I need to know how this happened!" Kerry yelled it so loudly that we both jumped. "Every detail!"

"We can't go to the diner," Henry said. "They'll never let us have a moment alone."

I let out a sigh. "Right. Have any other ideas?"

"Come with me."

Great. Judging by the way he uttered the words through gritted teeth, he *definitely* wasn't thrilled with me. He probably was taking me somewhere private to tell me what an idiot I was.

"Lead the way."

Henry gave one nod and we left the square, heading down a few roads. We came up on a two-story house with a massive garden, which happened to be the one he unlocked the gate to.

"This is your place?" I asked.

"Yes."

"Wow. This is very well landscaped. Do you hire someone for this?"

"No. It's just how I relax."

Oh boy. I had a feeling he would be doing a *lot* of gardening after this.

"All right, just get it over with." I crossed my arms. "You can yell at me now."

His brow pinched. "Yelling doesn't solve anything."

"You're obviously mad."

"A little, but it's because I have *no* clue what just happened back there. And I despise being *this* in the dark." He crossed his arms too. "Haven't felt like this since the first day of med school, honestly."

"I found a way out. One I should have discussed with you, but they can't make me date Jude if they think I'm dating someone else."

He stared and shook his head. "I'm still not following."

There was an edge to Henry's voice, a desperation I hadn't heard before.

"Fake dating," I said. "You and I pretend to be together to get Madison off my back about Jude. And then we go our separate ways."

"*Fake* dating? Like what you did with Jude?"

"Yes. We say we're together but we're really not. Just for the camera. You can have your normal life and I can work on the library without being forced to like a man I hate. It's a win-win! Well, kinda. For me, at least. But I'd make it worth your while. Name anything in your house and I'll fix it. Or out of the house. I'll do anything you need me to."

"Hang on. I just need a minute." He took off his glasses and rubbed his forehead while I lapsed into silence. I watched as he began to pace around.

My stomach sank. "You okay?"

"I can't even begin to comprehend this," he said. "There's dating and there's friends. This is in the middle. And I had no idea there was a middle before last week!"

Henry had always been so soft-spoken and polite. He wasn't that now. His face was red. He was tense, and had a deeper tone I'd never heard before. Horror dawned on me. I'd taken a mild-mannered doctor and sent him to the edge. *Fuck*, I needed to fix this.

"I shouldn't have done this. God, Henry, I'm *so* sorry."

"What was the alternative? Being forced to kiss Mister Tall, Dark, and Personality of a Paper Bag?"

Despite everything that was going on, Henry had Jude *pegged*. I would have laughed if I hadn't been so worried about him.

Henry saw it. "Sorry, I shouldn't have said that."

"No, you can say what you want. I'm just trying to figure out how to fix this. I really messed up here."

"At least I didn't . . . ." He trailed off and took in a deep breath. "There's nothing for you to fix. I shouldn't have reacted so strongly to this. But you have to know I'm not . . . cut out for this. Friendship is one thing. Dating is another. Blurring the lines isn't something that goes well for me."

"Okay," I said, any mirth gone. "That's understandable. I'm sorry I dragged you into this. I just . . . panicked at the idea of touching him, but that's my issue to fix."

Shame colored my cheeks. I needed to leave. Mull over my mistakes. Then figure out how to make this better. I walked backward down his porch, ready to run.

But a hand latched onto mine.

"Wren, wait."

I looked out at the sky and then back to him. "Yeah?"

"If I say no to this . . . What are the other options?"

"I . . . don't think there are any." I shrugged. "But that's okay. I got myself into this, so I can deal with it."

"No," he nearly snapped, and I blinked at the sharp tone of his voice. Then he winced and spoke in a softer tone. "No. You can't just accept this."

"I would love nothing more than to find some way out of it, but I don't think I can. You saw how Madison was. Even with the entire town *cheering* about us being together, she didn't wanna believe it."

"So, I should say yes."

"Henry, *no*. If it'll make you miserable, then don't. I'm the one who signed the contract. I agreed to this. It'll be fine pretending with Jude."

"*Wren.*" He said my name desperately. Like it was the last thing he could hold on to. "*I* can't watch you pretend with Jude."

I froze. I'd had no idea he cared so much.

"If this is the way out, then we're getting you out of it."

"We?"

"Yes. And let's be honest, no one else is gonna let it go, even if we tried to back out of it."

I could only stare at the sharp line of his jaw as I fought a massive wave of emotion. I wasn't sure what I was feeling, whether it be relief, guilt, or concern, but it made my throat close up.

"Fuck, Henry." I cleared my throat, trying to play it off. "Thank you. I owe you big time."

"You don't owe me anything, other than patience when I need very specific instructions. Fake dating is something that I have *no* experience with."

"Luckily, you're talking to the pro." I laughed, but his face was serious, so I thought about it. "Mainly, it's about the cameras. Being there when filming. When your work schedule accommodates, of course. Maybe I'll crash on your couch and come from your place to make it look like we're spending time together." I paused when he looked a little green at the suggestion. "Or not."

"Yeah, I don't . . . My house is my place. I'd like to keep fake dating out of that."

I could respect that. I even took a step toward his gate to give it space.

"Noted. All it would entail is hand-holding. Maybe a coffee or some other gift. A kiss here and there."

"Okay. Hand-holding. Gifts. A kiss."

After the last one, I was looking forward to doing that again.

"And off camera, we're friends. Just like before."

"All right. Clear rules. I can work with that."

"Seriously, I owe you whatever you want. Just say the word and I'll make it happen."

"It's fine." He shook his head. "Besides, you'll be busy answering questions. I'm sure people are still talking about it."

"At least Mollie's at home. I'm kinda glad she was busy today. I can at least explain."

Henry frowned. "It's probably already in the group. Actually, I bet it was in there the second it happened."

My face fell. "Shit, really?"

"Absolutely. No one wastes time here."

My stomach churned. "Oh no."

Like clockwork, my phone rang, and it was the one other person who would have wanted a warning.

"Shit," I said. "I need to go get yelled at by my best friend. And grab my stuff from the set. Thank you for literally saving my ass."

I waved as I ran away, sending Mollie to voicemail so I could book it to the farmhouse and tell her all that happened in person. And then I could freak out about fake dating Henry.

I had a ton to do.

"Facebook?" Mollie hissed the second I walked into the farmhouse. "I had to find out you kissed Henry from *Facebook*? What am I to you? Dirt?"

"No!" I rushed to say. "Kissing Henry was completely unplanned and kind of an accident."

"An accident? In front of the whole town?"

"Accidents always happen in front of the town," Cain said. His voice was at least calm. Hopefully he wasn't as mad at me as she was.

"Don't talk to me when I'm scolding Wren!"

Cain only shrugged and walked away. I rubbed my face and prepared for more.

"I'm all for you doing batshit-wild stuff whenever you want, but can you at least give me a warning?"

"Next time I'm running to make a split-second decision, I'll text you first. Or right after. This time, I had to make sure Henry wasn't gonna explode."

"He had *you* kissing him. I bet he felt like he won the lottery. God, when did this happen? When did you two get together?"

I braced myself for what I was about to say next. "Mollie, it *didn't* happen. Kissing him *was* a split-second decision because we were never together."

Her eyes went wide. "*That's* how you made a move?"

"It wasn't a move! It was to get out of doing it with Jude. It was *fake*."

"Oh . . . my . . . *God*."

"Yeah."

"So, you're not really dating?"

"Nope."

"Dale won all that money for nothing?"

I raised an eyebrow. "Is that your first thought here?"

"Well, no. My first thought is a bunch of confused exclamation points. But the second is that if he knows he didn't really win, that's gonna be *huge*."

"The goal is for no one to know. We look like we're dating and we have to."

"When did Henry agree to this?"

I cleared my throat. "After I did it."

Mollie gasped. "*Wren!*"

"I know, I know. Not my best decision. He wasn't thrilled with me, but we worked it out. I owe him big-time, but he's on board."

"So, he's dating you for show to get you out of everything with Jude, and what is he getting in return?"

"Nothing right now. He said he didn't want me to do it either."

"He's saving your ass and asking for nothing?" She let out a laugh. "What a guy."

"I'm gonna figure something out . . . eventually. I have to tackle one problem at a time. And the next problem is gonna be my director."

"Was she mad?"

"Furious."

"Well, maybe she shouldn't be pushing you with a guy like Jude. Or with anyone at all, for that matter." Mollie crossed her arms. "Serves her right."

"She's not gonna take this lying down. She wants Jude and me to pretend to be together, but I *can't*. Now that I have an out, I have to use it. Seeing him today was miserable."

Mollie narrowed her eyes at me. "You've been sad ever since you finished season one. What did he say to you to start all of this?"

"Nothing that's worth mentioning."

"Is it not worth mentioning, or are you not wanting to talk about it?"

I shrank into myself and looked out the window. "You're gonna hate him when I tell you."

"He's already not my favorite person."

"Okay, fine. He said he could never see himself being with someone so . . . manly."

Mollie's jaw dropped. "He . . . *what*? How dare he! You're a fucking *catch*."

"I know," I lied. "I'm definitely a catch."

Maybe if I said it enough, I would believe it. But deep down, I knew how off-putting I could be. It had happened many times before. To people important to me. People who should have loved me.

"I can't believe him. No wonder you wanna get away."

And I needed to. I didn't know how I would get through this season if I hadn't made up something to get me away from Jude.

My phone rang, and I cringed when I saw it was Madison.

"Time to go face the music. Be right back."

"Give 'em hell!" Mollie called as I went upstairs. When I was in the guest room, I filled my lungs with much-needed air before answering.

"I hope you're ready to see sense now," Madison said without any sort of greeting.

"I *am* seeing sense."

She let out another groan, which didn't mean anything good for me.

"You're under contract," she said. "Which means you do as I say."

"Did you give Jude this lecture when he kissed someone else?"

"He said that wasn't serious."

"And yet he started all of this. Henry and I connected when that happened, you know." It was a version of the truth. Sure, we hadn't actually gotten together, but Henry was one of the few who got me to open up.

"I don't care about Henry. I care about making this show what it should be."

"And as the star of the show, I'm telling you I can't be with Jude this season."

"*Renovating with Love* is based on you and Jude. You have no choice."

"I'm with someone else," I snapped. "So it's a no!"

"I don't care who you're with. You have an obligation, so whatever's going on can be put on hold."

Anger flooded me. Even though I wasn't with Henry, the idea of putting a real relationship on hold to act for a camera was ridiculous. "Are you serious?"

"Obviously, you don't know how show business works, but this is it. You do what's best for the show. Your personal life can wait."

"And if I don't?"

"Then I'll sue you for contractual breach. And considering you just wasted your money on a run-down library, I highly doubt you'd have the money for what I'd do to you."

My jaw dropped. "You have to be kidding me."

"Try me, Wren. I'll do what it takes to make this show successful. No matter the cost."

13

HENRY

Strawberry Springs Neighborhood Watch

Kerry Winsor: Anyone seen the lovebirds? I still have questions!

Comments:
Tammy Jane: They haven't been at the diner. I have some too!
Jade Clark: They're probably enjoying some alone time. *eyes emoji* Let's give them space. (Do you think they'll get married at the square?)
Kerry Winsor: Oh, that would be so pretty! We need to figure out who does all the flowers. I bet they'd decorate for the wedding!
Dale Garrett: Do you wanna take bets on when they'll get married now?

My brain felt like it was melting out of my ears. Google was *not* helpful when I looked up how to fake date someone. There was one legitimate site that popped up in my search. The rest were all Reddit posts about how fake dating was unrealistic and only happened in books.

If only they knew.

What I needed to do was continue with my routine. I was sure I would find comfort in my plants and silence, but I wanted to get this right. And I'd fallen down a rabbit hole to ensure that.

Eventually, I rubbed my eyes and tossed my phone on the couch. I was already frustrated from being flustered with Wren, and I knew she'd noticed. I couldn't let that happen again.

But my brain wasn't working with me, because when I wasn't thinking about how to be a fake boyfriend, I was thinking about the kiss with Wren.

I shouldn't. I needed to put it out of my mind, because it was only for the camera, but for a split second, it felt like she'd run to *me* and kissed *me*. And for that split second, I thought it was all real. That after this, we would go on a date and be something.

It was harder than I expected to get over the disappointment.

I should have seen it coming, though. Wren was out of my league. Even the most perfect version of me didn't deserve her. Others thought we had a connection, but a woman like her wouldn't look twice at a guy like me.

And it would get worse if I started to slip.

What if she looked at me the same way Norah had?

Fuck.

I couldn't let it happen, but I wasn't sure I could stop it either.

My phone buzzed with a text and I picked it up, hoping it wasn't an emergency.

CAIN

Hey. You good?

Are you all right? Does Eric need anything?

Nope. He's his usual self.

But I heard about what happened today. And what Wren told Mollie about it being to get out of her dating Jude.

I see.

I'm pretty bad at this, and if you don't wanna talk, I'll respect it. But if you do ever need an ear, I'm here for that.

I blinked at the screen. I'd heard of all the work Cain had put into being more open with the town. I just hadn't seen it for myself.

Thank you, Cain. I'm just gonna try not to make a fool of myself.

I'll be here if you do. But also if you don't.

I told myself I wouldn't take him up on that. The last thing he wanted to hear was me scrutinizing every single rule of how to fake date someone. Most people would probably be able to figure it out easily. Or could make educated guesses on how something like this worked.

Me, though? I never could.

I grabbed a notepad from one of the side tables and wrote out what I knew.

Dos:
Only touch her when the cameras are rolling
Hold hands
Give her gifts
Kissing (but not real kissing)

Don'ts:
Catching feelings
Touching her when I want to
Letting her stay over
Letting her see the real me

Normally, lists made me feel better, but this one would be hard to follow. My own fledgling feelings would make this difficult.

But I was the one she chose, so I had to do my best.

After I had my rules down, I forced myself to go through my routine and try to get it together. Once I was outside and with my plants, I felt more like myself. It only got better after I cooked and ate dinner.

Still, the nervousness simmered under the surface of my skin. I tried to find a book to read. Something in my house to calm the feeling.

When nothing worked, I knew I needed to go on a walk and hope no one talked to me. The roads were thankfully deserted. I didn't follow a path and allowed my feet to lead me wherever I needed to go.

Eventually, I found myself at the library.

But for once, the lights were on. After being here for so many years and seeing nothing but the same thing over and over, it was shocking to see it breathing again.

I looked around for the crew, but only saw a red truck. Wren was here.

It was a bad idea to see her so soon after this afternoon, but I was sure she was in there alone. And I didn't like the idea of that.

The second I entered, there was a bang so loud that it made every one of my hairs stand on edge. I jumped, wondering if she'd fallen. The bangs kept coming, and I ran into her on the second floor, swinging a sledgehammer against wooden shelves.

I would have left if she'd looked normal. But she was covered in sweat and her movements were wild.

"Fuck." She swung. "Everything." Again. "About." Another. "This!"

The final hit brought the old shelf down, and her chest heaved. She went to hit it again, but I stopped the sledgehammer mid-air.

"Wren," I said. "What're you doing?"

Her eyes were wide. "Henry? What are you doing here?"

"I was out for a walk and saw you here alone." I took the sledgehammer from her. "Now I wonder if it was on purpose."

"You got me. Now leave me to my meltdown. I'll be fine."

"Are you avoiding something again?"

Her eyes narrowed. "Does it matter?"

"Everything matters. Especially when it comes to you."

My words made her eyes widen for a moment. Then she blew out a breath. "Just go and let me smash things. It's how I process bullshit."

Wren took the sledgehammer and returned to the job, hitting the other shelf with all of her might. The noise was overwhelming and I cringed at every hit, but refused to move.

She was mad. Anyone could see that, but anger always had something simmering underneath, waiting to spring free.

Eventually, she stopped and she hiccupped. Her shoulders fell and I knew the moment had come.

"Are you ready to talk now?"

She jumped and turned to me. "You're still here?"

"Anger fades. It's what remains that you need to talk about."

Her eyes watered as she tugged off her gloves and set the sledgehammer on the ground. "All of that was for nothing."

"All of what?"

"Me kissing you. Saying we're dating. If I don't forget all of it and pretend to be starry-eyed with Jude, then they'll sue me." She put her head in her hands. "Why did I even try to fight back? It never ends well for me."

"*Can* they do that?"

"No idea! But I can't afford a lawyer at this moment because I just bought the library and used a lot of my money to do it. I'm literally stuck, and it's all my fault."

In a second, I was wondering if the STM grant would help. If *I* could help. I was sure there was some way to fight this.

But now tears cascaded out of her eyes, and I knew this wasn't the time to fix this. She needed someone.

"I'm sorry," she said. "This is so stupid to cry over."

"Wren, it's not." I stepped close to her.

I put a gentle hand on her arm and tugged her to me, giving her plenty of space to pull away if she wanted to. Instead, she pressed her face into my neck, melting into every inch of me.

She fit so perfectly. Like she was meant to be in my arms.

I shoved the thought out of my head.

Wren needs a friend, Henry. Not a guy with a crush.

I pulled myself back into the present, listening to her soft sniffles. My hands ran up and down her back and the tension slowly melted away.

"It's okay, buttercup."

The name slipped out, and I could only hope she hadn't heard it.

This hug went on for a while—too long for friends. She must have realized it right when I did because she pulled away.

"Thank you," she said. "Did you call me buttercup?"

"I was hoping you didn't notice that."

"It's a cute name. It's a shame you can't use it when you fake date me, though."

"We'll fix this."

"There doesn't have to be a 'we,'" she said. "It can be just me now."

"I'm still helping you with this. We'll fix it. But I think you need to take a minute and recover."

"I'm fine. I can destroy things all day."

I raised an eyebrow and looked at the wall. "You did a lot. You're sure that you're not feeling tired after you stopped for a bit?"

Her face fell. "You know too much."

"Comes with being a doctor," I replied. "What if you showed me the library? It looks very different with the lights on."

"That's probably a better use of my time." She stretched her shoulders, grimacing as she did so. "Dammit. I went too hard on that."

"Come here," I said. She blinked, but she did what I asked. I put my hands on her shoulders and pressed in. "You carry your tension here, don't you?"

"Yeah. Smashing things helps relieve it sometimes."

"There are other ways, you know."

"Like what? Bottling it up inside until I explode?"

"Nope." I pressed harder and rubbed circles into her tight muscles.

"Fuck," she said. "That feels good."

My body heated at the words, and I had to focus on my motions and nothing else. It was too easy to imagine this in a very different connotation. Her shoulders were warm under my hands, and I resisted the urge to pull her closer.

I recited my rules in my head. I'd need to put it on the fridge at this point to keep from breaking them.

Wren's body finally loosened as I worked on her. Her tension was not only in her neck, but all the way down her back. I got to touch far more than I should have, but eventually, she was like putty in my hands.

"If the doctor thing doesn't work out," she said when I finally pulled away, "you could be a masseuse."

"I'll keep that in mind."

Her eyes met mine, and for a long time, she held my gaze. I had no idea what she was thinking, but I knew I was thinking of how it felt for me to touch her.

"The library?" I asked, hoping to get both of us back on track.

"Right. Let me show you."

I followed her as she walked through. Even now, this place felt newer, thanks to the lights being turned on. But her plan was incredible. She was planning to make community spaces and also leave plenty of places to keep books. I saw her shine return as she talked about it, and by the time we were downstairs, she was her usual self again.

"I can't wait to see it," I said. "This is better than I ever imagined it."

"Hopefully, the town likes it too. I know some small towns are resistant to change."

"Some are, but not this one. The library is *good* change, and all of them know you'll do it right."

She turned and gave me the same full-on smile that I'd seen when I'd first met her, and it made my heart skip a beat. I hadn't seen it when she'd been on camera, which made it feel like it was all for me.

"All right, you've made me feel better," Wren said. "And now I have something to show you."

"What?"

"You like the history of the town, right? There's a reason I ended in the kids' section."

Wren pulled out a box from one of the corners. She flipped it open and revealed colorful masks and decorations.

"Are these puppets?" I asked, pulling one out.

"Among other things," she replied as she grabbed a dragon mask. "I think they were used for story time."

"If only I'd been here." I pulled it from her and put it over my face. "Would I be a scary dragon?"

It was easier to look her in the eye with protection, but she didn't let me hide for long.

"I think you'd do much better as the hero." Her hand gently pulled the mask away and her eyes met mine again. Unfiltered. "That's better."

All I could do was stare at her and wonder how she was real. She didn't move away, her hand still on my wrist. I would have given anything to know what she was thinking.

But then there was a sound of something falling, and then footsteps. Without thinking, I stepped in front of Wren and looked around.

"Jesus," she said, her hand now on my shoulder. "Is this place haunted?"

"If Henrietta and Marjorie were dead, I'd say yes. But ghosts aren't real."

"So, then a real person did that?"

"On the other hand, maybe we should blame it on ghosts."

"I'm glad I wasn't alone," she replied. "Thank you for coming to check on me."

"Yeah, of course." My mind was barely functioning, but the healthy dose of fear gave me enough of a reminder of my rules. "I bet it was someone sneaking in. A lot of people take walks on the square at night."

"Really? Is it safe to walk outside when it's dark?"

"Have you been at the square at night?"

She shook her head. "I got here right as the sun was setting."

"Come with me. You should see this."

I led her outside. The square was fully lit up as it usually was, giving the air an incandescent glow. The lights lined each building, something that had only started when I moved in.

"Whoa," she said. "This is incredible."

"It's mostly safe, but it makes it feel magical here."

"Like the sign?"

"Like the sign."

"This almost makes me forget about all of my problems."

"We should get some sleep and figure out the rest in the morning."

"I still owe you food. What about breakfast?"

I rarely ate breakfast in the diner. I preferred to make something for myself, but if she was offering, I wouldn't turn her down.

"Yeah, I'll meet you there at eight."

"It's a date," she said with a smile before beginning to walk away.

My heart skipped a beat at her words. "Don't you mean a fake one?"

"Right." She didn't turn around. "See you for our fake date, Henry!"

I took a shaky breath and tried to get my head back on straight.

This was another reminder that, when it came to her, I was absolutely and totally *fucked*.

And it would take everything in me not to break my own rules.

14

WREN

RWL Superfan Discussion Central

Bethany Perry: [Link: YouTube video of Wren and Henry embracing in a library.]

Comments:
Carly Ware: She already moved on? That was quick . . .
Jamie McCullough: A little too quick if you ask me.
Neve Bullock: They do have better chemistry, though. Jude never looked at her like that.
Kerry Winsor: I'm officially on the Henry train.
Neve Bullock: Weren't you just heartbroken about Jude?
Kerry Winsor: I'm easily influenced! Leave me alone!!!

"So, did you have fun at the library?" Mollie sipped on coffee as she stood at the bottom of the stairs as if she'd been waiting on me to wake up.

"How did you know that's where I went?"

"Lucky guess. You love to work on things when you're mad."

And I had been. I hadn't told Mollie everything that Madison had said, but I muttered the words *lawsuit*, *stupid*, and *forced* before I left the house. I was pretty sure she got the gist of it.

"Yeah, well. It mostly helped."

"Wanna talk about it over breakfast?"

Slowly, I said, "I'm . . . actually going to get breakfast . . . with Henry."

Her eyebrows raised. "Really?"

"Yeah, he's offered to help me figure out how to fight Madison on the Jude thing."

"I could also help."

"I know, but you said yesterday you have to pick the remaining strawberries so you could make jam. Don't delay that just for me."

Mollie rolled her eyes. "I hate it when you remind me of things I have to do. Have fun with your fake boyfriend."

"All of that's up in the air."

"Maybe." She was smiling a little *too* wide.

"You seem perky." I checked to make sure Eric wasn't around before adding, "Was the dick that good?"

"It always is." She laughed. "But I'm also happy you're here. And I know everything will work out."

"I don't know what to do with this positive side of you."

She shrugged. "You could be positive too."

I wanted to be, but my problems wouldn't let me. I'd come here to get a break, but all the worry had haunted me. I almost needed something to shut my mind up so I could actually breathe for a while.

"Go get breakfast with Henry," Mollie said at my silence. "Continue flirting."

"We're not flirting. He's a good friend."

"Yeah, and I pulled off being blonde."

She had *not* pulled that off at all.

"Terrifying," I said. "That's what you are now."

She did a little bow before pushing me out the door.

"Holy shit," I muttered to myself before yelling, "Say bye to Cain and Eric for me, then!"

"You have to leave first!" she called through the door.

When I got to the square thirty minutes later, Henry was walking up to the diner, eyes forward. He looked lost in thought.

I pulled into a spot near him and honked the truck's horn.

He jumped, looking startled for all of a second before he recognized me.

"Nice trick," he said as I got out.

"I was afraid you'd miss me."

"That would be impossible," he replied.

I ignored the swoop in my stomach at his words. "That's a good line. You should save that."

Henry opened the door for me, the picture-perfect model of a man. Tammy was at the front, wearing a name tag that said Myrtle.

"If it isn't Strawberry Springs' most famous couple."

Henry didn't miss a beat. "Give it a few weeks. The news will die down."

"You're giving Kerry something to live for, though. Even if she's mad that she lost a pretty penny."

I bit the inside of my cheek, and Henry's hand landed on my shoulder. It was so much easier to pretend with him. It felt natural. Like I could do it for a long time and never get tired.

"Do you mind if we get the table in the corner?" Henry asked. "We have a few things to discuss privately."

If Tammy was shocked, she didn't show it. "Of course. I'll

even pretend like I didn't see you. Though, if Kerry comes in, I can only do so much."

"Understandable."

Tammy led us right to the corner Henry had asked for. He sat across from me, but kept his hands in his lap.

We were in friend mode now that we had a little bit of privacy.

"Have you heard from Madison yet today?" he asked.

"No," I replied. "I doubt I will until we start filming again."

Henry huffed out a laugh. "I can't believe I'm saying this, but considering the public reaction, I expect you will soon."

"Public reaction to what?"

"You haven't seen it?"

I shook my head, dread swirling in my stomach. Henry took out his phone and passed it to me.

"Why am I seeing a video on glove sterilization?"

His cheeks went pink. "It's just an ad," he said. "The real thing is after."

I looked back down. Once the ad was done, I saw the library.

And then I saw us.

I gasped, a hand over my open mouth. "Someone filmed us?"

"Whoever was there must have taken a video of us and put it on YouTube. My bet is on Marjorie."

"And put it on YouTube as . . . HammerTime69?" The username would have made me laugh if they hadn't posted a video of *me*.

"I . . . suppose? I have no idea who posted this. You should read the comments."

I scrolled down, eyes widening when I finally hit them. A few were asking about Jude, but the majority were talking about *us*. Henry and me.

And how cute we were.

"That's what you meant by public opinion."

"Yes. And as mortified as I am that I'm on YouTube of all places, it might work."

He was *mortified*? "We could try to get it taken down if it bothers you."

"It's fine. If my mother sees it, I'll have to have a very unfortunate call with her, but I'll live."

"What's your mom like?" I asked, leaning forward. "I could try to—"

"I can handle her," he replied. "And my mom is . . . normal."

I waited for him to say something else, but he didn't.

Henry obviously didn't want to share information about his mom. He had the right to keep anything he wanted from me—I knew that.

But I was still disappointed.

"All right," I said. "But I still owe you for all of this. If I convince Madison to go with it, you'll have to give me something to help you with."

"Don't worry about it."

"Come on. Does your car need an oil change?"

"No."

"Does your house need any new light fixtures?"

"I like my house the way it is."

"What about the clinic? I bet it could use an upgrade."

"That's also fine."

"Henry," I groaned. "You can't just give me nothing to help you with. I'm not a taker. I'm a giver too, so let me give you something."

"There's really nothing."

"If you don't, I'll find it."

"There's *nothing*. Just let it go and don't look for it."

"Fine, I won't look for anything."

"Good."

"In front of you."

"*Wren.*" That firm voice returned, and I was tempted to push him just to see what he would do.

But I held back. I was sure my savior wouldn't appreciate me annoying him more than I already had.

And by the time I'd figured out what to say, he'd sighed. "Sorry," he said. "I got a little too firm there. I just want you to take care of yourself. I don't need anything."

"All right," I replied. "I can respect boundaries."

Mostly.

A shadow crossed over our table, and I did a double take when I saw the last person I expected.

"M-Madison? What are you doing here?"

She took off her sunglasses and placed them on the top of her head. "Filming resumes tomorrow. And I'm making sure things go off without a hitch. I see you two are cozy."

We could have been cozier.

"You caught us having a normal breakfast," I said. "What do you need?"

"Were you aware a video was posted of you last night?"

"Yes."

"And did you plan for everyone to see it?"

"Wren had nothing to do with that," Henry said, his voice tense.

"Is that true?"

"He was helping me feel better after *someone* threatened me. I didn't even know there was a video."

Madison rolled her eyes. "So, someone in this town did it. Whatever. The point is, our plan has changed. You can be with Henry. He can be a guest star."

"I can be a *what?*"

Shit. This was not what I expected.

"No, he can just be on the sidelines. He has a job as a doctor. Something he can't just stop doing."

"Yes, I know. But the network likes the romance element, and so do the fans. You chose Henry, so to keep the romance alive, we want him too."

I opened my mouth to argue more, but Henry cut me off.

"Wren, it's fine. We can work with this."

"But you said—"

"I know what I said." His eyes went back to Madison. "I can't commit to much. What were you thinking?"

"We film you seeing the library. Talk about what it means to you and this town. Make it a cute little story. Only a few hours a week. We can talk compensation."

"I don't need money, but I do have a request."

"What is it?"

"I want you to showcase the town. Not just as a place that needs this library, but as a real place. Which means highlighting the local businesses, like this one."

Madison's eyes narrowed, a sign she wasn't thrilled with the request.

It was a good one, though.

"Fine." Her voice was stiff. "I'll draw up a contract."

She walked away without another word, headed to her car.

Tammy approached the table. "Do I even wanna know what that was about?"

"Just business stuff," I said.

"Good business things," Henry added. "For more than just us."

"I don't know if I like you two planning things together," she said. "It's a little scary. But I have a feeling this'll be lasting a while. So, I guess I'll have to get used to it."

A while in reality meant only a few months. But I wondered if she expected "a while" to mean so much more. They saw

Henry and me as a real couple, two people who were dating for love and not for benefit.

I would have to remember that when this ended.

The second I saw Jude pull into the square on filming day, my heart jumped to my throat.

He didn't feel the same way. His entire body was loose and relaxed as he walked over to me.

"I hear you have a new boyfriend you'll be with on camera. Congrats."

"Yeah," I said. "Sorry about not pretending to date you."

"Eh, it's fine. I'm still the main guy on the show, and it frees me up a little. Hey, does this town have any hot ladies?"

"I . . . You're really asking me that?"

"What? You're seeing someone else. So, I'm free to do it too."

He was right, of course. But I hoped that he would remember that I'd once had feelings for him.

That was obviously asking for too much, though.

"Not sure," I said, shrugging. "Mostly kept my eyes out for the guys." I'd only met Jade, who was my age. She was gorgeous with her colorful hair and free-spirited personality, but I highly doubted she would give him the time of day. She had to have high standards.

He hummed. "Sometimes there's a diamond in the rough in places like this."

"Sure. Have fun hunting."

"Get ready," Madison called to me. "Henry's about to head this way."

"How do you know?"

"We're getting him mic'd up so we can hear everything. We want your hellos to be on camera."

When I did this with Jude, they told us what to say and how to say it. Jude and I got a few minutes to warm up before we were shoved into faking it.

But I supposed it was different this time. The cameras all turned in the direction Henry would walk from, and then he appeared.

He didn't look that different from usual, and I forced myself to forget that we were being watched. I wanted this to be as natural as possible.

All thoughts flew out of my head when Henry leaned down. His hand went to the side of my neck, and the air in my lungs rushed out of me as his lips moved over mine.

By the time he pulled away, my brain was a mess of exclamation points.

"Hi, buttercup," he said.

"H-hey," I replied.

"I brought you these." He pulled out a bundle of yellow flowers with five tiny petals. "These are buttercups."

My brow furrowed. "I thought those were the yellow flowers that bloom in early spring."

"Common misconception. A lot of people call those buttercups, but they're daffodils." He tucked the flowers behind my ear. "Now you're camera ready."

"I should hire you for my hair and makeup team."

"I'm free any day of the week for you."

"Cut!" Madison called. "Nice work. Henry, are you available for a tour of the library before work gets underway?"

"I've already seen it, but I can come by after I get done at the clinic."

"Sounds good. Head on over to get your mic taken off."

He turned to do so, but then looked at me. "How did I do?"

"Incredible," I said. So much so that even *I* got confused. "Thank you for being on camera. You're a natural."

"I'm only doing what you told me to."

And he had my attention every step of the way. I couldn't look away from him.

But then his watch went off. "I need to get to the clinic now." He held it up. "I set this to remind myself when I needed to get there."

I was disappointed, but I tried not to let it show. "I won't keep you. Thank you for filming with us this morning."

Henry looked at Madison, whose eyes were fixated on us, before he pressed a kiss to my cheek. My eyes widened as he did it, and the spot where his lips touched my skin felt hot.

He was gone after that, but his touch lingered.

"He could have brought *me* flowers," Jude muttered when I walked up to him. "You know, people in this town aren't all that nice. I tried to ask for someone to park my car, and they looked at me like I'd lost it."

"The town doesn't have valet service."

"I was gonna pay them!"

I shook my head. The town had been oddly cold to Jude since he arrived, and I wondered if it was because of what they thought he had done to me.

"Let's just get to filming," I said, looking at the library. I would have to coordinate the work and the show schedule, so I would be busy.

Time moved both too slow and too fast. Whenever I was taking something apart, it went by quickly, but when the cameras were on me, and I had to repeat work to get the perfect shot, my irritation grew.

Still, we got a lot of work done. The guys and I moved some of the shelves in order to rip up the old carpet from upstairs, then we went for the built-ins that weren't usable. My body was exhausted by four, but my work wasn't done.

"We need to do interviews," Madison said. "With you and Jude."

"I thought we weren't doing anything together."

"You're coworkers and friends. Obviously, you won't be touching him, but you have to give the audience an update."

That sounded like a nightmare. "What are we saying?"

"Something about how you're focused on the library. Whatever works. Now, come on. Henry will be here soon."

I didn't want to step away from tearing things down, even as my body told me I needed to be done. But we went outside where the library was in the background. Jude stood next to me and Madison told us to start.

"After we finished up last season," he began, "things changed. Obviously."

Changed? He was caught kissing someone else.

"But now we're completely focused on our projects," I said quickly. "It's better this way."

"We're still friends, though," Jude added.

I tried not to glower. We weren't friends. He wanted nothing to do with me.

"Yeah, friends," I ground out. Madison's lips pressed into a thin line, but she didn't cut the cameras.

It didn't take long to finish it up, and I was glad that Jude was many steps away from me. This was far better than the alternative, which would have been trying to stomp out this feeling and force myself to look like I liked him.

He was too perfect and too shallow.

And now I had Henry, who was far too easy to fake date.

15

HENRY

Strawberry Springs Neighborhood Watch

Atticus Thompson: Need a lawn mower.

Comments:
Kerry Winsor: I thought Simone mowed your lawn?
Atticus Thompson: She made a phallic crop circle so now she's banned.
Marjorie Brown: You got pics? For science?
Jade Clark: You want pictures of the crop circle penis? YOU?
Marjorie Brown: This is bi-erasure!!!
Jade Clark: You've got a good point. Sorry, Marj.
Marjorie Brown: Jk I hate penises.
Kerry Winsor: Do I need to post the admin rules again?

MID-AFTERNOON CAME AND WENT. Normally, I still had energy at this time of the day, but my feet were dragging. I'd left early to grab the flowers for Wren and get ready for filming before the clinic opened. Doing that single interview took more prep than I expected, which meant using up more of my energy.

I was more than happy to help Wren. She looked vibrant today, like she was enjoying life, and I didn't regret saying yes.

I would just need to stick to the rules, go home alone, relax at every moment, and be the perfect man when I left the house.

No big deal.

I debated closing the office for a while so I could eat lunch in peace, but before I could get up and turn the sign, Jade walked in.

I instantly scanned her for injury. Other than her hair now being purple, nothing was new.

"Hey," I said. "Is everything okay?"

"Your girlfriend is a fucking lifesaver!" She bounced on the balls of her feet. "The show put up all of our shops online and posted about it. Do you know how many online orders I've gotten?"

"A lot?"

"Two, but that's way more than ever! Imagine what it'll be like once the show starts airing. I might even sell out!"

There was another reason I had to make this work. The town. Putting up information about the town was one of my ideas, but Wren had ensured it was included in the contract and that they followed through. While no one was hurting for money because of the STM grant, I knew we all wanted to stand on our own two feet in case the money ran out.

"I'm so happy for you," I said. "Did you come in here just to tell me that?"

"Mostly. I was honestly hoping you'd pass on the message to Wren. She's been busy all day. I don't know how she does it."

"To the detriment of her health," I said. "I'll definitely pass on the message."

"And can you put in a good word for me? I have a feeling I

said something wrong when we first met, but I wanna get to know her. She's so cool."

It was one of my worst nightmares to be in the middle of a social situation, but I nodded anyway. Jade was a good friend of mine, and I wanted her to get to know Wren if she could.

"I'll do my best."

"Hey, maybe she'll drag you to the bar. It's the one place I've never seen you at."

And there was a reason for that. By the time the clinic was closed for the day, I was more than ready to get home and be alone. The last thing I wanted to do was go be around more people.

"Y-yeah, maybe."

Jade's eyebrows pinched. "Are you okay? You seem . . . off."

I *was* off.

"I'm good. No need to worry about me."

"Right, but I also know you. Usually, you're so happy. If you're feeling weird about all of the change, you can tell me. I'll make sure it doesn't get to the Facebook group."

For a second, I was tempted to. But a younger version of me had tried that. Not only with Mom, but with Ace and Norah.

I was able to seem normal most of the time, and everyone had certain expectations of me. But under the surface, there were needs I had that no one understood. To some, sights and sounds never bothered them. They were fine with anything that happened around them.

But to me, it was like a cheese grater on my brain.

I loved this town and the people in it. I loved it so much that I made sure they only saw the best in me. The Henry that they could deal with. I didn't think I could take it if they saw the real me and gave me the same confused look everyone else had.

"No, I'm really fine. Just a little hungry."

"Oh, say no more." She laughed. "I get it now. You're way nicer than when Tammy's hungry. Or, God forbid, Hugh."

"I try," I replied. "You just happened to catch me right when I was gonna eat lunch."

"I'll leave you to it. Thank you for listening to me rave about Wren." She waved and left. I walked up to the door and watched her walk away before my eyes went to the library where Wren was.

I would need energy to make it through the tour, so I locked the front door and turned the sign to closed. When I did, I walked back to the office, where I was completely and blissfully alone. As I loosened my tie for just a moment, I was able to breathe deeply and feel like myself.

As time went on, I would have to rely on stolen moments like this. It would have to be enough, because I refused to let everyone know everything about me, only for them to be disappointed in what they saw.

And if that happened with Wren?

I wasn't sure I would ever recover.

If I'd had time to get another flower for Wren, I would have. But Madison expected me at the library at five on the dot, so I had to make my way over without a gift in hand.

Wren had shed a layer. She was only in a tank top and shorts now, and her long hair was tied up in a bun. She looked incredible after a long day of work. Dimly, I wondered if she needed another massage, then I shoved it out of my mind. That was an excuse to touch her again and I didn't need to be thinking that way.

When I saw her, I did the same thing I had this morning.

Pulled her in for a kiss, ignored the way my body insisted I let it go on for far too long, and then moved away.

"Wait!" Madison called. "We don't have your mic on."

I resisted the urge to tense. The mic had been a nuisance when I wore it.

"Madison, chill." Wren said, glaring over my shoulder. "You don't need to hear what's going on here!"

"I absolutely do!" Madison said. "Henry, come over here. We'll redo the kiss when I'm done. Wren, freshen up. We want you to look good on camera."

"Is it a bad thing for me to look like I'm working?" she muttered.

My eyes followed her as she walked away, tracing the freckles on her shoulder. She didn't need to do a damn thing.

After my mic was on, Wren walked out of a makeshift trailer. Her hair was brushed and fell over her shoulders, and her skin was patted dry of any sweat.

She was still in the tank top. I wasn't sure if that was a good or a bad thing.

"All right, redo time!" Madison called.

Wren rolled her shoulders and her eyes met mine.

Then she ran at me.

I had to brace myself when she ran into my arms. This time, instead of being shocked by my kiss like she had been this morning, she was ready. Her lips pressed against mine, but instead of keeping it chaste, she immediately moved to capture my bottom lip between hers.

The very few things I saw on fake dating told me to keep it as respectable as possible, but there was no way to once she was all over me like this. I put my hand on her cheek and returned the favor, but this time, my teeth caught her lip. My other hand gripped her hip and I pressed her closer to me.

"Really?" Madison yelled. "That's so overboard!"

Wren pulled away. "You're the one who said you wanted every bit of this!"

Madison rolled her eyes, muttering about them hopefully being able to use something. I came back into myself. Was that kiss just to make Madison regret redoing it?

I must have gotten caught up again.

No matter what everyone said about us, Wren wasn't into me. She was sweet, she was kind, but she was still out of my league. She trusted me to do this, and I needed to stick to my rules rather than get caught up in my own head.

"Is it time for the tour?" I asked. "I want to see what Wren worked on today."

My hand trailed down her arm to grab hers. I was the perfect boyfriend. That's all I needed to be until this was over.

"Yes!" Wren said. "Wait until you see the wall where the shelves were. I found the coolest old wallpaper."

She dragged me inside, with Madison following us to tell us to slow down for the cameras.

Wren did no such thing, and I only had seconds to take in the state of the first floor. Some of the older furniture was cleared out. The faded tiles were still there, but they would be replaced soon.

We went through the kids' section and then up the stairs. The second floor was completely different. More open and inviting. I didn't know someone could work so fast.

"Look at this," Wren said, showing me where the tan plaster had fallen. Under it was green and white striped wallpaper.

"Whoa," I said. "That has to be from the seventies."

"Groovy, right?" Jude said. I'd forgotten he was following us to stay included. It was hard to remember he existed when he only talked to the camera and never to us.

"I bet Marj and Henrietta remember this," I said, pulling

out my phone. "They ran the library from the day it opened. Then fell in love during the process."

"You should put it in the group," Wren said. "I bet all of the locals would love it."

I nodded and took a picture. Once that was done, Wren told me her plans. She was all excitement. Her limbs moved as she talked and her smile only grew. I couldn't wait to see what it looked like when it was done.

But mostly, I loved seeing her this happy as she talked about it.

"All right, I think we've got what we need." Madison cut the cameras. "And now we can talk about the future."

Wren's hand tightened in mine, but she turned to Madison with a nod. "Okay, what's next?"

"First, we need to decide what businesses we will showcase in what order. We can do some B-roll in the diner, then have you two shopping for candles at the candle shop. Then a night at the bar."

"A night at the bar?" I asked. "I'm not sure if that's my thing."

"So you wanna skip that one?" Madison asked. "I'm only doing it if you're there."

No, I didn't. I knew Mark would want the publicity.

I would just have to deal with all of the sounds.

"No, never mind, I can do it."

Wren's eyes moved to me, and I hoped she didn't pick up on my misstep.

"Okay, so most of the things I wanna showcase we have plans for. I did notice a clothing shop. Maybe it's time for a makeover, Wren."

"I'm not changing my whole look," Wren said. "I deal with the makeup, but my main goal is to *work*."

"You'd be prettier in a dress," Jude said. "A lot of people agree with me."

"We won't be doing that." I said it flatly. A miracle considering the curling anger in my gut.

"I'm not demoing a library in a dress. *You* probably could, though." Wren looked at Jude as she crossed her arms. "Since most of your stuff is for the camera anyway."

I had to cover a laugh with my hand.

Jude rolled his eyes. "I meant for the other things we do around town."

Madison nodded. "Exactly, we could—"

"We won't be doing that." Now my voice was louder. More firm. "Wren is exactly how she should be."

A silence stretched across us, and I wondered if I'd overstepped. But then Wren reached for my hand and squeezed.

"Thank you," she said. "And obviously, I agree with my boyfriend."

"Your boyfriend isn't the director."

"But I have a vested interest in making sure my girlfriend is treated right. The answer is no."

Madison glared, but I held firm.

"Fine. We can skip the shop."

"I shop there," I said. "There's no need to punish the woman who owns it because Wren doesn't want a new look."

"Do you two have any more demands?" Madison asked. "Because the list keeps growing."

"I'm sorry boundaries are hard for you," I replied. "Hopefully, over time, you figure out that they're helpful for making a peaceful work environment."

Usually, I would wonder if my attitude was too rude. But when Wren pressed her lips together to smother a smile, I didn't regret a thing.

"I'm done here," Madison muttered. "Jude, you're free to go."

"Finally," he said. "Hopefully, the bar has some hotties tonight."

Wren rolled her eyes, but her hand stayed in mine until we were blissfully alone.

I stepped away the second I could, even though every cell in my body screamed for me not to. Now that they were gone, we were friends. Only friends.

"It's working. And I still owe you. Want some food? I could take you out to eat. Hell, if you're tired of diner food, we could go to the next town over. Or even the bar—"

My control was slipping with every given second. I was *exhausted*. And this was only day one.

"No, not tonight. I need to get home."

"O-okay. Of course. See you tomorrow."

The way her smile faded was almost enough to get me to stay, but I needed to go. I couldn't be the Henry she wanted me to be if I did. So I waved at her and walked out of the library, ignoring every part of my body that wanted me to take her up on her offer of more time together.

16

WREN

Strawberry Springs Neighborhood Watch

Henry Connor: @Marjorie Brown, do you recognize this wallpaper?

Comments:
Marjorie Brown: Holy hell, Doc! It's been years since I thought of that ugly stuff. It was up when I met Henrietta.
Henrietta Brown: I still think it's cute.
Marjorie Brown: Good lord, honey. Are you blind? That's the ugliest thing I've ever seen! Who puts green on walls?
Kerry Winsor: Green is trending on walls right now! Everyone loves it.
Marjorie Brown: What is wrong with people these days???

A WEEK PASSED. Henry came to visit me every day before work, and I was making steady progress on the library. He took to filming well, and I started to look forward to our morning chats, especially when he would smile and press a kiss to my lips.

Even if it was fake, it felt intimate and steady. Henry was always there, and I was used to getting my morning kiss before starting work for the day.

Having him around helped when I worked with Jude. We still had to film together, though this time, there was far more distance between us. We did interviews too, but those were mostly professional, except when he would smile over at me like he would in season one.

It was only on camera too, just like it had been before. Many would call it a friendly smile, but it was so similar to the ones I used to get that it felt disorienting.

Instead of getting a thrill, I was filled with dread. Henry and I weren't really dating, yet it felt like a betrayal to him. I never returned them and only focused on the job.

And the job was demanding. Demolishing a library was hard, especially when I had taken on most of the work myself to save money on paying for travel expenses for my contractors. Jude didn't help when he wasn't on camera, so it left me to do most of the work.

After three days in a row, Henry had demanded I get some time off to showcase the town. I'd tried to tell him I was fine, but he wouldn't take no for an answer.

The rest *was* needed, though. The day that I had off, I slept for twelve hours straight and had to nurse my sore muscles.

The day after that, we were filming at Center Point.

"You're alive," Mollie said when I came downstairs. "I thought you'd need to sleep in again."

She and Cain had only seen me at breakfast and dinner. The rest of the time, I was playing on my phone in bed.

"I'm *mostly* back." I rolled my shoulder. "Could use a massage. But I'm not doing heavy lifting today."

"Good. About the break thing. I'd totally take you to see a masseuse, but we don't have those here."

I opened my mouth to inform her of Henry's secret talent, but then snapped it shut. That would open up far too many questions.

"So, what are you up to today?" she asked.

"Filming at the diner," I replied. "And getting a bit of the farmers market."

Mollie perked up. "You'll be able to see my booth! I finally have enough jam to sell."

"You're gonna be a vendor at the market?" She'd been working hard, and I knew that she was planning on selling her new items, but I had no idea she was ready now.

Mollie nodded. "I was gonna see how you were feeling before inviting you. The booth isn't gonna be the *best*, but I'll have a few things."

"Is Cain going?"

"I'm dragging him for heavy-lifting purposes. And to grab things I want from the other vendors."

Cain didn't seem like the kind of guy to socialize. "And he's . . . okay with that?"

"Okay might be a strong word, but he'll do it if I ask." She set down a cup of coffee. "He just texted that he's done loading the car, so we need to get going. See you soon?"

"I'll be there," I replied.

The whole square was packed when I pulled my truck into the last free parking spot. The air was already heavy and hot, which promised a miserable day, yet it didn't seem to stop anyone.

"There are *way* too many people," Madison grumbled.

"This is nothing compared to Nashville."

"I can reserve a street in Nashville," she said with a roll of her eyes. "When will your boyfriend be here?"

"Any minute," I said. "He might be fighting all of the people."

"You can come in, you know," a rough voice said as the door opened. We both turned to see Tammy staring at us. "I don't bite."

She was in a nicer outfit today, though her name tag still didn't match. She didn't want much filming done since Ron hated the idea of cameras in the diner. The B-roll footage Madison had planned was more than enough.

"I'm just waiting on Henry," I said. "Though, I do have a question."

"Hit me with it."

"Should I call you Tammy or Mickie?"

"Is that what this one says?" She looked down at her name tag. "These days, I just grab one and run with it. Ron would say to call me Mickie. But I probably won't answer if you do that."

"That's so confusing," Madison said.

"I call it a quirk," Tammy said. "I bet people will find it endearing."

Madison shook her head and walked off.

"That one's a real social butterfly," Tammy announced.

"Yeah, sure. She's just mad she has to do something for a small town."

"I'm sure she'll survive. I'm not gonna let it get me down. Truth be told, I'm a little excited about today. It's nice to have some attention coming to the town. Think we'll get tourists?"

"Probably a few," I replied. "The first episode airs soon."

"You've done a lot for us, and you haven't even finished the library yet."

"Some of it was Henry. I'm only making them follow through."

"It's more than a lot of people do for a small town like this."

"You guys took Mollie in. So I owe you."

"You don't owe us anything." She shook her head. "We take care of the people in town. The world is a dark and shitty place. It's nice to be the light sometimes."

"Literally," I said. "The square is absolutely gorgeous at night."

"It is. I don't know who keeps up on all of that, but it makes me happy. I come in when they're just about to turn off in the morning."

I could see why Mollie stayed here. Anything like that in Nashville was done to attract tourists. This was just here out of love.

"So, kid, how are you?"

I blinked. "Wh-what?"

"Hasn't anyone asked you that before?"

"Yes, sorry. I'm just not used to people caring to ask." And certainly not from someone who was old enough to be my parent. The little kid inside of me loved being checked in on. I had never had that before.

"You'll get a lot of that around here. So?" Tammy looked at me expectantly.

"I'm good. Busy."

"Henry treating you right?"

"Is there a world where he wouldn't?"

"Not to my knowledge, but just say the word. Some men get real weird when they get into a relationship."

Henry did have his moments, but nothing like what she was talking about. He was the perfect boyfriend when he had to be, but avoided me at any other time. I wouldn't lie and say I wasn't curious about his life outside of what he showed me, but he'd been clear that it wasn't my business.

Still, we were friends. I wouldn't have minded seeing more of him.

"Henry's great," I said. "I'm lucky to have him." Tammy

hummed and went to say something else, but I saw Henry walking down the sidewalk. "We'll have to get mics before we come in. Mind if I grab him?"

"Not at all. See you two in a few. You'll have to tell me how good my acting is."

Henry made it to me as she went back into the restaurant.

"Hey," I said. "Ready to get filmed again?"

"As much as I can be." His voice was muted today, making me wonder if he was as okay with this as he said. I'd asked him if he needed anything or if there was something I could do to help him, but every time, he said no and that I should relax.

But I could tell something was up. He was quiet as our mics were put on.

Jude met us by the door. I wasn't sure if Madison was aiming for this to be as awkward as possible, but having a meal with my fake boyfriend and fake ex-boyfriend wasn't high on my list of fun things to do.

The cameras started rolling, and Jude finally turned to me. "I can't wait to hear more about this town you like so much."

"Henry did all the selling," I replied, trying to match his energy. "That and the people of the town."

Jude nodded, but his mouth was tight. The town hadn't been so friendly with him.

We walked into Center Point. Despite his tiredness, Henry filled us in on what he knew about the diner.

Tammy met us at the front, wearing the oddest, fakest smile I'd ever seen.

I blinked, wondering if she'd been replaced with a robot version of herself, but then shook it off.

"Table for three?" I asked.

"Of course. Follow me."

Henry and I exchanged a look. At least he was as weirded out by this as I was.

"How am I doing?" she whispered to me as I sat. The cameras would definitely hear that, but it could be cut.

"It's . . . something," I said.

"My mama always told me I couldn't be a movie star," she muttered to herself. "Now, Henry. Coffee or water today?"

"Coffee. I need it."

"One for me too, please," I ordered.

"Oh, you're both tired? I don't even wanna know the reason why."

My cheeks grew warm. I *wished* it were what she was hinting at. My life would be better if it was sex that kept me up late at night.

But I wasn't going to look at another person. Obviously, Henry wasn't interested in that with me, but I knew better than to try to look for anyone else while I was technically with him. I would have to either charge up my old vibrator or find something to take its place.

"And I'll have a beer," Jude said.

Tammy's smile fell. "It's ten in the morning."

"Still. You've gotta have my favorite." His smile went to the camera. "Bud Light is all I ever drink."

I suppressed an eyeroll. "Tammy doesn't usually—"

"Oh, I'll make it happen." She was smiling again, but this one looked sinister. "Be right back."

"Is it just me or is she kinda weird?" Jude asked.

"The cameras are on," I hissed back. "And she's doing her best."

I crossed my arms, feeling an odd sort of protectiveness making my spine straighten. Tammy didn't have to do anything for the camera. And she certainly didn't have to find a way to make Jude's beer order happen.

Henry's hand landed on my knee, and I took a breath to calm down. Any tension on camera could be used in a negative way. Madison had gone with my plan to be with Henry, but that didn't mean she wasn't cooking up something else in the background.

"Wren's picked up on what we all feel. No matter how much we annoy each other, we care." Henry's voice was soft but firm. I didn't know when I'd started to feel this way. Maybe it had started from the second I drove in.

"Seems like a good way for people to know everything about you." Jude looked around with a frown. "And I bet nothing even happens here."

"Things definitely happen here," Henry replied. "Even if they're not what you'd expect."

Jude shrugged, seemingly unable to care. He always wanted the biggest and best of everything. He'd once told me it was how he'd gotten to where he was. He'd hit it big as a teen and then made his way through life always working hard. Or so I thought.

I loved working hard, so I'd thought we were made for each other. But his version of it was paper thin. It was being friendly for a camera. Kissing ass when they were rolling, and then nothing when they were off.

I didn't know what I saw in him. All I knew now was that I regretted the time I wasted on him.

"All right, I have drinks. Coffee for the cutest couple in town." She smiled at Henry and me, then it fell when she looked at Jude. "And a Bud Light for you."

Jude didn't waste time. He grabbed his glass of foamy liquid and drank it, but then his eyes bugged out.

"I've . . . never had it taste like that before."

"I thought it was your favorite?" Tammy tilted her head, looking like the pinnacle of innocence.

Henry used his free hand to hide his mouth, but I could have sworn he was smiling.

"It's good," Jude said, eyes on the camera. "Best I've ever had."

"Glad I could scrounge one up for you." Tammy pulled out her notepad and took our orders. Henry and I didn't need the menu since we knew what we wanted, but Jude made a big show of asking about all of the best meals.

Tammy's lips were fixed in a permanent frown by the fourth question.

"What about the burger? Is it butchered locally or . . ."

"Cain would kill anyone who suggests that. He loves his animals more than anything, and they're only for dairy. These are from a town a little north of here. There's a big ranch up there." She tapped her pen. "How about you try one and—"

"Are they grass-fed?"

She let out a sigh. "I'm not sure. Like I said, you should try it first. It's good. I promise."

"Fine. I'll get a burger."

Madison cleared her throat in warning. This was getting awkward and fast.

"Coming right up," Tammy replied. She gave Henry and me a roll of the eyes before she walked off.

"They're gonna have to cut that," Henry said under his breath.

"They'll have to cut most of this, I fear."

"What's with the people here?" Jude asked. "Everyone usually loves me."

"They care about Wren. The other woman you kissed was big news." Henry's voice was light, but it had a slight edge to it, like he was as unhappy about what Jude had done as everyone else was.

"But that was—"

Now Madison cleared her throat harder. There was no talk about fake relationships on camera.

Jude sighed. "I'll have to change their minds then."

I wanted to tell him that I doubted the people here would care about his surface-level platitudes. But I kept that fact to myself. Seeing people not be fooled by him was refreshing.

Henry's thumb ran circles over my knee, reminding me that we'd been touching the entire time. It was easy to pretend that we were sitting in a diner on a date. That we were here and enjoying it, just the two of us.

Oh God, I wanted that, didn't I?

It would never work out. I had a whole life in the city, one that I was excited to get back to once the library was done. He liked small-town life, and probably didn't like me that much, if the way he constantly left right when we were done was any indication.

I didn't enter this thing hoping that we would end up together. I thought that after Jude, I would have learned my lesson.

Apparently not.

Because I was crushing *hard*.

The cameras, and by extension, Jude, were around until we got our food, but after our first bite, they announced they were done. Madison packed up and Jude abandoned his burger.

I was glad when they were gone, and Henry was too, judging by the way his shoulders slumped.

"Do you wanna leave now? I can take care of the bill."

"No," he replied. "Not having the cameras around is helping. And I wanted to tell you that the local businesses have already felt the show's benefit."

"They have?"

"Jade came to tell me that just having her shop on the show's website helped. She makes candles, by the way. And sells different crystals."

"Where is that at?"

"Jade's Goodies." He pointed out the window. "Mollie goes there often."

"I should try to make it over there."

"Jade wanted to know if she said something to upset you when you met her."

I blinked. "She asked you?" Jade had done nothing wrong, and I felt terrible for being wary of her. She'd been here with Mollie when I couldn't. I picked at my cuticle as I wondered if Mollie liked her more for that.

"She asked me to put in a good word for her, which I can. She's a good person."

"I don't doubt that," I said. "And Jade didn't do anything wrong. This is all on me."

"She mentioned being Mollie's friend while you were gone. Is that what made you nervous?"

"Yep." I sighed and leaned back. "But I'll work on it. It's not her fault. She *does* seem really cool. I might try to see her after I go to Mollie's booth at the farmers market."

Henry raised his eyebrows. "She has a booth today?"

"Yep, it's her first one. I have to buy her out of everything she has."

His eyes went to the farmers market and then back to me, lips pursed. "I don't usually go since it's so busy, but it would be nice to see her booth."

I perked up. "Wanna join me?"

He considered it for a long moment. I wondered why he wouldn't want to go. Was it too hot? Did he have plans after this? Just *what* did this man do in his free time?

"It'll be a good chance to drive home that we're seeing each other," I added. Henry's eyes flicked to me.

"That's not a bad point. We'll go after we eat."

I'd never finished a meal so quickly in my life, but I was excited to see Mollie and get to act like Henry's girlfriend in public. Tammy must have been keeping a close eye on us because she brought us the check shortly after.

"Did you do anything to Jude's food?" I asked. "He barely touched it."

She crossed her arms. "I have a reputation to uphold. That is nothing but the best."

"And the beer?" Henry asked.

"Well, I served beer about ten years ago. Found an old can and brought it out."

Henry gasped, and I let out a laugh. "That's evil," I replied.

"He should learn his lesson about cheating." She said it easily as she grabbed his unfinished plate. "Though I doubt he will. There're plates deeper than him, aren't there?"

I laughed one more time, but out of the corner of my eye, I saw Henry reaching for the check. I cut him off.

"I've got it," I said. "Don't worry about paying."

I still hadn't figured out how to repay him for doing all of this. A meal was but a drop in the bucket, but it was a start.

"No, I'll cover it." His voice was firm. "I'd be a bad boyfriend if I didn't."

"Don't tell me you think the guy has to pay for everything."

"I don't think that. *I* just want to do it for *you*."

My stomach flipped. The few dates I had been on, they took one look at me and decided that I could pay for my own food. It went against everything I needed to do to pay him back, but I wanted this.

"The classic 'who will pay' discussion," Tammy said with a laugh. "How about this? It's on me."

Both of us turned to her at the same time.

"Tammy," I said, shaking my head, "you can't cover everything."

"We ate, and we need to pay."

"Oh, *now* you're on the same side." She rolled her eyes. "I just thought about it while you two were arguing. I don't know why I even bothered with bringing it. I got my diner on TV. I'm good with you two having free food."

"But—" Both of us said it at the same time.

"I'm walking away now," she said as she snatched the check off the table. "You better leave before I kick you out!"

Henry sighed. "She *will* actually kick us out."

"Fine." I stood. "But I would have paid."

"No, you wouldn't have." He said it like a fact, and I wondered if there was a future where we would be eating together again.

"Don't underestimate how stubborn I am."

"Oh, I'm not. But I also have a feeling you'd listen if someone told you to do something the right way."

I paused, body warming at his words. I didn't think of myself as a good order-taker, but there'd been a few times, particularly when I was in the abandoned library, where he'd firmly told me not to do something, and I hadn't.

Maybe *he* was the key.

But Henry was already backpedaling. "I just meant . . . I mean—"

"So, the farmers market," I said, deciding not to push it any further. He already looked like he'd started to regret every word he'd said. "Any tips as a resident of the town?"

"I don't usually go to it, so I'm as new as you are."

"So, we're winging it."

"That's not my favorite way of doing things."

I laughed and tugged him along.

I found Mollie on the far side of the square from the diner. She looked radiant in the sun and was talking to people animatedly.

I waited patiently for her to be done before I slammed my hand on the table and said, "I need all of the jam you have."

"Well, you're in luck. I have two left."

"*Two?*" I asked with a gasp. Sure enough, her table was nearly empty. "You're killing it!"

"This was a great idea," she said. "And now I'm adding income when the strawberries slow down. I already have new blueberry bushes planted, and next year I can do something with that." Her eyes landed on Henry as he stepped closer to me to let someone through. "Oh, hey. You're hanging out with Wren today?"

"She wanted to come, and I hardly ever make it to these things. They're busy, even on a hot day."

"You get used to the heat after a while," she said with a shrug. "How did filming go?"

"It was short and sweet," I said as I grabbed the two jam jars. I inspected them, wondering how I would add it to my regular breakfast, and by the time I looked up, Henry was handing his card to Mollie.

"Quick, before she sees." His voice was hushed.

"Henry!" I said. "I was supposed to—"

"It's too late," Mollie said. "I have the card and I'm running it."

I crossed my arms. Henry looked so smug. I wasn't sure if I wanted to smack the look off his face or kiss it off.

"You know I owe you."

"Breakfast was paid for. I had to do my boyfriend duties somehow."

"Boyfriend duties, huh?" Mollie asked with a laugh. "He's serious about this."

"Very much so," I replied.

"I aim to be the best."

Mollie hummed, and she had the same facial expression as the day Henry had given me the four-leaf clover. My developing crush must have been so obvious for her.

"Where are you going after this?" Mollie asked.

"I wanna see all the vendors," I replied. "Maybe Jade's Goodies, if Henry can tolerate me for that long."

"I absolutely can," he replied.

"Would you go so far as to say you *enjoy* Wren's presence?" Mollie asked.

Damn her.

"I'd go further." Henry's eyes met mine. "I look forward to it when I wake up in the morning."

Shit. My heart skipped a beat, and for a second, I thought this was all real.

Then I brought myself back to reality. We were in public. The town thought we were together. That's all this was.

"Have fun then," Mollie said, but she gave me a smile that told me she'd caught all of that.

"We will."

"Oh! And let me know if Jade has the strawberry-scented candles," she said as we were walking off. "I have an addiction that must be satisfied!"

"I will!" I called back as I tried to get my heart to slow down. I couldn't take Henry when he was treating me like this.

He stopped me only a few steps later. "Is the heat getting to you? Your face is red."

"A little," I lied. In reality, *he* was the one getting to me.

"Let's get some water before you get dehydrated."

"I see iced coffee."

Henry crossed his arms. "You should get water instead."

"Coffee is mostly water. With some brown added in."

"Please don't mention anything brown being in a drink."

"You're a doctor. You've seen poop before."

Henry sighed. "That's beside the point. Water is good. You should have that."

I tilted my head. "Don't tell me you care about my well-being. Is this a doctor thing or a Henry thing?"

"It's a boyfriend thing."

I ignored the heat in my cheeks as I tried to remind myself that he meant *fake* boyfriend. "So cute. You deserve a raise in whatever currency boyfriends get paid in."

He raised one eyebrow, and I realized the insinuation I'd made.

Diversion. I needed a diversion and *fast*.

"I'm still getting coffee, though," I added quickly, trying to dart away.

Henry grabbed me before I could make a break for it. "Nice try." I tried to tug away from him, but his grip tightened on me. "Water first."

There was that voice again. This was doing things for me. Things I didn't know could be done. My entire body felt like it was on fire from this alone.

Then his hand was gone and he was grabbing water. I tried not to be disappointed. He could have had me in his grip a lot longer.

What did it say about me that I was so turned on by that?

I really needed to dig out my vibrator.

"Sorry about that," he said. "Here."

I took the offered water, but it did nothing for me. Still, he watched me closely until I drank some.

"Are you done making sure I don't get dehydrated?" I asked. "We have more to see."

"Lead the way," he said, gesturing for me to go ahead of him.

Henry bought some fruits and vegetables from one place while I grabbed cookies to share with Eric.

Both of us were red in the face from the heat by the time we ducked into Jade's Goodies. The air-conditioning felt incredible on my sweaty skin. Henry tugged at his shirt, and I knew he felt the same. He was in more layers than I was.

"Regretting the fancy clothes?"

"A little, but this is what I usually wear."

"You could get away with a T-shirt or something."

"I don't—"

"Oh, shit!" another voice said. "Hi!"

I saw a streak of purple, and Jade was suddenly in front of us. "Hey," I said. "We were just at the market and I figured I'd drop in. Mollie has a request for strawberry candles."

"I saved one for her. And one for you."

"I'll take one. Though Mollie might steal it."

"She's a fiend for these things. It's almost like she owns a strawberry farm and loves it."

"I've never seen her so happy," I replied.

"Then we're doing something right. Let me go grab those candles while you look around. Be right back."

She darted to the back and I let my eyes linger over the shop. There was a bit of everything from crystals to candles. I never burned candles at my place, mostly because I was never there long enough in between work to enjoy it.

"I need to get the linen one," Henry said. "I burned through all of mine reading the other night."

"Oh!" I nearly ran over. "I'll—"

"Don't even try," he said. "I'll buy my own candle and whatever you want, thank you very much."

My mouth snapped closed. Apparently, I'd listen only to him when he pulled out that tone.

Jade walked back in, two candles in hand, and went right to the register. "You know, from one woman to another, if a guy wants to buy things for you, let him."

I couldn't say that I owed him, not without inviting questions from Jade, so I put up my hands. "Fine. I'll let this happen."

"Thank you, Wren."

Henry grabbed the candle he wanted while I continued to look around. When I made my way to the crystals, I asked, "Do you have anything for filming a show and trying not to kill your costar?"

"Unfortunately, no," Jade replied. "Though, there *is* one you might like." She grabbed a purple stone. "Amethyst for inner peace."

"I'm not great at being peaceful."

"It also *looks* cool," she said.

The smooth stone was cold in my hand. "Now that I agree with." I flipped it over. "What else does it mean?"

"Healing, clarity, and manifesting love, though I get the idea you're pretty good with all of that stuff. I mean, you bagged Henry, and you're a badass." She said it with a flick of her hand, like it was obvious.

But I didn't always feel that way. I didn't want to think about all of the things I needed healing from. At least not emotionally. "You know what? I'll get it. If it only heals my sore muscles."

"You're sore?" Henry asked.

"A little, but I'm good."

"I could—"

"I spent all day resting," I replied. "I'm *fine*."

His lips pursed, and I knew wandering around in the heat wasn't technically restful. I walked over to the register with Jade. She excitedly told us both about all of the new things coming in since her customer base had grown, and I focused on that while I put the crystal in my pocket.

"Are you sure you're feeling okay?" Henry asked when we walked out. "You shouldn't overwork yourself."

"I promise I'm fine," I replied. "You made sure I got time off."

Henry shook his head. "They ask for way too much."

They did. Even I knew that. "I could always go for another massage. Your house isn't too far from here, right?"

His face fell. "I can't."

It was all he said. He didn't owe me an explanation. I knew that.

But I wanted to know *him*.

"Okay, yeah. I get it. I'll ask Mollie. Or just take a hot bath."

"Epsom salt could help." His voice came out low, and I wondered if he was late to whatever he had to get to. He certainly didn't seem to like the words he spoke.

"I bet it will. Thanks for hanging out, Henry. I'll see you at filming on Monday and then the bar that night."

"*This* Monday?" he asked.

"Yep. That's the date I texted you. Mark is so excited. It'll be fun!"

I turned before I could think too hard about him turning me down and ran for my truck, completely missing the way he had only grown more tense when I mentioned the bar.

HENRY

Strawberry Springs Neighborhood Watch

Mark Bell: Folks, if you've ever wanted to be on TV, this is your chance! Come on down to Bell's Brews TONIGHT. Our star couple will be there as well as Lucas's band!

Comments:
Jade Clark: Technically, we all have the chance to be on TV all the time . . . But I'll be there.
Kerry Winsor: I'm looking for a babysitter. URGENTLY!
Marjorie Brown: Time for me to break out my go-go boots. I wonder if I can figure out what these kids call twerking.
Jade Clark: Wow, I wish I didn't have eyes.
Henrietta Brown: They still have to make it TV appropriate, Marj. And that sight would get any show taken off the air.
Marjorie Brown: My own WIFE? How could you!

Monday came far too quickly. I'd put it out of my mind, ready to forget I'd ever agreed to it, but Wren's reminder told me time was moving far too fast.

I dreaded going, but hoped that I would have an easy work day before it started.

That did not happen. I had a slew of physicals with kids and many shots to give, which led to a lot of distraught children. After the third crying fit, my ears were ringing.

I closed for lunch again to get some peace and quiet, and while I felt better, it was only temporary.

The plan was to get footage of us getting drinks with Jude to highlight how much fun we were having in town. To top it all off, Lucas would be there, which meant the bar would be louder than usual.

Wren was waiting on me, hair down. She looked cute in a flannel and jeans. I wanted to tell her that, but I was exhausted. By the time I saw her, I didn't want to talk to anyone.

"Hey," she said when I walked up to her. I gave her a kiss on the cheek as a greeting since Jude and Madison were nearby. "Have a good day?"

"Yep," I made myself reply.

She watched me, and I wondered if she was waiting for me to elaborate. I couldn't say much due to patient-privacy rights, but I also had no idea how to tell her why I was so worn out.

I couldn't say my day was too loud and I was tired because of it. That made no sense.

We got our mics on, which consisted of me getting touched in ways I didn't want. My mood wasn't great when we walked in.

But the *noise* instantly made it worse.

"Wow!" Wren said. "This is like an actual concert in here."

I'd never been to a concert. Was it normal to feel your bones rattle with every beat?

Wren dragged me to the bar, ordering something for us both. I had no idea what she got because I couldn't focus on a word anyone said. My attention was split between the music, the people, and the cameras following us around.

A cold drink made its way into my hand, and I looked at it warily. Wren grabbed my arm and put her lips close to my ear.

"It's just a cocktail made with wine," she said. "I can get you something else if you want."

I shook my head, not wanting to cause any problems for anyone else, and managed to clink glasses with her before taking a sip.

Thankfully, it wasn't too strong, but immediately, I felt some of the noise blur into the background as the alcohol hit.

I didn't usually do this, but if I were to be here for hours, I needed something to help. And drinking was the only thing everyone else was doing.

"There she is!" a loud voice said, and we both turned to see Kerry approaching us. She pulled Wren into a tight hug. "You look so good!"

"Thanks," Wren said. "Though I'm wearing a version of what I worked in today."

"You look great in anything you wear." She then turned to me. "You look good too. I don't think I've ever seen you here before."

"This isn't really my scene," I replied.

"I bet you'll change your mind once you get Wren on the dance floor!"

Absolutely not. If I had to focus on dancing, not making a fool out of myself right by a speaker? That would be a disaster.

"We still have our drinks," Wren said, holding up her glass. "We're good here!"

"Still, you have to dance at least *once!*" She laughed. "It's tradition for the couple to do. I hear Mollie and Cain did."

"We'll see where the night takes us."

"At least Jude has the spirit!" Kerry pointed to him, and true to her word, he was on the dance floor near Brooke, who he'd obviously taken an interest in. Brooke was one of the few people who wouldn't have cared about Jude kissing someone else, and the star seemed to be soaking up her attention. "You could always join him if you wanted to dance, Wren. You're still friends, right?"

I normally liked Kerry, but this was the first time I felt a true spark of annoyance toward her. I had been trying my best to be better than Jude was to Wren, but as always, I wasn't the best choice. This was not something I was having fun doing. And I knew it would show. I wished I could easily force this feeling away and be exactly what I wanted it to be, but that wasn't something I could do.

Thankfully, the cameras had moved toward Jude showcasing his dancing skills. Wren's eyes followed the camera, and I wondered if deep down she wanted to go and be with him. The thought did nothing for my mood.

I took another sip, letting everything fade into the background. For a second, I closed my eyes and tried to pretend like I was at home. By the time I opened them, Jude had walked over.

"Wanna dance?" he asked Wren, and I swore I saw red. "I'm free."

Wren's eyes widened as if she was as shocked by his question as I was.

"N-no, I'm good."

"Seems boring over here."

"Boring is just fine, thanks."

She shifted closer to me, pressing her body into my side. Somehow, it made me more grounded in the moment.

"Lemme know when you change your mind. I'd hate for you to miss a second."

"Sure." She shrugged.

He walked off, returning to the fun. The camera followed his every move.

"You could have gone with him if you wanted," I said.

She rolled her eyes. "Not you too."

"I'm terrible at dancing. And at this. But that doesn't mean you should miss out."

Wren's gaze moved to me, and now her eyebrows were furrowed. She studied me for a long time, and I wondered what she was seeing.

Then she reached for the mic pack and flipped the switch on it. Before I knew it, she'd reached behind my sweater and done the same for me too.

"Okay, what's wrong?" she asked.

"Don't worry about it," I replied. "Go dance." Her eyes narrowed. "I just need a minute. Then I'll be fine."

And I really did. I looked around, noticing there was a camera between me and the door. If I left in a rush like I wanted to, that might look bad. And despite how overwhelmed I was, I didn't want that.

I scanned the rest of the bar, remembering one place I'd heard about.

I'd seen Mark post about his closet. Normally, it was off-limits, but he would have to understand if he caught me. I let Wren go and crossed the space. There was only one hallway with two bathrooms and a third nondescript door. I breathed out a sigh of relief and entered the dark room.

But it was only for a second because it quickly opened.

"Wren," I said, turning to her. "Go back out there."

She stepped in and closed the door. "No."

I sighed and put my hand over my eyes. I needed to get her to leave so I could recover. She would ask questions—ones I had no answers to.

A long beat of silence stretched between us, both in the bar and the closet. She didn't ask, and when I peeked at her, she was watching me. Giving me space but keeping me close.

Almost like she was simply making sure I was okay.

I was aware of every one of her breaths, and I waited for my irritation to grow.

It didn't.

My clothes were too tight and the music resumed outside, but at least I wasn't around the cameras. I tugged at my collar, getting momentary relief from it before I opened my eyes and looked at Wren.

But her eyes didn't meet mine. She was now focused on my shirt, and her cool hands slid to the top button, undoing it.

"What're you doing?"

"It's obviously bothering you."

"But—"

She shushed me. "Let me help you for a change."

Her fingers opened two buttons before she pulled off my tie. I could already feel relief.

"I used to try to wear skinny jeans a long time ago. I'd feel a little like you do if I were in them." Her voice was soft, but instead of adding to what I couldn't take, she was like a beacon to focus on.

"I'm sorry, I'm not cut out for this."

"It's just a bar, Henry. Not exactly my scene either."

"But if you wanted to dance—"

"I would do it alone. But I don't. I'm fine here."

A part of me wanted to know if she was lying, but I also wanted her here.

Even though I should have wanted to be alone.

I hung my head, wishing more than anything that I didn't *need* to be in this closet. She stepped forward and pulled my head down to her shoulder. One ear was pressed into her neck, and her hand moved to the other momentarily as if she was moving to run her hands through my hair. I grabbed her hand and left it there.

I could feel her heartbeat, but her neck and hand drowned out most of the sounds. I sagged in relief, taking in this moment of peace.

I could get *far* too used to this.

Time passed, one second after another. Slowly but surely, I felt like I was okay again.

"Better?" she asked as I pulled away.

"Yeah," I said. "I'm sorry. It was a tough day at work."

"I figured," she replied. "You came to the bar right after closing down for the day. Not everyone is built for that."

"But most are."

"You aren't most people, though." She tilted her head to the side. "That's what I like about you."

My throat went dry. Would she say that if she knew that this wasn't a one-off thing? That this was my life?

I pushed away the thought, taking stock of how I was feeling. I was still tired, but I could at least think straight. The music wasn't as pounding, and now that I thought about it, I wanted to prove that I could be just as fun as Jude was.

"Let's go back out there."

"Are you sure?" she asked.

"Yes. I'm good now." I reached down and grabbed her hand. "And I owe you a dance."

Wren's eyes narrowed, but she must have seen that I wasn't lying because she nodded.

"All right, we can dance. But first, I have to do something." She stepped back and moved some things around.

"Wren, what are you doing?"

"Making it look like we had a fun time in here."

For me, this was nearly fun, but my cheeks grew hot as I

thought about what she truly meant. I could see it all, me pushing her against the wall, hands all over her as I made her—

I threw the thought out as soon as I had it. I highly doubted Wren would like *that* side of me.

"Is that really necessary?" I asked as she ruffled my hair.

"There's a good chance a camera is out there waiting." She winked at me. "Let's give them a show."

She finished it off by flipping her hair and messing it up, then pulled me out of the closet.

Just as she had said, a camera waited for us.

"Whoops," she said with a giggle. "Sorry. Had to have a private moment."

My entire body was hot as we headed toward the dance floor. The music was still poundingly loud, but I was able to think through it as she turned to face me. I didn't know how to dance, but neither did anyone else in town. Most of the people around us were either jumping or swaying to the music. I was planning on doing the second one, but Wren pulled me to her.

After what I'd thought about in the closet, it was easy to pull her close and move with the beat. She rewarded me with the same grin she got every morning when I kissed her.

I wasn't completely drunk, but the alcohol was still very much in my system. Instead of trying to keep my mind blank, I let it wander. I let myself revel in the feel of her hip bones, of her neck against my nose when I leaned down. She felt incredible, whether we were in silence or in chaos.

Eventually, I twirled her, earning a laugh. She settled facing away from me, with my entire front pressed into her back. My thoughts ran wild as I pressed a kiss to her neck, keeping her tight to me.

This was getting out of hand, but I had nothing in me to stop it. She felt so good, and I wanted to enjoy it rather than overthink it.

But then I realized there was another part of myself that was growing hard, and I pulled away.

The song finally faded and I came back into myself. The cameras were packing up and a PA was waving us over.

"I guess our job here is done," Wren said, though she sounded out of breath. "The dancing was fun."

"Yeah, it was."

Too fun, even. I was losing myself in her, making mistakes I shouldn't.

I needed to get home, and by myself, before I made any more mistakes.

Strawberry Springs Neighborhood Watch

Mark Bell: For the last time, MY SUPPLY CLOSET IS NOT FOR KISSING! Especially if you're gonna get so wild that you knock stuff on the floor.

Comments:

Kerry Winsor: Oooo who had too much of a good time?

Jade Clark: Wasn't me. There were NO decent guys at the bar last night.

Kerry Winsor: Did you not see Jude?

Jade Clark: Oh, I saw him.

Henry Connor: I am so sorry, Mark.

Kerry Winsor: WHAT

Jade Clark: HENRY YOU DOG

I had never been more grateful for the weekend. After having to make it through the four days after the bar, it took me far too long to even get out of bed.

After my smoothie was made, I sat on my couch in complete silence to drink it. Within my four walls was quiet and peaceful, and I enjoyed the silence while it lasted. Then, I made my way outside and worked in the garden as the sun rose in the sky.

Since summer was in full swing, I was sweating after only a few minutes. I couldn't stand to be outside for long since I was already battling a headache, so I got the watering done and then headed inside for a shower.

Once I was in the cool spray of water, I thought back over the night at the bar. Flashes of Wren holding me, of me holding her, while we danced played through my mind. I tried to decide if I needed to apologize to her or not for getting too handsy.

She hadn't seemed angry when we gave our mics back, but still. I'd let myself slip. Every day I'd thought about it, especially when I greeted her each morning before filming, but I hadn't allowed myself to fully give in to the thoughts I'd had in the bar. I'd kept myself too busy.

And even though I knew it was wrong, I wanted to do it again.

I was using my own body wash, but my mind conjured the smell of hers instead. Whenever I was close to her before she got to work for the day, I could smell the faint scent of roses. Somehow, I'd memorized it and was able to conjure it up.

Before I knew it, my cock was hard again.

I closed my eyes, trying to will it away. I had plenty of other nonsexual things to think about, but the second I tried, she would pop back in.

It was no secret that I was attracted to her. I had been since I met her, but touching her, even under the guise of a fake relationship, was hard for me to forget.

We're not together. It's not real.

If only desire could have been controlled by thoughts. I would have won, but instead, the feeling stayed, and my will slowly lost.

Had it been too long? Possibly. I rarely ventured out, and if I did, it was for a one-night stand. There could never be the possibility of more. I always kept myself in check, no matter who I was with, and the result was a mediocre release with no desire to do it again.

Everything about Wren was a turn-on, though I hoped it was because of my dry spell. If I were lucky, I only needed a release, and then I could think clearly about her.

Wrapping my hand around my cock, I emptied my mind. I would focus on the feelings. Not the woman who had started all of this. I gave it one long pump, feeling heat spread through my body.

Slowly, I moved more, leaning my head against the cool tile of the shower. My hand didn't fully satisfy the urges, and my mind flashed to what someone else would feel like. Her mouth would encase my cock, taking me as deep as she could go, before I told her to get on the bed and spread her legs.

In real life, I forced myself to be polite, to let all of my partners take the lead, but in my mind, I could take control. She would do as I said, her freckled chest on full display. I'd take a second to let my mouth kiss each one before lining myself up and plunging into her.

"Yes," she'd moan. *"More. Give it all to me."*

I wouldn't be gentle. She'd take my cock like she was made for it, and I wouldn't slow down as I barreled toward an orgasm.

"Fuck yes, Henry. Come in me."

I would look up, seeing Wren looking up at me.

And I came.

"Fuck," I said the moment I was able to think again. I

shouldn't have done that. Nothing good would come of me thinking about her as I jerked off, because we were only fake dating. There was no future where any of my fantasies were real.

I needed to follow my rules and stay sane.

But as more time went on, that seemed impossible.

When I got out of the shower, I still felt guilty, but I saw I had a text from the very woman on my mind.

WREN

> The first episode is coming out tonight. Mollie is having a mini watch party. Want to come and hang out? I'll have popcorn. Or vegetables, if you wanna be healthy. 😉

And now I felt worse. I wanted to spend time with her, but there was no way I could be the version of Henry she wanted. I was a mess, falling apart at the seams. She didn't deserve that.

> It was a long week, so I need rest. Maybe some other time.

> Take as much time as you need. Do you wanna skip filming tomorrow?

> No, I can film.

I wasn't going to let her down *that* much. No, I was taking the day, and I would be normal by tomorrow.

I had to be.

18

WREN

RWL Superfan Discussion Central

Carly Ware: First episode of the second season drops TONIGHT! What are you most excited for?

Comments:

Jamie McCullough: I need an update on Wren and Jude! They better get back together!

Alicia Parrish: What about that other guy? Do you think he'll be in it?

Neve Bullock: He's just an off-season side piece. She better be with her soulmate!

Kerry Winsor: As a resident of Strawberry Springs, I can tell you he's not a side piece! And he might be in the show . . .

Neve Bullock: NO

Alicia Parrish: Is he cute in real life too?

"I'M SO EXCITED!" Mollie said. "We get to watch the new series while the star of the show watches it with us!"

She had ice cream in her hand. Cain followed behind her with popcorn. Eric grabbed a massive handful and Cain sighed when pieces went everywhere.

"How are you feeling?" Mollie asked, sitting next to me.

"Nervous," I said. "I know they went a new direction with adding Henry, but it feels too good to be true."

"I get it," she said. "But they did such a good job on the first season. I bet this one will be even better."

I hadn't seen the first season. By the time I wasn't filming it, I had no desire to see Jude and me flirt.

I'd never considered seeing myself on TV, not even when I was a kid dreaming. I never thought I was the kind of woman for that. Some days, I still didn't.

Pulling out my phone, I checked it again, hoping Henry had changed his mind. He was a balm on my frayed nerves, and I knew he would know the perfect thing to say to put my worries to bed. I didn't want to make him feel bad for taking time for himself, because he more than deserved it.

I just foolishly wished he didn't shut me out from it.

We'd been spending a lot of time together, but I had a feeling that there was something I was missing. Usually, I didn't think this hard about people I hung out with, but I wanted to know everything about the man who'd helped me. All that was in my mind was the put-together version of him he showed me.

And I wanted more.

The bar had done nothing for my crush, especially when he'd pulled me close during our dance. I'd been serious when I told him I was fine skipping the dance floor, but now I regretted not staying longer. There was something about him that made me unable to look away, even though I should for my own sake.

He was good at keeping up boundaries and making sure we didn't spend too much time together and get confused.

Still, it stung.

"All right, we're ready." Mollie turned on the TV and did a little dance before passing the ice cream to Cain. "It's a shame Henry couldn't come."

It was. "Yeah, but he's literally saving my ass here. He deserves a day off."

"Is that disappointment I detect?" Mollie asked with an eyebrow raised.

I shrugged as the show started.

The first episode opened with my interview with the camera, in which I talked about how things had changed between Jude and me. The tension was obvious on my face when Jude called us friends, and I was surprised Madison had left that in there.

Then, a drone shot of the library took up the screen, and my voice told the story of how I'd found it.

I left out the part where Henry and I had snuck in, but everything else was true. I felt like it was a forgotten centerpiece of a community. The town was tight-knit but needed a little love. How it had inspired me.

All in all, it was a good beginning. Madison easily could have put me in a bad light after the stunt I pulled.

Then, Jude came on the screen. He told the story of us. How we didn't work out. And he sounded . . . disappointed?

In all of the time I'd worked with him, he'd never given me the time of day. There was no indication he'd missed me at all.

Was he acting again?

"That's odd," I said. "I didn't know they were gonna go for that angle."

"They could just be wrapping up loose ends," Cain said.

"They better be," Mollie said as she grabbed the ice cream from him.

The episode moved to the tour of the library, then to me kissing Henry. My cheeks grew hot the second I saw us, because that looked . . . *real.* And my best friend was watching it while she covered Eric's eyes.

"Look at that hand placement," she said. "Did you notice that?"

"No," I hissed. "I was more focused on his other one on my face."

She whistled.

"Can I see now?" Eric asked.

"I feel like I'm watching something private," Cain said. "But it's better than the first season."

"You didn't like the first season?" I asked. I wasn't sure I could handle it if he didn't, but my curiosity was piqued.

"I loved the work you did," he said immediately. "But the romance was . . . a little forced."

"He unfortunately called the fake relationship." Mollie rolled her eyes. "Rude."

"It was unnecessary, that's all. I only cared about the mansion. No offense."

"None taken," I replied. It was refreshing to hear someone care about the work. All I'd seen online were people freaking out over Jude and me.

But I'd started this whole thing to show my work to more people. I hated that everything was about a fake relationship and not the beautiful piece of history I was working on.

I focused back on the show. They were showing the first few days of work I'd done, though making it look like Jude and the crew did more than they had. The contractors hired were there during the day, but Jude was a true TV guy and preferred to only do work on camera.

Which meant he didn't get much done at all.

Seeing it now made me roll my eyes. And it only got worse when they kept showing him watching me. I'd not noticed while we were filming, but there were loads of shots of him glancing over.

"Are they making it seem like he misses you?" Mollie asked.

"He doesn't," I said. "He was the one caught with someone else. He started this whole thing."

But then the camera cut to another scene of Henry and me, and I wondered if what I'd seen was real. They weren't making either of us look like the enemy, just a happy couple.

When the episode was over, I was tense. Looking at myself through a camera was far more uncomfortable than I expected.

"That was interesting," Mollie said. "Especially now that I know the whole story."

"It's show business," I muttered. "They want the good ratings."

"Is that what you want?" she asked.

I frowned, trying to decide. I knew Mollie would want an answer eventually.

But by the time I'd come up with something, she was covering her mouth and running to the bathroom.

I blinked. I'd been the one to get the ice cream and popcorn. "Please tell me Dale doesn't stock expired stuff," I said.

"Oh, no. It's fine."

"It's fine?"

"Mollie throws up sometimes," Eric explained. "Any time I ask, they say they'll tell me later."

I frowned. "If Mollie's sick . . ."

"She's not," Cain said.

"Then—" I froze when I realized what was going on. Then I tore after Mollie.

She was hunched over the toilet bowl and didn't spare me a glance as I hovered in the doorway.

"Cain, don't be a mother hen. I'm *fine*. Stay with Eric and Wren."

"I'm not Cain."

She let out a groan. "Shit."

"You're . . . Are you . . ." I didn't even know how to ask.

Mollie sat back on her heels. "Yes, I'm pregnant. Not very far along, but enough to make me throw up randomly. If you see a spot in a field, stay away from it."

I could only stare. I knew they were discussing kids. But she was pregnant? Already?

"Wren?" she asked. "Are you . . . You have nothing to worry about, you know. You're welcome here, and my due date is way after you go back to Nashville, but even if you stay longer, we still have Cain's old room we could use."

I heard her words, but couldn't say anything. I was in such a state of shock that I didn't know what to do.

Mollie played with the hem of her shirt. "Please say some-thing," she begged.

I pulled myself out of my thoughts. I wasn't sure what I was feeling other than total and complete shock. "I am so *happy* for you."

She perked up, her back straightening. "You are?"

"Of course!" I pulled her into a tight hug. "You're gonna be an amazing mom."

She was. And I knew it more than anything. Mollie was kind, funny, and selfless. Cain was dedicated and caring. There was no reason I shouldn't be thrilled.

And I was.

But there was also a deep sadness, one I carried with me everywhere. Mollie hadn't done this, and all she deserved to see was my happiness. But I couldn't shake the grief that rocked me to my core.

My future niece or nephew was going to have the greatest mom in the world.

And I'd gotten one of the worst.

19

HENRY

Strawberry Springs Neighborhood Watch

Kerry Winsor: The first episode of *Renovating with Love* was so good! I kinda feel bad for Jude, though.

Comments:
Jade Clark: He can have the heiress he kissed then. Friendly reminder that Henry is in the group and can see everything you say.
Nicole Rudder: What streaming service is it on? I swear there's like a million of them.
Mollie Wilson: It's mainly on live TV right now.
Nicole Rudder: Who has cable anymore???
Henry Connor: Not me. You'll have to keep me posted on how I'm doing on camera.
Kerry Winsor: You're not even watching the show you're in??? I'd never be able to look away from myself.
Hu Gh: Hey, has anyone noticed that the new girl looks kind of like the girl in the show?

Jade Clark: You're kidding, right? Please tell me you're kidding.

I FELT Wren before I saw her. Instead of giving me my usual wave, she crashed into me the second she saw me. I had to keep what was in my hand pulled away so it wouldn't get crushed.

"Hey, buttercup." The pet name slipped out, but I told myself it was because I was wearing the mic. "What's going on?"

"I just need this," she said, her face pressed into my shirt.

I stayed still, letting her have whatever time she needed. I looked around and saw Jude watching us, and I hoped for his sake that he hadn't been the one to do this.

"Okay," she said, pulling back. "I'm good."

"Are you sure?"

"Good enough. I can't really talk about it under the best friend code, so don't ask too many questions, but I just got a shock. That's all. What's in your hand?"

I was content to figure out what had upset her, but she was already trying to peer behind me to see what I was hiding.

"This is a morning glory. They just started blooming." I delicately put it in her hair. "I thought you might like it."

"Is there a florist in town that I don't know about?" she asked. "You always find the best flowers."

"No florist. I grow them myself."

I tilted her head to kiss her. I wanted to talk to her all day, but she pulled away and turned. "They told me to keep it short today since we have a load of work to do. At least I can keep you with me." She gestured to her hair.

"I understand," I said. "Have fun and don't work yourself too hard."

"No promises," she said before she walked over to Jude to do whatever she had to for the day. After checking my watch, I needed to get to the clinic.

But as I turned, I saw Jude reach out to touch Wren's shoulder. She moved away, eyes narrowed at him, but the action alone made my fists tighten. As far as I knew, she wanted nothing to do with him.

Why was he trying it now?

I was tempted to stay and make sure he didn't try anything like that again, but work called.

The sight weighed heavily on my mind until eight, when the door opened, and I was shocked to see Hugh walking in.

Hugh was one of the oldest people in town, and he avoided me like the plague. He didn't need to, considering all of the things I knew about him.

"Tammy won't give me any coffee until I come in here," he grumbled. "Damn woman always getting in my business."

I crossed my arms. "Does she have a reason to be worried?"

"I stepped on a rusty nail a week ago."

"Wha—*Hugh!* You have to come in when things like this happen, especially considering your age. Come to the back right now. We'll check it out."

"Can I get coffee first?"

"Will it make you let me do my job without complaining?"

"Maybe."

I let out a sigh. "Get a cup, but then we're talking about this rusty nail and why you're avoiding coming to get treatment."

It was lunch before I got a breather. Hugh's unscheduled appointment put me behind for the day and I had to rush through every visit to stay on time.

I was tempted to close the clinic, but as I walked up to the door, I saw one of the PAs running to me.

"The ladder . . ." she panted. "It . . . She fell."

My heart jumped in my throat. "Who fell?"

"Wren."

My heart dropped. Wren fell? *My* Wren?

I tore out of the clinic without another thought. It was rare that I dealt with an emergency, but I was trained for it.

But in *this* emergency, I couldn't think of anything else but *getting to her*.

I loved the people I shared the town with, but I was able to put up a professional wall to do my job when I needed to. This time, my mind was filled with all the things that could have happened, and I'd never moved faster in my life.

I found her on the ground, thankfully in a grassy area. She was slowly sitting up, eyes on her arm that dripped blood.

Most importantly, she was conscious.

"Wren," I said, skidding to a stop in front of her. She looked up at me, and her eyes seemed clear. "Are you okay?"

"Yeah, I think so."

I put my hands on her cheeks to get a closer look at her eyes. They were clear and alert.

The cut on her arm was more than likely going to need stitches, and I trailed my gaze over every inch of her to check that it was the only injury.

"What happened?"

"It was an accident, I swear!" Jude was the first one I heard, and I turned to him, glaring.

"What did you do?" I nearly growled.

"I was just trying to talk to her."

"Next time, don't use the ladder I'm using," she snapped.

I was going to break my Hippocratic oath and *murder* him.

"I'm fine," she said. "Luckily, I fell on my ass."

"I'll be the judge of that," I said. "You're coming with me."

"What? *Now?* But I—"

I didn't give her a chance to argue. I slid one of my arms behind her back and the other under her knees and hoisted her up. She yelped, arms coming to wrap around my neck.

"I've got you."

"I-I can walk. I *think*. Seriously, I'm fine."

"Buttercup, I'm gonna lovingly ask you to shut up and let me do my job. Adrenaline is still in your system, and you could easily have injured something."

Her cheeks went pink, but her mouth closed.

Everyone gave me a wide berth as I took her back to the clinic. After setting her on an exam bench, I immediately locked the door.

"Henry," she began. "I don't need—"

"Stitches first. Hold your arm out. Do you know what cut it?"

"A tree branch, more than likely. That was all that broke my fall."

"Are you up to date on your vaccines?"

"Yeah."

I nodded. At least there wasn't a risk of tetanus.

I cleaned everything up before numbing the area and working on the stitches. I listened to every breath of hers to make sure she wasn't in pain.

"Done," I said. "I'll take them out in two weeks."

"Thanks. Listen, I—"

"I'm not done. Can you move your wrists?"

"Of course I can."

"Then let me see."

She moved both wrists.

"Elbows."

She did that too.

"Knees."

They seemed fine.

"Ankles."

And now she paused. "Okay, one might be hurting a little, but I can—"

"We're gonna skip the part where you say you're fine and order an X-ray for you. We'll make sure it's not broken."

Her cheeks were still pink, but thankfully, she didn't argue. I was struggling to keep my anger at Jude and my worry for her in check. But right now, it only mattered that she was okay. We could deal with everything else after.

I helped her get in position for her X-ray and then double-checked the resulting image.

"You got lucky. Not broken. Just sprained. You'll need to wrap it and keep it on ice."

"Okay." She blew out a breath. "I'm sorry."

"Why are you apologizing?"

"Because you're mad."

"I'm not mad at you."

"You're acting completely different. I probably should have realized that Jude was that stupid, but you don't have to do all of this—"

"Stop," I said. "Do not put this on yourself, and do not think for one second that I won't take care of you if you're injured."

Wren stopped in her tracks. "Is that what this is?"

"That, and me trying not to go kick Jude's *ass* for compromising your safety." I ran a hand over my face. "When I heard it was you that fell, my heart stopped."

"You care that much?"

"Is it not obvious?"

"All of that could have been for the cameras. And it'll make a great scene."

"I care about you," I said firmly. "I care about your safety.

Your happiness. If you ever fall like that again, I don't care where you're at, I'll come running."

"Why?"

"Because you're—" *The woman I wanna break rules for. The first thing I think of when I wake up.* "My . . . friend. One of my closest ones." The words were so wrong, but I knew she didn't want any of my real thoughts. She couldn't.

"A friend, huh? You do a lot for your friends, then."

I tucked a strand of hair behind her ear. "It's you I'd do a lot for."

But then I remembered myself and stepped away.

"Let me take you back to the farmhouse. I'll get you set up with ice, and you have to *rest*. Doctor's orders."

"Who can argue with orders?" The words gave me pause. Was I ordering her around? "Thank you for taking care of me. Do you have any crutches? I can try to walk."

That made me lose my train of thought. "I'll carry you."

"I can just walk on my good ankle."

"Not an option." If it meant I got to have her in my arms again, I would do anything. "Let me go get my car and we'll head out."

It was only a short walk, and I avoided everything to do with the set while I was out. Wren was still on the exam table when I got back. I picked her up and took her to my car, helping her into the passenger seat. I'd need to get her truck to her, but what was most important now was making sure she was taken care of.

When I got into the driver's seat, she was looking over every inch of the interior of the car.

"It's just a Honda. I promise there's nothing I'm hiding in here."

"You have CDs," she said, pointing to where they were folded into my visor.

"Oh, yeah. Sometimes I like to completely disconnect when

I'm not in the mood for a podcast. CDs are easier. I know what to expect."

"Did Spotify shuffle play the wrong song?"

I laughed. "I like to enjoy it as the artist intended it. And not have a distraction while I do it."

She hummed. "I bet it's nice to slow down every once in a while."

"It's how I stay sane."

Wren nodded and leaned her head against the window. Her eyes closed and we lapsed into silence. She had to be exhausted after falling off a ladder. It was normal for it to hit after the adrenaline faded.

I didn't mind the silence. It gave me time to think about how I'd slipped today, how I'd ordered her around because I was so worried about her. I needed to be the Henry she wanted, not the one I hid.

We pulled into the farmhouse and there wasn't a car in sight.

"Wren," I said softly. "We're here. Do you have a key?"

"Yeah." She reached into her pocket. She handed them to me and opened her door. I was at her side in a second. "I wanna walk. Just help me do it."

"Fine. But only because I have to unlock the door."

She put her good arm around my shoulder and we slowly made our way inside. She didn't protest as I carried her up the stairs, and she led me to the guest room, where she fell on the bed with a sigh.

"I forgot how nice being indoors is when it's hot."

"You need this day off," I said. "I'll get you ice and be right back."

It felt odd going through Cain and Mollie's house, but I was able to find what I needed and put it on her ankle. Her eyes were closed again and I was sure she was asleep.

But then she caught my arm as I was about to leave. "Can you stay?" she asked. "Wait, you have the clinic. Sorry. I just hate being alone when I'm sick . . . or injured."

I went over the schedule for the day in my head. My heaviest workload was behind me, and I could easily reschedule my last two appointments over text.

"Yeah," I said. "I'll stay."

"Really?"

I nodded, and she moved over on the bed, patting the space next to her. I took off my shoes and joined her. I thought she might go to sleep, but she laid on her pillow and turned to me.

"I can't believe I fell off a ladder. I've never done that in my life."

"What happened?"

"Jude was being weird today. He kept trying to talk to me while we were filming. Usually, he's busy making himself look like he's working, and nothing bothers me. I kept telling him I was busy, especially since I wanted to work on the windows on the second floor, but then he followed me up the ladder and knocked it over. A tree caught it. Just not me."

"He's a fucking idiot."

"He is," she replied. "And he's only doing this when we're rolling, which makes me think he's been told to. Plus, there was something about the editing of the first episode. They're making him look like he misses me."

"So, the show's pushing a different narrative." One that I didn't like.

"It could be nothing, but with the way he's acting, I think so. It could be a love triangle thing."

"A love triangle only works if you give him the time of day. I suppose we'll have to make sure our fake relationship stays strong."

"Yeah." She sighed. "When are you gonna let me help you in return, by the way? I still owe you one."

"I don't need anything." And I didn't. Any help she could offer would mean opening up more of my life.

"I wanna do something. Especially after you dropped everything to make sure I was okay."

Shaking my head, I said, "I'm doing this because I want to."

"Still. It feels wrong to take this much."

"You've had a long day," I replied softly. "Rest until Mollie gets back."

Wren's lips pressed together, but she shuffled closer until her cheek was pressed against my arm. Her eyes slowly closed and her breathing evened out.

I leaned my head against the headboard, trying to process everything she'd said. I was still out of sorts from her being in danger at all, and I hated the idea of Jude wanting anything to do with her. She'd been hurt by him once. She'd said she didn't want to fake anything else with him.

And she was mine.

No, she wasn't mine. I was helping her out.

With a sigh, I knew I *had* to get myself back on track. But there was something about her. Whether it was the freckles dotting her skin or the way she smiled at me—it made me lose all of my sense of control.

I had no idea how long we stayed like that. I lost track of time after I closed my eyes too. But the slamming of the front door jolted me back into the present, and I gently moved away from Wren's still-sleeping form to make sure Cain and Mollie knew what happened.

I met Mollie as she was running up the stairs. But she was in the bathroom with the door shut before I could even say hello.

"Mollie, dammit," Cain said as he came up the stairs. "I told you, we should—Henry. Hey."

"I was about to leave," I said, raising my palms. "Wren fell at the library and I—"

"Wren *fell*?" Mollie yelled from the bathroom. "What the *fuck*—"

The sound stopped and was replaced by retching.

"Is she okay?" I asked Cain. "Because I can check on her."

"This is *supposed* to be normal." He crossed his arms. "But I feel like I'm losing my mind here."

My brow furrowed as I tried to think of a time when throwing up would be normal.

Then it hit me. "She's pregnant."

"Yep. Please don't tell anyone. Not yet, at least."

"Has she seen a doctor yet? I could probably confirm it and get her a referral to an OBGYN."

"We have a doctor in Nashville. It's a long drive, but they're one of the best in the state. Her mom found them."

"Does Wren know?"

Cain nodded, but then his eyes moved to the bathroom door, which had just opened. "All right, throwing up is completed." Mollie sighed. "Now, can someone tell me what happened to Wren?"

"She fell off a ladder."

"A ladder?" Mollie's voice climbed in pitch.

"She needed stitches and has a sprained ankle. All because of Jude."

"That asshole. What did he do? Did he do this on purpose?" If Mollie's anger was directed at me, I would have feared for my life. But I agreed with her.

"He's been trying to talk to her. She didn't want to and had work to do. He followed her up a ladder."

"What an idiot," Cain said.

"She's fine. I took care of her and got her back. I'll need to get her truck and bring it here, and she needs to rest for at least a week. Maybe more, if she heals slowly."

"I'm on it," Mollie said.

"And you can rest too," Cain added.

Mollie rolled her eyes. "Don't start on that again. I'm fine to do normal activities. I was in the fields for eight hours a day before I got pregnant."

"You'll just need to hydrate and stop if you feel off," I added.

"See? Henry's on my side."

Cain blew out a breath. "Traitor."

"Nothing good will come out of telling Mollie no," I explained. "Even I know that."

He shrugged, but we both knew I was right. "Come on, Henry. I'll help you get Wren's truck."

"Really?" I asked.

"Might as well. Mollie probably wants to stay here and make sure Wren's okay."

"Definitely," she added. "And the proximity of the toilet helps too."

"That leaves you and me."

The quiet end of a stressful day gave me enough energy not to worry about the drive to get Wren's truck, so I agreed. Mollie grabbed Wren's keys and gave them to Cain before we left.

"So," he said as we got back on the road. "How is fake dating going?"

The Cain I'd met hated small talk, especially in person. The gruff man who'd barely talked to me had vanished when Mollie came into town.

He was trying, and I knew that.

"It's going fine. Though I don't trust Jude."

"He's always looked like a fucking tool," Cain muttered. "Even in season one."

"I try not to judge people by their looks, but yeah. He has one of those sports cars, too, and revs it for no reason."

"Jackass. At least Mollie also hates him now that she knows everything. I always thought something weird was going on. It seemed fake."

"Hopefully, Wren and I don't look the same."

"You definitely don't."

There were a lot of implications one could take from that. Were my feelings too obvious? How did I play the perfect boyfriend and not let it slip through?

"You know, you're a good guy, Henry. I don't think it would be bad if anything happened between you two."

"I'd probably have to get Mollie's approval if I even wanted to. But Wren and I are friends. That's all we'll be. And she's leaving when this season is over."

Everything had come out of the library already and they were going to be putting it back together soon. Once that was over, *we* were over.

And it would be for the best.

"Mollie thinks she could be convinced to stay."

"Is that what Mollie *thinks*, or what she *hopes* for?"

"You might have a point there," Cain said. "But it's worth a shot, isn't it?"

"You're saying that as a man who got the perfect relationship."

He shrugged. "You're right, but it's been nice not being alone."

I never let myself even think about a life where I wasn't alone. I was certain I would have that with Norah, and when she left, I didn't think of it ever again.

Even if Wren did want to try, I knew I was losing the battle within myself. I got firm with her. She would grow tired of that.

I was better off by myself.

"I'm glad," I said. "But I'm fine where I'm at. And once this season is over, I'm sure she'll be too."

We were nearing the square and we lapsed into silence. Cain gave me a quick glance before saying, "I don't know who you're trying to convince. Me, or yourself."

Then he was gone. I watched him as he got inside Wren's truck to drive it home. When I was alone, I let out a long breath, hoping to get what he'd said out of my mind.

It didn't work.

20

WREN

Strawberry Springs Neighborhood Watch

Madison Heines: Hello. I've joined the group to post a friendly reminder to NOT shoot the drones. They're only trying to get shots of the library. We've lost three now.

Henrietta Brown: @Marjorie Brown
Marjorie Brown: Wasn't me! I'd use the bat.
Hu Gh: I HAVE A RIGHT TO DEFEND MY LAND AND MY SKIES AGAINST INVADERS!
Jade Clark: Whoa, calm down there. You know it's just a machine, right? To take pictures?
Hu Gh: I did NOT consent to Facebook using my pictures!
Jade Clark: It's not for Facebook!!! Can't you read???

"This is a terrible idea," Mollie said. "Literally one of the worst you've ever had."

It had been three days since my sprain. I'd been sitting dutifully in bed, icing it the best I could.

But I was losing my mind.

And so was Madison. We were losing valuable time, and she demanded that I come back to filming. I was so bored that even being in front of a camera sounded fun.

"I have stuff to do," I said. "I won't work, just do interviews and come back."

"Henry said to rest for at least a week."

"It's not even my driving ankle," I said. "Seriously, it's fine."

I hoisted myself up on my good foot and gently tested the waters on the injured one. It was sore, but not the worst I'd ever had.

Henry didn't need to know this, but I'd twisted this ankle many times. Sure, it wasn't from falling off a ladder, but this wasn't the first time I'd walked on a bad joint.

"You're a nightmare patient." Mollie shook her head.

"Like you wouldn't do the same."

She blew out a breath. "You don't have to call me out like that, you know."

I slowly made my way toward the front door. "I'm your best friend. I definitely do."

"You're really going for it, huh?"

"I need to get out of these four walls."

"Fine, but I'm helping you down the stairs."

"Won't Cain be mad, considering he thinks you're *so* fragile right now?"

She shrugged. "We both do things our boyfriends don't like. Whoops."

I was tempted to correct her, but the words got caught in my throat. It was nice, even if only for a second, to pretend that this was real.

My crush was getting worse. And I had no idea how to get a handle on it.

"All right, the coast is clear," Mollie said as we got to the bottom of the stairs. "No one caught us."

"And hopefully no one will. I'll be back early today. Unless I go try to find hardware."

"Then I'll kill you. You still don't need to be doing your full workload."

I rolled my eyes, but she was right. "Thanks, Mollie. I'll see you in a bit."

"Have fun getting yelled at if Henry catches you!"

I waved her off. Henry didn't expect me to be there. I highly doubted he would even notice me.

Slowly, I got in my truck, cursing how high it was, and drove to the square. I parked right in front of the set, letting a PA pull my truck around to a better spot, and hobbled over to where we would do interviews.

"I'm here," I told Madison. "What do you want me to do?"

"Finally." She folded her arms across her chest. "The contractors have loads of questions for you."

"They could've called me."

"They would have if your little boyfriend hadn't told them not to. I swear, two injuries and he's acting like you almost died!"

She walked off in a huff, and I realized I had a line of people wanting to talk to me. I kept my weight on my good foot and listened to all of them. We were at an important part of the renovation, and my injury couldn't have come at a worse time, so I tried to be as patient as possible, even as I grew tired.

"All right, enough questions." Jude walked over and then stopped in front of me. "We have interviews to do."

"I need to sit down," I informed him. "Give me ten minutes."

"The faster we do this, the faster you're done for the day."

"Jude, seriously. Stop pushing me. Didn't you learn when I fell off a fucking ladder?"

He frowned. "I said I was sorry for that."

"Was that as I was falling to the earth? Because I didn't hear it."

"Just—"

"No, Jude, my ankle fucking hurts and I need to sit for a bit! What's gonna make you listen to me?"

"Maybe a doctor telling him to," another voice piped in. "Because I specifically said she needed rest, and I'm sure you don't want me to report you to OSHA for endangering her *again*."

Every hair on my arm stood. That was *Henry*. And he was using his hot doctor voice.

I slowly turned. "H-hey, Henry."

His chest puffed as he glared at Jude. He only spared me a glance. "We'll be talking about *you* later."

I probably should have been worried. That would be a normal reaction in the face of anger, but there was something about Henry that was so *hot* to me at that moment.

Maybe there was something wrong with me.

I wasn't trying to do it on purpose, but every time he did this, I thought about it for days after.

"Fine." Jude threw his hands up. "I guess I'll just keep waiting and doing nothing! God, this is all so *boring*!"

Once Jude was gone, Henry was on me. "Wren. Sit. *Now*."

I did what I was told, even though my thighs clenched at the order.

"In my defense, I was bored." I said it the second I sat.

"So that's a good excuse to work when I specifically told you not to?"

"I was only planning on doing an interview, not any real

work. I couldn't help that every contractor had a question for me, which kept me here for way longer than I intended."

He blew out a breath and knelt, not giving me an answer. My mind went blank when he gently took off my shoe.

"What are you doing?"

"Making sure you don't get sore."

Holy shit. He was rubbing my ankle while pissed at me? My body was warm already from the hot day, but this was taking it to new levels.

"Why are you doing all of this?"

He didn't look up as he answered, his fingers trailing my sore ankle. "If there's anything I learned about you falling off that ladder, it's that I can't bear to let anything happen to you."

"Nothing is happening to me. I'm just in a little bit of pain."

Now he looked at me. "That's included in what I said."

I could get lost in his eyes, but then I remembered where we were. The cameras were rolling. This had to be for them.

"I'm trying to rest. I'm just not the kind of person to do nothing all day."

"Then sit. Do your interviews on a chair. If they give you a hard time, send them to me."

"O-okay." My brain was fuzzy. His hands and words were too much.

He spent a few minutes focusing on my ankle, and for the entire time, I was unable to think straight, much less talk to him.

Afterward, he told Madison to do my interviews with Jude from the park bench. She tried to argue, but he didn't let her.

Once all of it was set up, he turned to me. "Can I trust you to take care of yourself?"

"I'll try my best."

"Okay." He pressed a kiss to my cheek. "I'll see you later, buttercup."

And he was gone. I watched him until he disappeared into

the clinic, noticing that he didn't stop to take off the mic pack. In fact, I wasn't sure he had even been wearing one in the first place.

Which meant I wasn't sure if all of that was for the cameras at all.

***

Almost two weeks later, I walked into Henry's clinic to get my stitches removed. I'd done my best to take it easy, but he had also made sure I was listening. I did have a lot to do when it came to the show, especially when I was taking more time off right after the injury, and Madison wanted the all clear to put me back on my usual work.

The door jingled to announce my presence, and Henry poked his head around the corner. "Wren?"

"Hey," I said. "Have time for a walk-in? It's been two weeks."

"I do," he replied. "Come on back."

"No waiting time? Perks of dating the doctor, I guess."

"More like perks of a small-town doctor."

I laughed and followed him. At least he didn't correct me on the dating thing.

"How are you feeling?" he asked.

"About the same as this morning. My ankle is mostly fine. The stitches seem fine."

He hummed and took off the gauze. "You're healing really nicely."

"I aim to please." That might have been a lie. It had been over a week since he'd gotten bossy with me, and I was already missing it. I was torn between following orders and pushing him to get more.

Henry was focused on my arm, and I had to resist the urge

to sigh in disappointment. Ever since he'd said he couldn't bear to see me hurt—for me and me only—I'd been hoping to see any sign that he was into me in any other way.

But he'd been the picture-perfect fake boyfriend. As always. He stopped when the cameras were off. He walked away at the end of the night.

Except for when I asked him to stay the day I'd fell.

Henry finished taking the stitches out and turned to wash up. "You should be fine for some stuff, but take it easy."

"Does this mean I could make sure the clinic is in good shape?" I asked. "I can do small repairs too, you know."

"No." There it was. The voice. I ignored the thrill that shot down to my toes.

"I have to do something for you in return. And it would be a start."

"It's not the priority."

"My priority is helping you out while you're helping me out." I moved to hop off the table, but his hand appeared on my midsection.

"Did you miss the part where I said to take it easy?"

"I can check things out and take it easy."

I moved again, but his hand was firmer.

"Why are you so worried about helping me?" he asked lowly.

"Because you literally saved my ass and asked for *nothing* in return. If you don't give me something to do, I'll find it."

I met his eyes, even as they narrowed. I was used to pushing people, but *this* gave me a thrill in my chest. Henry had this vibe around him. A side that he hid from me. I wanted to see what it was.

His hand moved from my midsection to my hip. "I don't need anything in return."

"Let me decide that."

"No." He let out a sigh. "Why do you insist on pushing me?"

Because it made him like *this*. "I don't take handouts."

"Take this one."

He was close. So close. This wasn't how friends acted.

"No," I said, repeating his own words back to him. "There's something I can give you, Dr. Henry Connor, and I *will* find it. Whether you like it or not."

A frustrated growl erupted from low in his throat. It sent every inch of my body on edge. Gone was the mild-mannered doctor I liked.

In his place was something I *more* than liked.

Henry let out a breath, our eye contact breaking. I saw him fighting for control again. "You're all cleared, Wren. You can get back to work."

My stomach sank. I didn't want him to be like he was with everyone else. I wanted more of him. All of him.

He went to step away, and I knew I couldn't let it happen.

I grabbed him by his tie, yanking him to me.

Pure desperation was the only reason for my next move. It wasn't smart, and it could easily get me in trouble, but I couldn't let him walk away.

So I crushed my lips to his.

I got a minute of his lips sliding against mine. Of his hand tightening on my hip. In that minute, I thought of all the ways I could push him again.

But then he pulled away.

"What are you doing?" he asked. "There's no one around."

"I-I know, I just . . ." Words failed me. What was I doing pushing the boundaries of our fake relationship? "Sorry. That was me acting on an impulse."

"An *impulse*?" He seemed so confused, like me kissing him was the last thing he expected.

Shame made my cheeks hot. "I got my wires crossed. I thought maybe we could—we were heading toward doing something more."

"We're not," he immediately said. "We *can't*."

Oh, *God*. I was never allowed to fake date again. I'd now been rejected by *both* men I'd done this with. That feeling—the one I hated—infected every inch of me.

"Of course," I replied. My voice didn't shake, but I didn't sound like myself.

"You're . . . disappointed?"

"I mean, yeah. But I'll get over it. You don't like me that way, and I got confused. Sorry about that."

I gave him a tight smile. At least I'd gotten an apology out. Hopefully, this wouldn't ruin things between us too badly. Now I needed to get the hell out of the clinic and process what I'd just done.

But his hand was back on my midsection. "I never said I didn't like you."

"You don't have to say it. I can figure out why you're saying no." Even if it hurt like a *bitch*. It was tempting to cry, but I refused to let it happen. At least until I was alone.

"Wren, stop. I'm not saying no because I don't want you. How could I not want you? You're . . ." He looked at me, gesturing up and down. "You."

"It's stopped many people before, trust me."

"Not me. God, never me. I've thought about it since the day we *met*."

My heart jumped at his words. He had? "Then why are you saying no?"

"Doing this changes things between us. We're supposed to be fake dating for the cameras, and friends in private. That's already complex enough. Adding more in? It could end terribly. We have rules for a reason."

"Fuck the rules."

"That's not how I operate. You're saying your wires would get crossed. Mine would too, and then when it's over, we're both hurting."

He was seeing this logically. I knew he was. And deep down, I knew he was right. But Henry's hand was still on my midsection and that clouded everything else. I wanted him. He wanted me.

So, how could I make this happen?

"We can make it so both of us know this is a one-time thing."

His brow furrowed. "A one-time thing."

"Yeah. We're getting it out of our systems. I don't know about you, but thinking about this has definitely clouded my judgment a little. We could clear the air."

He blinked, *actually* considering it. "It's been distracting for me too."

"Exactly. We do this once. Have fun. And then go back to what we were before. We can even make it a rule."

"I *do* like rules." He bit his lip. "So, one time—"

"And we do whatever we want." I tugged on his tie again.

"That could be a terrible idea." His words ghosted over my ear.

"I love terrible ideas." My teeth scraped over his earlobe. "So, are we doing this?"

"Fuck, Wren." His voice wavered. "Yes. We're doing this."

My pulse jumped again. I wasn't sure where to start or what I wanted to do with our one time together. I could picture it all, yet none of it seemed good enough for this single chance I had.

Henry's lips captured mine in a bruising kiss. He tugged me toward his body and I wrapped my legs around him to keep him close. Most of the people I'd been with let me take the lead. Usually, that's what I said I liked. But there was something so delicious about Henry making the moves here. I didn't have to plan it all out. He'd taken over.

His tongue darted across mine as he deepened the kiss. I opened myself to him and he pulled me tighter, our tongues still tangled. My mind whited out. I'd thought I would need to direct him to what I wanted.

But he was simply doing it. Taking it.

And my mind was silent.

I trailed my fingers to the buttons of his shirt, eager to take off his layers. His hands followed mine and he unbuttoned it himself without even breaking the kiss. My hands trailed over warm, smooth skin. His shoulders were taut, as was his back.

My hips ground into him, desperate for any friction. I cursed my jeans. For work, they were great, but if I'd known I'd be grinding against Henry in his office, I would have opted for leggings.

Henry's hand moved from my hip up my side.

"You're so soft," he groaned into my lips. I was pretty sure this was the first time any man had referred to me as *soft*.

"My jeans," I said. "Get them *off*."

"You'll have to be patient," he replied.

I whined as his hand cupped my breast. "Why?"

"Because I'm about to find every part of you that sets you off with my mouth."

I was about to tell him no, that I only wanted him to touch me more, but then his lips ghosted behind my ear and I let out a gasp.

"Right there," he said with a chuckle. "Noted."

Henry trailed downward and his mouth settled on my neck for a long moment. I could feel him tug my skin into his mouth, and *fuck*. I would have one hell of a hickey, but I didn't care. He continued pressing kisses into my skin.

I was covered in gooseflesh when he finally took off my shirt.

Each of his kisses were setting my nerve endings on fire, but the soft area above my collarbone caused me to cry out.

"You're torturing me," I whined.

"It'll be worth it, buttercup."

I writhed as his mouth moved, my core desperate for attention. I'd never felt like this from kisses alone, but Henry was organized. Methodical.

And it was driving me up the wall.

My legs gripped him like a vise, desperate for anything. I was sure I could feel the outline of his cock in his pants. And God, I wanted that inside of me.

I'd never been this wet in my *life*. And only from kisses. What the hell was happening to me?

After he found his fifth spot, the area under my ribs, I was begging.

"*Please*," I groaned. "I'm losing my mind, Henry. You have to touch me."

"I have you begging just like this," he said, still not moving. "What would happen if I . . ."

His teeth grazed under my ribs, and I gasped when I felt him suck the skin into his mouth again.

"Ah, *fuck*." He was nowhere near my clit. How did this feel so good?

Now one of his other hands went under the band of my bra, tracing my nipples. The sensation was almost too much, but he kept me right on that edge. Usually, I had to direct a man to where I needed him. This time, I was only feeling pleasure.

Henry's hand finally moved behind me as he bit into my sensitive skin, lavishing it with attention. I wasn't sure how much time had passed when he unhooked my bra with one movement.

My tits tumbled out, and my bra was tossed across the room.

"Every inch of you," he said. "Gorgeous."

"H-have you tortured me enough yet?"

"There's not enough time in the day," he said, mouth lowering. "If I had unlimited time . . ." He lowered a kiss to my rib cage. Then to my stomach. "I'd find out which of these freckles made you gasp. I'd kiss each and every one."

He was now at my hip. Slowly, he undid the top button of my pants. I was about to come out of my skin as he slid the fabric off of me. I sat up, wanting his pants off too, but he laid me back down.

"We're not rushing this," he ordered. "Slow down, Wren."

Who was I to fight that voice of his? I paused, even though I wanted nothing more than to touch him too. Henry brought my core right to his face, and I knew I'd made the right choice in letting him lead.

I thought I was prepared for the feel of his tongue on me, but I wasn't. There wasn't enough preparation in the world for how it felt to have him lick all the way from my entrance to my clit and then back down again.

"Dear God." I threw my head back, screwing my eyes shut as he worked. His tongue fucked me like a promise. Like I'd never get over this one-time thing. And when I was close to coming, he moved up to my clit and sucked on it, bringing me to the edge. My hands tangled in his hair, forcing him to stay right where he was.

Henry rewarded me with an almost punishing amount of pressure. It didn't just push me over the edge, it rocketed me there.

I let out a cry so loud the entire town square might have heard me. I rode wave after wave of pleasure on his face.

It took a long time for me to remember how to breathe, and when I finally could, his mouth covered mine. "That was the best meal I've ever had in my life, Wren. It's your turn to taste it too."

And I did. But I still tasted him, and I was ready for more.

I tried to wrestle out of his grip, determined to get his pants off too, but he broke the kiss and whispered the hottest thing I'd ever heard in my ear.

"Do I need to tie you down to make you listen to me? We're doing this my way."

I immediately stilled. Who was this man and why did I want him to fuck me a million times?

Henry's teeth sank into my bottom lip before his hand covered my breast. My nipples were sensitive from my first orgasm, and I whined and shamelessly ground myself against his hardness.

His hand applied pressure. "Stay still."

It killed me to follow his order, but I did. He let go of my breast and trailed down to my pussy again. This time, a finger pressed inside of me.

One finger was enough for my core to clamp down on.

"You're so fucking tight," he said into my lips. "Are you always this wet?"

I could only tell the truth. "No."

"Then it's all for me."

He thrust his hand, his finger plunging deep before pulling nearly all the way out. I tightened with every movement.

"You're gonna need some work if I'm gonna fuck you."

"N-no." I needed him inside of me. I was losing my mind. "I can take it. I promise."

"Can you?" He added a second finger.

"*Fuck*," I managed, though barely. I wanted to prove that I was ready so badly, to be so good that he would fuck me. But I couldn't help that my pussy was contracting, tightening around the first thing it would find. I was so revved up. So ready.

And yet I was going over the edge just by his fingers alone. "I'm gonna . . ." I trailed off as the first wave started, body tightening as I came again. Henry didn't slow down the pace. In fact, he picked it up, curving his fingers to my G-spot, which only made pleasure rush through me even harder.

"I could do this all day," he said.

"No," I whined. "I want your cock. I fucking *need* it. Stop being a giver and take something."

"Buttercup, I think *you'll* be the one taking it."

"Let me. Please, please, *please*."

His hand *finally* went to his own pants, and he took them and his underwear off in one go. When his cock finally sprang free, my mouth watered.

Seeing it was so much better than only feeling it. I reached out and pumped it, reveling in the way he shuddered. Finally, I was affecting him for once.

"I have so many ideas," I said, running my hand up and down him again. "So many ways to drive you wild like you did me."

"I thought you wanted me to fuck you."

I did. But I also wanted to take his cum down my throat. I bit my lip, unsure of what to do for our first and only time doing this.

"You said you wanted to take it," he added.

A thrill of excitement rushed through me as he reached into a drawer to pull out a condom. Once it was slid on, he lined up with my pussy.

I wrapped my legs around him again, not letting him escape. He responded by pushing in, just an inch.

I gasped again. One inch and he was stretching me wide. What would all of him do?

"This is why I wanted to take my time," he said, his mouth kissing the sensitive place under my ear, then he leaned over me. "This is why you listen."

He had that voice again, the one that made all thoughts leave my mind.

"Are you gonna order me around, or are you gonna fuck me?"

Now his teeth grazed the skin. "I can do both."

I tried to think of a smart-ass reply, but he pushed in deeper, stretching me even more. He pulled out before going back inside, working me open with slow, controlled thrusts. I struggled to breathe each time that I thought he was fully inside of me. He kept getting deeper and deeper in.

This method was true torture, but I must have loved it, because I could feel the heat again. My core was tightening around him, even though he was opening up all of me.

"You're about to come again," he groaned. "I can feel it."

"I don't know what's happening," I said. "This isn't how it usually goes for me."

"Good. I want you to remember this."

I would. Even if it ended right that second.

But he pulled all the way out. I only had a moment to feel empty before he surged all the way in.

"*Henry.*" His name came out like a curse. Or a prayer. I wasn't sure which.

"Wren," he responded as he pulled out again. "Are you gonna come on my cock? Are you gonna let me feel it?"

My toes tightened. "I want to."

"You will. I know you will." His thrusts sped up, and with this new force, he was reaching parts of me that I didn't know existed. I dragged my nails down his back, eyes closed again. He was so fucking hard. So fucking deep. There was nothing else I could do but come again.

Everything tightened one last time, releasing in a perfect explosion. My sight went black and every one of his movements sent another wave jolting through me. I screamed his name as I felt it hit me over and over again.

Henry cursed under his breath and slammed into me one last time. I held onto him hard, my orgasm still racing through my body. Then I felt him jerking inside of me as his lips captured mine one more time.

Or one last time. One last time for just the two of us.

Henry pulled away, eyes meeting mine as I caught my breath. I was heaving, both totally satisfied and begging to do it again.

"W-Wren," he said. "I—"

My phone rang, breaking my focus.

"Fuck," I said as I checked the time. "I have to get back to the set. I'm late for, like, five things."

I gathered my clothes and dressed quickly before running out the door.

Henry didn't get a word in, not even to tell me to take it easy.

That should have been my first sign something was wrong.

21

HENRY

Strawberry Springs Neighborhood Watch

Kerry Winsor: Isn't it state law to pull over if you have more than five people following you and you're on a TRACTOR ON THE HIGHWAY?

Comments:
Jade Clark: Bold of you to think people care about laws here.
Kerry Winsor: It made a fifteen-minute drive thirty minutes!
Hu Gh: Leave me alone. I just needed some beer from the town over.
Kerry Winsor: So your first choice was a TRACTOR?
Hu Gh: You complained about my car backfiring. Then you complain about my tractor. Get a life!
Tammy Jane: This coming from the man who complained in this very group about me giving him decaf?
Hu Gh: COFFEE IS DIFFERENT

I saw myself and Wren over and over again. It followed me home, played behind my eyelids as I went to sleep, and restarted the second I woke up.

I'd had sex with her in the *clinic*, of all places. I'd bossed her around, done only what I wanted to do, and completely lost control.

Wren was right to leave the second we were done. I had no idea if she was really late for anything. It could have easily been an excuse to get away.

There was so much that I should have done. I should have asked her what she liked, if she even wanted me like that. If she wanted to be the one leading.

But I didn't. I blacked out. I was so driven by my desire that I let myself slip.

And I needed to apologize to her.

I wasn't sure how. My morning walk was always invaded by cameras. The second I passed, one of the PAs from the show got me mic'd up and ready to be present. There would be no time to have a private conversation.

I could call her, but this was something that needed to be done in person. I had to force myself to look her in the eye when apologizing, just like Mom always expected me to.

But how did I say that I was sorry for getting so forceful? That I should have held back? I had no idea how to even begin, and I needed to figure it out.

Instead of walking, I drove in and parked at the back of the clinic, completely avoiding the set. I barely looked at anything in the exam room while getting it ready for the day, focusing purely on work.

The deviation from my schedule was killing me, but I doubted Wren wanted to see me anyway.

My first patient was someone from the town over, and I was relieved to be able to fall into professionalism while I worked with them. It was proof that I could still be the Henry people wanted. I just needed time to get there.

I saw a few more patients after, falling into my usual routine with ease. I felt marginally normal by the time the day ended.

Then the door jingled and one last person walked in. I turned, expecting it to be a walk-in.

It was Wren.

My heart jumped into my throat as I saw her in overalls and a T-shirt. I couldn't even look at her face yet.

I'd fucked up *so* badly.

"Hey," she said. "I must have missed you this morning."

I fiddled with paperwork. "I drove in. Needed a change of pace."

She was silent for a moment, and I was so tempted to see what expression she was wearing. But I *couldn't*. "Okay. I can't imagine getting stopped every morning is fun, so I get it. Have you had a good day?"

"Yeah, it's been fine. Can I help you with something?" I hated not saying anything else to her and getting straight to the point, but I needed time to figure out how to be the version of me she wanted. And I hadn't had that.

"The producers want an interview about the changes in town. They said you were the one the audience knew the most. Are you up for it?"

No, I wasn't. But I needed to be.

"Yeah, I can do it. Now?" I finally looked up at her, catching only that her cheeks were flushed as she looked at me.

Was it out of disgust?

"That would be best."

I bit my cheek and followed her over to the set, still unable to look her in the eye. It was *loud* today. Contractors worked on the facade while Jude hammered something near the front of the building, where we did a lot of the interviews.

Every bit of it pounded into my head.

This was a bad idea.

I couldn't even talk to the PA putting my mic on. All I could do was stay calm. My shame was turning into annoyance at every sound that hit me.

The seconds couldn't tick by fast enough.

"You and Wren come over here," Madison called.

I didn't know it was possible for me to tense even more, but I did. Would she even want me next to her after how I'd acted?

When I got close to her, she linked our arms.

"You don't have to do that," I told her under my breath.

Her eyes widened, but there wasn't much she could say that wouldn't give us away. Her arm remained firmly wrapped around mine, though.

"Let's get this started!" Madison said, getting the camera on us. Wren blinked and turned to it. I wanted to be able to focus on it, but the hammering was *still* going on.

"Shouldn't we wait for it to be quieter?"

"Jude's also filming something," she said. "The mic packs should filter out what we need."

I gritted my teeth. How was I supposed to focus on what I was being asked when I had to listen to the slamming of a hammer, the drill of machinery, and feel Wren standing close when I wasn't sure if she wanted that?

Madison said something else, but I wasn't able to take it in.

All I could hear was *clang*.

Clang.

Clang.

"Henry?" Madison asked with a groan. "Come on."

Clang.

"No," I finally snapped. My head had already been pounding from the noise, but now my heart was racing too. I needed it to *stop*, and *now*. "I can't be interviewed while listening to Jude hammer the same thing over and over. Does he even know what he's doing if he's still trying to get the same fucking nail in?"

Everyone was silent for two seconds. It gave me a second to realize that I had just raised my voice and cursed in front of people, which is something I never wanted to do.

Then Jude hit the fucking nail again, and I was right back where I started. My ears rang, and I knew I needed to get out of here.

"If you can provide a decent environment for an interview, then we'll talk. But this is ridiculous."

"It's just *sound*," Madison hissed.

"Henry," Wren said softly. "Are you okay?"

I pulled away, but she followed. Why was she doing that? She should hate me.

"We'll do this later. I can't right now."

It was tempting to drive home, but I didn't want to be behind the wheel of a car. I made it to the clinic, slammed the door, and went to my tiny office to try to cool down.

The second the sounds had stopped, I knew I'd messed up. While it might have been overwhelming, most people didn't completely shut down and lose it like I had. I'd finally snapped.

Just like I never wanted to.

Who had been there? Who all did I need to smooth things over with?

Wren, for sure. I'd already messed up with her yesterday. I was sure her view of me was decimated, and I didn't know if an apology would fix this.

I also had to say sorry to Madison and Jude, which would be next to impossible considering I was still so frustrated with their lack of care for how Wren felt. But I would if I had to. After all these years, I couldn't lose how people saw me. I'd done so much work to show the better side of myself.

Closing my eyes, I tried to remember if anyone in town had been watching the filming. Now that the newness of the cameras had faded, most people didn't watch the day-to-day anymore. I was pretty sure the square had been empty.

And thank God for that.

The door to my office opened and the lights shut off. I looked up and found Wren.

I couldn't even look at her.

"Misophonia," she said softly. "Is that what it's called when noises can make you tense and angry?" I blinked. How did she even know the word? "I won't bother you for long, but I wanted you to have something." She slid a case across the desk. "They're my ear protection for loud noises. If you have to go outside or anything, you're welcome to use them."

She turned to leave, but I managed to speak before she could. "Why are you giving me these?"

"If Google was right and sounds make you upset, I want you to have something to help."

"I shouldn't need *help*," I hissed.

"And yet we do. Tell me, did you feel the same way when you got your glasses?"

"N-no."

"It's similar, isn't it? They help you function. They make it to where you can drive and go through life normally. I'll admit that noise sensitivity isn't something that's super talked about, but it's all the same to me."

"It's not *just* noise sensitivity," I said with another sigh. "It's part of a whole spectrum of issues. Most people don't under-stand it."

"I would. Or I'd try to."

"Why?"

"Because you mean a lot to me." She said it like it was obvious. "And that means leaving you alone if you want to be alone, but also staying if you want me to stay."

"I do. Want you to stay, I mean."

She nodded and sat. "Then that's what I'll do."

"I don't know if I'll be fun company."

"If you want to simply sit here in silence, I'll do that too."

I didn't deserve this, not after yesterday. But, despite that, I needed her to know.

"The misophonia is something I struggle with, but it's a part of a bigger picture. I'm autistic. I can accommodate myself and mask it, but only when I follow a strict routine and make time to rest."

"And you haven't been able to do that," she said. "Shit, Henry, I'm so—"

"Don't apologize. I'm the one who agreed to it, and I pushed it too far." I put my head in my hands and we lapsed into silence. I didn't hear the door open and close, but I wouldn't have been shocked if she had left without a trace.

The sympathy would fade, eventually replaced by annoyance. It was what had happened before. I'd had an inkling of what it was, and both Norah and Ace promised to help.

But then it got too rough for them both.

It was easier to hide it and pretend I was normal. Seeing others grow tired of me was far worse.

As the moments ticked by, I was able to breathe deeper. Pure silence and darkness were exactly what I needed.

Finally, I looked up, and Wren was still there, typing on her phone without making a noise.

"You're still here?"

"I am. Are you feeling better?"

"Somewhat."

She nodded. "I talked to Madison. The interview isn't happening today."

"Wh-what?"

"If you wanna continue, which you don't have to, then we need to make sure the construction site isn't ridiculously loud some other time. And I ordered you a pair of your own earplugs, ones that are recommended by other autistic people. They'll be here in a few days."

"I don't understand."

"Don't understand what? That I'm helping you? I told you I would."

"Why aren't you angry with me?"

She blinked. "I mean, I could be, but I'm not. I knew something was up, but it was your choice to tell me or not. Obviously, I'd like to know everything about you, but some things are yours to tell. I won't force them out of you."

"You want to know everything about me? Even after yesterday?"

"Yesterday?" she repeated. "What about yesterday? Did you mean when you and I . . ."

I looked away, images flashing in my mind. Things I wish I'd done differently.

"Do you regret it?" she asked after a long silence.

"I do."

She jerked back. "Oh . . . okay."

Wren had the same look on her face as when she thought I'd turned her down. I was sure she thought I didn't notice when she was hiding her hurt, but she always curled inward on herself as if trying to make herself smaller.

I needed to explain. "*You* should regret it too. I acted like a jerk, ordering you around like that. I tried to be way nicer and more communicative, but I snapped, and I'm . . . I'm really sorry."

"Wait, hang on. *That's* what you regret? Just how you acted?"

"Yes. I hold myself to a higher standard. That's not how I should be."

She could only stare at me, crossing her arms. "And were you gonna ask me how I felt about it, or were you gonna just assume I was mad?"

I opened my mouth to say that it was obvious she was mad. How could she not be? But then I thought about it. The only time she appeared angry was just now, when I'd told her how she should feel.

Rubbing my face, I let out a long sigh. I couldn't stop screwing up with her, it seemed.

"No, you're right. I'm sorry. I don't get why you wouldn't be. That's not a side of me that I like."

"Just because you don't like something doesn't mean I feel the same way."

Now my eyes cut to her. "You . . . *what?*"

"I liked yesterday. A lot, actually. I'm always making decisions and ordering others around. It was a nice change of pace."

I blinked. "What? But I told you what to do. I was rougher than I should have been."

"It was still hot, even when you left a hickey and I had to hope Mollie had some foundation that was a decent match for me." She rubbed her neck right where my mouth had been. "And we probably should have talked more about it, I'll give you that, but we can talk now. And I'm fine. Really, I am."

I couldn't believe what I was hearing. I'd done all of that and she'd *liked* it? "But I'm the mild-mannered doctor. That's who I am, this other side of me isn't . . . I'm not supposed to be like that."

"Did you enjoy it, though?" she asked.

"Yes." There was no hesitation. "Very much."

"Then this is a part of you too. Like being autistic is. And the misophonia. You don't have to tell everyone about it, but you also don't have to hide anything. Not with me. And judging by the way you're looking at me, I'd say I'm the first person who's told you that."

She was right. I hadn't heard any of this before. It was so strange to hear that I was half tempted to say I was asleep and this was all a weird dream. "My mom doesn't get it. Neither did . . . others."

"Sometimes we're around the wrong people for a while, and that lasts." She let out a humorless laugh, and I had a feeling she was talking from experience. "So I wanna understand."

"Thank you. I'll be better—"

"Don't worry about being better. Just be wherever you stand for that day." She gave me a smile before she stood. "And right now, you need a break. And now that I know that you're okay, I'm gonna go make sure Madison doesn't try to come here and change your mind."

Wren leaned down, and for a second, I thought she was going to kiss me. I would have let her. But she didn't. We must have both remembered the rules at the same time. The sex was a one-time thing. We were back to being friends in private.

She moved away, waving at me as she left. I could only do the same, letting a different kind of regret take me over.

Wren had seen it all, and she still cared about me. She didn't see any part of me as a fault, but as a side of me. Some of which she even *liked*.

I wanted nothing more than to explore that. To see if it was a fluke, or if there was some way that I could do all of it again. To be with her not as a one-time thing, but for as long as she was here.

But that was against the rules we set.

For once in my life, I hated the rules.

22

WREN

Strawberry Springs Neighborhood Watch

Jackie Anne: Does anyone know if any local stores sell raccoon food?

Comments:
Tammy Jane: Jackie, NO.
Jackie Anne: The poor things must be starving!
Tammy Jane: But if you feed them, they'll never stop coming.
Henry Connor: Jackie, I'm all for animals, but raccoons can carry rabies.
Jackie Anne: You have the shots for that, right?
Tammy Jane: I repeat: JACKIE NO.

I RAN into Jade the second I left the clinic. My mind was occupied with the heavy conversation I'd had with Henry, but her bright hair pulled me right out of my thoughts.

"Oh, hey!" She hid her hands behind her back. "Is every-thing okay?"

"It's all good. Is everything okay with *you*?"

She laughed. "Never better."

She went around me and walked into Jade's Goodies. I turned and watched her. Was she carrying . . . nails?

I had a lot of questions, but I didn't have time to follow and ask. Instead, I walked back to the set, only to find Jude talking to Madison.

"I *swear*, this town is weird!" Jude threw his hands up. "They just disappeared."

Madison scrubbed her face. "That's not possible."

"Well, it happened!"

"We still need the shot. It's gonna look good when you're watching Henry talk to Wren—"

"Like I texted, that's not happening," I told the both of them. "Henry's done for the day."

"Where is he? I can—"

"You're not doing anything," I interrupted. "He's not filming today."

Madison slowly blinked and then she crossed her arms. "After trying to film one scene?"

"It was ridiculously loud."

She rolled her eyes. "We need the interview *today*."

"I can ask someone else from the town," I offered.

"No, the audience doesn't know any of them. You can have Jude do it since his nails apparently *disappeared*."

"They did!" he said. "I don't know how to explain it."

I couldn't have cared less about Jude's nails since I was more focused on the way she continuously wanted me to interview with him, even when we could have done it with someone else.

But I wouldn't fight it. Not when it would give Henry the time he needed.

"Should we stand as close as she did with Henry?" Jude asked.

Was he *kidding*? "No. Henry's my boyfriend. You're not."

"But it was a good shot."

"Stand close!" Madison called as she walked to the camera.

I stood near him, but not close.

"You're so tense on camera," Jude said. "What's with that?"

"I'm a taken woman now," I replied. "We're not gonna have the same dynamic as season one. I don't know why you keep forgetting that."

"I'm just doing my job."

"And that now involves charming the audience. Not me."

"Get ready!" Madison called. "And Jude, get closer!"

"Seriously?" I snapped.

"Your boyfriend could have been here if he didn't need the day off."

I let Jude get one inch closer to me, but I wasn't thrilled about it.

Madison called out a question, asking us how we've noticed the increase in tourism. I answered it honestly. I was happy to see the businesses grow and get more customers. They deserved it.

Jude was quiet, but I doubted he knew anything that was going on. When he wasn't obligated to be here, he was either in Nashville or flying to one of his other houses all around the country.

But at the end of the interview, just when I thought we were wrapping up, he put an arm around me and said, "We're just so happy to be able to help this small town."

I was so shocked that I went still, but I saw red.

"Cut!" Madison called.

"What the hell was that?" I snapped, shoving his arm off of me. "Why are you *still*—"

"It was a moment of bonding," he replied. "We still need those."

"We're broken up."

"The people still like seeing us be friends."

"Not with your arm around me! Jesus, how clueless can you be?"

"How dramatic can *you* be?"

I wanted to smack him upside the head.

"I'm done for the day." That should have been the last thing we needed anyway, but I wasn't fit to be on camera anymore. If Henry were in a better place, I would have found him, but instead, I stalked to my car.

Jade was waiting for me.

"Want me to tie him up?" she asked.

I blinked. "Wh-what? Why would you tie up Jude?"

"He's being weird. To you and Henry. And I'm not liking it."

"Is that why you were acting weird earlier?" I remembered what she'd been holding. "Wait, were you carrying nails?"

"They were so easy to swipe. He's not very observant, is he?"

"Not at all, but *you* are. You saw what happened with Henry, didn't you?"

"I didn't hear it all since I was inside my shop, but he was mad. It takes a lot to get him mad, so I figured I'd step in. You did better than me, though. He probably needed the break."

"He's doing a lot for me." I blew out a breath. "The least I can do is make him take care of himself."

"At your own expense?" Jade raised an eyebrow. "Madison seemed really happy to push you and Jude together."

"Don't remind me."

"He'll be gone once filming is done. We're all doing our part in making sure he hates it here."

"You are?" I asked.

"He cheated on you. Of course we are." She said it like it was obvious, but I'd seen everyone else who watched the show treat me like a commodity. The center of the drama. Not a person.

God, I loved this town.

"Thanks," I said. "You guys are nicer than the show's fans."

"That's a low bar, but we'll take it." Jade leaned forward. "And if you find anything else for me to do to piss off Jude, let me know. Annoying men is *very* cathartic for me."

I let out a laugh and thanked her once again before heading to the farmhouse. While I was worried about her and Mollie before, I saw now that Jade was a good friend. Even to me, and she barely knew me.

Mollie was home and more than likely working on dinner with Cain. I thought I was safe to let out the longest sigh known to man the second I walked inside. Jade had helped, but I was exhausted.

Then my best friend came around the corner. "Uh-oh. Bad day?"

"You could say that. Jude's still acting weird. He put his arm around me in an interview."

"What?" Her jaw dropped. "In front of Henry?"

"He wasn't there for the filming today."

"I thought he came by every day."

Guilt hit me. He must have added that to his routine when we'd started. And then it all became too much. "Things were different, but it's fine. He's fine."

"Is something going on between you two?" I opened my mouth to answer, but she cut me off. "And don't even try to lie. You asked me for foundation to cover up one hell of a hickey this morning."

Heat rose to my cheeks. "Yeah. Something happened."

She was still, but then she pumped her fist so hard I thought she might fall over. "*Yes!* I knew there was a connection there."

"It's not . . . It was a one-time thing."

She groaned. "Why would you ruin my happiness like that?"

"You said you didn't want me to lie."

"Was it at least good?"

"It was the . . . *best.*" The heat only intensified as I thought about it. God, I would do that over and over again. "But he doesn't want things to get complicated. We're fake dating, remember?"

"You could make it real."

"Not if that's not what he wants."

She let out a sigh. "Why would he not?"

There were loads of reasons. He might have been into me but didn't think I was relationship material. Or he didn't want to deal with all the long-term implications of being with me. I wouldn't blame him for any of that.

But I knew Mollie would disagree with every single one of them, so I shook my head.

"What's for dinner?" I asked, desperate to change the subject. "Do you need any help?"

"Pancakes," she said slowly. I was sure she was going to call me out, but she let it slide. Thank *God.* "Cain's making them."

"Didn't you have that for breakfast?"

"It's the only thing I can keep down," she said with a sigh. "I wish I was one of those women who didn't get morning sickness, but on the bright side, we got the genetic testing done, which means in a few weeks, we'll know the gender."

"You're there already?"

"It's early, but I'm ready to know." She put a hand on her slightly rounded belly, and my stomach sank as it always did when I was reminded what a perfect mom she was going to be.

"Are you doing one of those gender reveals?"

"That's what I was gonna talk to you about. We definitely are. Jackie has been begging to plan it."

"Does this mean she's the one who gets to know?"

"Not really. I was gonna ask you, if you're not too busy."

I blinked in shock. "Me? Seriously?"

"You're my best friend. Of course you'll be the first to know. You get to pick out the cake and everything."

Feelings were fighting a war in my gut. On one hand, I was so honored. I wanted to do this.

And yet I was so fucking sad at the same time.

"Of course I will," I said slowly.

"Are you sure? If this isn't your thing, I won't force you."

"No, I'm excited. I promise. It's just been a long day."

"I know," she said, pulling me into a tight hug. "You're so busy, which is why it's totally okay if you can't."

"No, I want to. It's gonna be so fun." And it would be. Once I figured out why I was so sad about it. Was it that I felt like I was losing her?

Or was it connected to Mom, like most of my sadness was?

"Go get some rest before dinner," she said. "You sound exhausted."

I nodded, grateful for the escape. I went to my room and flopped on the bed, trying to work out everything I felt.

And how my mom managed to still haunt me after all of these years.

I didn't expect to see Henry for a while. The plan was to give him as much space as he needed and worry about the show later.

So when I saw him walking down the sidewalk as usual, my

heart jumped into my throat and I abandoned the contractor who'd been asking me a question.

"What are you doing here?" I asked as I ran up to him.

"Hold on!" one of the PAs called. "He doesn't have a mic yet!"

"This is a private conversation," I told her. "I'll let you know when he's ready."

She huffed and turned around.

"Wren," he began. "I'm fine."

"Are you? Yesterday was a dumpster fire." In more ways than one. My emotions felt more tangled than my hair after a roller coaster ride.

"I took the whole day off. Rest does wonders." His eyes went down to my ankle. "And I'm pretty sure you don't need to be running on a freshly healed sprain."

Something in my chest loosened. He was back.

"I was making sure my boyfriend wasn't doing something dumb," I said with a roll of my eyes.

"That's *my* job."

My jaw fell open. "Are you *roasting* me right now? Who are you?"

"We can switch it up," he said with a smile. "Now, go back over to what you were doing. I have something to give you, and Madison will come after us if it's not on camera."

I blinked, realizing he had something behind his back. "You're killing my curiosity."

"It'll only take a few minutes."

"That's forever," I moaned as I returned to my contractor. It was hard to talk about crack filling while I knew Henry had a gift for me, but I did my best.

It didn't take much acting for me to be happy to see him. Or for me to run up and kiss him. In fact, I would have done that any day. Especially now that I knew how it felt when he—

My thoughts flew out of my mind when he brought out a massive blue hydrangea. "This is for you."

I stared at him in awe. "This is . . . Wow, are you *sure* you don't have a secret florist connection?"

"No, they're from my house. I grew it."

And I killed any plant I touched. "Thank you," I said, looking at the fluffy flower. His gestures had been so sweet that I decided to dry all the others he'd given me. But for a flower this massive, I'd need to figure out how to do the same thing.

"I can open the clinic a little later if we need to do that interview."

"Oh, don't worry about it. I figured it out."

"Cut!" Madison yelled. "No business talk!"

"I'm not gonna apologize for communicating!" I snapped back.

"So, you're still being difficult?"

I rolled my eyes and turned back to Henry.

"I have a feeling things didn't go well here yesterday," he said.

"Most of it was fine, so don't even try to feel bad."

His cheeks went red. "How did you know?"

"I might do dumb things sometimes, but I know you. And I'll tell you later."

"I can come by. I have an evening appointment, though."

"I'll be here. I have to deal with a few things now that I'm fully healed."

"*Mostly* healed." He looked at me pointedly. "Don't overdo it."

"I guess you'll have to make sure I don't," I said with a wink. "See you tonight?"

He pressed a kiss to my lips. "I'll look forward to it all day."

My stomach did a flip, and as he walked off, I had to remind myself exactly what this was.

I had a feeling I would be doing that more often.

Thankfully, I was pulled into work, which kept me busy. Though I gave Henry shit for it, I did try to not go too overboard with all that was on my list. My ankle was doing well, but it would hurt if I kept at it for too long.

Everyone left at five, and I took off my mic before going back inside to work upstairs. About thirty minutes later, the front door opened with a creak.

"Wren?" Henry called. "Are you here?"

"Yeah, give me a second!" My voice echoed off the walls as I finished what I was working on and started to slowly get up.

A hand helped me up halfway. "Still working?"

"I was doing easy stuff. Planning out tile." I gestured to the ground where I'd laid out a few samples. "What do you think?"

"I don't miss the old carpet," he said. "Are you making this similar to the color scheme downstairs?"

"I am."

"It'll look great," he replied. "Now, what happened yesterday?"

I blew out a breath. "I did the interview with Jude. Madison insisted on it."

His brow creased. "I didn't realize he cared for the town."

"He doesn't. He just pretended, which is what he's good at. At the end of it, he put his arm around me and made this weird comment."

Henry's shoulders tensed. "Did he now?"

"Yeah. Don't worry, I shut it down. No need to get fake jealous for me."

"I'm not *fake* jealous. It's very much real."

Jealousy wasn't an emotion I usually liked, but him feeling it for me sent a thrill down my spine. "Really?"

Henry brushed a strand of hair over my shoulder. "Yeah. I

don't like the idea of anyone making any moves on you. Not while I have you."

I waited for him to clarify. To say that he only had me when we were in public. But the correction never came.

And I didn't want it to.

I was tempted to ask what he was thinking, but for just this moment, I could let myself pretend that this was all real. He was mine. I was his.

The fantasy was too good to ruin with reality.

"I think he's gonna keep trying, though. On Madison's orders."

"We'll only wind up disappointing them."

"My thoughts exactly. With that and . . ." I trailed off, thinking of what Mollie asked me. "Some stuff at the farmhouse, a lot is on my mind."

"Stuff at the farmhouse, huh?" He raised an eyebrow. "Does that have anything to do with Mollie being pregnant?"

"You know?" I asked.

"I do. I saw her rushing to the toilet after you fell off the ladder."

"It's pretty easy to figure out, isn't it?"

"Very. And it's also easy to see that you have mixed emotions about it."

"I'm happy for her," I insisted.

"I know you are, but it's normal to feel uneasy when friends have major life changes."

I shook my head. "I'm not upset about that either. She deserves this, and I want her to have everything she wants."

"So, what *are* you upset about?"

I could lie. Say it was nothing. Henry would see right through it, though. "It's just that . . . life didn't end up the way I expected, I guess. It's hard to accept, but it's not her. And honestly, I don't want her to see anything other than happiness, because that's what she deserves." I shook off thoughts I didn't want to have. "It just keeps coming up. Sometimes work helps, but now there's all this stuff with Jude, and even being here feels wrong. I need my brain to shut off for a while."

"Need another task to do?"

I laughed. "If you say it as an order, it might actually work."

Henry went rigid, and I realized what I had said.

"That was a joke. A bad one, obviously. Ignore me. I know the rule."

And he didn't break them. Ever. I might have loved the sex. He did too, but it was over. Our one time was spent.

"A joke?" he asked. "You didn't mean that at all?"

I winced. Of course he would want to know if I meant it. "It was a joke with a nugget of truth in it. I *do* like the way your voice sounds when you tell me what to do. Especially when I make you get really firm. And when we had sex, it felt like I didn't have a problem in the world. My brain was quiet. But that's over, and we're back to friends. I guess I'll figure something else out."

"Don't."

"Don't *what*?"

"Figure something else out. If it works, it works."

"Are you suggesting that I annoy you enough to order me around?"

"I'm suggesting that we explore this."

"This as in *us*?"

"Yes."

"But there was a rule."

"Rules can be changed."

Somehow, this was the most shocking thing he could have said. My eyes grew wide. "You're suggesting we bend the rules? *You*?"

"It's new for me too. But you make me want to." His hands were in his pockets, but his eyes were firmly on me.

I couldn't believe this. He was willing to change rules. For *me*.

Had anyone done that before?

It was tempting to stare at him forever, to memorize this moment.

But he needed an answer before he changed his mind or took my silence as a no.

"You said we would explore this. Explore it as in it's another one-time thing?"

"Honestly?" He shook his head. "I don't know if it *can* be."

"Me either."

"We should still have some rules, though."

I nodded. The idea of it was a little comforting. My Henry was in there somewhere. "Please don't tell me you'll only be nice."

He laughed. "No, not that. But this is . . . risky. I want to be sure we don't have regrets when it's time for you to go back to Nashville."

I nodded. I'd be back to visit Mollie, but the point still stood. I would be living in Nashville and spending most of my time there. "Yeah, that's probably a good idea."

"We still fake date. We're still friends in private, with the added benefit of . . ."

"You telling me what to do while you give me orgasms?"

"Exactly," he said with a smile. "And not at our houses. That's a slippery slope. At least for me."

I nodded, trying to hide my disappointment. I still wanted to see every part of him. And that included where he lived.

But he was right. I was leaving, and getting our wires crossed was a bad idea.

"And if you ever wanna change things, you can tell me at any time."

He said it like I would want to. I was pretty sure I wouldn't. "Okay," I said. "I'll let you know if things change. Anything else, Mr. Rule Man?"

"That's *Doctor* Rule Man, and no. That's it."

"All of that sounds good to me." I stepped close, running my hand up his tie. "Are you open to some exploration now?"

"I'm up for it any time I'm with you." Henry's hand traced my cheek. "And I have an idea for the desk that's just over there."

He didn't have to say anything else. I was running for it the second he suggested it.

HENRY

Strawberry Springs Neighborhood Watch

Kerry Winsor: Can someone tell these tourists to use the crosswalks??? Were they raised in BARNS?

Comments:
Henrietta Brown: They're just confused. Kind of like a goose when it's first born.
Dale Garrett: It's good for business! No complaints here.
Kerry Winsor: Good for you, Dale, but I'm wearing out my brakes stopping for these idiots.
Hu Gh: Don't worry about stopping, Kerry. Keep going. It's ten points if you knock their shoes off.
Jade Clark: VEHICULAR MANSLAUGHTER? ON MAIN???
SherriffMike Finch: Hugh, don't make me come find you again. I have three reports with your name on it already, old man.
Hu Gh: You ain't got me yet!
SherriffMike Finch: I'm leaving this damn group.

Wren didn't waste time—not that I would have let her. The old desk was still upstairs, and I knew she was saving it to refinish and put in the renovated space.

I wanted to desecrate it first.

The second I could, I had my lips on hers, putting her ass on the desk. I could smell her usual rose scent mixed with a hint of sweat, and I couldn't get enough of her. I'd never met someone who liked to be told what to do, and now I got to experience it all again.

I couldn't stop thinking of her. When I'd arrived at the library, I wasn't sure how I was going to keep myself in check in front of her.

Now I didn't have to.

Wren's hands went to the buttons of my shirt, but I stopped her with a firm grip on her wrists.

"Always so eager," I said into her mouth. "But we have all the time in the world, buttercup."

I nibbled on her bottom lip, earning a gasp. "Are you gonna torture me again?"

Normally, I would say no. Normally, I wouldn't dream of something like that.

"If you mean am I gonna make this last as long as I possibly can, then yes." Now I was going for the spot on her ear, the one that made her moan the last time I kissed it.

"Fuck," she said as I pressed my lips to the sensitive skin. "But we can do this as much as we want to."

"Doesn't mean I'm gonna rush. All those kisses for the camera have to be chaste. But here, when I have you like this, I can do whatever I want."

And I brought my mouth to hers again, dipping my tongue to taste her. The kiss turned messy as her tongue rolled against mine, and I bit down. She made a sound that would haunt my dreams and pressed in closer, body tightening.

I was tempted to take it further and make her do whatever I wanted, but I did have one last polite cell in my body.

"But if you ever wanna stop—"

"I won't."

"Wren," I said, pulling away. "I'm gonna let loose."

Her cheeks turned a dark red. "And you should."

"But I have to at least tell you that you can stop me at any time. If you push against me or—"

"I *like* pushing against you, especially when it makes you mad at me."

My eyes shut. I was very tempted to shut her up, but I had to make this known.

"We need a safe word at the very least."

"It can be Jude."

"*Jude?* Really?"

"He's a fucking turnoff for me at this point. And I'm sure he is for you. I don't like men without brains."

I couldn't help but laugh. "Using an ex's name as a safe word. That's a new one for me, but it'll work."

"Perfect. And trust me, I won't be using it."

"We'll see about that."

She grabbed my tie and tugged me close. "Yes. We will."

I was done being polite, but her brattiness sealed the deal. My mouth covered hers again as I pressed her deeper into the desk. I'd been hard the second she mentioned that she thought about it still, but now I was aching, so ready to take her for myself.

But I would be patient.

I swirled my tongue around hers until her hips were bucking against me, until she was whining into my mouth, desperate for more. I gave in for only a few minutes as she ground her core against me, before I pulled away.

"No," she moaned.

I hauled her up before turning her around and bending her over the desk.

"I said I had an idea for this desk." I bit her earlobe. "And I'm gonna take you like this."

"Oh my *God*," she said. "Yes. Fuck yes."

I yanked down her pants, eyes lingering on her round ass for a moment too long. She even had freckles there.

Then I took off mine, freeing my cock to rub into her folds. I angled myself downward, feeling her whole body jerk as I hit her sensitive clitoris.

"*Ah*, fuck me, Henry."

"I don't take orders." I moved forward again with more pressure. "You do."

"*Shit*." She was panting. So soaked already and I'd barely done anything. I wondered if her pussy was quivering. She moved her hips up, chasing my hardness. I nipped at her shoulder blade before whispering into her ear.

"Come on my cock. Take what you need. Use me."

Her only response was a muffled moan, but she jerked upward, still rubbing her pussy on me.

Wren's entire body shook as she came with a cry. I found her shoulder, where I sucked her skin into my mouth.

I moved my hardness backward, hitting her entrance.

She gasped. "Yes. Finally."

There would be nothing final about this. Even when I was fully seated inside of her, I'd drive her back to the edge as much as I wanted to. I pressed in until the head of my cock was fully encased in her wet heat.

But then something broke through. One last shred of control.

"Wren, I don't have a condom."

"*Fuck,*" she said. "I don't either. *Why* don't I carry one on me at all times? I need to be prepared."

I pulled out of her, another idea already forming in my brain. "Get on your knees."

She turned and looked at me with wide eyes. "Please tell me you'll be fucking my mouth."

I pulled off my sweater and threw it on the ground. Then I grabbed her by the hips, pulling her off the desk and making her kneel on the floor, using what I'd been wearing to soften it for her.

"Yes," I said.

"None of this nice guy stuff, right?"

My hand was firm on her jaw. "Wren. Suck."

Her mouth enveloped the head of my cock, and I thought I was going to black out. Wren hollowed her cheeks and I surged inside, keeping her close. She moaned and tightened her mouth.

She was too good at this. She was too good at everything she did. I had her on the floor of the town library, moaning while I fucked her mouth. How was this even real?

I wasn't gentle. I gave her what she asked for and she didn't complain. I never thought anything could be like this, where I wasn't grappling with myself to be the man I wanted to be.

My orgasm built with every second. Her hands tightened on my thighs, and she took me to the back of her throat right as I was going to come, swallowing every last drop.

"Next time, we have a condom," she said as she finally pulled off of my cock. "The fact that nothing fucked me is unfair."

"Do you want more?"

"Yes, but you finished, so we're done."

"Sex isn't done just because I had an orgasm. Get back on the desk, Wren."

She stared at me with wide eyes for one second before she scrambled and laid back, her entire pussy on display. She was soaking wet, and I wasted no time with inserting one finger inside of her.

"Fuck." She was so responsive, so tight. I wasn't sure how I'd even fit inside of her. I moved my thumb to circle her clit. She arched up, scooting down to try to get my finger deeper. I rewarded her with a second one.

"H-Henry, I'm gonna—" She was wrecked, but I paused.

"Not yet."

"You're so mean," she moaned.

"It'll be worth it," I replied as I pressed a kiss to her hip.

"Still, you do know this is killing me, right?"

"You could always use the safe word if you want me to stop."

"Don't you fucking dare."

I resumed my motions. If she was talking, she wasn't feeling good enough. The library was filled with the sounds of her moans and gasps as I worked her to the edge, only to pull back again. She grumbled about it once more, but then I added a third finger and she went silent.

"Please, Henry," she muttered this time. "I need to come. Please let me."

"Since you asked so nicely . . ." I didn't slow down, and she cried out, pussy fluttering as she came again.

She was out of breath for a long moment, and my spent cock gave a twitch at the sight of her. I already couldn't wait to do it again.

"You've killed me. I'm dead." She threw her arm over her eyes. Then her stomach growled.

"You sound hungry. Not dead."

"I am. I skipped dinner."

"Wren." The edge to my voice was back. I waited for her to grow annoyed, especially since I wasn't using it during sex.

But she didn't.

"Sorry, I forgot." She slowly got up. "Up for grabbing something with me?"

It was tempting to offer to cook for her, to bring her back to my place and do this all over again.

But that was against the rules.

"Center Point is still open," I said. "As long as we hurry."

"I could go for diner food." She grabbed her pants. "Let's do it. After we wash up. At least the library bathrooms are mostly working again."

Washing my hands in the bathroom of the library was a little like washing up with a fire hydrant, but it did the job.

Wren met me outside and we made the walk to Center Point. Tammy was sitting at a booth reading when we walked in. She did a double take.

"You just made it," she said with a smile. "I was thinking about closing early."

"If you still are, we can go," I replied. "I know we're here right before you're done for the day."

"No need. I wouldn't mind someone to talk to. Ron's quiet today."

"I'm tired!" a gruff voice said in the back. I'd lived in this town for years and barely knew what he looked like. Tammy was definitely the face of the couple.

"Been a long one," she said. "With the people filtering in and out because of the show, we're busy. I finally got a few girls from the high school to take over some shifts. After they get fully trained, I'm going to the *beach*."

"Too hot," Ron called out. It was the most I'd heard him talk in years.

"You can stay here alone, then! I deserve some time in the sun."

"There's always the fall," I said. "Might be a good middle ground."

"You might be onto something," Tammy replied. "Sit wherever you like. What are you having to drink?"

"Water," Wren said. "I'm so dehydrated."

My eyes slid to hers. I could see why, after what we'd done. Her cheeks turned a beautiful shade of pink, like the roses in front of my house.

"Same for me." I sat beside Wren; it felt so natural to be close to her. Plus, it gave Tammy space to join us if she wanted to.

But I was only doing this because we were in public. Or at least that was what I told myself. We were dating here, and when we were alone, we were friends with benefits.

"How's the library going?" Tammy asked as she brought us two ice-cold waters. "It looks like you guys are working hard."

"We're putting it back together," Wren said. "Replacing the floors and making sure everything is in working order. Then we'll be ordering books and opening it up."

"It's all Marjorie and Henrietta can talk about," Tammy said. "It's all *anyone* can talk about. We're excited to have a piece of the town back."

"Hopefully it lives up to the hype."

"Oh, it will." Tammy liked Wren. That much was obvious. She was friendly with everyone in town, even Hugh—when he was being nice. But I could tell by the way she perked up whenever Wren was in a room that she was excited to see her. "What are you two having?"

"The apple pecan salad," I replied.

"I want the biggest plate of chicken tenders you have."

I immediately regretted my choice. Chicken tenders were

my food of choice before I realized that I needed to eat vegetables too.

"Sounds good." Tammy turned and yelled out the order to Ron before sitting with us. "Now, I've got some opinions on books to stock it with, by the way. Can we get an erotica section?"

Wren choked on her water. "A what?"

"Erotica. Don't look so shocked. Old ladies need their books too."

"Will the grant even let us stock it with that?"

Tammy shrugged. "They've never cared before. At least do the romance books. What do they call that now? Pepper, or something? Oh no, *spice.*"

"I'll start a list," Wren said. "Erotica for all the ladies is at the top of it."

"I have a few authors to recommend. I'll send you a list. Give me your number."

Wren blinked but recited it anyway. She seemed so shocked by Tammy's attention, and I had no idea why.

"How are you doing after your fall?" Tammy asked. "We were pretty worried about you."

"Oh, I'm fine."

Tammy's eyes cut to me. Clearly, she didn't believe Wren.

"She's healed well," I said. "But she has a bad habit of not resting."

"Really? You're gonna call me out?"

"Someone has to."

She rolled her eyes. "I get bored way too easily."

"Same here," Tammy agreed. "But no one wants to see you make it worse. I'm watching you."

Wren laughed, but I could see her hands move under the table. I grabbed them without a second thought, running my thumb over her knuckles.

I wanted to figure her out, to know every detail of her life.

But it wasn't my place to. I was temporary. Only a comfort for now.

And I needed to figure out how to be okay with that.

The next morning, there was a new PA putting on my mic. She had strawberry-blonde hair, and the only reason I noticed was because it was the same color as Wren's.

"It's really nice of you to do this every morning," she said while she fiddled with the mic pack. "It must get annoying."

"I don't mind. It helps Wren out."

My eyes drifted to the woman that was always on my mind. She was doing an interview with Jude, gesturing to the library. She did them all the time, but this time, he was only watching *her*.

My chest tightened. Both of us knew either he or Madison was angling for something, but I refused to watch the show, so I didn't see it.

And now it was right in front of me.

For this, Wren was *mine*. And only mine.

"So," the PA said, "um, you know, I hate to do this, but I wanna shoot my shot."

I turned to her. "What?"

"A lot of people think Jude and Wren might get back together. And if they do"—she stepped close to me, putting her hand on my chest—"maybe we could go out."

"Absolutely not." The words were out before I could stop them and I threw her hand off my body before taking three healthy steps back. "I don't consider other women when I'm in love with someone else."

She blinked, color darkening her cheeks. "B-but—"

"No. It's a firm no. I'm Wren's. *Only* hers."

Wren suddenly appeared behind the PA. "What's going on here?"

"Nothing," I said quickly. "On my end, at least."

The PA stammered before running off.

"Okay." She drew out the word before looking at me. "Wanna explain?"

"She asked me out."

Her jaw dropped. "*That's* why she was so close to you?"

"God, she touched me. I feel like I need a shower." I took off my dress shirt, leaving only my T-shirt remaining. "Take this. I don't want it."

"At least I never have to worry about you fake cheating," she said with a laugh. She wrapped my dress shirt around her jeans. "I'll take the accessory. What did you say to her?"

I thought back, remembering my declaration of *love* and being hers. "What any taken man would."

It might have been too much, but thankfully, there was no camera around to see it.

"Nice work, though I think Madison wanted that to go another way. She looks pissed."

"She'll stay that way," I muttered. "Now get back over to your station. I have a flower to give you."

"I love it when you bring me flowers," she said before walking back.

The pink rose weighed heavily in my pocket as my words to the PA played back in my mind. I'd grabbed it not for its meaning, but for how it looked like Wren's cheeks when she blushed.

But now I was wondering if its meaning was like all of the other ones I'd given her.

Perfectly accurate.

I did the usual song and dance of seeing her, ignoring Madison's glare the whole time. Despite my possible slipup, I was proud that we were outsmarting whatever plan the director had. The good mood carried until I was in my office.

And snapped the second I saw I had a text from my mom.

MOM

> When were you gonna tell me you're in a TV show??? A few episodes are already out and I didn't know!

This was *not* good. Mom had always felt left out of my life, and I knew this was just another thing to add to the list. Scrubbing a hand over my face, I prepared for a call, which would turn into a visit this weekend.

I could only hope Wren wouldn't be mad at my absence.

WREN

RWL Superfan Discussion Central

Jamie McCullough: When are Jude and Wren gonna get back togetherrrr? I'm so done with the love triangle.

Comments:
Neve Bullock: So ready to see Jude and Wren again. How it should be!
Alicia Parrish: Honestly, she should dump Henry so I can have him.
Kerry Winsor: She's really happy with Henry, guys. And he's a super sweet guy! Besides, aren't we all watching for the library?
Jamie McCullough: Nope.
Alicia Parrish: HA. Not at all.
Kerry Winsor: But Wren's whole thing is her work? The romance is fun but she's changing our community for the better! Isn't that important???

I'll be out of town this weekend. I'm sorry, but I need to go visit my mom. She wants updates on the show and how all this happened.

WHEN I GOT Henry's text, I tried my best to remember all of the things he'd told me about his mom. The main one was that she didn't understand him. So when he said he was visiting her because of the show, alarm bells rang in my mind.

When are you leaving?

Eight on Saturday morning. I'll be back by five on Sunday evening.

It was great that he was so detailed because it made my job easier.

I got to Henry's house at seven fifty-five on Saturday and leaned against his Honda.

Four minutes later, he was coming out the door and jumped when he saw me. "Wren? What are you doing here? I said I was leaving *this* Saturday, right?"

"You did. I'm going with you."

"What?"

"Do you need me to repeat it?"

"Why would you . . . You're resting from the show."

"And I can rest at your mom's."

He shook his head. "That's not how she works. She'll be incessant with the questions, loud too."

That only hardened my resolve. "Sounds like your worst nightmare. You'll need backup."

"Wren, this isn't a good idea."

I straightened. I hated it when he said that. All I could do was rush to prove him wrong. "I figured the fake dating applied to your mom too. If she's seen the show, then she knows. And I still owe you."

"You don't owe me anything."

"But I do. And I'll find more ways to help you. This is included." I gestured to his car. His eyes narrowed and he opened his mouth, but I rushed to stop him. "And if you boss me around right now, I'll use the safe word."

"That's for sex."

"And this very moment." I pointed at him. "Don't try me."

"Wren," he said firmly. "I'm staying the night."

I held up my bag. "That's why I have this."

"We would be sharing a bed. You coming with me would feel . . . intimate."

"There's a floor." I shrugged as if it were nothing. I'd planned for this too, but having to actually offer was making me struggle with disappointment. I wanted to share a bed with him more than anything, but I knew he didn't want things to get complicated, and I had to respect that.

"You have this all thought out, don't you?"

"I do. You haven't talked about your mom much, but what you *have* said tells me this might be a hard weekend. Let me help."

Henry stared at me for a long time, and I was preparing myself to have to keep arguing with him to do this.

Instead, he walked over to the passenger side and opened the door.

"Help would be nice. Get in."

"Yay!" I ran to get into his car before he could change his mind, throwing my bag in the back seat.

"So, tell me about your mom," I said as he got in the driver's side. "I barely know anything about her other than she doesn't get you. And that she's loud."

"She can't help it. She's partially deaf in both ears."

I blinked. "Oh, does she know sign or anything?"

"No, she's determined that she doesn't need it. She has hearing aids, but she doesn't realize how loud she can be at times. And when I tell her to quiet down, then she can't hear anything herself. I mostly deal with it."

"Not this weekend." I reached into my pocket. "Earplugs. Just for you."

"That's sweet, but I'll survive."

"Why survive when you can live? And these are blue! Like the hydrangeas you gave me."

He glanced over at them. "I'll try them," he said. "But it might not work."

"Then I'll figure something else out."

Henry let out a chuckle before putting a hand on the back of my seat to reverse out of the driveway. I watched him, eyes trailing over his face before I tore them away.

"So, where are we heading?" I asked.

"Knoxville," he replied. "It's where I'm from."

"I haven't been there in a while. There are a few suppliers based out of there, though."

"It's a nice town. Just . . . a lot over time."

"Is that why you're here?"

"Yeah. I could have made it work, but small-town life is for me."

"I can see why." We drove through the square. How many hours had I looked out the windows of the library and admired the town for how cute it was? "I really can."

"But you love Nashville?" he asked.

A few months ago, my answer would have been yes. In a way, it still was. But I hadn't missed it since coming here. When I thought about it, life there seemed *fine*.

Life here was . . . warmer, somehow.

"Wren?" Henry asked.

"S-sorry." I shook myself out of my thoughts. "I do love Nashville. And I have a huge renovation coming up. It's an old house. I'm going back to my roots."

"Are you excited?"

"Very. The owners seemed to want a complete gut job when I did the consultation on the phone, and that'll keep me busy."

"And after?"

I had barely thought about after. "I'll be visiting when Mollie has her baby. I can't let them go without knowing their aunt. And you and I could go to the diner!"

"We'll make a habit of it," he said. Henry's voice was soft, and I wondered if he dreaded the idea of me leaving.

Or if he would miss me at all.

But I couldn't think about it. Not when he was already heading to a difficult weekend.

"Can I go through your CDs?" I asked. "We need some road trip music."

"They're all yours. But please don't pick the Metallica one. I'm not in the mood for my mother's favorite band."

"Noted," I said as I went through them. I went for one of the newer Lila Wilde CDs. Once I put it in, I looked at the rolling nature out my window and tried to ignore the excitement at being able to see more of Henry.

The open country roads turned into the highway about halfway through the drive and then buildings started popping up. Before I knew it, we were in the city again.

Knoxville was smaller than Nashville, but still had traffic. Henry was a safe driver, though I could see him get antsy as more people were around.

We pulled into a small house on a hill. There was one blue car in the driveway and roses blooming in front of the door.

Henry took a breath. "Here we go."

"Put these in."

"I'll be—"

"Nope. These will help. You got tense when we hit the city. So don't add to it."

Henry slowly took the earplugs and put them in. I tried and failed not to feel proud of myself as we got out.

"There you are!" a voice yelled as the door opened. "We have so much to catch up on, Henry. To think you've been on actual TV and I didn't—"

A woman with graying brown hair and thick glasses froze when she saw me. She was nowhere near Henry's or my height, but she had his same facial structure.

"You brought her! I thought you said she was busy!"

"I thought so too," Henry said. His voice was louder than usual, yet still soft in comparison. "But she rearranged her schedule."

"Wow." Henry's mom walked close, appraising me. The hairs on my arms stood. "You are something. Very different than the woman I imagined he'd bring home!"

And there it was. I was used to it, but it stung each time.

"Mom." Henry's voice was flat. "I like her the way she is."

"It's not a bad thing! I just expected someone who likes books and is as quiet as he is. You're still incredible." She held out a hand. "I'm Colleen Connor."

"Wren," I replied as I shook it.

"Now that's a handshake your dad would have loved," Colleen said.

"I thought the same thing," Henry agreed.

"Come in, come in!" She waved us both in the door. "I'm so excited you're here!"

Henry followed me in, and I tried to observe how he was doing. With his hands in his pockets, he seemed to be doing what he always did.

The tension line in his shoulders wasn't completely gone,

but it was far better than it could have been. He hadn't been kidding. His mom's base volume was a yell. I wasn't sure how he would have fared if I hadn't stepped in.

Colleen's house was homey. There was a simple love seat on one wall with a TV and a dining room table set for two people. Despite the small furniture, it felt full. Everything was older, looking like it came out of a nineties magazine, but just like the farmhouse, it was warm.

I'd always been inspired by charm, but usually I would say this needed work. Instead, I felt like it was exactly what it should be.

Maybe my definition of charm was changing.

Colleen turned to Henry, mouth open as if she was about to say something, but then she zeroed in on him.

"What are those things in your ears? Please tell me you don't need hearing aids already!"

Now Henry tensed. "N-no, Mom, they're not hearing aids."

"They're a gift from me," I said. "Earplugs, so he doesn't get overwhelmed."

"Plugs? Can you even hear?" Her voice grew louder, and Henry blinked against it.

"Yeah. I can still hear pretty much everything. Just not as intensely."

Colleen hummed. "Weird."

"They'll help him have a better time staying over," I said. "Isn't the quality time what matters?"

She hummed as she considered it. "You're right. He's always leaving early. Maybe these will help. Ear*plugs*. Who would'a thought?" She shrugged, accepting my explanation easily enough.

"I can take them out if they bother you," Henry said.

"No," I hissed. "If they help, we use them. Just like glasses."

"Wren—"

"She's got your best interests in mind, huh?" Colleen laughed. "Don't take them out if they help. I'm just trying to wrap my old head around it."

I rubbed Henry's back. "Don't make it worse just so other people are comfortable."

"I'm trying," he said. "This is all new to me."

"You're doing great."

"Huh?" Colleen interrupted. "I didn't catch that."

"Nothing. Just making sure he knows he's all good."

"Of course he is! He's home! What could be better than that?"

"Yeah, Mom." A soft smile graced Henry's face. "I'm home."

He must love her. As he should. Sometimes it was hard to love, and be loved by, those who didn't understand you.

And some people failed at the whole thing entirely.

I looked in between them, heart panging as I thought of myself. But I shoved it aside. Henry was the important one here. Not me.

Walking to the wall, I eyed all of the pictures. Some were old, possibly of Colleen when she was younger. There were a few wedding pictures and some of a young boy with glasses.

"Please tell me this is Henry," I said.

"It is," Colleen replied.

"The *wire glasses!*" I turned to him. "You were so cute."

"Mom picked those out," he said. "They were a product of the time."

I followed the pictures. They were in order of age, which allowed me to see him grow up. He grew taller and taller, just like I had. I was fascinated with childhood photos, mostly because I had none. Mom didn't think I was photo worthy. Dad didn't have enough time to take them.

Eventually, I paused over one where Henry was in a suit. He still had the soft angles of a teenager and was with a shorter girl with blonde hair. She was in a yellow dress and had a carnation. She was beautiful.

"That was his prom," Colleen explained. "You and Norah were a cute couple."

I blinked. He'd said he'd been with someone who'd moved on very quickly. Was this her? Was this why I'd heard from people in town that he'd never dated anyone?

Was he hung up on her?

I could see why.

"She lives down the road now," Colleen mused.

"She's married," Henry added. "To Ace. He took this photo."

"Still think that was weird. I mean, your ex and your best friend? I thought there was some sort of code for that."

"It was years ago, it's fine."

It didn't sound fine. I turned to Henry, whose shoulders were now tense.

I wanted to know everything, but he made it clear that he didn't want that from me. Even as friends, he had walls up. I doubted he wanted me to know this.

"Oh well." I feigned calm, something I was too good at. "He ended up where he was supposed to."

"He has you," Colleen said with a smile. "Let me get you two some snacks. Now, I'm sure you know this, but Henry's favorite is string cheese, but only one particular brand."

We followed her into the kitchen where she rummaged through the fridge.

"I can eat other things now," Henry said. "Like vegetables."

"But only the carrots cut like chips."

He winced. "The crunch is better. The other ones are too loud."

"That's adorable," I said. "Does Food 'n' Things carry that?"

"I asked Dale to order them."

I was going to soak up every second of this. I was finally getting information on the man who was in all of my thoughts. Colleen brought out the string cheese and Henry wasted no time grabbing one. I did the same.

"Mollie and I tried to make queso from these once by melting them in the microwave. Her mom had to explain that they were two totally different kinds of cheese."

"You ruined good string cheese in the microwave?" Henry looked at me like I'd stepped on a puppy.

Colleen laughed. "You've committed a sin."

"Oops, sorry," I said before taking a bite out of the top.

"Wren!" Henry grabbed the cheese from my hand. "You monster!"

"What?"

"That's not how you eat string cheese. You peel it." He demonstrated and peeled off one edge.

"Is that why they call it string cheese? I thought you just ate it like regular cheese."

"How did you—*why?*"

I shrugged as I took it from him and ate one of the smaller pieces. "This is *way* better."

"He feels very strongly about his cheese," Colleen said. "He likes you. He even gave it back!"

"I'm debating that choice," he muttered.

"I'm very sorry that I'm not educated on string cheese. Does that help?"

"Don't let it happen again."

"You two are something else! On the show, they made it seem like a fairy-tale romance, but almost *too* fairy tale. You better watch out for that Jude guy."

"Trust me, I'm aware." Henry's voice was dry.

"That's *not* happening," I assured her. "They're spinning it in a way I didn't agree to."

"Show business," she muttered with a roll of her eyes. "There's a reason I hate reality TV."

"Didn't you watch *Ru Paul's Drag Race*?" Henry asked.

"That's not reality TV. That's *art*."

I laughed and ate another part of my string cheese before Colleen led us back to the living room. She pulled out one of the dining room chairs and sat in it, leaving the tiny love seat to the both of us. Since it was so much older, it meant we were practically sitting on top of one another.

Not that I was going to complain. I tucked in my legs and leaned into it, half of my body pressed into Henry. He gave me a glance before wrapping his arm around my shoulders.

My heart skipped a beat.

"Now you two need to tell me every detail of how this happened." She leaned forward. "Start from the beginning."

"Well," I began, "it all started when Henry sent me on a wild-goose chase for irises."

"Him and those flowers. He loves them!"

"Of course he does," I said without missing a beat. This was the one thing I did know. "And he was trying to keep me busy, but then we broke into a library, and it all went downhill from there . . ."

"These are lifesavers," Henry said that evening when he took the earplugs out. We were in the tiny guest room, which used to be his old bedroom. She'd gone to bed at nine and left us with a pile of pillows and blankets to use for the night. "I mean, she's still loud, but it's tolerable."

"The reviews on those are great. Apparently, people use them for concerts too."

"Thank you," he said. "You were right about them."

"And right about coming?"

"I'm not so sure about that. Did you *have* to mention us breaking into the library?"

"Her lecture was hilarious."

"For *you*," he said, crossing his arms.

"You were just doing your doctorly duty," I replied, rolling my eyes. "Nothing to it."

"Still. That and the string cheese has you on thin ice."

"I shared my chicken tenders with you, though."

Henry and I had gone out with Colleen. He'd ordered grilled chicken and vegetables, but I saw him eyeing my fried version. Dinner had been fun up until Henry and I once again debated over who would pay.

In the end, I headed to the bathroom and covered our check on the way back.

He wasn't amused.

"Sharing earned you a few points," he said. "Sneaking off lost them."

"You're just mad that I pulled it off."

"I am. I'll remember this for next time."

Would there even be a next time? I had no idea, but I didn't need to think too hard about it. I was determined to soak up as much as I could about Henry, and this weekend had already been a gold mine.

I riffled through my bag, grabbing at the T-shirt and shorts I'd brought for sleeping in. "Be right back. Gonna change."

I headed to the bathroom down the hall. My hair was up in a ponytail, and I tugged out the hair tie. As it tumbled down around my shoulders, my reflection stared back at me. I'd worn a flannel and jeans on the way over, but as the heat pressed on, I'd stripped off my outer layer and was now in just a white tank top.

Before I could stop it, my mind wandered. I wondered if the

woman—Norah—had dressed up for him. I wondered if he looked at me and thought of her.

Many people looked at me and thought of someone else. It was a curse of mine.

I focused on brushing my teeth. I hated these thoughts. Over the years, I'd gotten good at ignoring them, but ever since Jude had turned me down, they followed me around.

Mom had left wounds. Ones that I wasn't sure would heal.

Everything reminded me of it these days, and all I wanted to do was be normal.

And now I knew about his ex—the one that he could still have feelings for.

I had a bad habit of comparing myself.

I changed into my pajamas. The large T-shirt had the collar cut out years ago and hung off one shoulder. It had been a work shirt before I made it a nightshirt. The shorts were short, not even coming below the hem of the tee.

When I got back to the room, Henry had changed too and met me at the door. He had on more casual clothes, but they were still far nicer than mine.

"Wren." His eyes trailed down my body, lingering on my shoulder. "You . . . uh."

"They're old. Sorry. I don't do traditional pajamas." I brushed past him, feeling the way his eyes followed me. But by the time I'd put the clothes for the day in my bag, he had left.

While he was gone, I looked through the blankets. I pulled three and made a tiny makeshift bed on the floor.

Henry was back in mere moments. "You don't have to do that. We can make the bed work."

I was smoothing out the area I would lie on while I answered. "Colleen gave us a hundred and one blankets. I'll be fine down here."

"There's barely any room. You have maybe a foot and a half to sleep on."

I did. This was *not* going to be a comfortable night. "I can fit."

"But your ankle."

"It's healed. I'll be fine."

He blew out a breath. *"Wren."*

"Henry." I still didn't turn.

"You've been messing with the same part of that blanket this whole time. Something's wrong."

He was right, and I should have known he would see it right away.

But I still clung to the hope he would let it go.

"Don't worry about me."

"I'm going to."

"Seriously, Henry, you're tired. Go to—"

"Wren, look at me." There was an edge to his voice. One that still made my body feel hot despite the mix of emotions running through me.

I gritted my teeth against everything I felt and turned. Henry had knelt behind me, but when he saw my expression, his eyes went wide.

"Oh, no. Wren, I didn't mean to—I shouldn't have gotten firm."

Something broke through everything—a question. "Why are *you* apologizing? I'm the one trying to cling to the idea that you'll let it go, which you never do."

"I'm pushing you."

Which others don't care enough to do. "That's not the issue here. I'm not mad at you for making me look at you. I'm not mad at all. I'm just . . . having a difficult time."

"Was it Mom?" he asked. "Me?"

"No, nothing like that. I'm just trying to keep our boundaries in place. Even when I have . . . questions."

"Questions about what?"

"Norah." I said it lowly. "But you're saying that we shouldn't get too close, and I wanna respect that. I'm having a hard time with curiosity."

And wondering if I was enough.

"You can ask whatever you want," he said. "You don't have to make yourself miserable to make me comfortable."

I fiddled with the corner of the blanket. "Do you still have feelings for her?"

He answered it immediately. "No. I'm not sure if I ever did, to be honest. She was a part of the group, and at the time, Ace was dating around. I think she chose me because I was around more. But in the end, she wanted him. I think she always did."

"So, she broke it off with you and got with him?"

"It didn't go exactly like that," he said with a sigh. "I made mistakes. A lot of them. I didn't know my limits then. I felt different from others, but didn't know why or what to do about it. And I went along with Ace a lot of the time. I wound up in a lot of situations I couldn't handle. So, I'd get overwhelmed. Then I'd get angry."

"Like the day when you snapped at Jude?"

"Worse. I'd go to a club and lose it. Or be in a crowded mall and go off on a person who pushed me. I'm not proud of it, but I learned to control it. Unfortunately, I learned all of that when it was too late. They'd been pushed away by my actions. Toward each other."

"They didn't try to understand why?" I asked.

"I was being a jerk."

"The only time you're anything close to a jerk is when you're overwhelmed. Unless you've completely changed your personality, you're not always upset. There's a pattern."

He shook his head. "No, but we were all kids. I don't blame them. I just wish I'd been better."

"You didn't know either. And your mom is sweet, but she's not exactly an expert."

"No. I suppose not." He let out a sigh. "But they're happy together, and I realized that I couldn't do things long-term. Not with the snapping. The need to have quiet time. It's a lot."

"It's not. At least not for me."

"You're the exception," he said. "But not everyone is like you. When I moved to Strawberry Springs, I told myself I wouldn't let it happen again. I would be kind and put together. No one would ever see what I showed Ace and Norah. It's one of my worst fears, actually. To find a home somewhere and then mess it up."

"Oh." I thought about the day in the square when he'd gotten mad. That must have been terrifying—that he'd slipped up and people saw. So far, I didn't think they did, or at least I hadn't heard that they had.

I didn't know the people of the town as well as Mollie did. I didn't know how they reacted to things like this, but I could relate to the fear of losing others. Almost *too* well.

"We'll make sure you're taken care of," I said. "So all the construction doesn't bother you."

He smiled and looked over at me. "You're incredible, you know. I'll miss you when you leave."

That was the issue, wasn't it? I was leaving.

And I had to. The jobs were in Nashville. That was where I could keep on fixing things.

What was I without that?

"I'm sorry," I said.

"Don't be. We'll see each other again."

"As friends, though."

He nodded. "As friends."

I was crushed by this. My heart ached in ways I didn't know it could.

"I should sleep on the floor," I said.

"I don't want you to."

"But the rules—"

"Don't friends share beds at sleepovers?"

"They do." But I wasn't thinking of him as a *friend*. Not after this. I wanted it all with him. The sex. His life.

But I had to go back to Nashville, and I would never ask him to follow me. Not when he loved Strawberry Springs so much.

"We'll figure out the rest later."

"*You're* the one suggesting we just figure it out?"

"I can be flexible." His hand brushed my cheek. "When it comes to you."

I should have said no. I didn't need to make this worse.

But I wanted him. In all the ways.

I climbed onto the mattress, finding it softer than I was used to. Our shared weight made it to where we were both in the center of the bed, arms pressed against one another.

"Does your mom believe in firm furniture?"

"Nope," he said. "I try to tell her it's terrible for her back, but she doesn't listen."

"It's gonna be impossible to stay on our sides of the bed."

"It's a full-size bed. There aren't sides."

"All the more reason to sleep on the floor."

A hand landed on my hip and squeezed. "Wren." There it was. That warning.

"Fine." I turned away before I could do anything stupid. "But don't say I didn't try."

"You always try," he said as he turned off the bedside lamp. "It's what I like best about you."

I lay awake in the darkness for a long time, and I was pretty sure that he did too.

All of my life, I slept alone. There was never someone else in the bed with me; I wasn't used to sharing heat and warmth.

But I liked it. *God*, I loved it.

Henry's breath evened out and I turned to him. Other than the hand on my hip, he hadn't moved any closer. We were still close because of the bed, but I wanted more. I wanted to burrow into him. To make this moment last forever.

Instead, I rolled away and got all the distance I could. My heart ached, but this was for the best. I'd stay away and wake up on my side of the bed.

Or at least that was what I told myself.

HENRY

Strawberry Springs Neighborhood Watch

Kerry Winsor: The fence DID NOT work! I put my clothes out to air dry in this beautiful weather and a deer ATE MY UNDERGARMENTS

Comments:
Jade Clark: Which undergarments?
Kerry Winsor: DOES IT MATTER?
Jade Clark: Very much so. Bras could be dangerous. Panties on the other hand . . .
Kerry Winsor: I will ban you from the group.
Jade Clark: Don't make me tag Marjorie.
Kerry Winsor: Don't you DARE.
Marjorie Brown: You called?
Marjorie Brown: I'd make a joke here, but this one writes itself.
Mollie Wilson: Did you say "Oh, deer" when you saw it?
Kerry Winsor: MOLLIE

The room was dark and the house was quiet. Usually, I didn't wake up in the middle of the night, but one sound pulled me from sleep.

A soft moan from Wren.

There hadn't been much distance between us when we fell asleep. Mere inches, if anything. But the little space there had been was gone, and her back was pressed tightly to my front.

I was still groggy, but I knew without a shadow of a doubt that I was hard, and I was pressed between her thighs. Only her thin sleep shorts and underwear separated us.

Before I knew she was upset earlier, I'd nearly lost it at the sight of her slightly tanned skin, dotted with freckles, all on the curve of her shoulder. I hadn't even been sure she was wearing *shorts*, and it was tempting to throw her onto the bed.

And then we'd talked, and I pushed all thoughts of that away. I needed to again.

But she made the sound again, arching back into me.

"Wren," I managed to say. "What're you doing?"

There wasn't a response. I sat up on my forearms, barely able to make out her face. Her eyes were closed, and when I put a hand on her cheek, she didn't respond.

She was *asleep*. Asleep and grinding against me.

I grabbed her hip to still her, head swimming from the friction alone.

"Wren, buttercup. Wake up." I tightened my hand. She didn't stop. *"Wren."* My voice was louder, bordering on desperate.

"Huh?" she said, her voice low with sleep. "What's happening?"

"You must have been having a *very* good dream, and it woke me up."

"Shit. I'm sorry."

"No, don't be. This is an incredible way to wake up."

"I tried to stay in my space, but I guess my brain did its own thing in my sleep."

I buried my face in her neck, picturing what it would feel like to be inside of her again. The thought of her pussy quivering around me was almost enough to make me say yes.

But I didn't. We were in my mother's house. In a bed I'd grown up in. I'd already made so many mistakes with her. I was letting her get way too close. Even sleeping in the same bed was pushing it, no matter how much I wanted it.

And as tempting as it was, she was leaving. We'd go from seeing each other every day to only seeing each other when she visited Mollie.

If I went down this road where she was in every part of my life, it would never be enough.

My spiraling thoughts were interrupted as I felt her shift against me once more.

"Wren, I *can't*. Not here."

She stilled, going silent. It killed me to tell her no, but it was the right choice.

"Okay." Her voice was quiet. "I get it."

"When we're back, I'll make it up to you."

"We do have a library desk calling our name."

The thought made me have to resist the urge to press into her again. "I'm sorry."

"Don't be. There are some rules that shouldn't be broken." She angled her hips away. "Do you want me to sleep on the floor?"

"No." The words were immediate. "No, please stay here."

"I can't complain about that. You're not a bad cuddler."

I huffed out a breath, tightening my arms around her midsection. "You're better than any pillow."

"Happy to be of service," she said before yawning. She fell asleep not too long after, and I lay awake, wondering if I'd made the right decision.

I woke up alone with the sun streaming through the curtains onto my face. I blinked with a groan. Mom never let me sleep in this late. She always woke me when she got up for the day, usually insisting that we spend time together before I left. I put on my glasses and slowly climbed out of bed.

The earplugs were still on the nightstand. It was tempting to say I didn't need them, but they helped *so much.*

I'd always prided myself on acting normal, on hiding the things I struggled with every day.

But I didn't realize how much easier life could be if I allowed myself to have just a little help.

I grabbed them and put them in my ears in case Mom was waiting for me. I shaved and got ready for the day.

As I walked down the short hallway, I heard Mom's voice. "Good grief, you're strong! How are you managing that?"

"Years of practice," Wren said, her voice tight. "There, is that what you were hoping for?"

"This is incredible!" Mom clapped, a sound that would usually set me on edge. I came around the corner, jaw dropping when I saw the scene before me.

Nothing was where it was before. The love seat was on the other side of the room, and the TV was on the wall. Mom's bookshelf had been shoved in a new location and Wren was in front of it.

"Hi!" she said when she saw me. "What do you think?"

"I think you've been busy. How's your ankle holding up?"

She rolled her eyes. "I've done more on worse."

"Do I need to once again remind you of how that's a terrible idea?"

Wren laughed. "Nope. But it's seriously fine. This is nothing for me."

"What a woman she is. I only asked if Wren had any ideas on how to set up the living room better so I could get another couch, and here we are." The look on Mom's face was one of pure joy.

"Using the space wisely is key in smaller homes," Wren said. "And it's better to see it too."

"Now we'll all have space to sit when you bring this one back."

Guilt clogged my throat at the sight of them getting along so well. I would have loved to have Wren back here, but I didn't know if it would happen before our arrangement was over.

Mom was completely oblivious to the silence that stretched between us.

"Oh! And Wren offered to go to breakfast with me! I know you always have a hard time with brunch on a Sunday. She's so good at explaining things." Mom threw an arm around her.

"I-I'm fine," I said. "I'm well rested and I have the earplugs."

Mom gasped. "So, you'll go?"

"Yeah."

Wren's eyes narrowed on me, and I knew she would notice if it were too much, but I laced my fingers through hers and walked out the door.

"Are we taking your car?" Mom asked. "The back seat is bigger."

"Yeah, I'll—" I paused when I saw a couple walking down the road hand in hand.

Ace and Norah hadn't changed that much since graduation. He still worked out every day, and she was as slight as ever.

I paused, waiting for the usual pain to hit.

It didn't.

"Is that—" Wren began, but was interrupted.

"Oh! Ace! Norah!" Mom waved at them. "Nice morning, isn't it?"

They both paused and waved.

Norah saw me first. The color on her cheeks was apparent from this far away as she tugged Ace's hand.

I waved back, hoping it didn't look as awkward as it felt.

"Henry," Ace said. "You're looking good."

"He's on TV!" Mom said, patting my shoulder. "Can you believe that?"

"No," Norah said immediately. "I can't."

A hand curled on my shoulder and warmth pressed against my right side.

Wren.

"He's great at it," she said. "He's great at anything he does when he has the proper support."

The message was clear.

Norah appraised Wren, eyes wide. I was sure she saw what everyone else saw—that she was effortlessly gorgeous. Bright, and the light of every room.

"Oh yeah," Mom said. She was completely oblivious to the tension that had settled on us all. "Wren got him something to help with his ears. Isn't that great?"

Should I have been embarrassed? Once upon a time, I would have. I'd wanted their approval. I'd wanted to be a part of that group.

But I had new people I surrounded myself with. Over time, Ace and Norah had become an unpleasant memory. Not people that I cared about in the same way.

"Yeah, sure." Ace gave us a smile. "As long as he's not still bossy as hell."

It was meant to be a joke. Ace was always kidding around, but it hit right in the center of my chest.

"Some people like that," Wren said. "Henry is exactly as he should be."

The pain turned into warmth. What had I done for a woman like Wren to be in my life?

And what had I done to deserve the fact that she was leaving?

"I'll let you guys get back to your walk," I said. "We're on the way to breakfast anyway."

I could tell both Ace and Norah were shocked I was even going out to eat when it was busy, but they knew a different version of me. They were people who knew my past, not my present. Wren had that sole honor.

I'd let what happened with them dictate so much of my life, but they had been young too. Kids could hurt one another. It was easy to.

And now we had gone our separate ways.

"Are you okay?" Wren asked quietly when we'd gotten in the car.

"Yeah, I am. They're just people."

"They're quiet," Mom complained. "It's like they're guilty of something."

"It doesn't matter," I replied. "What happened is done. I have other things to focus on."

My eyes landed on Wren, who gave me a bright smile.

It was four by the time we were getting ready to head back, much later than usual. My ears weren't ringing, and for the first time in a long time, I didn't feel totally wiped at the end of the day. Having Wren here helped more than I could say, even if she tried to steal my keys and drive back.

Her stubbornness about driving delayed us from leaving. The keys were firmly above my head while she tried to grab them. My slight height advantage worked against her, which was obviously something she wasn't used to.

Wren's body was pressed against mine as she tried to grab them from my hand.

"This. Is. Ridiculous!" She fumed.

"It is. Are you ready to admit defeat yet?"

"No," she huffed.

My hand went to the small of her back. "The faster you give up, the faster we get back to Strawberry Springs where we can pick up where we left off."

She immediately went still.

"Got a picture of that!" Mom nearly yelled from the doorway, startling us both. "You two are so cute, you know."

"Yeah, cute." Wren stepped away, still breathless from my offer. "I try to help, but he plays dirty."

"Always has," Mom said. "Now come here and give me a hug before you head out." We did as we were told, and when Mom had her arms around me, she tried to whisper, "Keep her."

I wanted to. More than I could say. "I'll try."

A noncommittal answer was the best, though it hurt me to say.

"And *you*!" Mom pulled Wren into a tight hug. "Thank you. You're good for him."

"I try," she said. "Thanks for having us."

"Come back anytime. I mean it!"

Wren smiled, though it didn't reach her eyes. "Of course."

I waited until Mom's house was out of sight before I asked, "Is the lying getting to you too?"

"The lying?" she asked. "Oh, about us. Yeah, it doesn't feel great if I think about it."

"Your smile was off when Mom hugged you. What were you thinking about?"

"Oh, uh . . . nothing." She picked at her cuticle. I reached over to grab her hand.

"Wren, I know you. I know when you're upset about something. You don't have to tell me, but I'd love to know."

She looked at her hands. "I don't . . . have a great relationship with my mom."

"So it's hard to see others with it."

"It's not that I'm jealous, because I'm *not*. I'm just sad."

I squeezed her hand. "I'm sorry, Wren."

"Most of the time it's fine, but it's been popping up lately. The thoughts of her."

"If coming this weekend made it worse—"

She shook her head. "No, it didn't. I had fun, and I don't regret it."

"Do you want to talk more about it?"

"Honestly, I just wanna move on. I spent a lot of my life thinking about her, and it gets old after a while."

"Understood. But if you ever change your mind, I'm here."

"Thanks, Henry." She gave me a smile. "I'm already feeling better."

For a while, we drove in silence, her hand curled in mine. Having her here was comfortable. It had been the whole weekend.

I always thought that it would exhaust me to be around *anyone* for a prolonged period of time. It was why I valued my privacy so much. But with Wren, her presence never got old, and she didn't wear on me. I didn't want to walk away. I wanted to keep her.

Even if it wasn't possible.

The thoughts were pushed out of my head when she untangled her hand from mine. For a second, I thought she was done and going back to us acting as friends. Then her hand ran through my hair and I fought the urge to gasp.

"You always know what to say. Out of curiosity, do you know how hot your emotional intelligence is?"

"I thought it was a basic thing."

Her nails traced my scalp. It felt incredible. "It's really not."

"It's not a good idea to distract someone when driving."

She kept playing with my hair. "Tell me to stop, then."

She would if I told her to, but I didn't want that just yet. I didn't realize how much I soaked in all of her touches. Her fingers were on my jaw, lightly tracing the skin, leaving behind a tingling feeling with every place she caressed.

It was a struggle to keep my eyes on the road, especially with a goddess of a woman beside me. Despite all the work I'd done on myself, it felt unreal that such a confident, capable woman wanted *me*, of all people.

My hands tightened on the steering wheel as she drifted lower, brushing over where my dick was rapidly hardening.

"How far are you gonna take this?" I asked lowly.

"As far as you let me." She fiddled with the button of my pants before taking me into her hand. We were on country roads, ones that I'd driven a hundred times, but the second she touched me, my mind could only focus on her. She pumped up and down, running her fingers over the slit where precum was already accumulating.

"*Fuck.*" Could I break the steering wheel from gripping it too hard?

Wren jerked me off as I drove, her hand firm and steady. I kept my eyes ahead, but I felt her fully pull it out of my boxers.

She shifted, and suddenly, her mouth was around the head, sucking.

That was it. I could take no more.

I pulled off on the side of the road. "Get in the back seat," I ordered.

"*Fuck* yes," she said before doing exactly that. I didn't bother buttoning my pants as I followed her.

This woman. She pushed me to my very limits.

And I loved every second of it.

There was no way the two of us could fit in the back seat, so I left the door open, thanking God that I always took the back ways no one else did.

I yanked her leggings down to her ankles and put my mouth on her pussy as she lay back.

Wren let out a loud moan, running her hands through my hair.

I didn't go easy on her. I fucked her with my tongue before sucking on her clit. I drank every drop of her, knowing that we were on borrowed time on the shoulder.

She was breathing heavily within the first few minutes, and I didn't let up. There'd be no torture for her today, only the release we'd both waited too long to have.

Her thighs clenched around my jaw as she tightened. I felt it when she came, wave after wave of it jolting through her body like electricity.

"There's a . . . condom in my bag."

"You came prepared, didn't you?"

"I learned my lesson."

I reached onto the floorboard of the back seat where she'd tossed her bag and grabbed the condom. After rolling it on, I teased the head of my cock against her wet pussy, knowing I'd not done enough to prepare her.

"If you stop, I swear—"

"No need for threats, buttercup. I'm gonna fuck you."

"Thank *God*."

"But we'll be taking this slow."

"Henry," she whined. I pressed just inside of her before she could complain any more.

That movement alone was enough to make her gasp, and I took the opportunity to snake a hand down to her clit.

Wren let out the prettiest noise as I circled her sensitive bud. I pressed in just a little more, feeling her wetness flutter with every one of my movements. Every few pushes, I would pull out before surging back in.

Her legs wrapped tightly around me, coaxing me in even more. Her breathing quickened as she arched into the seat.

I knew she was close, so I tipped her over the edge by finally pushing all of the way inside, still keeping my movements steady.

"Oh my *God*."

And then I felt it. The quiver of another orgasm. Tiny little pulses on my cock.

It made me see stars.

I growled low in my throat, unable to keep myself still for long. I jerked my hips forward, mind hazy as I fucked her like I'd been meaning to. The car shook with the force of it, but I didn't care. All that mattered was the feeling radiating from my cock and the way she sounded as I fucked her.

I was completely lost in her. There wasn't a part of me that cared that we were on the side of the road, out in the open. All I felt was *her*. It's all I wanted to feel.

As the sensation built, I covered her mouth with mine. She was breathing as heavy as I was as I pounded into her.

My orgasm felt like an explosion rocketing through every part of my body. Everything tightened and then released, and I almost lost my footing.

"There's no way," Wren said as she caught her breath, "that sex on the side of an empty road in a car felt that good."

"I can't believe we just did that."

"Don't let the logic in now. We threw that out the window the second we left the city."

I laughed and pressed my forehead against hers, a movement that was far too intimate.

"We should get back," I said. "I bet you want to see Mollie."

"Oh, yeah. Of course."

I pulled out of her and threw the condom in the trash bag I kept in the car. When we got back on the road, I tried to remember we were friends. Only friends. Who pretended to date. And who had sex.

But my body buzzed. Rushing things with her wasn't satisfying. I wanted her in my bed where I could do whatever I wanted for as long as possible.

When we got back to my house, the desire to ask her to come inside was overwhelming. I liked spending time with her, and she might have been the only person I wanted in all aspects of my life.

But I had to remind myself she was leaving.

So I kept the words to myself.

"See you tomorrow?" I asked as she climbed out of the car.

"Yeah, see you."

I expected her to walk away, but her eyes flicked between me and the house. I swallowed the words threatening to break free.

Come inside.

Join me.

Don't leave.

But none of it would be fair. She had a career, and so did I. I wouldn't ask her to stay, and I had a feeling she wouldn't ask me to leave.

Wren straightened and grabbed her bag. She was gone only a few seconds later.

And I was alone again.

WREN

Strawberry Springs Neighborhood Watch

Hu Gh: @**Dale Garrett**, you want some turkeys to freeze for the Thanksgiving season?

Comments:
Dale Garrett: No . . . that's not how this works.
Hu Gh: I've got fresh meat right here and you're turning me down?
Tammy Jane: My man wants to know how much you're selling them for.
SherriffMike Finch: Hugh, it is NOT hunting season. You can't be going after turkeys right now.
Hu Gh: If I'm packing heat, it's the season to me.
Jade Clark: Oh my God, Hugh's gonna get arrested.
Marjorie Brown: Can you get a video?

Mollie kept staring at the cake in my hands as I took it out of the fridge.

"There are no hints on the top of this cake," I said. "And you're not finding out early."

"The suspense is *killing me*," she whined.

"It's killing all of us," Maribelle said. She'd stayed the night in Cain's old room. I'd been happy to see her since I'd spent a lot of my childhood with her. She seemed thrilled that Mollie was pregnant, and doted on her daughter much like Cain did.

I shook my head. "You guys only have to wait an hour."

The day I'd learned the gender of Mollie's baby had snuck up quickly. After one of her appointments, she'd shoved a sealed envelope in my hands and begged me to look and then burn it because her curiosity was too much.

I'd done that and then ordered the cake.

Her need to know what she was having was only getting worse. Cain hadn't asked, but I could tell he was giving me double glances when he thought I wasn't looking. Mollie had resorted to following me around, begging for a hint.

"An hour's too long," she said. "Gimme something."

"You've made it weeks while the results came in. One more hour won't kill you."

"No," she moaned. "I just need to know if Cain's right or not."

I looked at him with a raised eyebrow. "What's your guess?"

"Boy."

"Interesting," I replied.

"Is that a hint?" Mollie asked.

"Nope."

Mollie groaned.

"I think Cain's wrong," Maribelle said. "You're carrying like I did."

Mollie's eyes cut to me, but I kept my face blank.

"I'm leaving for the diner early so you don't ruin the party."

"*Wren!*"

"Bye!"

I loaded the cake into my truck and took off before Mollie chased after me. Tammy offered to host the gender reveal at the diner since it was raining and nearly the entire town wanted to come. Mollie wanted to have it at the farm before Cain begged her not to let that many people into their house.

Forty minutes later, I was pulling up to Center Point. I'd driven like a grandma to make sure that I didn't accidentally knock over the cake, which not only earned me a honk from a woman I didn't know, but also made my drive that much longer.

When I walked in, the neon sign was covered with a banner that said "CONGRATS MOLLIE AND CAIN" in both pink and blue letters. There were balloons *everywhere*, and Kerry was at a booth blowing up more.

"Whoa, this is . . ."

"Too much?" Tammy asked from beside me. "I tried to tell her, but she told me this was the first gender reveal she's gotten to host in years, and she was going all out."

"Nothing can stop Kerry."

"Now you know how the town works." Tammy winked. "Let's go put that in the back before someone tries to sneak a peek."

"I'm being respectful!" Kerry yelled.

"It's not only you," I said with a laugh. "Mollie isn't playing around today."

Tammy laughed too. "Follow me. I'll show you where all the fun happens."

The back of the diner featured stainless steel counters and a massive coffee pot. Ron was sitting on a chair reading a newspaper. He had longer gray hair and a thick, gray mustache.

"Did ya hire someone else?" he asked.

"Nope. She's just putting the cake up."

"You brought a customer back here?"

"Oh, come on. She's not a customer."

Ron narrowed his eyes. "Then what is she?"

"A woman who's good at forgetting what I saw," I said with a wink.

"Just don't go lookin' through my books. All my recipes are there." He went back to his newspaper.

"Don't mind him. His secrets have secrets."

I nodded, trying not to let my eyes linger. He reminded me of my dad, if he were still alive. Dad had been there when no one else was, and though he was quiet and gruff, he'd made sure I ate and taught me everything I knew.

Like all grief, I missed him at random intervals. But that hadn't been my first brush with losing someone, and I'd been able to lose myself in work until the pain wasn't as unbearable.

Tammy took me to the cooler, where I hid the cake behind a bunch of eggs from the farm.

"So," she said as we walked out, "how are you and Henry?"

"We're good. He'll be here later today."

"No feelings for Jude or anything?"

"Nope," I said. "Ignore the show. They're making drama out of nothing."

As more episodes came out, the love triangle grew more obvious, though I refused to play into it even for a second.

Others, though? They were seeing the wrong side of all of this. While Henry hadn't been made into a villain, he also didn't get the attention that Jude did.

I counted down the days until I was done filming. My house reno projects were so much easier than the drama of television.

"Good. No one but Kerry cares about Jude. He's nothing more than a visitor. Not even a good one."

"Small-town life doesn't agree with him."

"But does it agree with you?"

I blinked. "Me? It's great, but I have things planned after this. I'll be back in Nashville."

"Are you not gonna visit Henry?" She raised an eyebrow.

I paused. At the end of this, Henry and I would be broken up.

The thought made my chest ache. It had been nearly two months since he'd entered my life and I was used to having him around, even with his rules to keep our distance.

"I . . . suppose I'll have to figure that out."

"I hope you do."

"Were you this friendly to Mollie?" I asked, eager to change the subject.

"I was friendly, though not like this. I like you."

I thought changing the subject would make the ache in my chest go away. Instead, it only made it worse. "Why?"

"*Why?* Do you want the whole laundry list?" She held out her hand and began counting them off. "You're redoing our beloved library. You're kind in a way a lot of people aren't. You work your *ass* off, and you remind me of Kelsey."

I didn't know what to do with three compliments, so I focused on the last thing.

"Who's that?"

"My daughter. She moved away a while ago."

"Do you miss her?"

If Tammy caught onto my topic change, she didn't mention it. "Of course I do. I'm proud of her, but these days, she's so busy with her friends and job hunting that we barely get to talk."

"I hope you get to talk to her more."

"I'm not the kind of mom who'll hover. She's got her life, but she always did this thing that drove me up a wall."

"What's that?"

"She'd change the subject when someone was getting a little

too close to a painful topic. And if I pressed, she would say she's fine." Tammy set her hands on her hips. "How similar are you?"

My stomach fell to the floor. "I-I don't . . . You caught that?"

"Yeah, I did. I notice things, kid. And you"—she pointed at me—"you have something going on. Something you're really trying to avoid."

"It's nothing major."

"Problems make themselves known. You can run, but they're always faster. The best thing to do is find someone you trust. Have you told Mollie?"

"No," I said. "I'm not ruining things for her."

"Henry?"

"A little, but I don't wanna go into details with him."

"Have you told *anyone*?"

I paused. My mantra was to pretend it wasn't happening.

And how had that been going for me lately?

"You know, I'm some woman you barely know. And I bet it's hard for you to trust. But if you need someone, and you look around and can't find anyone, I'll listen."

"Because I remind you of your daughter?"

"And you just seem like you need someone. Whatever this is, it's deep. It's been following you since you got here."

"I don't even know where to *begin*." I let out a sigh. "And the party starts soon."

"Begin with a feeling. The bad ones. When you feel that again, come find me."

"You're busy with the diner."

"The high school girls can handle it for a bit."

"Thank you," I said. "I might take you up on that."

"You can even have your little chat back here," a deep voice said. "I won't listen."

"Ron!" Tammy admonished. "You're way too quiet."

He shrugged one shoulder. "It's a talent."

I laughed, wondering if this was what life could have been like with Dad if things had been slightly different, if he'd married her when they were young, if Mom had liked us enough to stay.

And if I had been enough for her.

I rubbed my chest. Tammy was right. These thoughts were chasing me.

"Where's my cake?" I heard from the diner. Mollie had arrived, and she wouldn't be deterred for long.

"I guess we're starting."

"Whoa, when did all of these people get here?" Tammy peered out the door.

"Probably when you were yapping," Ron said, flipping a page of the newspaper.

"Keep it up and I'll make you come out with the cake and announce that it's time to cut it."

His eyes slid upward. "You wouldn't dare."

"Try me."

I resisted a laugh as Mollie called my name. In the seating area, she waited for me in a floral dress. Her bump was getting bigger, though that didn't seem to slow her down.

It was one of the things I loved about her.

"There you are!" Mollie ran over to me and pulled me into a hug.

"We just saw each other an hour ago."

Her arms squeezed. "I know. I just like hugging you."

That was exactly what I needed to hear. For a second, I felt normal.

"Mollie!" another woman called. "You look so good!"

My best friend pulled away and turned to Jade, who had another woman with long, curly black hair with her.

"Thank you!" she said. "Oh, Wren, have you met Grace?"

"I've probably seen you around," I said, forcing a smile.

"Sorry, I've been so busy with the show and . . ." I gestured to Mollie.

"It's totally fine," Grace said. "Although I'm *dying* to give you a makeover at the clothing shop."

My heart sank. "O-oh. I mostly stay in work clothes."

"Uh, duh. It *so* suits you. I just got in some new colors that would work so well with your vibe. Oh! And a set of comfortable clothes for your days off."

"You're not trying to force me in dresses or anything?"

"No!" she scoffed. "The best outfit is what you're comfortable in."

"She's so good at dressing people," Jade added. "But the work clothes she's found are so cute *I* might wear them."

Jade was in combat boots and a skirt. I couldn't see her wearing anything other than those.

Which meant the collection must have been good.

"I need to make sure we're going to local businesses too. Henry could also shop."

"Oh, Henry. I order sweaters just for him." Grace sighed with a fond expression on her face. "What a little nerd."

"Are you close with him?" I had to talk around the cotton in my throat.

Grace's eyes widened. "Not like that! Only as a friend!"

"Girl code is in session here," Jade said. "The second one of us is into someone, they're off-limits."

"Is that what you did with Cain?"

"Cain was never an option," Jade said. "I don't do things with men I know too well. Tried it once, and it didn't work out for me."

"Gabriel talk is *banned*," Grace said. "He's dead to us."

Jade put up her hands. "Sorry!"

I felt like I was missing a ton of context, but I wasn't sure if I was mad about it. They seemed welcoming, even though my time here was limited.

"I can stop all talk about men," Mollie said. Then she turned to me, all joy gone from her face. "Where's the cake?"

"Henry's not here yet."

"Yes he is," she said, pointing to the door. I turned to see him striding in, his hair in its usual pushed-back position. I wanted to go to him, but Mollie grabbed my shoulders. "Wren, I'm dying here!"

"Jeez, okay! You've been pushy since you got knocked up."

"At least I'm making sure everyone's on schedule."

I put up my hands in mock defense before heading to the kitchen.

Mollie bounced on the balls of her feet as I brought it out and Cain smiled while looking at her. I set it on the table and gave her the knife before stepping back.

The whole room waited on the edges of their seats as the knife dipped into the cake.

And then Mollie saw the pink center.

The whole room erupted in cheers. But no one was more excited than Mollie and Cain. She jumped and hugged both him and Jackie. Cain reached down to talk to her rounded belly, and tears of joy leaked out from her eyes.

They were the perfect little family, and I knew that their daughter was going to have the best life.

I'd seen pictures of a party like this. In them, a woman with strawberry-blonde hair was holding up a cupcake with pink in it. She'd been excited like this too.

And then she met me.

My whole chest ached as I remembered the photo. It hurt so badly that tears prickled my eyes.

Fuck. I was spiraling, and that was the last thing I wanted to do on Mollie's big day. Out of habit, I searched for Henry, who was congratulating Cain. I was tempted to get his attention and tell him exactly what was going on.

But that would mean cracking open the deepest secret I had, and he'd been clear that neither of us needed to get things confused when it came to this fake relationship. I'd met his mom, but hadn't even seen the inside of his house, which was just a short walk away.

No, I needed to deal with this alone. If he knew, then he would know everything about me.

I stumbled to the back of the restaurant, glad that Ron was still engrossed in his newspaper. I rounded the corner and fell to the floor, pressing a hand to my eyes.

Tammy was right. I'd run from this for too long. I'd hidden this until I couldn't anymore.

"You okay, kid?"

I looked up and saw Tammy. "What are you doing here?"

"I saw you come back here. Thought you might need to talk."

"You don't have to miss the party."

"But *you* are," she said. "And I'd told you I'd be here. So, scoot." I let out a breath before moving over. Tammy got onto the floor next to me. "Are you gonna tell me, or do you want me to guess?"

I had a feeling she wouldn't guess this one. I reached for my phone and scrolled back to one of the oldest photos I ever had and passed it over to her.

"My mom had a gender reveal like this."

"You look a lot like her."

"If you keep scrolling, you'll see where she kept everything. Logs about how I kicked, excited notes on all the things we'd do." I squeezed my fists. "I found it two years after she abandoned me."

Tammy sucked in a breath and looked over at me with wide eyes. "What?"

"You know how most kids with divorced parents live with their moms and visit their dads? It was the opposite for me. I lived with Dad and went to go see Mom when she would have me. She started a new family and had the daughter she wanted. And when I proved I wasn't who she wanted, she . . . ghosted me. Disappeared. Told Dad I was too much for her."

"Then she's not a mother." Tammy's voice was low.

"That's the thing, she *is* one. Just not to me. She wanted to be, judging by these pictures. She was *so* excited. I still wonder when she decided I wasn't worth it."

Tammy was quiet, and in the silence, I wondered if she had started to see what Mom did. If she looked over and wondered what was wrong with me that made my own mother leave.

Eventually, I gathered the courage to look over at her. Tammy's entire frame was tense, from the clenched fists to the thin line of her mouth.

"Bullshit," she eventually ground out. "You don't decide your kid isn't what you want. You get what you get, and you do your best by your kids."

"She wanted a *daughter*. Not . . . me. I thought I'd gotten over her leaving, but maybe I never will. Even Dad's death got easier over time, as sad as it was. But she's alive. She's walking around every day and never thinking of me." I looked at my phone. "But she used to. Somehow, it's worse than her being dead."

"She failed you. I bet she's failing all of her kids."

"My half-sister Ginnie probably doesn't feel the same. She's a great mother to her. Which means she was always capable of it. I just wasn't good enough."

"Who could look at you and decide you're not good enough?"

"My mom."

"Then that's her fucking problem. Not yours. Look at me." Slowly, I dragged my eyes up to her. "You didn't deserve that, you hear me?"

"I want nothing more than to believe you, but it's hard. I'm not normal. I don't like dresses or wear much makeup. I never wanted to go to get my nails done, and it's not just her who's told me that I should change. And sometimes I wonder if I *should*."

"No," she said. "I was never a normal girl either. Should I change?"

"Of course not."

"Who's tellin' you that? It better not be Henry. I'll give him a piece of my mind."

The fact that she'd go after the man she'd known for years for me was sweet. "No, not Henry. Never him. But Jude did. The show has also hinted at it."

"Then screw those idiots. You don't have to listen to narrow-minded people. All they wanna do is make you fit into whatever the hell they think's right. And trust me, kid. You're way bigger than them."

The words helped. I might have to fight what Mom taught me my entire life, but for once, the pain eased. "Thank you."

"When did Jude say this?"

"Right before I came here."

She shook her head. "So, he hit right on something that bothered you and you came here trying to be fine. Then, Mollie gets pregnant and it adds to it."

My shoulders slumped. "Exactly. I feel like such a shitty friend."

"You're not a shitty friend for having problems. We all have them. No one can help it. You're not taking away from her day because you're sad."

"I just wanna be happy for her. That's it."

Tammy's hand landed on my shoulder. "We can feel two things at once. I saw your face when you looked at her. You *are* happy. But you're also sad. And that's okay. This'll pass and you'll be the best aunt a girl could ask for."

"You think so?"

She laughed. "Absolutely. That baby's gonna adore you. Just like Mollie does."

Despite everything, I managed a smile. "I think I needed this chat."

"I meant what I said earlier. Anytime, kid." She put an arm around me, and I let myself lean into it. My own mom might not be here, she might not have chosen me, but I'd enjoy the moments of love I could find.

We sat for a few minutes, listening to the party going on outside. Once I felt more like myself, I helped Tammy up and could go back out and pretend that nothing happened.

It almost felt true.

The second I was back out in the dining room, Mollie found me.

"Where did you go?" she asked. "And why are your eyes red?"

I blinked. "Oh, you know. Emotional stuff. I'm fine."

Her hands settled on my shoulders. "What's going on?"

"It's your day. Don't worry about me."

"I can multitask," she said. "Were you hoping it was a boy like Cain was?"

"No. It was stuff about my mom."

"Your mom?" Her eyes widened. I didn't talk about Mom, mostly because I hadn't realized she'd abandoned me until it had been years since she'd answered the phone. Mollie had tried to ask about her many times, and I'd always changed the subject.

"Yeah."

"What made you think about her?"

"Sometimes when I see people win their lottery with their moms, like your future daughter has, it's hard. But that's a me problem—"

"No," Mollie interrupted. "It's not a you problem. I know something happened. Something bad enough to where she isn't in your life."

"Mollie, nothing happened. That's the issue. She just . . . stopped wanting to talk to me."

To anyone else, something like that made no sense. A mother's love was usually guaranteed, unconditional, and to have it end *had* to come with some falling out.

But not with me.

"I don't . . ." Mollie's voice was strangled. "What do you mean she just stopped talking to you?"

"I called and she didn't pick up. It's gone on for years."

"When was the last time you talked with her?"

"The day I met you."

"But that was . . . You were having a rough day. She seriously never talked to you again?"

"Nope."

Her voice raised in pitch. "What is *wrong* with her?"

"No idea. I'll never know."

She wiped at her eyes, but I knew she wasn't only sad. She was *pissed*. "She lives in Mom's neighborhood, I could go kick her—"

"I tried visiting her once. Dad did too. She didn't answer the door. She's not worth all of that."

"She ignored you at her *door*?"

"It was years ago. Before I figured it out. Most of the time I don't even think about her. Until . . . until Jude said something similar to what she used to tell me. It's been haunting me since I got here."

"Wren," she said. "I'm so sorry. Is there anything I can do?"

"Just continue to be the amazing friend you are. That's all."

Mollie pulled me into a hug. "She sucks, by the way. I thought that the first day I met her."

"She does," I replied. "She always had something negative to say."

She pulled away. "I hope you know that whatever she said was wrong."

"You don't even know what she said."

"I don't need to, because I know *you*. There's nothing on this earth you could do to deserve that."

"Mollie," I whined, wiping at my eyes. "You'll make me cry again. You know my eyes get super red."

"It's okay if you do. Trust me, people have seen all the bad sides of each other here. You're safe."

"It's nice," I replied, thinking of Tammy. "Really nice."

Mollie pulled me into the tightest hug of my life and rubbed my back.

"Uh oh, here comes the boyfriend," she said as she pulled away. "And he looks worried."

I nodded as my eyes searched for Henry. He walked up to me, concern written on his face. Never had I experienced so many people being worried about me.

Mollie was gone by the time he arrived. He didn't seem to notice she'd run off.

"What's wrong?" he asked.

"Mom stuff," I replied. "It's a long story."

"Do you wanna talk about it?"

"I do, but the rules . . ."

"There're no rules saying we can't talk," he said with a shake of his head.

"But there *is* one about not getting wires crossed, and if I tell you everything . . . I think I might." It was true. I already felt closer to Tammy, and I'd have to leave her too.

His eyes widened. "I didn't know it was a risk for you. At least not like *that*."

Was it one for him? I wanted it to be. Maybe I would feel less alone. "This is a thing I've kept hidden for a long time, and if you handle it like you do everything else, then I'm gonna get attached."

"And you don't want that."

I forced myself to nod. I shouldn't want anything more than this.

But dammit, I did.

"I understand."

The words were painful to hear, but it would be best when I left.

But did I *want* to leave?

It had always been a fact. My projects were planned out, and my time here had a deadline.

Only now, the idea of going back felt terrifying.

I would miss Strawberry Springs.

27

HENRY

Strawberry Springs Neighborhood Watch

Jade Clark: **@Jackie Anne**, why did I see about ten raccoons scurry behind your house?

Comments:
Mollie Wilson: Uh-oh. She's been caught.
Jade Clark: Caught with what?
Mollie Wilson: She told me she's building an army.
Jade Clark: Of RACCOONS??
Tammy Jane: Well, at least they're not in my trash.
Marjorie Brown: Have you taught 'em tricks?

"Honestly, Theo, I'd say you're in perfect health," I told the patient in front of me. "Other than the knee pain, of course."

He rubbed his knee with a sigh. Theo had moved in before I did, but was one of my first patients. Usually, men in their thirties avoided doctors, still thinking they were invincible. But

Theo came to his yearly visits like clockwork. I didn't know much about his past, but he was a nice enough guy. He mainly kept to himself, though Marjorie seemed to like him, judging by how much she tagged him in things in the Facebook group.

"I knew I shouldn't have helped Hugh with his carpet issue," he grumbled.

"He can be demanding, but it should heal. Just rest for a bit."

"Thanks." He glanced at the door before looking back at me. "How long is Wren gonna be in town?"

I nearly dropped my clipboard. "Why do you ask?"

"I wanted to ask her about something. I saw what she was doing with the library and wondered if she was doing anything after."

"What kind of things?" I hadn't heard of Theo ever dating anyone, but it would be my luck that he would be interested in the most gorgeous woman in town.

"A project," he immediately said. "Not anything else. I don't make moves on other people's partners. Or . . . anyone, really."

"Oh." I let out a breath of relief. "Wren will be in Nashville after filming ends, but I'm sure you could convince her to take a job here."

"It might be a few months. I need more money saved up."

She would be gone in a few months, but if I had her back for a project . . . I'd get more time with her. Even if it was as just friends.

"You should still ask. Since she's so close with Mollie, I'm sure she'll visit."

"She's close with you too, right?" he asked.

"Oh, uh, yeah. Of course." I laughed awkwardly. If Theo thought anything of it, he didn't say anything.

"I'll have to ask her once all of the cameras are gone. Thanks, Doc."

We wrapped up the appointment after that, and I took a breath of relief as I walked to the door to lock it.

Before I could, however, Tammy walked in.

"Hey, Doc. Got a minute?"

"Yeah, I do. Is something wrong?"

"Not with me. Just wanted to chat."

That was . . . concerning. I gestured to one of the waiting room chairs and sat next to her. "What's on your mind?"

"You and Wren."

I blinked. "We are?"

"Yeah. You guys are serious, right? Are you going with her when she goes back to Nashville or . . .?" She trailed off.

My shoulders tensed. In all of our planning, we hadn't talked much about the end. I didn't want to think too hard about what life would be like without her. "I'm sure we'll figure it out."

Tammy wasn't convinced. "You two are serious enough to be on camera and you're fine with saying you'll 'figure it out?' Who are you, and what have you done with Henry Connor?"

"I'm trying to be more relaxed with this one."

She raised an eyebrow. "You have a woman like Wren and you're choosing to be relaxed?"

"Yes?"

"She's the kind of woman that you go on one date with and start planning the wedding. What the hell are you doing?"

I wasn't sure I could tense any more, but I did. "I'm not doing anything, just keeping it . . . chill."

The words sounded wrong coming out of my mouth.

She narrowed her eyes. "Something's fishy here."

"Nothing is fishy! In fact, I make sure nothing ever smells like fish. I use a lemon-scented cleaner and—"

"Henry," she said slowly. "You know I'm not gonna be fooled."

"Could you try to be?"

"No." Her voice was flat. "Listen, if it were anyone else, I'd let it go, but this is Wren. So, I'm figuring things out. I came here hoping I would find out some info on you and her, something that would tell me if you could get her to stay, but this is off. You two are off."

"Do you always do this much digging?"

"For her I do." She crossed her arms. "Now, spill."

There was something about the way she looked at me that reminded me of my mother when she would catch me reading at two in the morning. I knew I couldn't keep lying.

"Wren and I aren't dating."

"What?"

"We're pretending to . . . so she doesn't have to be with Jude."

Tammy looked like she was trying to remember all of the numbers of pi. "I don't . . . But you look—"

"She's a good actor."

"And you?"

"I'm . . . not acting as much, but I'm making sure I don't get attached." It was hard to admit, but somehow also easy to. I didn't realize how much I needed to talk about this until Tammy forced it out of me.

"Is this why no one ever sees her at your house?"

I reared back. "People are keeping track of that?"

"Kerry is. Not closely, but your house makes more sense. It's closer to her work. So, she's never there?"

I rubbed my face. "That's one of the ways I'm managing, yes."

"I can't believe it. You're lying to us all. You even had *me* fooled." She let out a laugh and then paused. "Wait a second, you're in denial and it's been months. I won the damn bet!"

"Tammy, you can't let this get out."

"You mean I know I won and I can't even get the money out of it?" She threw her hands in the air. "You're a cruel man."

"Sorry, but it was needed. You saw her the first day of filming. She was miserable."

"And what did you get in return?" she asked. "One doesn't just do all of this for nothing."

"I didn't ask for anything. I just wanted to help. She's the one who made sure she did things in return."

"Sexual things?"

"*What?*" My cheeks felt hot. "No! I mean, not *directly* in return. But that's beside the point."

"Don't tell me you're using her for—"

"Tammy, *no*. I would never."

She eyed me. "You're right. You wouldn't. But I'm still worried about her. About you both, at this point."

"We'll be fine."

"Even when it's done? You're just gonna let her leave?"

I slumped. "I guess so."

"You're not happy with that, are you?"

"Not really, no. But it's the plan."

Tammy frowned. "Why don't you just ask her out? See if she'll come back when she's done with her projects."

"She's famous in Nashville."

"And now she's famous here."

I still shook my head. "She doesn't feel that way about me."

She let out a barking laugh. "Yeah, *right*. What, do you think I'm old *and* stupid? That girl definitely likes you."

"I'm sure in some ways she does," I said, thinking about the sex, "but in others not so much."

"Have you asked her?"

"Well, no."

"Then, how could you possibly know?"

"I—okay, maybe you have a point."

"I have *all* the points, and then some. So, are you gonna do it?"

Letting out a sigh, I added, "This could go wrong. What if she says no and it gets weird?"

"So, you're scared? Are you gonna let a little fear stop you from getting a girl like *Wren*?"

When she put it like that, it felt simple. I wasn't the kind of guy who let fear stop me. If I did, I wouldn't have gone to medical school or moved here.

"You are . . . alarmingly convincing."

"It's a talent of mine. One of many."

"I'm glad Wren has you."

"And I wanna keep her. So you better do your part, Doc." She pointed at me. "She belongs here. She just doesn't know it yet."

28

WREN

RWL Superfan Discussion Central

Alicia Parrish: Henry in just a T-shirt? He looked so HOT.

Comments:
Neve Bullock: Still waiting for more Jude content. They're dragging this one out WAY too long.
Kaitlyn O'Brien: Why is this group so anti-Henry? He's way better than Jude.
Kerry Winsor: THANK YOU!

ONE STRING of the fairy lights on the square had stopped working.

It had been bothering me since the sun went down. I was supposed to be sealing the windows, yet all I could see was a dark spot over one of the buildings. The Strawberry Springs town square was incredible each night.

And I wanted it to stay that way.

The fondness for the town had crept up on me. Now that I'd realized how much I liked it here, it was all I could think about.

I tried to finish the work, but I couldn't focus on it. Eventually, I abandoned my station and trotted across the street. These types of buildings always had some sort of roof access, and I snuck around the back to find it.

There was a metal staircase. I would find out how the lights were installed and figure out what I could do. I got to the rooftop and saw a figure already there.

They turned the second I came up, and for a brief moment, I wondered if I was finally about to witness a crime in this tiny town.

Instead, it was the last person I expected to see.

"Henry?"

"Wren?" His eyes were wide, just like mine. "What are you doing up here?"

"The lights aren't working."

"Ah, well. You don't have to worry about that." He put a plug in. "I already have it."

"You're a doctor *and* you do light maintenance?" I crossed my arms. "You have a lot of secrets."

"It's not a secret. It's just something I don't advertise." He rubbed the back of his head. "When I moved here, these were all broken, and I asked if there was any funding to fix it. The STM grant sent it to *me* and I've . . . been taking care of the square ever since."

"By yourself?"

"Normally, people aren't out at night. When I finish up with my hobbies, I do this and the flower pots."

"The ones always in bloom?"

"Yeah."

"You're taking care of the whole square and no one knows?"

"No one knows because no one's ever asked. Besides, I like to take care of things," he said. "And people."

I could see it. He was always in tune with how I was doing. Just like Mollie and Tammy.

"That's . . . so sweet," I said around the wad of cotton in my throat. So this was what he was like when no one was around.

I was glad I caught him, but sad that I didn't get to see it as

. . .

As his girlfriend.

Fuck. It was getting harder and harder to ignore. I thought I'd done well by not telling him about Mom, but the feelings were already there. I wanted this. All of it.

"Wren, I—"

"I think I need to get back," I said, turning away. "I probably shouldn't have delayed what I was working on to come over here anyway."

"Hang on." His hand wrapped around mine. "I need to talk to you about something."

"Is it important?" *Because I have to go hide for a bit.*

"Yes, it is. It's about us."

Ice made its way into my chest. Was he done with this? Had he grown bored or met someone else?

That would be my luck. I found a friend in Tammy and then would lose Henry.

"Y-yeah?" I asked. I kept my eyes on the stairs, unable to turn back.

I was terrified someone else was going to leave.

"Wren, turn around." This wasn't like his usual orders. It was soft and gentle.

Would his rejection be like that too?

I slowly faced him, heart in my throat.

He let out a breath. "You know, I spent hours trying to figure out what to say and . . . I have no idea where to start."

"Start anywhere." *I can take it.*

I was lying.

"I broke a rule." He gulped. "Most of them, actually. I don't think I can just fake date you anymore."

The words washed over me. He was done. It was over. I'd—

"Did you say *just?*"

"Yeah, I did. I have feelings for you." He rubbed the back of his neck. "A *lot*, actually. And I want this to be real."

I could only blink at him. He *what?* This wasn't the end? He wanted more, with *me?*

A voice distinctly like Tammy's sounded off in my head. *"Duh."*

"You can say no," he added. "And I won't back out of anything. I realize we never talked about what could happen if things changed, but I'd be willing to work it out with you."

He liked *me*.

He wanted more with . . . *me*.

Once, when I thought I could be something with Jude, I had an image of what it would be like for the guy I liked to return my feelings, but after his rejection, I'd silently accepted that people never liked me back.

And now I had no fucking clue what to say to Henry.

But I could show him. I could tell him with actions.

I grabbed him by the tie—one of my favorite things to do— and brought his lips to mine. I had no idea how to say yes because no one had ever offered me *more* before.

Henry hesitated for only a second before his hand cupped the back of my neck and brought me closer, pressing my body tightly against his.

"Is that a yes?" he asked. "Or did I misread the situation?"

"It's pretty hard to misread this."

"I do have a talent," he said.

"Then I'll say it. Yes, I'd love to be more with you."

"Thank God." Henry let out a breath of relief. "I was preparing myself for you to turn me down."

"I was preparing for *you* to say it was over."

He gave a disbelieving laugh. "Why would I *ever* do that?"

I shrugged. "It happens."

"No, Wren. It's not gonna happen with me. I've been yours since I saw you on the side of the road."

Seriously? Had it been that long?

I didn't get a chance to ask. Henry's lips found mine again and I lost myself in his embrace. Had anything ever been like this? Would anything top it?

A moment later, he pulled away. "Come back to my house."

My eyebrow raised. "I thought that—"

"I'm inviting you over. Screw all that I said before."

A thrill of excitement made its way through my stomach. All I could do was nod eagerly before he grabbed my hand and pulled me in the direction of his home.

Henry grabbed his keys as my gaze trailed over the front door of his house. I'd done all of this before, but now I had the excitement of going inside.

"So, what should I expect?" I asked. "Hoarding? No decorations?" I shuddered. "Bikini model posters on the walls?"

Henry paused and turned to me. "You *really* think that's what'll be in here?"

"You were pretty secretive," I said. "Sure, you said you didn't want this to be too real, but you could have some massive skeletons in your closets. Or on your bed."

He turned the key with a laugh. "No skeletons. I was telling the truth. If I invited you into everything, then I'd never let you leave."

"Are you never letting me leave now?"

"We'll see," he replied as he opened the door.

The space was clean. This was an older home, a craftsman that was built when the rest of them went up. Each room was separated a lot like the ones in Mollie's, but here, all of the walls were a simple yellow, though it wasn't a bachelor pad by far. Decor was on nearly every wall. It was mostly paintings of mountains or florals.

Henry had an office with a massive bookshelf on one side and a small table on the other. Pictures of his mom and places he must have visited were on the walls, as well as floral artwork.

"Who's your decorator?" I asked.

"This is all me. I wanted it to feel like a home." He took off his sweater and folded it over his arm. "I reset here, so it needed to feel like mine."

"It's *nice*," I said, eyes trailing over it.

"Are you saying that as my girlfriend or as a contractor?"

"Your girlfriend, huh?" I liked the sound of that.

"That's what you are now. And I *am* curious. You've seen hundreds of houses, and other than basic maintenance, I have no idea what's going on."

"It *is* in good shape for its age. If it were mine, I'd change the color on a few walls. The floors could use a recoat. Usually, I wouldn't go for honey oak stain, but it's growing on me. A lot of things are." I walked through the short hallway to a modest kitchen. "No dishwasher?"

"I prefer doing it myself. It's calming."

I hummed as I looked at the old wooden cabinets. "Original cabinets too. They're in good shape."

"You'd change them, wouldn't you?"

The old me would have said that I needed to completely change it. But now, I wanted to change only what was needed.

"I'd change the layout, mostly because washing dishes sucks. No matter what you say."

He laughed. "You've just never listened to a podcast about bone density while doing it."

"You're right. I haven't, and I won't be. I'll leave that to you."

I went through the kitchen, stopping when I saw something on the fridge. It was a list in Henry's handwriting, attached with a magnet.

"What's this?"

"That's nothing you should worry about." He tried to grab it, but I moved it behind me.

"Now I'm really curious." I pulled it out to read it. "Is this a list of dos and don'ts?"

He huffed out a laugh. "I made it the night you asked me to fake date you."

I read off the things he'd allowed himself. "Only touch her when you're on camera. You struggled with that one."

"Yeah. I figured that out quickly."

"Hold hands, give her gifts. Kissing but not real kissing." I laughed. "This was exactly what I told you to do."

"I like to remind myself," he replied.

And then I went down to the off-limits section. "Catching feelings. We both failed that one."

"Immediately."

"Touching her when I want to. You could have failed this one sooner."

He crossed his arms. "I had to at least *try*."

"Letting her stay over." My voice went quieter. "And here I was thinking you had secrets. Or just didn't want me around."

His hand tilted my chin up to make me look at him. "That was *never* the issue."

"You had me fooled." My eyes went back down to the paper

as I read the last one. "Letting her see the real me. Is *this* the real you?"

"Partly. The frustration at noise and bossiness in the bedroom is a part of it. I thought they were bad things."

"Not for me." I shook my head. "I like it all."

"I didn't think it was possible for someone to." He pressed a kiss to my lips. "Now I see I was wrong."

I could have stayed there all night in his embrace, but I also knew I had more house to see.

"How many bedrooms?"

"Three."

"That's a lot of space."

"Most of the houses here were built for families. I use one to store my massive collection of sweaters."

"Seriously?"

The corner of his mouth quirked. "No, I just use the closet."

Henry led me to the bathroom, which was also original. I couldn't help but notice every single part of him everywhere, including the aftershave he used and the razor on the vanity. This was his life, and I finally got to see all of it.

"You know, if you'd met me when I first got here, I would have said a lot more needed changing. But after living in Mollie's house, I like the history. This house has it too. What matters is that *you* like it."

"I do," he said. "But we could make it work if you did have changes."

"How long do you think I'm staying for?"

"As long as you want," he replied.

"I would take you up on that, but I do have projects lined up. Huge ones. Three hours away."

"I know. We can make it work. How long will they take?"

"A few months."

"And then what?"

"Then I find the next thing to fix." I shrugged. "Or at least, that was the plan. The show was supposed to allow for bigger and better things, but after this . . . I don't know if I can keep going."

"You don't have to. You could come here."

I thought about it. Mollie was here. Tammy was here. *Henry* was here. "You'd really be okay with that?"

"A lot of people would," he said. "More than you know."

"I always thought my life would be fixing things. And I still love it but . . . maybe it doesn't have to be *all* work."

"It doesn't. You could spend it doing other things."

It was a future different than I thought possible.

But I wanted it.

I brought him back to me, kissing him only for me. No one else. And I liked it this way.

"You know, the one downside to this surprise trip is that I don't have any extra clothes."

"Wear mine," he said as his hands roamed up my sides. "You can have anything of mine, actually. Though the pants might be a little long."

"I'm *not* that much shorter than you."

"You're not at all, but it makes your cheeks go red whenever I remind you that I'm taller than you." He pressed a kiss to my warm skin. "It's my favorite color."

***

I thought I was adjusting to the guest room of the farmhouse, but it didn't compare to the night of sleep I got at Henry's. His room had the most comfortable mattress I'd ever put my body on, and he only had on low lights to read. I wanted to talk to him more after my shower, but the second I lay my head on his shoulder and he started rubbing my back, I'd passed out.

I'd been in a lot of houses, but they never felt like *homes*. Henry's did.

Natural light was what finally stirred me the next morning, as well as Henry's soft breathing next to me. He was still in the position we'd fallen asleep in, me on his shoulder and him on his back. His book was on the nightstand next to him with his glasses on top, and I wondered if he'd even moved before joining me in sleep.

I curled in tighter, trying to take in the moment. My leg hiked up, only to hit something *very* hard as I did so.

My eyes popped open. I'd barely woken up yet, but already my mind was flooded with all of the things we could do. My hand trailed his stomach as I tried to wake him up. He didn't stir.

But my pinky grazed his warm skin, and *God*, he felt so good.

My leg was still pressed against his cock and he let out a sigh as his hips jerked up for friction. I bit my lip and gave him what he obviously craved. His brow furrowed as his eyes finally opened.

"W-Wren?"

"I really hope you weren't expecting someone else."

"Absolutely not. I was making sure I wasn't still dreaming."

I sat up and swung a leg to sit on top of him, his erection pressed against my ass. "Nope, but you have my mind on one thing. I hope you can handle me messing with your schedule."

"Fuck the schedule," he said, reaching for my cheek to pull me down into a kiss. He rarely ever cursed, but it sounded incredible. I'd done that to him. I'd made him do something new. As my lips moved against his, I shifted downward, rubbing against him.

I hadn't slept in much. The lingering heat outside made me turn down the sweatpants Henry offered, and I'd made it work with my underwear and his shirt. I'd thought I would have stayed away long enough to enjoy my outfit choice with him the night before, but this was just as good.

"It's like you were made for me," he murmured into my skin. "Only me."

His words felt so good, almost too good. But I took them in, remembering that Henry was like no one else I'd ever met in my life. He was incredible in every way, and he'd asked me to be his.

Nothing else mattered.

"And you were made for me," I said.

I craved friction as our mouths met again. The kiss turned dirty as I moved, letting myself get lost in us.

His cock felt so good on my clit, even when we were separated by clothes. My hands tightened on his shoulders as I chased after the feeling I needed.

I came when he cupped my breasts under his shirt. His palms rubbed against my nipples and I cried out, body tightening as my vision went dark. Heat poured from my core into the rest of me. Henry pulled back, his eyes tracing every one of my features as I came down from it.

"You're so beautiful every time you do that," he said.

"Is that why you always make sure I come?"

His expression went flat. "No. I make sure you feel good because I want to. This is just an added bonus."

I sat back, eager to feel more of him.

"Do you have condoms here?"

"I grabbed a few when you were in the shower. Check the nightstand."

Sure enough, they were there, and I grabbed one. I fumbled with his boxers, but I freed his cock. After the condom was on, I moved my underwear to the side before guiding him to press into my opening.

His hands tightened on my hips. "Go slow, buttercup. Don't rush this and hurt yourself."

"I'll do what I want."

"Don't make me flip you over," he warned.

I stilled. I was tempted to make him order me around, but we had time for that. We had time for a lot.

"Fine, but only because I really like being up here."

He pulled me in for another kiss as I pressed downward. My body was ready for him in most ways, but he'd been right. I always underestimated how long it took me to fully let someone in, and that went for multiple things in my life.

I was lucky Henry was so patient. We were both breathing heavily when I finally had him all the way inside of me. This position was like nothing else we'd been in, and he felt deeper than he'd ever been before.

Taking one experimental jerk of my hips, he somehow went even deeper, causing both of us to groan.

My hair was falling down on him. His eyes cut to it once and then twice before he grabbed it and wrapped it around his fist. "I wanna only focus on you, and this is distracting."

His hold made my body heat up. "No, *fuck*, this is good. I love this, actually."

"When are you going to stop being perfect for me?"

Despite how good every part of my body felt, my stomach flipped. When had I been perfect for anyone? "Hopefully never."

His hand drew circles on my hip. "I can agree to that."

He jerked up this time, making me bounce on his lap. I let out a gasp as he did it over and over again, pounding into me while I sat atop him.

Maybe this was my new favorite thing. Maybe *he* was my new favorite thing.

Henry fucked me like this for what could have been seconds

or minutes. I couldn't think of anything else but how he felt while moving inside of me.

One of his hands pressed to my clit, eliciting a groan. That was exactly what I'd needed to climb one last peak while he fucked me.

"H-Henry, *yes*." I gasped. "Just like that."

He kept the pace, eyes on me as I chased after the feeling. I crashed over the apex of another orgasm, body stuttering as that familiar heat took over.

"Fuck," he said as he slammed into me once more.

"That gets better every time," I said, still out of breath.

"Agreed."

I rubbed my eyes, feeling my stomach rumble. "So, what's next on the list?"

"Well, there's only one thing to do. Breakfast?"

HENRY

Strawberry Springs Neighborhood Watch

Kerry Winsor: Was it just me or were some of the lights on the square out for a bit? But then it was fixed!

Comments:
Tammy Jane: They've done that for a while. No idea who fixes them. Maybe it's gnomes or something.
Jade Clark: How do we all live here every day and not know who maintains it? The town can't be outsourcing that.
Tammy Jane: Huh. You're right. Weird.
Henry Connor: Ah. Well, if you guys want to know, I can tell you who it is.
Jade Clark: !!! HENRY TELL US
Henry Connor: Me. I take care of it.
Kerry Winsor: WHAT? All by yourself?
Henry Connor: I want the town to feel beautiful.
Kerry Winsor: I do too! We should start a committee!

"Finally, I can use this cookbook Mom got me," I said as I grabbed a massive tome from one of the bookshelves. "They usually only have recipes for multiple people."

"I can eat for multiple people," Wren said. "What were you thinking?"

He flipped through it. "She always tells me there's a good pancake recipe in this book."

"Like homemade?" she asked. "I've never had homemade anything before I came here."

I paused and looked up at her. "Really?"

She shrugged. "My dad was a busy guy, and he did what he could. Most days I wound up eating McDonalds."

"And I'm guessing your mom didn't cook either?"

She winced. "She knew how to, but she didn't really cook for me the rare times I saw her. Then she decided to be done with me, and I have no idea what she does these days."

Wren said it like a fact, but her turned-down eyes said it was anything but that.

"Decided to be done with you?" I asked slowly.

"Yeah. She ghosted me." She laughed, but there was no humor in it. "Kinda like a guy does to a girl, except she was the person who birthed me. How lucky am I?"

Far too much fell into place. Why she stayed so busy with work. Why she never mentioned family. And why she'd been upset at the baby shower.

"Is that what you didn't want to tell me before?"

"Yeah." She cleared her throat, obviously trying to push away the emotions. "I try not to talk about it. Mostly because it's so sad. Mollie knew my mom wasn't great, but even she didn't know that she disappeared. I'm trying to get better about it."

I was tempted to ask why her mom had done what she had, but there was no appropriate reason. None at all. Wren was incredible. Kind, smart, and strong. And even if she wasn't always this way, even if she was flawed as so many people were, it didn't matter.

No one deserved to be abandoned.

I took a step toward her. "Wren—"

"Don't pity me." She held up her hand, eyes on her feet. "The situation sucks, but I can't do pity. I wanna still be the Wren you know, not the woman who was left behind."

"You're still the woman I know," I said as I grabbed her hand. "And I don't pity you. I just know more now. Part of this dating thing means I'm here for you when you're bashing things in and building them from nothing, but also when you're feeling sad when someone did something terrible."

"I think that's what Tammy wants to do too. It's weird to be supported."

"It won't be for long," I tugged her close to me and pressed my lips to her forehead.

"Thank you," she said. "You're the best fake-to-real boyfriend a gal can ask for. Though, I *will* drop you down a level if we don't start on these pancakes soon."

"Understood. I should have everything to make them. Let me pull it all out."

I grabbed everything I would need—flour, sugar, salt, eggs, baking powder—but froze when I realized I didn't have buttermilk.

"Shoot. Turns out I don't have one thing."

"Buttermilk?" Wren asked as she looked at the recipe. "We could probably skip that, right?"

I stared at her. "Skip a key ingredient of the recipe?"

"You have regular milk. Add some butter to it."

I let out a shocked gasp. "Wren, that's not how it works. And you can't deviate from a recipe, it's sacred!"

She laughed. "*Sacred?* Do you mean you've never added anything to a recipe before?"

"Not the first time I make it. I need to learn the method first and then can experiment from there."

She put up her hands. "All right, fine. You're lucky you don't live too far from Food 'n' Things. I'll go get it."

"I'm already in trouble because it's gonna take a little longer to make this. I'll go get it. Will you mix the dry ingredients?"

"Sure."

"And you'll measure them, right?"

She rolled her eyes. "No, I was gonna dump a bunch in there and hope for the best."

"You're a monster."

She laughed. "I'm *kidding*. I'll measure. Especially since this recipe is *sacred*."

"When you eat them, you'll see," I said before quickly getting dressed and walking out the door. I made it a few streets down before my phone rang. I pulled it out and saw Cain's name.

"Hey," I said. "Everything good?"

"No, it's not," said a voice that was definitely *not* Cain. "I haven't heard from my best friend in over twelve hours, and if you haven't seen her, then I'm dragging Mike out of the diner and making him hunt her down!"

That was Mollie, and she sounded more tense than I'd ever heard her.

"Wren's with me," I said immediately. "She must not be checking her phone."

"Her location said the library. Did you two spend the night there or something?"

"N-no, we were at my place."

Mollie gasped. "Your place? Wait a second, did you two—"

"Maybe I should wait for her to tell you this."

"There's no telling now, I've figured it out! I'll get the details from her later, but you two are like . . . a thing now? Or are you both still in denial?"

"We're together," I said. "No more denial."

"Yes!" she nearly yelled into the phone, the sudden explosion of unexpected noise making me cringe a little. "Finally! You're my favorite right now."

"Hey!" I heard Cain say in the background. "Take that back!"

"Favorite person I've never had sex with," Mollie said. "And Henry, you better have given her the time of her *life*, do you hear me?"

"I'm sure you've already heard that I'm very capable of that," I said, rubbing my now warm face.

"You're right. I did. It needs to continue."

"This is a very weird thing to overhear," Cain said. "Can I have my phone back now, princess?"

Mollie sighed. "I have to go. Thank you for the update. I'll also be stealing your number from Cain's phone. Bye!"

She was gone before I could say it back.

I let out a shocked laugh. I'd never let myself fall for someone, but I could only hope that I made a good enough impression on those who were close to Wren.

When I walked into Food 'n' Things, Dale was behind the counter talking with Kerry about all of the changes in the town. Even in the store, there were a few people who'd come to visit. Some I knew from neighboring towns, others were obviously tourists. I gave polite waves to a few of them as I grabbed what I needed and got in line.

"We're gonna need a hotel," Kerry said. "Or use the apartments that used to be above the square."

"A hotel? Here? That would make things even worse. And those apartments are terrible. They're falling apart."

"And raccoon infested," Kerry muttered with a sigh. "I just think we should capitalize on this."

"We're a tiny town with just a few people. I love this new business, but it'll pass."

"The people who do come here love it, and we'll have the largest library on the town square."

"The second they're done here, the library will be gone again. It's just how things work."

"What about the STM grant? It's helping."

"Some billionaire temporarily cares about us. It won't last forever."

Kerry crossed her arms and looked away, eyes meeting mine. "Oh! Sorry, Henry. Didn't see you there."

"Just need to get this," I said. "Though I agree. It would be nice if Strawberry Springs were more self-sufficient."

"It would require a lot of work," Kerry said. "Maybe it's best that we leave it."

I didn't want to leave it, but Dale had a point. Whoever was behind the grant would lose interest, and then we would be right where we'd always been.

Dale grabbed the buttermilk and scanned it. "Big plans?"

"Making breakfast for Wren."

Kerry gasped. "Are things going well still? You two are always so cute together."

"Still feel bad for Jude?" I asked.

Her cheeks colored. "I mean . . . in the show I do. Obviously, you're way better. I definitely see it."

Dale laughed. "Busted by the Facebook group."

"It's fine. I'm only messing with you. Things are good. Better than good, actually."

"I called it," Dale said. "From the second he saw her, I knew they were gonna be together."

"You'll never let us live it down," Kerry said. "You better get back and make breakfast. I bet she's hungry."

"Shoot, you're right." I nearly ran out the door. "See you later!"

When I walked in, I found Wren in the kitchen glaring at a bowl.

"Would it be too cheesy for me to say what's up, buttercup?"

"Save the niceness for later. I tried to make homemade buttermilk and created a science experiment instead."

"You mixed butter and milk, didn't you?" I asked it warily. The idea of what could have been in that bowl made my whole body cringe.

"Yep, and then I thought it tasted good, except for the chunks. Then I realized dairy should *not* have chunks, and now I'm regretting everything."

I walked over and slowly took the bowl, not looking inside of it. "Buttermilk is the leftovers from churning milk once the butter is taken out."

"So, I traumatized myself for nothing?"

"You learned what buttermilk is in the end."

She sighed, though she looked less green now that the milk and butter weren't in front of her. I walked over to the bowl with all the dry ingredients. I collected the remaining pieces before mixing it together.

The cabinets opened and closed before Wren finally set down a skillet. "It's the correct size," she said. "I'll get it warming up."

"Thank you. Also, after breakfast, we'll need to go to the library."

"Why?"

"You forgot your phone there and Mollie had no idea where you were."

Wren's eyes were round. "Shit. I knew I was forgetting something. Did she call you?"

"Yes. I told her where you were and some of what happened. She figured out most of it."

"She's smart like that." Wren opened the drawers and pulled out a spatula. "I can't wait to get the twenty questions when I get back."

"I know breakfast took a little longer than I intended, but hopefully it'll all be good things."

"They'll be the best." She attempted to dip her finger in the batter, but I held it up.

"What are you doing?"

"Trying the batter."

"This has raw eggs and flour in it. It's risky to eat it before it's cooked."

"Have you never had raw cookie dough?"

"No."

She gasped. "Now who's the monster? It's the best part!"

"Until you get salmonella."

"High risk, high reward." She jumped and sat on the counter, which gave her just enough height to grab the bowl and get a taste of it, but she frowned. "I expected that to be better."

"I expected it to be pretty bland."

"We could have added something to it."

"Maybe you can talk me into it next time. But for now, we follow the recipe. And try not to get salmonella."

"Would you take care of me if I did?"

"I would. And then I'll tell you that you shouldn't have eaten raw batter." I flipped the first pancake and had to fight Wren to make sure she didn't eat it the second it was done. I wound up giving up on the third and fourth pancake and let her snack while I cooked.

Eventually, we were at the small table with a stack of pancakes each.

"With the syrup? These are incredible. I'm always eating homemade food from now on."

"My mom is right sometimes," I said. "I'll happily try new things if it's with you."

She grabbed my hand. "Me too."

My schedule was thrown off entirely. I'd probably be late to work, and Wren would be late to filming. While I didn't love the idea of not having time to do paperwork in the morning, I did love the time I spent with her.

Eventually, we would fall into a new routine that I could follow, but for now, I would make it work. It was more than worth it.

WREN

Strawberry Springs Neighborhood Watch

Hu Gh: Drone for sale. Hole in the bottom. Full price only. I know what I've got.

Comments:
Tammy Jane: Are they ethically sourced? Or were they hunted?
Marjorie Brown: Can I get a picture of the hole?
Kerry Winsor: Marjorie! Don't encourage this!
Marjorie Brown: WHAT? Maybe I'm into drones!

I WAS CAREFULLY WEEDING the irises when a shadow crossed over me. I tensed, hoping it wasn't Jude, who was trying to get me to interview with him.

"Hey, kid," a very different voice said. "How are you?"

I looked up, shocked to see Tammy.

"Hey yourself. What's up? Do you need anything?"

"Can I not just check in on you?"

"You can . . . It's just not normal for me."

Tammy huffed. "Still hate that woman who pushed you out of her."

"Not even calling her my mother?"

"She'd have to work for that." She rolled her eyes. "I was just on a break. I called Kelsey, but she's busy, and then saw you out here. How's the library going?"

"It's almost done. We're installing tile starting tomorrow, and then we furnish it. I can't wait."

Though I almost could wait, because once I was done here, I had a ton to do when I went back to Nashville.

And I didn't even want to go back.

"Me either. The only people more excited than me are Marjorie and Henrietta. And maybe Henry. And Mollie." She scratched her head. "That's a longer list than I thought."

"I'm gonna try to do my best," I said. "But if I mess it up, it gives me more reason to come back and fix it."

"Do you have to have a reason to come back?"

I paused in my weeding as I thought about it. For most of my life, I was always in search of something to fix. I couldn't imagine not finding a bigger and better house to renovate, but now that I thought about it, I didn't *have* to fix anything. I loved my job, and I would want to get back to renovations eventually, but I felt like I could take a break.

I could be with Henry.

"You know, you're not wrong," I said. "I guess I can come back for my boyfriend."

Tammy narrowed her eyes and looked around. "You don't have to lie to me, kid. I know."

"You know?"

"I *know*," she repeated as she leaned in. "It's all for the show."

I gasped. "What? How did you find out?"

"I figured it out when Henry got all cagey. This is the face of a mother. He couldn't lie to me."

I could see Henry crumbling under Tammy's hard stare. I'd probably do the same.

"Ah, well. I guess the secret is out. In a way."

She raised an eyebrow. "Did he talk to you like I told him to?"

"You told him to do that?"

"No miscommunications on my watch," she said with a laugh. "So, he did it?"

"He did," I replied. "And I said yes."

"Finally! I might have only known the truth for a day, but that was too long!"

I laughed. "I'm glad no one else knew. They wouldn't have been able to keep their mouths shut."

"Definitely not. And you two owe me, considering technically *I* won the bet."

"Oh, God. I hadn't even thought of that. How much money did you lose out on?"

Her flat expression told me it was a lot.

"Let's just say you're lucky I like you or else I'd be asking to get paid back."

"Back pay for bet winning is a new one for me."

"We take them seriously around here. You'll get your chance to join in on one soon. Something tells me you'll fit in just fine once you're settled."

Had I ever fit in anywhere? Sure, I had with Mollie, but it wasn't like this. It wasn't a community.

"I honestly can't wait to be done with my work in Nashville so I can get back. Hopefully I won't miss anything good."

"What all do you have planned?"

"You wanna hear about all of the things I'm doing back in Nashville?"

"Yeah. I'm fascinated by what you get up to, kid. I'll hear it all."

Cotton made its way into my throat. I'd come here to escape and spend time with Mollie before the show resumed. It was supposed to be temporary and fleeting.

And instead, I found a family. And I was starting to really like spending time with them.

"Wren!" Mollie yelled the second I was through the door. She ran over to me, hugging me despite how sweaty I was. "Thank God I can actually *see* that you're okay."

I winced. "Sorry I missed your twenty calls. Last night was . . . unexpected, and then I had to film today."

She was smirking when she pulled back. "I hear someone isn't single."

My cheeks heated and I laughed. "You're right. I'm not."

"Henry is a sweetheart. Even Cain agrees. He would have even agreed before he liked the town, which really says something."

I laughed. "It does."

"We're almost done with dinner, by the way. Are you hungry?"

I paused. "I was actually gonna hang out with Henry tonight."

Mollie raised an eyebrow. "You're spending another night with him?"

"Is that okay?" I wouldn't blame her if she felt exactly like I did when I first came. Like I was moving on without her.

But she shook her head. "Why would I be mad?"

"Because . . . we don't get as much time together, I guess?"

"You're in a new relationship, and I know how it is. When you find your person, you wanna share a life with them. I mean, look at mine." She gestured to the house. "We'll make time for hangouts, girls' nights, or just a night with Eric to play, but if you're happy with Henry, I'm happy for you."

"I am happy," I said. "I almost don't know what to do with it."

"You've been dealing with a lot for a long time," she said. "Some that I didn't even know about. I hate that you don't know what it feels like to be happy. Then again, with Trevor, I didn't either. But I saw your misery, just as you would have if you were here."

"I wish I had been," I said with a sigh. "I felt terrible about it for a while."

"You were busy with your show."

"And look how that turned out." I rolled my eyes. "I hate the show, and they tried to force me to do things I didn't want to. What would have happened if I'd stayed in Nashville and didn't come here? You could've forgotten me." As I said the words, emotion hit me hard. My eyes prickled, though I tried to stop it.

The idea that people left was something I carried with me every day. Once Mom vanished, it left a crack inside of me, and from that, whispers arose from the depths.

Everyone leaves. Protect yourself.

If I wasn't memorable enough to my own mother, why would anyone else care?

"Wren, I would *never* forget you." She stepped close, eyes also shining with tears. "You're like a sister to me, even when we're apart."

"But people have before," I said with a shrug. "It can happen again."

"If I ever start to forget you, find me and kick my *ass*. I would deserve it."

"Bad word!" Eric called.

Mollie blinked. "Hey! Were you listening?"

"No!" he lied as he came into view. "I was just around."

"I'm not dumb." She pointed at him.

"My marble run fell over. I wasn't listening for long, I promise!"

Mollie crossed her arms, watching him closely.

"It's okay," I said, shaking my head. "We were just talking about adult stuff."

"About people leaving, right?" he asked.

My eyes went wide. "Uh, yes."

"I'm sorry your mom did that," he said quietly. "My dad did too. My biological one, I mean." The word came out slowly, as if he'd recently memorized it.

"He did?" I asked.

"A few kids asked me about him, but I never cared."

"Why?"

"Because I met new people. Ones who really care about me. My *real* dad is Cain, and if I have him, I feel okay. Is there someone like that for you?"

My eyes went to Mollie, who was looking at Eric with a small smile on her face. Then I thought of Tammy, who'd come to chat with me simply because she saw me, and Henry who rushed to my side when I'd taken a tumble off of the ladder.

"I do," I said slowly. "And I'm lucky to have them."

"It's good to have people that really like you. Not ones who want to change you."

"He's *five*?" I whispered to Mollie.

"Almost six, but *still*," she whispered back, wiping at her eyes. "He's so mature."

He'd said exactly what I needed to hear.

"Thank you," I said. "And I can't stay for too long, but I absolutely can help you with an amazing marble run before I go!"

"Yes! Can you make sure it goes down the stairs?"

"Absolutely not!" Cain yelled from the kitchen. "I'm not breaking a leg because of a marble!"

"When I have some time, I'll get you more pieces to make something *huge*," I said. "But for now, let's see what I can do that won't get you in trouble with your dad."

HENRY

Strawberry Springs Neighborhood Watch

Kerry Winsor: You people are way too into your phones! Look around! Notice your neighbors! JEEZ.

Comments:
Jade Clark: Is there something you want us to notice, Kerry?
Marjorie Brown: Probably that silly hat she's wearing.
Kerry Winsor: It's a BERET and it's not silly! I was trying something new and no one even noticed!
Hu Gh: I noticed. I thought you were going through one of those midlife crisis things. I didn't wanna be called rude again.
Kerry Winsor: IT'S NOT A MIDLIFE CRISIS! IT'S A FASHION STATEMENT.
Jade Clark: Do you have the urge to buy a sports car, Kerry?
Marjorie Brown: Aging is very normal! Just look at me!
Kerry Winsor: I HATE YOU ALL.

As usual, sunlight woke me up from my slumber.

But what was unusual was the woman I was curled around.

Night two of her being in my house only proved that I would never let her go, especially since she fit into my home like she was meant to be here. She let me read while she worked on planning out the books she was getting for the library, and we tumbled into bed by nine, though we stayed awake far longer than that.

There was a bite mark on her shoulder, and my cock stirred at the memory. Every time we were together, it was right. I felt whole.

And I owed it to her.

"Is that a flashlight in your pocket," Wren asked softly, "or are you happy to see me?"

"Why would I have a flashlight in bed?" I laughed. "And neither of us are wearing clothes."

"The joke made much more sense in my head. Give me a break, I just woke up."

I kissed her cheek before sitting up.

"Your beard grows fast," she mused as she turned around.

"I have to shave it every morning."

"So, this is just for me?"

"There are a lot of things that are just for you," I said softly, leaning down to kiss her. "But I do need to get ready for the day."

I wondered if she would pout and ask me to stay, but I forgot that she was just as busy as I was.

"Me too," she said, stretching. "I hope I brought my good overalls from Mollie's. I'll need them."

Wren was easygoing in a way I didn't expect. I spent as much time as I could with her, but both of us had careers and lives. She wasn't bothered when I had work. Back when I was with Norah, she'd been annoyed when I even *studied*.

I got up and shaved before getting dressed. Wren was heading for the door when I came downstairs.

"Wait," I said. "Are you not having breakfast?"

She paused. "I'll eat a big lunch."

"Really?"

She slowly turned. "We're both pretty busy today. I'll figure it out."

"There's a reason I follow a routine, you know. I usually make a smoothie in the morning. Can you spare five minutes for me to get you one too?"

"That sounds great," she admitted. "Do you use frozen fruit? I bet that would be *so* good with how hot it is."

"I do, but I also have something else for you." I reached down and grabbed one of my extra water bottles. "I'll fill this up before you go. You need to hydrate."

"I'll have a bottle of water a day."

"Those are sample sizes," I reminded her.

Her cheeks went red. "*Fine.* I'll take care of myself. But no promises on refilling it if I finish it. That's always the step I don't have time for."

"I'll come by on my lunch and refill it for you." I was used to being on camera and finally relaxing at home. I was starting to feel like myself again, so taking care of her was easy.

"You have work to do. Don't worry about me."

"Rule number one of having me as a boyfriend is that I'll always worry about you." I set down the bottle. "And take care of you."

Her cheeks only grew redder, and now I knew why. Her mom hadn't done this for her, and she'd gotten the bare minimum from her father. I bet all of this was new.

Though it wouldn't be for long.

"I suppose I should say thank you." She gave me a soft smile. "And sorry for being such a distraction."

"You're not a distraction."

"But I am," she said. "I would know because we were up until midnight last night."

There was a tiredness behind my eyes I couldn't shake, but it was nothing coffee couldn't fix. "I don't regret that."

"I didn't say anything about regret. And I won't, even when I cover up the hickey you gave me."

"You could wear it loud and proud."

"And risk Madison's wrath *again*? You're playing with fire."

"She's pushing you with a man who isn't me. She deserves it."

Wren laughed and raised an eyebrow. "Possessive, are we?"

"Only for you." I grabbed her by the waist and pressed a kiss to her lips. I was tempted to give her more, but she pushed me away.

"The smoothie? Then your job?"

"Sorry," I said. "I'll get to it."

"And I'll start mentally preparing for being on camera. Madison wants you to come by today. And you have plenty of flowers to bring. I don't know how you would choose with everything you have."

She wasn't wrong. I'd forgone having a lawn a long time ago in favor of more native plants.

"It wasn't all that hard," I said as I grabbed the ingredients for the smoothie from the freezer. "I picked them based on how I felt about you."

She turned to me. "How did you do that?"

"Each flower has a meaning. You probably don't remember the ones I gave you, but—"

"I do remember," she replied. "I've kept them."

My heart skipped a beat. "You did?"

She tucked a strand of hair behind her ear. "They were so

beautiful. What was I supposed to do, throw them away? I dried them and put them in a scrapbook Mollie gave me."

I didn't know she'd cared enough to do that. All this time, I thought she was out of my league, yet she was exactly the person I'd been waiting for.

"It started with the irises."

"On the second day I was in town?" She raised her eyebrows.

"It wasn't totally intentional. They *were* blooming, but when I met you, I was so impressed by you that I thought they fit."

"What do irises mean?"

"Many things. The one I thought of was valor. You're . . . so incredible, Wren. You're brave, even when you don't see it. When I met you while you had that flat tire, I knew . . ."

"That I wasn't normal?"

"That you were way out of my league."

Now her eyes were wide. "That's *really* what you thought about me?"

"Yep."

Her face flushed as she brought me in for a kiss. I would have stayed there forever if I didn't have more to tell her.

"The next were the buttercups."

"You forgot the clover," she said. "That's the first thing you picked for me. It got dried too."

"I think that one is obvious."

"Still." She shrugged as she looked at me through her lashes. "It was adorable. What did the buttercups mean?"

"Joy. I mainly thought that it was a good idea for the show, but then I realized I feel joy whenever I look at you."

"And that's why you gave me the nickname?"

"It's why it stuck." I brushed my thumb over her cheek. "Then there was the morning glory. It means unreturned love.

Or it could mean undying love. For the show, I meant it to be the second one."

"And for you?"

"A few weeks ago, I would have said the first. Now, I agree with the second one."

"Then the hydrangeas?"

"Gratitude. For being there for me when I had my issues."

"Of course. Those were beautiful, though a pain to dry."

"You didn't have to."

"The flowers are the sweetest thing anyone has ever done for me. I wasn't throwing them away."

"You'll have to show me the scrapbook," I said. "And the final one was—"

"The rose. Which usually means love." She tilted her head. "Was that one for the show too?"

"They were blooming, and I thought of you. And then I justified it by saying it was for the show. But after . . . I knew."

Wren straightened. "No way did you say you loved me through flowers."

"Technically, I *realized* I loved you through flowers."

"Both are equally nerdy. And equally adorable." She tucked back more of her hair, and I saw that her entire body was flushed. "What made you finally figure it out? So I can do it all the time, of course."

"There wasn't a moment that did it, just a lot of little things that added up."

"Still, there has to be *something*."

"It's just you, Wren. You're what I love. You don't need to do anything to earn it or keep it. You just have it." She blinked, and I could have sworn I saw wetness in her eyes. But I knew her well enough to let her process, so I continued. "You don't have to say it back—"

"I want to, though." She cleared her throat. "I do love you."

My cheeks heated at her saying those words. I knew that, without a shadow of a doubt, those words would become my favorite to hear.

"Dating for one day and we're already saying the L-word? We're moving fast."

"Technically we've been dating for months."

"That doesn't count." I shook my head. "Because I didn't have all of you."

"And you like having all of me?"

"I do."

I wished I could have said my day went well from there, but the construction on the community center echoed around the square, invading even the clinic.

It didn't help that my schedule was packed and I was busy from the second I unlocked the door through lunch.

There wasn't much I knew about tiling, but workers were cutting a lot of it. The high-pitched squeal followed me around, giving me a headache by midday, and it only got worse when I refilled Wren's water like I promised to.

My mood was rapidly declining, something I usually would have gone home for. But in the afternoon, I had to go to Food 'n' Things again to get ingredients for dinner. Most of what I had at the house were portions for one, and Wren had already asked to come back over.

I didn't want to cancel, so I put in the earplugs. They didn't block out everything, but they made it all more manageable. I had to take a few minutes to sit in the near silence before I left, but I was already more like myself.

As I walked, I hoped no one noticed them. It had been very tempting to take them out and never use them again when Mom had asked what they were. It was always tempting to hide what I struggled with, even when it was to my own detriment. Having Wren there made it easier to explain.

Thankfully, she had taken what Wren had said easily. Maybe she didn't understand it, but she didn't argue. I wasn't sure if my neighbors would have the same reaction.

Maybe I wasn't giving them enough credit. Or I could be exactly right. It was hard to tell how people would act when they heard about a disability.

Food 'n' Things wasn't busy, and I was able to grab what I needed for chicken alfredo. When I turned the corner, I ran into Henrietta and Marjorie, who were talking by the freezers, ice cream in hand.

"I swear, every time you get ice cream, you regret it!" Henrietta's voice was tight. "Why do you insist on making yourself suffer?"

"It's *ice cream*," Marjorie said. "What else am I supposed to do?"

"Not eat it?"

"That's miserable!" Marjorie's eyes cut to me. "Henry, tell her that life without ice cream isn't worth it!"

"Everything is good in moderation, but if it makes you sick, then even less of it is probably best."

Marjorie sighed. "What a doctor answer."

"He has sense," Henrietta said. "So get the sorbetto."

"That's boring," she complained as I walked around her. I thought I was free to check out with Dale, but she grabbed my arm. "Hey, what do you have in your ears?"

My shoulders slumped. I was caught. "Earplugs. It's a little loud today."

"You're telling me," Marjorie said. "I don't care, but Hen here can't deal with it. I keep telling her she'll adjust once we get back to work, but she's been in a bad mood all day."

"I'm fine!" she insisted. "I just hate loud noises, especially when they're repeated like that. Couple that with the stress of having to socialize, and I'm ready to crawl out of my skin and into a quiet cave and stay there."

"That sounds similar to what one of my autistic students experiences," someone else added. We all turned to see that Nicole, the local teacher, had joined us. I rarely spoke with her, though I knew she and Cain had had problems in the past. "The girl I'm talking about is autistic, though. It often goes undiagnosed in women, and our understanding of it is more recent, so plenty of older adults were never evaluated. Might be something worth talking to Henry about."

My shoulders grew tight as I watched the two older women carefully.

"We don't need to get her evaluated. Have you seen this woman's doll collection? I *know* she has autism. Knew it the second they had a word for it!"

"Marj!" Henrietta hissed, her face darkening. "Don't mention the dolls."

"At least you know," Nicole said. "Where did you get those earplugs, Henry? I wanted to gift some to the girl in my class, but haven't been able to find a set yet."

"Wren got them for me, so you'd have to ask her. I think the brand is on the case, though."

"Give them to me too," Marjorie said. "I'm staging an intervention."

"I'm—" Henrietta began.

"No, you're not fine. Usually, I annoy you, but this time I think you're close to divorcing me. If we're getting back to running a library, you'll need something to make sure you don't lose your mind."

"Do they get rid of humming?" Dale called. "One of the freezers is broken and I can't take it anymore."

I looked in between all of them. Even though I hadn't admitted anything about myself, I felt welcomed. As if being different didn't make me worse off. I should have seen it coming. Strawberry Springs was a family, even when we made each other mad. There was a reason I chose to settle down here and not in a city.

"So, do you have an obsession?" Marjorie asked.

"Me? Why?"

"Henrietta has her dolls, and while you were zoned out, Nicole was telling me the little girl in her class loves Barbies. Do you have one?"

"H-how did you know—"

"I'm not dumb. Or maybe I am, in which case, feel free to tell me I'm wrong."

"You're not," I said. "It's just hard to admit it. Where I came from . . . it wasn't understood. Or accepted."

"It still isn't in some areas," Nicole said, hand on her hip. "A lot of people think it's a disease or something to be cured. Really, it's just a different way of experiencing the world, one that's on a spectrum."

"Exactly," I said.

"Yeah, yeah, we're all being sweet," Marjorie said, waving her hand. "I wanna hear about Henry's thing."

"My special interest is growing flowers."

"Oh," Henrietta said. "That's a good one."

"Is that why your garden is so massive?" Nicole asked.

"Pretty much."

She hummed. "Nice."

"Can I steal some?"

"Marjorie!" Henrietta chastised.

"I'll let you *have* some," I replied. "As long as you don't cheer on Jackie's raccoon thing."

"You drive a hard bargain. The truth is, it won't go on forever. They'll turn feral when they slow down in the winter."

"And how do you know that?"

She shrugged. "I've trained a bunch of them."

I raised an eyebrow and turned to Henrietta. "You let her do this?"

"Do you think I could stop her?"

"God forbid a woman has a hobby." She threw her hands up and grabbed at her ice cream. "Now if you'll excuse me, I'm getting this and will be having a date with my toilet later."

"Oh my *God*," Henrietta groaned. "I faced homophobia for this."

"You love me, baby. You know you laugh when no one's looking!"

32

WREN

RWL Superfan Discussion Central

Jamie McCullough: Any predictions for how much longer it'll take before Wren and Jude are back together? I'm getting bored.

Comments:
Neve Bullock: I'd bet on it being the finale. They'll drag it out as long as possible to keep us watching.
Alicia Parrish: I don't know, maybe Wrenry is an actual thing? I could see it.
Kerry Winsor: Wrenry?
Alicia Parrish: It's a couple name. Their names combined. Everyone knows that.
Kerry Winsor: Well I hate to break it to you, but "Wrenry" is absolutely an actual thing. Far better than "Wrude" which is exactly how Jude has been since he came here. He doesn't talk to any of us!
Jamie McCullough: You take that back! We are so not here for the Jude slander.

"Are you really making a pregnant woman cover her eyes and walk?"

"I'm making sure you don't fall," I replied with a roll of my eyes. "And don't play the pregnancy card. You know you wanna see it before anyone else."

She huffed out a sigh. "I do. Curse you."

"All right," I said, placing her right in the middle of the library. She was the first to see it mostly finished. A few of the books were around, though more were on the way. "Ready?"

"So fucking ready," she said. "Move that bus!"

"We definitely don't say that. Pretty sure it's copyrighted."

"I can say whatever I want. I'm not on camera."

I laughed and gently pulled her hands away from her eyes. They went wide as she took in everything. The bottom level was full of color since the kids' area was here. The tiles were different shades of every color, and the white walls were covered with murals.

"Holy *shit*," she said. "This is . . . It feels exactly like it did when I was a kid."

"I wanted it to be magical. I didn't change much, other than brightening it up."

"How did you even do all of this?" she whispered as she walked.

"You saw most of it. A lot of long hours." I looked around. "Hopefully it was worth it."

"It absolutely was," she said with a smile.

Mollie walked toward the tables set up for the kids to either read or play on. The puppet area that Henry and I had found was placed on a tiny stage, ready for anyone who wanted to put on a show.

She gasped. "Eric is gonna love this. And so will this one. We'll be here all the time."

I looked out at the space. Instead of seeing ghosts of the past, I saw what could be. Mollie would be hanging out with Eric while helping her daughter read. All of the faces I'd grown to know would filter through as they visited the new and improved heart of the town.

When I'd been working here, I only saw the work. Now I saw it all.

Pride filled my chest. I'd done this. I'd made it happen.

"You haven't even seen the upstairs yet."

"I bet it's even better," she said, linking her arm through mine. "There's a second staircase back here, right? We can take that."

"Let's take the main one."

Her eyes narrowed. "Why?"

"There's just something I wanna save for the end that you'll see if we go any farther."

"Wait, what is it?"

"If I tell you, it ruins it."

She groaned. "But now I'm curious! Is this the special surprise from months ago?"

"Yes."

"Aw, come on. You know I'm terrible with surprises. Especially after the gender reveal." She paused and then she raised a single eyebrow. "What if I ran?"

"Do you really think you can outrun me?"

"I did back in gym class."

"You're several months pregnant."

"Wanna try me?"

"Mollie, don't ruin it for yourself."

She let out another loud groan and stalked to the main

stairs. Her mood quickly changed when she saw all of the new working stations as well as the massive bookshelves.

"Wait a second, is that an erotica section?"

"Yep. Tammy requested it."

"*Tammy?*" Mollie's jaw hung open. "I mean, good for her, but that's not what I expected."

"I wonder who'll use it. You know Marjorie is gonna keep track."

"I'll have to keep you posted."

There was a pang in my heart. I loved it here, and I wanted to see how it looked when it opened. Hell, I wanted to read books from here, just like everyone else would.

But what Henry and I had discussed was fresh on my mind.

"You might not have to do that for long."

Mollie turned to me. "You're coming back after your project, aren't you?"

"I think I am. I really like it here and I wanna stay."

"Yes!" She pulled me into a tight hug. "I was *so* hoping for this! So, will you find work out here?"

"I'm not sure," I replied. "I don't know what all there is to do. I might be traveling a lot, but I'll make it work."

"If anyone can find something in a small town, it's you." Mollie continued to hug me tightly. "I'm so glad you like it here."

"Me too." I wrapped my arms around her. When she pulled away, her eyes were misty, but she went through the other sections as she sniffled.

"I wish I could be here for opening day, but I have that big scan. *Why* did I schedule it for that day?"

"You didn't know," I said. "Neither did I. It was all up in the air until now."

"They're gonna love it. They'll call you a hero."

I laughed. "I don't know if I'm that."

"You went to bat for this library, and we all know it. It's incredible."

"I was happy to. This was the first project in a while that I genuinely loved."

"Now, what was this last thing you wanted to show me? I'm trying to be patient, but it's killing me."

"All right, all right," I said. "Let's go see the final thing."

We walked down the back stairs, and Mollie bounced on the balls of her feet as I opened the door that led to the first floor.

I gestured for her to turn around to look at the mural. We'd cleaned it up and hired someone local to come and restore it. Most of it was the same, though I'd had the artist update a few of the buildings.

"Oh my God," she said, hands flying to her mouth. "I remember this!"

"It's perfect for the center of town."

She walked close, her hands tracing the details. "I thought it would have been painted over. Or vandalized. This was the surprise the whole time?"

"It was. We got lucky with how good of shape it was in. It was just here, waiting for us to come and find it."

"The farm's on here!" She walked closer. "It has my name!"

"It's supposed to reflect the town residents as they are now."

Mollie stared at it for a long time. When she finally turned to me, her eyes were wet. "It's amazing." She hugged me once more. "I didn't know you were doing all of this."

"When I saw it, I knew it had to be done. I'm glad you like it."

"Like it? I *love* it." Her arms tightened. "You're the best friend ever."

"Like you're not too."

"What's happening here?" a voice called. We both turned to see Madison.

"I'm showing my best friend the library," I said. "I'll be back to work in a few."

Mollie blew out a breath. "You're just taking a break."

"If you're showing someone the library, we should get it on camera." Madison crossed her arms. "We could use it in the finale."

"I don't wanna be on camera," Mollie said.

"But she's your best friend."

"You do know that no means no, right?" Mollie's voice was cold. "Or do you need a lesson on consent?"

"I don't think I like your attitude."

"And I don't like how you make Wren feel, so we're on the same page."

Madison's jaw dropped for one second before her glare turned bad. She'd been steadily getting more and more frustrated with me. And I'd done the same with her. "Wren wanted this."

"*Wren* is right here," I said. "And I wanted some of it, not to be forced to be with Jude after it looked like he cheated on me."

Madison shook her head. "Then you don't have what it takes to be on TV."

"You're right," I replied. "I don't think I do."

The implication was heavy. If I didn't have what it took, then it meant the show was over. Madison had always talked like we'd be doing this forever. This was my first hint to her that I was done.

"You'll get there," Madison said. "Especially once we're back in Nashville."

"I don't wanna be back in Nashville."

"And neither do the people," Mollie added. "You know the ratings. People are *talking*."

"Yes, they are. But it's about the storyline *I* created. That little video did nothing. They want you with Jude."

"I'm sure if another one got posted, people would see why she's choosing Henry."

"Another won't pop up."

Mollie raised an eyebrow. "Are you sure? I had fun posting the first one."

Madison's nostrils flared, and what Mollie had said hit me at the same time it did her.

I blinked. "Wait, the video. You posted that? Were you at the library?"

She snickered. "I wanted to take some inspiration from my best friend and see the inside before it was all done. And then I saw who Wren has the most chemistry with."

"I don't take advice from nobodies," Madison hissed. "I know what's best."

"Sure. Sure. We'll see about that."

"It's *my* show."

"I have a say too," I said.

Madison's jaw tightened and she shook her head, beginning to stomp away.

"Really?" Mollie called after her. "You're giving up that easily?"

"You won't listen anyway. Besides"—she turned with a smile that looked anything but kind on her face—"I have a finale to prepare for."

33

HENRY

Strawberry Springs Neighborhood Watch

Marjorie Brown: I've been in such a good mood that I deserve to be taken down a few notches. Got anything mean for me? You know you want to . . .

Comments:
Kerry Winsor: @**Marjorie Brown** I'm not over you calling me fat!
Mark Bell: Or the time you made me lose a drinking game in my own bar.
SherriffMike Finch: You also will not update your tags. Good grief, woman, you're gonna get a ticket from anyone else!
Hu Gh: This is a fun game. You suck.
Marjorie Brown: I did NOT consent to this! Henrietta did this when I left my phone unlocked. She's not as nice as you think she is!!!

THE WHOLE TOWN square was alight with celebration. Kerry had arranged for banners and balloons to be brought out, and as the person who'd maintained the square, I'd told her where to put them all. She'd gone one step further, deeming that we should make a collective to ensure Strawberry Springs stayed beautiful, and I'd somehow agreed.

Now, she sent me texts with her plans. Most of them wouldn't work, but some could easily improve the town.

But today, she was with a sea of other people. I'd seen everyone in town individually, but never all together like this. It showed how excited people were to have the library up and running.

As Wren's boyfriend, I got special privileges. I was closer up, which helped, considering how *loud* everything was for the library's opening. I focused my attention on running my eyes over every inch of the new space, wondering how Wren had made this all happen.

In just a few months, the library was alive again. It had been turned from an eyesore to a beautiful space. That was what I wanted to feel for the day. Pure joy for Wren.

She and I had already discussed a quiet night back at my place, so while I was pushing myself by not wearing my earplugs and being around the whole town at once, I knew it was going to calm down soon.

For now, I got to take it all in.

Wren and I had arrived together, but one of the assistants had insisted she use some type of new mascara, so she'd been delayed while they put that on her. She'd rolled her eyes, but told me to go hang out with the town while she finished up.

When she was finally ready, the entire town clapped when they saw her. Even from where I was standing, I saw her freckled cheeks darken as she gave everyone a wave.

They all silenced when Jude came out too. I could tell he

was ready for the applause, and the town's refusal to be friendly with him ensured he'd never come back.

Good.

Filming started with Wren and Jude talking to the camera. Even though she was next to a man she didn't like, she still glowed when gushing about the library. It was obvious she was proud of it.

They let us in shortly after. Even though I had started out ahead of everyone else, they all swarmed to get in. I could see why. The inside was as beautiful as the outside. Maybe even more so. There was color and books everywhere, like a painting come to life. I'd seen it every step of the way, but nothing prepared me for the final walkthrough.

Despite the near chaos, it was incredible to see the town's reactions to the space. I focused on one at a time, taking it all in.

"It's so beautiful!" Henrietta said, tears in her eyes. "Can you believe we get to work here?"

"No, I really can't." Marjorie's voice was quiet. "I thought this day would never come."

It was rare that she was so serious.

On the other side, Kerry followed her son, Tommy, as he excitedly talked about all the books he wanted to read. He bounced around like a little ball of energy.

"We'll never leave," she said with a laugh. "To think, all it took to get you to read was a library!"

I didn't get a chance to see anyone else's reactions because I had an armful of Wren. She'd launched herself at me and I pulled her into the air while I squeezed her tight.

"The face!" she said as she pulled away. "You made the face!"

"What face did I make?"

"The look of shock and awe. My favorite one."

I remembered when we'd been in the square and she'd

grabbed me by my arms when she'd mentioned she was excited for me to see the finished product. And here I was now, with her in my arms.

If only I'd known then.

"But while you're making the face I was waiting for, I still need to know what you think."

"I think it's incredible. Just like I knew it would be."

"For once, I agree. A lot of the time, I'm fixing something to simply fix it. But this felt . . ."

"Magical?" I asked.

"Yes. Just like the town slogan says." She pointed to the mural behind me. I turned and couldn't help but look at everything we had in this updated version of the town.

"It looks magical," I said. "And I haven't even seen the upstairs yet."

Her hand slid into mine. "Come on, I'll show you."

We walked up the stairs, and I was greeted with more books than I thought possible. It was quiet up here in the new space. I took a moment to enjoy the reprieve from the noise. "You got *everything*."

"Oh yeah, it'll take everyone a long time to make their way through these. Mollie said the original was endless. I tried to make it match."

I perused the shelves, looking at each genre that was available, but came to the end of the room sooner than expected. There once had been an unsafe overhang here. Now it was a white wall with a wooden door.

"Did you wall this off?"

"Yeah, I did." She pushed open a door to a meeting room. The lights were off, but when she flicked them on, I saw a couch, table, and chairs.

"A study room?" I asked. "I thought those were downstairs."

"They are," she replied. "These are quiet rooms." One of her hands traced the wall. "They're soundproof."

"Seriously?"

"Yeah. I knew this area was a little *too* big, but I got the idea while I was looking up things to help you. A lot of people struggle with things being too much. Now they have a safe space."

My eyes grew wide as she talked, and my heart skipped a beat. "You're incredible."

"It's what anyone would have done."

"No," I said, grabbing her hand. "Trust me, there aren't a lot of people who would put this much thought into something like this. You were planning to be here temporarily, and you could have done this quickly to get out of here to work on other things. But you didn't. It goes to show what kind of person you are."

"Thank you," she said. "It's still a little hard for me to accept compliments, but I'll get there."

"You will."

"Do you need some time to enjoy the quiet?" she asked. "I know the sea of people was a lot."

It was tempting to take her up on her offer, but I wanted to see it all. Shaking my head, I brought her in for a kiss, sliding my hands in her hair.

"Don't let this go too far," she whispered. "The cameras might have followed us."

"They didn't," I murmured into her mouth.

She pulled away, frowning. "Really? They didn't?"

Looking out into the main room, there were a few people who had made it upstairs, but no cameras.

"They could be interviewing Jude."

Wren's lips pursed. "I'm gonna go check."

"I'll come with you."

"Are you sure? I'll be fine on my own."

"I'm sure you will be, but I'm celebrating you today. There's no reason I can't go downstairs with you."

She eyed me, and while it *was* a lot, I was so happy for her that I didn't care. I grabbed her hand and tugged her out of the quiet room.

We headed downstairs into the fray again, but the cameras were gone. Wren checked all the corners while I looked out the open door.

I blinked when I saw an older version of Wren. She had flowing hair and was in a sundress and heavy makeup. Madison was with her, and she was getting a mic pack on.

All of the joy melted out of my body. There was *no* way they could have . . . *Why* would they have done *this* of all things?

"Shit," I muttered.

"What?" Wren asked as she walked up to me. The second she saw the woman, her whole body tensed.

"Please tell me that's not your mother."

Wren took in every inch of the woman. "That's exactly who it is." All of the excitement was gone from her face and her cheeks were turning a deep red. "I can't . . . I never thought I'd see her again. Why is she here? Is it for the show?"

"This might be the finale. Something to get people talking."

"No," she said. "*No,* they wouldn't."

The disbelief in her only added to my anger. This was her day to celebrate, to feel nothing but happiness after all the work she'd put into this.

"I think they would." My voice was low.

"I can't. I need to *think*. I need to get out of here."

"Go to the quiet rooms. Lock the door."

She nodded before darting off. I watched her go, wondering if I should follow. Noises were blending together. I was angrier than I had been in a long time. In any other situation, I would have cooled off. Walked away and thought it through.

But they were actively hurting Wren. That was just unacceptable.

I hadn't been in town yet when Cain had let his anger get the best of him, but when people told me about it, I had always wondered what could make someone lose their cool in such a way.

Now I knew.

"What the hell?" I asked as I stormed out of the library. "Her mother, really?"

A hand landed on my shoulder. "Come on, man. It's just—"

"Don't touch me, Jude." My voice was low and deeper than I'd usually let myself be. "This is what you people do, huh? Whatever's good for the cameras? If you knew a single thing about her, you'd know this is fucking unacceptable."

All the voices quieted down. In the back of my mind, I knew that I shouldn't do this so publicly. I didn't need the town to see me like this.

But *fuck* anything I was afraid of. Wren had run like her life depended on it. Whatever happened, I would deal with it later.

Madison rolled her eyes, unfazed. "We needed a good finale. When I did research on Wren, I saw that she never talked about her mother. What better way to end a show than to have Jude find her?"

Jude was going to take the credit for this? "What, so you could paint him as a caring boyfriend when he's never cared about her at all?"

"Hey, I care—" he tried to interject.

"What's her favorite color then?" I asked.

His face went blank.

"I thought so," I muttered. "You never cared to know *shit* about her. You never cared about anything. None of you have! Despite the fact that she worked her *ass* off, you'd make her face the woman who left her."

"That's an interesting way to refer to me," a smooth voice said. "But I suppose I can't complain too much. You seem to care about her very much. It's . . . interesting."

I slowly turned. She sounded like Wren but . . . wrong. Like she was colder. "It's easy to."

I didn't have anything to say to the woman who'd left her. I didn't care about her excuses or whatever she'd used to defend herself.

She gave me none of that. "You're not what I imagined for her."

"You'd have to know her to have a good idea of what's good for her."

"So defensive. How long have you known her again?" Wren's mom tilted her head. "Not as long as I have, that's for sure."

"Not as lo—lady, you haven't talked to her for *years*."

"I'm sure she told you some version of the truth."

The *gall* of this woman. I opened my mouth to give a sharp retort, but Madison interrupted.

"Does this really matter? Go get Wren."

"No," I said. "If you think I'm making her do this, you've lost your mind."

"Whatever," she muttered. "Hey! You! Old man, go get Wren!"

Hugh slowly turned, his face in a grimace. "I don't take orders from you!"

"All right, I'll get someone else. How about you?" She pointed to Atticus. "Can you get Wren?"

He crossed his arms. "I'm not a fan of forcing someone into a confrontation they aren't ready for."

"Oh, please. You don't even know her."

"I know *of* her. And I'm not a jerk." Atticus shook his head and walked off.

Madison found someone else. They turned her down too. After the fourth or fifth person, she stomped her foot. "What is with the people of this town!"

"Seems like you've hit a wall," I said. "Now, I'm gonna make sure Wren is *actually* okay. Then we'll figure out a plan." I turned to the rest of the town. "Make sure no one follows me."

Madison yelled my name as I walked away, but I didn't stop. Not until I saw Wren.

34

WREN

Strawberry Springs Neighborhood Watch

Jade Clark: God damn, I've never seen Henry so MAD.

Comments:
Marjorie Brown: I heard him from inside. What the hell happened?
Jade Clark: The show brought Wren's mom without asking her. Apparently they haven't talked in years.
Atticus Thompson: Absolutely deplorable behavior. They got what they deserved.
Jade Clark: Seriously. Henry needs to show that side of him more often. Maybe Hugh will take him seriously.
Kerry Winsor: I MISSED THE WHOLE THING? WHAT?! Is Wren okay?
Jade Clark: No idea. This is a freshly developing situation. Just low-key proud of Henry. He said what I was thinking.

THERE WAS a loud knock at the door. I ignored it, but when it happened again, I peered out.

"It's—" I froze when I saw Henry. "Hey."

"You okay?" His voice was tight, just like it had been when he'd been overwhelmed before and gone off on Jude.

My feelings crashed even more.

I opened the door to let him in.

"What the *hell* were they thinking?" he asked. "I mean, really, bringing your mother here?"

"Are you okay?"

He turned to me. "Am *I* okay? Who cares about me?"

"I do. You're so angry. I know you hate that."

"I'm angry because they hurt you." He ran a hand through his hair. "And they don't seem to fucking care that they did."

"Did you talk to them?"

"'Talk' isn't the word I would use."

Shit. He'd yelled? In front of the whole town? Wasn't that exactly what he'd been trying to avoid?

"Henry, you should—"

"No." He shook his head. "We're not talking about me. I wanna be sure *you're* okay. And if you need to leave, then we leave."

"But—"

"Wren, we need to handle this thing with your mother. Everything else can wait."

My heart lurched, but he wasn't wrong. I was hiding out like a coward when I had things to do.

"I'm mostly fine." At his narrowed eyes, I added, "I *am*. I'm honestly just shocked she's even here. At first, I thought she was an actress. I mean, she's avoided me for so long, why let it change now?"

Had she missed me? Did she have some explanation for not

ever reaching out? These were questions I didn't expect to ever have the answers to.

Until this moment.

"What are you feeling right now?"

There were too many things happening. My heart pounded. My chest was tight. Honestly, it felt like I was having a heart attack. I took a shaky breath, remembering how tense Henry was. I didn't want to add to anything.

"I'll survive once this is over."

"Wren, you don't have to do anything right now."

"I could get answers."

"Do you *need* them?"

My fists tightened. To anyone else, it should have been easy to write off Mom as a monster. And ninety percent of the time, I would agree. But she was *here*. And I needed to know if there was some other reason she left. Or if she regretted it.

I had a feeling Henry wouldn't like that answer.

I shrugged. "I still have to finish filming."

"You don't *have* to do anything."

"Henry, she's here." I shook my head. "I mean, I'm shocked, and I didn't know what to do, but at least I could get some answers after faking it for the camera."

"Are you convincing me, or yourself?" he asked.

"I have no idea," I replied, slumping my shoulders. "Honestly, this feels like a fever dream. And you seem tense."

"That's an understatement. I can't believe they would do this."

"Neither can I, but they did. They obviously had this planned out." I forced myself to move. "So, I'll deal with it, and hopefully figure out where the hell she's been for the last decade."

"And if this hurts you?"

"It won't be any worse than when she abandoned me." At

least I hoped it wouldn't. "The way I see it, once this is over, it's over."

"I hate this."

"I'll be fine," I said. "You stay here and calm down. I've got this."

His lips pressed into a thin line, and I brushed past him. My feet stilled as I got to the door and I thought about turning back, but I knew I needed this season to be over with.

I felt his heat at my back and I blinked. "What are you doing here, you—"

"Wren. You're not facing your mom alone."

Would she tell me the truth if Henry was there? I had no idea. I'd never considered the idea that she would ever meet him.

Turning back to Mom, I was able to take her in without shock running through me. She had barely aged in the many years since I'd seen her. She was like a doll version of me.

"Are we ready to film?" I asked before I could stop myself. Everyone's eyes turned to me. Most of the townspeople looked shocked, as if they didn't expect me to come out at all.

Mom turned, her eyes traveling up and down my frame. I saw her pause to consider me for a second, and tension shot up my spine.

Then she smiled. "I'm *so* ready," she said. "Look at you, all grown up!"

"Start filming!" Madison yelled and got out of the shot.

Mom walked up and hugged me. I wasn't sure if I returned it or not.

Had she just . . . complimented me?

"H-hi."

"Oh, it's been too long. You're as tall as your dad was!"

"Not all the way. I'm a few inches shorter."

"Still, you have his personality. It's one of my favorite things about you." Her hand touched my face. "I'm so glad Jude found me."

I blinked. *Jude* found her? There was no way. My eyes cut to him, and he was playing the same man who I'd almost thought liked me.

My stomach felt like the second of weightlessness on a roller coaster before plummeting down to earth.

"Um, thanks."

"Cut!" Madison called. "That's it. That's what we were looking for!"

Mom stepped away from me and Henry was at my back. "We should go," he said.

Going sounded like a great idea, but I turned to Mom, who was still looking at me.

"Actually, do you mind if we talk for a minute? It's nearly dinnertime, and I want to catch up with my little girl." Mom linked her arm through mine.

Henry only looked at me, and I saw an eyebrow raise with a silent question.

Is this what you want?

I knew that no matter my answer, he would help me through it. If I wanted to run, he'd drive the getaway car. If I wanted to stay, he would do that too.

"I think dinner is fine," I said. "There's a diner around here."

"I'll come too," Henry offered.

"But I haven't had one-on-one girl time in so long. Can we all talk later? I've wasted so much time here. I just want her all to myself for a few hours!"

She wanted *me* all to herself?

"Are you sure?" I asked.

She nodded. "Totally sure."

"Okay, then." I turned to Henry. "I guess I'll meet you at the house."

Henry's entire body was a rigid line, and I knew he needed to be home. He needed to recover from the surprise and anger he'd been feeling. I doubted he would admit it. He probably hadn't even realized what had happened yet. He would likely be devastated when he did.

"I'll ask one more time. Are you sure?"

Mom tried to cut in. "Of course she's—"

"I'd like to hear it from her."

Despite everything, my cheeks warmed. "I'm sure. Thank you for looking out for me."

"No problem, Wren." He placed a kiss on my cheek and then he was gone.

"So, the diner?" Mom asked.

I nodded and led her toward it.

"This is a quaint little town," she said.

"I like it." I tried to tamp down the instinctual feeling to defend myself. I hadn't known it would be there, but old habits died hard. Even when they were over a decade old.

"I'm sure you do." Mom opened the door to the diner. "The people seem to like you. They've been watching."

I wondered if Tammy had seen us walk in. Would she approve of this? She hated Mom.

I didn't get my answer right away. Tammy wasn't even at the front.

"Slow service," Mom muttered after we waited for a few minutes.

"I think we can just seat ourselves. Tammy's always busy."

I walked to a table before she could say anything else. I'd told Henry I would be fine, but every part of me screamed that I'd done something wrong.

Maybe Tammy would come out soon. She would know what to do.

"You know, I've followed the show since the beginning," Mom said.

"You have?"

"The second I saw the name, I knew I'd be watching." She smiled, but it didn't fill me with joy. Only fear. "Why did you not let them do something with . . . this?"

She gestured to all of me. Every single inch. I looked down. I was in work pants and my green T-shirt. It wasn't elegant, but it was me. "I didn't want them to."

Mom laughed. "Then I don't know how you got yourself into a love triangle. Unless all of it is fake, of course. I know about Jude. Madison told me it was for the cameras. But Henry?" She leaned forward. "There's just no way." There it was. The plummet to earth I was dreading.

"Did you bring me here to insult me?"

"I'm giving you some motherly advice."

I rolled my eyes. "Yeah, because you gave me a lot of that over the years."

"You're the one who acted miserable around me."

"You made me miserable!"

She rolled her eyes. "Sure, make it all my fault."

"You didn't even reach out."

"How was I supposed to know your number? You could have changed it!"

"I *never* changed my number. I was always waiting for you to call."

And I had been, whether I knew it or not. There was always a version of me, a little girl in overalls and pigtails, that waited for the mother I wanted to have.

Over time, I shut her away. I had thought she would never get her dream. Now I knew for sure.

Her eyebrows shot up. "You kept the number your dad got you in high school?"

"I did. Spam calls and all. And you never once tried to reach out. Not even on social media."

She shook her head. "I didn't come here to do this."

"Then why did you come here?" I asked. "Why do any of this?"

"Because I was hoping you wouldn't be the same stubborn girl who never did what I said!" she snapped. "And yet you are. You're wearing cargo pants!"

"They're practical."

"You're just like your father."

"And? Unlike you, he was there for me."

"And he died *alone*."

Rage made my spine go rigid. Had she really said that? "He had *me*."

"And who will you have, huh? Henry isn't gonna stay."

"How do you know that?"

"Because I heard about him. I heard he's a doctor who came to see you at the same time every day. How he swept you off your feet with little stolen moments, but he's *way* out of your league. He's the kind of man you *marry*, and no man would ever want this." She gestured to all of me again.

My rage turned into hurt. Here my mother was, sitting in front of me for the first time in over fifteen years, and she hated me all the same. "You're wrong."

"Am I? It'll start with resentment, Wren. How you mess up his schedule." Which I'd done. "How you never listen." He had to *order* me sometimes. "It might be cute now, but as the years pass, he'll hate you. He'll hate what you do. How you are. I know it'll happen, because it's what I did."

I didn't have an answer for her. I couldn't speak.

Suddenly, I would take Jude's comments. I would take them and be happy. I would take Madison's eye rolls. They were nothing compared to *this*.

"Save him the trouble, Wren. If you're so dedicated to being dusty from construction, constantly battling the kind of woman you *should* be, then you're not worth it." She stood, grabbed her purse, and left.

And *wow*, the second time was worse.

I looked down at my outfit. Should I have dressed up for the show today? Should I have let them do my makeup?

Should I have given in?

Henry would tell me no. Tammy would too.

I wanted to believe them. I'd spent years fighting back against that very thought. If it were anyone else, I would have told them to fuck off. I was who I was. But this wasn't just anyone. This was my *mom*.

For my entire life, there was never a question of changing myself.

And look where that had gotten me. Mom had *left*. What if I had changed? Would she have stayed?

I wanted to say she was wrong, but she wasn't entirely. She wasn't wrong about Henry. I *did* mess him up. I took him out of his comfort zone time and time again. Since I'd started staying with him, he'd been late to the clinic and kept putting off what he had to do, all because he was talking to me. Today he'd pushed himself past his breaking point.

All because I was throwing him off.

He didn't say that, but how long did I have until he did?

Tears gathered in my eyes, but I blinked them away. I looked up and saw Tammy walking out with a massive grin on her face.

"Wren!" she said. "I'm *so* happy to see you."

At least someone was. "Yeah?"

"I am. Not only did you open the library today, which I need to see, but you'll never guess who's here!"

"I have a few guesses," I said, thinking of Mom.

"Kelsey!"

A young woman appeared at her side. She was Tammy's height with brown hair and dyed tips and the same blue eyes.

Her daughter? The one she cared about?

Fuck.

"Wow," I managed to say. "It's nice to meet you."

"You too," Kelsey replied. "I can't believe I'm back, it's been too long. I'm even staying with Mom again."

"Long-term?" I asked.

"I'll be trying to find a job here." She slung an arm around Tammy, who leaned into it. "Mom's thrilled."

So, Tammy had her daughter back. Her real daughter.

She had no need for me anymore. Why would she? I was a temporary replacement for the real thing.

"That's so exciting," I said.

Tammy eyed me. "How did today go? Can I get you a drink, you look—"

"Actually, I have to get back. There are some final things to film." I stood and gave them what I hoped was a decent smile. "I'm so happy for you both."

The second I was out on the sidewalk, I broke out into a run. The crew was packing up, and I caught my break in the garden behind the library.

The irises had finished their bloom a long time ago, but I could remember Henry telling me to find them.

Only now, it hurt to think about. I needed a voice of reason. I pulled out my phone.

Are you free?

> Unfortunately, no. They didn't get the whole scan done, so I have to stay another night. Booooo! At least Mom drove out to take us to dinner.

I didn't answer. There was no need to. Mollie was busy with her family, the one she'd made. The one she'd never resent like mine did.

I wasn't sure when it happened, but my space in Strawberry Springs had been filled. Mollie had her baby to plan for. Tammy had her daughter.

And Henry? Henry had no room for me in the first place.

My phone buzzed with a reminder. I had twelve hours to get to my first meeting on the home renovation in Nashville.

I took a shaky breath. Once I was gone, they'd all forget about me. Mom certainly had.

But now I thought it might be better that way.

HENRY

Strawberry Springs Neighborhood Watch

Kerry Winsor: I think I speak for everyone when I say I am SO glad the filming is done. The extra attention was nice, but that lady Madison was kinda rude . . .

Comments:
Jade Clark: And so was Jude, while we're at it.
Kerry Winsor: Ugh. Never meet your heroes . . . except for Wren. She's staying, right?
Jade Clark: I sure hope so. But she's gotta be busy with the other stuff she did. You know her schedule is BOOKED.
Kerry Winsor: @Mollie Wilson, do you know anything?"
Mollie Wilson: I might, but I'm sworn to secrecy.
Kerry Winsor: UGH. Tell me!!!
Jade Clark: Nope. Best friend rules. She can't. (You can text me though, right?)

THE ANGER MADE me crash the second I got home, though I had my ringer on, waiting for Wren to either call or walk in the door and wake me up herself. I didn't even dream, though I woke up with an anxiety churning in my stomach that I couldn't place.

It had to be the fact that it was *daylight* and I must have slept through the night.

The bed was cold beside me, and the nightstand that I'd told Wren to use as her own was barren, except for one thing. A handwritten note. I immediately grabbed it, my entire body tensing.

I want to start this by saying how sorry I am. You've been going above and beyond for me since I got here, and I'm not sure I deserve that.

My meeting in Nashville is today. I know we said we would make it work long distance, but after the meeting, I'm going to stay here for a bit and give you a break from all of my chaos. Take that time to recover.

And when you don't miss me, you don't have to call.

I'll get the message.
Wren

I had to read the note multiple times. She was *staying* in Nashville? She thought I wouldn't miss her?

What the hell was going through her mind?

Reaching for my phone, I called her. She needed to know

she was wrong, and I needed to know what the hell would have made her think any of this in the first place.

But Wren didn't pick up. It didn't even ring.

I stood and ran my hands through my hair. My heart pounded. I needed to find her. I needed to go wherever she was. The only person who could have made her do something like this was her mother.

What had happened when they went to dinner together?

Tammy had to know. She was always watching Wren.

I didn't give myself a chance to get dressed. I needed to get Wren back.

Center Point was busy, and Tammy was running around taking orders. I was about to stop her when I saw the very woman who did this.

She didn't have the nerve to look guilty. She was on her phone, dressed up like she was having a day on the town.

I saw red.

"You," I said to Wren's mom. "What did you say to her?"

She blinked. "The boyfriend. Here you are again."

"Wren went to dinner with you last night and then disappeared with only a note. What did you say to her?"

"First of all, we never got dinner because there's no service in this town!"

"Hang on a second!" Tammy snapped. "Can you not see I'm busier than a hotel bed in a hoo—" She paused as she looked at the woman. "Wait, you're Wren's mom."

"I am. How did you know?"

"The Facebook group has a lot to say about you. I didn't think you'd be dumb enough to come into *my* diner."

"Oh, she's dumb enough to do a lot." I slammed the note on the table, and dimly, Tammy gasped.

"The group wasn't kidding," Tammy said. "Who are you, Dr. Connor?"

A spark of rational thought broke through my rage. I couldn't fully rein it in, but I lowered my voice. I'd have to worry about the damage I'd done later. Maybe I could bring Tammy flowers and ask her to forget what she saw.

"I'm the man who woke up to a note from Wren saying she *left*."

"She left a note that said *what?*"

Wren's mom read over the letter. "Well, she's bolder than I gave her credit for. Relax, I did you a favor."

"Did me a *favor?*" I hissed. "What the fuck is wrong with you?"

"Nothing's wrong with me. There's no one who knows Wren better than I do, and when I saw her on TV still like *that* —" She shuddered. "I was so disappointed. I thought I would surely get through to her, but obviously not. It was time to do my community service. When she said no, I told her what would happen. You would get tired. Everyone would, really. It's what I did."

"You . . . said . . . *what?*" I barely managed to get it out. My chest was in a vise. I was torn between yelling at a person like I never had in my *life* or running to tell Wren what bullshit that was.

"Can you not hear or something? God, what is with this place?"

"You think it's the town that has a problem? You're a fucking terrible mother—*no*, a terrible fucking person, and I pity anyone who has to spend time with you." My knuckles popped from the sheer pressure my clenched fists created.

An eerie silence settled over the diner, broken only by Tammy. "Get out."

"Excuse me?"

"You heard me." She jabbed her finger toward the woman's

face. "And you heard Henry too. I don't open my doors for lowlifes, and I never will."

"You know nothing about—"

"And none of us care to," I interrupted. "You may think you have some reason to do what you did, but it'll never be enough to justify all the shit you've put Wren through. You got to her once, but you'll never fucking do it again. Not while I'm around."

"Or me," Tammy added, arms folded tightly across her chest. "You wasted your chance with that girl and broke her soul. And now I hear you did it again? *Here?* You can take your little attitude, get out of my diner and our town, and go straight to hell."

"I never—" Wren's mom stood and nearly ran for the door.

"And you'll never again, because you sure ain't coming back here!" Tammy yelled as she left. "What a stupid fucking cu—"

"Don't say something you'll regret," I said. "Though I agree."

"You're not following your own rule." Tammy crossed her arms. "Why can't I call her what she is?"

"I'm . . ." The heat of the anger faded now that Wren's mother was gone. Had I really just cursed her out in front of Tammy? *Fuck.*

"Hang on, Doc." Tammy's hand landed on my shoulder. "We can't all have meltdowns right now. Someone has to go get Wren."

She was right. I *needed* her back. I *needed* her to know her mother was full of shit.

Everything else would have to be fixed later.

"Did you see Wren last night?"

"I did, but I was so excited that Kelsey was back that I didn't notice she was upset. Well, I did, but then she ran out before I could ask anything. I thought maybe it had been a long day for filming until I saw the Facebook group. When she didn't answer, I figured she was with you. Guess I should have hunted her down anyway. Dammit!"

"Mom?" a voice from behind Tammy asked. "What's going on?"

I turned to see a woman with brown hair and blue tips staring at us. I'd never met her before, but I knew of her through Tammy.

If Kelsey was back, then there was another reason Wren was upset. Tammy hadn't kept it a secret that Wren reminded her of Kelsey. If her daughter was back, then Wren wouldn't have wanted to overstep.

"Wren left," Tammy said.

Kelsey's eyes grew round. "What? But I just got here! The whole reason I came back was because I wanted to meet her."

"I have a feeling Wren didn't see it that way," I said. "I'm Henry, by the way."

"Her boyfriend?"

"Yep."

"How would she have seen it?" Tammy asked.

"Like you wouldn't have time for her."

"Fuck," Tammy groaned. "That's not . . . I would never! Have you called her?"

"She's not answering her phone."

"Then we go to her."

"I don't know where she lives in Nashville."

"Doesn't she have a best friend?" Kelsey asked. "You said her name was Mollie, right? We can call her and tell her what happened."

"But the diner—"

"I'll watch it," Kelsey said. "You two go."

"Are you sure, kid? It's busy."

"I've worked here before, and I was looking for a job." She

shrugged. "Might as well help out while you two go talk some sense into my new sister."

"Sister?" I asked.

"Mom's been talking about Wren since she got here. I knew I'd be welcoming someone into the family." Kelsey held out a hand to Tammy. "Give me your apron, Mom. I'm about to ruin Dad's whole day while you're in Nashville."

"Thanks," Tammy said. "I'll be sure she knows she's coming back. Henry, we're taking my car."

"I can drive."

"You strike me as a slow-ass driver. I'm not wasting any time." She dragged me out the door without another word.

I didn't have time to say that I wasn't going to waste a second either, but with the dangerous mix of emotions, I didn't need to be behind the wheel anyway. There was no way I could focus on the road when all I could think about was how awful Wren must be feeling.

And I knew I had to make sure she didn't stay that way for long.

Strawberry Springs Neighborhood Watch

Tammy Jane: If you see this woman, she is BANNED from the diner.

Comments:
Atticus Thompson: That's Wren's mom. I knew I had a bad feeling.
Henrietta Brown: Is Wren okay?
Jade Clark: I heard she's not, and that she left. I saw Henry at the diner. He went off on her as he should have, but it was intense. I can't imagine how he has to be feeling right now.
Kerry Winsor: No! I loved having her here! What kind of mother upsets her daughter that much???
Jade Clark: Maybe she didn't feel like a part of the town? I know she was so cool that I struggled to talk to her.
Kerry Winsor: And I only talked to her about the show. There must be something we can do so she knows how much we care!

THE HOUSE I was working on made me jump for joy when I saw it in pictures months ago. It was an old four-square design with white siding and black mulch. I could tell even then that the outside was original.

The inside was too. It should have been perfect.

But nothing felt perfect. In fact, everything felt . . . wrong.

Getting out of the car felt like a chore. Much like getting to Nashville had felt the evening before.

I'd had to fight myself every mile I drove. I didn't want to be back here, even for a house I thought I was excited to work on. I wanted to be with Henry and Mollie and everyone I'd met in Strawberry Springs.

But there was no room for me.

I kept my phone off, certain that Henry would call and try to convince me that he was fine. He always did that. He was fine until he wasn't. Just yesterday, he'd been pushing back on his own needs over and over. Just for me. I couldn't ask that of him, because I knew how it ended. One day, he'd wake up and resent it all.

It was easier this way. Cleaner.

And yet, it hurt so much.

The goal was to keep moving. To fix this house to feel better. I'd call some of the other people on my waitlist who had submitted interest forms and go from there. Eventually, fixing other things would lift this weight off my chest. It had to.

This would linger for a while. It always did, but I'd stay away until it was a dull ache. Until people forgot me, just like they always did. And when I was a warm memory, just a woman who had come through and done a nice thing, then I'd try to visit Mollie and no one else.

I was better from a distance.

Pushing all thoughts of Strawberry Springs out of my mind, I knocked on the faded red door. It would look great with a new paint job.

It swung open and a woman with shoulder-length brown hair was on the other side. She was followed closely by a taller man with lighter brown hair.

And *fuck*. Glasses.

Why did it have to be glasses?

"Hi," I said, holding out my hand to each of them. "I'm Wren."

"You're right on time!" the woman said. "I'm Violet, and this is Charlie. Thank you so much for seeing us."

"I know you're busy," Charlie added.

"I like being busy," I replied, even though the words tasted sour in my mouth. I'd also liked the peace I'd found with . . . *No.* I wasn't going there.

"Come on in," Charlie said. "We'll show you around."

The house looked just as it did in the photos, with metal cabinets and wood tones everywhere. When I'd seen it, I wanted to brighten it up. Most of it could be updated, but I'd keep the small things in place. Like the trim, the original floors, the color scheme.

But this felt like a *home*.

Usually, I'd jump out the gate. I'd tell them what I saw their space looking like, how I could preserve history, but make it modern.

This time? I had nothing.

"This is a beautiful space," I started. "Tell me again, what all are you wanting? It's okay if it changed in the last few months."

Charlie and Violet looked at each other. They must have had a lot of talks about this in between then and now.

"We're still thinking about having kids," Charlie said. "And I want this to be more . . . modern. Kid friendly. It has old wiring, and a lot of sharp edges. I mean, the stairs alone are a tripping hazard."

"No offense, but I've been trying to convince him to tell you we didn't need much of anything," Violet added. "This is his family's house, so it means a lot to him, but he insists we need to upgrade things. But he says he's fine with a complete renovation and you keeping the small bits of charm that you usually do."

Charlie looked over the space as he crossed his arms. He trailed over every detail. He must have looked at it a million times. Violet watched every moment as if she *knew* he wasn't ready for all of this.

I could relate to that feeling.

"My best friend is having a baby too," I said. "Another family home. Passed down for generations."

"Did she upgrade it to make it safer?" Charlie asked.

"Not a thing. In fact, she told me not to."

Charlie's eyebrows raised. "But with a kid, it has to be . . . something. I wouldn't be a good dad if I didn't consider it."

"He has daddy issues from abandonment. We both do, actually."

I blinked. For the first time, I felt a smile trying to creep onto my face. She reminded me of Mollie.

Then the crushing guilt came back. Was she trying to call me too?

"Violet," Charlie said with a sigh. "Really? We talked about keeping that to ourselves."

"Hey, I'm just letting her know what she's getting into."

"It's fine," I said. "What's a little parental-abandonment talk between strangers? I get where you're coming from. You want to be better."

"I do," he said. "And I feel like I *have* to do this."

"Even if he doesn't want to," Violet added.

"You know, you would be doing a lot better than a lot of

parents if you're just *there*," I said. "You don't have anything to prove other than that."

"I'll be here every step of the way," Charlie said. "I know that, I just—we saved up for this. We *can* do it. We can give them a house they'll love."

"But will *you* love it?" I asked. "Because if not, if you'll miss this, then it's not worth it."

"Wow," Violet said. "You're taking the words right out of my mouth."

"When I was staying with my best friend and"—I paused, thinking of Henry—"someone else, it made me rethink what I feel like a home is. It's the people, not the aesthetics."

"See?" Violet said. "Now you have even more people on your side."

Charlie's shoulders slumped. "It must be obvious if even professionals see it that way. Even if we don't update the wood, it still needs work."

I eyed the house. "Yeah, I could see that. The wiring is old. Radiant heat could be swapped for a central system, but we don't have to touch anything cosmetically."

"Isn't that your favorite part, though?" Violet asked.

"I like fixing things," I confirmed. "I think it needs love. And I'll go out on a limb and say it has that."

"She's good," Violet said to Charlie. "And I can—"

"You're not working on wiring," he interrupted. "That one's too risky for you. Anything else, sure, but not that."

"You work on the house?" I asked.

"I used to live in awful apartments, so I did the work myself. And now I do it here. Though, some things are above my pay grade." She eyed me. "And maybe below yours? You're *so* busy."

I needed to be, but what they needed mattered more. "I work with some people who can get the work done. I can do a lot, but I'm not certified to rewire a whole house. I do know a guy who does great work."

After I'd given them the phone numbers they needed, I went back to my apartment. I'd done the right thing, and I knew I had. But now I had nothing to fix.

And I needed to find something.

Usually, my motivation was always there, but this time, I was scraping the bottom of the barrel. I didn't want to fix things. I wanted to be in a *home*. Something that felt like what Violet and Charlie had.

All my life, I'd made homes for other people, but I never had a home of my own that felt like *mine*. The trailer I grew up in, the nice house I wish Mom had accepted me in, and the apartment I'd decorated myself—they were just places to sleep.

Home was with Henry. With Mollie. With Tammy.

And I'd left it behind.

When I shut the door to my apartment, all the emotions I was trying to run from hit me. I missed it. So much more than I could ever say. It was so easy for people to leave me, but it was much harder for me to leave them.

Did that make me weak?

Or should I have taken advantage of every second I could in Strawberry Springs?

It didn't matter. Henry would have been through his day by now. I bet he'd realized how far he'd pushed himself the day before. He was probably recovering and barely thinking about me. Mollie had to be excited about her scan and all that came with a new baby. And Tammy had Kelsey.

None of those facts helped. They only made me feel worse. I collapsed on the couch and felt like I was somewhere else, somewhere I didn't belong.

Tears leaked out of my eyes, and I knew I couldn't go back.

I'd started them on the path, and they would continue on until I was nothing in their minds.

A knock on the door brought me out of my misery. I wiped at my face, hoping for once that my red eyes didn't give me away.

Oh well. The only people who'd ever come to my door were salespeople for security systems. They deserved to feel bad for interrupting my misery.

To my surprise, it was Henry and Tammy.

I blinked. Had I finally lost it? Was I hallucinating now?

Tammy was in her usual work outfit, complete with a name tag that read "Dolly." Henry, on the other hand, looked like he had just rolled out of bed. He *never* left the house looking like that.

Guilt hit me. What was he doing? What were they *both* doing here?

"Hi," Tammy said. "Surprised?"

That was an understatement. I went to say just that when Henry pulled me into a hug.

"Never do that again."

Why was I getting hugged? Shouldn't he be taking his break from me? Shouldn't he have seen what he'd done?

"Why are you two here?"

Tammy scoffed. "To talk some sense into you. Obviously you need it after what that demon spawn of a woman said."

"She's wrong," Henry said near my ear. "She's so wrong."

"I—she's not, though. I've completely messed up your sched-ule. You've pushed yourself too far for me, and I'm not worth that." Henry's arms tightened at my words.

"Wren—" he began, but I wasn't done.

"Tammy also has her daughter back! She doesn't need me anymore. Neither of you need me." Henry pulled away, his eyes as wide as Tammy's. Neither of them knew what to say, so I continued. "Over time, you'll forget me." My throat felt tight as I said the words, but I *had* to get them out. "Go back home, I'll be fine."

"That is the biggest pile of bullshit I've ever heard in my life." The words sounded like they were from Tammy, but they were from *Henry*.

Now it was my turn to be shocked. "But—"

"Wren." His hands were tight on my shoulders. "I know your mother played on your fears, and I know it brought back thoughts you used to have, but you have to know deep down that this isn't true."

It was hard not to believe him when he was in front of me. Here he was, in *Nashville* with Tammy. They'd driven three hours after I left. They hadn't forgotten about me at all.

"I *want* to," I struggled to say, but emotions were bubbling up. Ones I couldn't ignore. "But I can't do this again. I can't care about someone and have them leave me when they're done. And I care about you *both*. Too much. If I stayed and then you were done with me, I don't know if I could handle it."

"We're not going anywhere," Henry said.

"But I messed you up. So many times. I'm not *for* you. You deserve someone who's more feminine, who's willing to—"

"Be what your mother wants?" he asked. "That's not what *I* want, Wren."

"You're perfect the way you are." Tammy's voice was softer than I'd ever heard it. "I'll tell you that every day if you come home."

"But you have Kelsey now, you don't need—"

"It's not you or her. Besides, she came back to meet you."

"Why would she wanna meet me?"

"Wren," Henry added. "Who wouldn't? You brought back the library—"

"I'm not worth it," I said desperately. "Guys, if I wasn't worth it to my own mother, then why would you care?"

"She said you weren't . . ." Henry's eyes were wide.

"What the hell did she mean by that?"

"I don't know, that I wasn't worth her trying? That I wasn't worth anything? At this point, it all feels the same. And I must have done this somehow. She *wanted* me at one point, and then she didn't."

"Wren," Tammy said, getting into my line of sight. "When we talked outside of the library, I told you what I thought of her. What did I say?"

I closed my eyes and thought back to it. "You said it was . . . her problem."

"And it's her problem now," she said. "She's the unfit parent. You're not unfit to be loved."

I knew that. I did. But I was *so scared*. Scared of feeling like I had when she said all of this to me. Scared of being someone's regret. Scared of giving it my all and it not being enough.

"Wren. Are you happy being back?" he asked. "If *you* need space, say the word and we'll leave."

"I didn't agree to that," Tammy said.

"But if it's what she wants, she can have it."

That was the Henry I knew. His voice was finally back. Was he okay?

I needed to know what had happened. I needed to know how he felt about all of this.

Tammy looked at me. "Is that what you need? Do you need time to think?"

I'd had time to think, and the whole time, I was thinking of them. What Mom had said shook me to my core. It made me rethink everything I'd grown out of.

And I'd run.

They'd followed.

"I . . . don't want space."

"Thank God," Tammy said.

Even Henry's shoulders slumped in relief. "Okay," he replied. "I'll stay here with you until you're done with what you're working on."

"What? No. You have things to do."

"My choice, remember? I know your mom didn't choose you, but we do. And we will."

"Why?"

"It's what you do when you love someone."

"Real love," Tammy added. "Not whatever the hell your mother says she does."

My body was warm, something I didn't think was possible with how awful things had been.

"You don't need to stay," I began.

"Wren, let me help." The tension was back in his voice, and I rushed to explain what had happened.

"You don't need to stay because I canceled my project."

Both of their eyes widened.

"But you said you were excited to work on it."

"I was . . . a while ago. But today I went to see a house that I could have easily turned into something different. But they didn't want that . . . and neither did I. I thought I could fix something and feel like myself. Now I just wanna be home."

"Sounds like you did the right thing," Henry said softly. "And we'll get you home."

"And to be clear, you're stuck with us." Tammy pointed at me. "If you run off again, we *will* find you."

"I think I've learned my lesson." And I had. I'd left to try to protect myself, but I didn't need protection. I had everything I needed back in Strawberry Springs.

Back *home*.

HENRY

Strawberry Springs Neighborhood Watch

Kelsey Rose: Who tattled on me buying beer last night to my mom? I'm NEARLY THIRTY! I CAN DO WHAT I WANT!

Comments:
Tammy Jane: You bought the worst beer known to man. It was a public service for someone to tell me!
Kelsey Rose: You're driving to Nashville. WHY ARE YOU ON YOUR PHONE?
Tammy Jane: Ever heard of stopping for gas?
Kerry Winsor: Is she really that old? It feels like yesterday she was trying cheerleading and broke her arm.
Kelsey Rose: WHY would you bring that up? Everyone had forgotten.
Tammy Jane: Sorry, kid. No one forgets things here.

WREN WAS quiet on the drive to Strawberry Springs. I'd ridden with her in the truck to make sure she wasn't alone while Tammy took her car. We'd pulled into the diner three hours later in order to finish all of our conversations. Now that she was back, so was my rational thought.

I had a *lot* of people to apologize to. A lot of people who I'd have to look in the eye and find some sort of explanation for how I'd acted. Most of the town had seen me lose it both in the diner and in front of the cameras. I didn't regret standing up for Wren, but I knew there would be consequences for this.

Wren's hand squeezed mine as she put the truck in park.

"You okay?" she asked.

"I'm . . ." *Fine* wasn't right. No words were.

"It's hitting you, isn't it?" she asked.

She knew me too well. Better than I knew myself, even. I nodded, knowing I couldn't say much more since Tammy had pulled up next to us and gestured for us to get out.

"You good?" Tammy asked as she looked at me. "I told you two to use the bathroom before we left but did you listen? No."

"Not that," Wren said. "It's—"

"I'm sorry," I said as I gathered what courage I had. "I shouldn't have acted like I did in the diner."

"You mean when you called Wren's mom dumb to her face?"

Wren's eyes went wide, but she didn't say anything. I knew this was what I had to do. "Yeah. That."

Tammy let out a snort. "Like I care. She had it coming!"

"Still. I try to be better than that. That's not the best version of myself."

"Kid, your girlfriend left you after having a bomb dropped on her. No one expects the best side of you after that."

"But yesterday—"

"Yeah, that was justified too."

"I highly doubt the town saw it that way."

"It's fine," Wren added. "We can smooth it over."

"There's nothing to smooth over. Here." She pulled out her phone and tapped on the screen as she pulled something up. Then she handed it to me.

"What's this?" I asked.

"The Facebook group. They're talking about you."

Wren got close to me and peered over my shoulder.

I started to read, my stomach sinking. But then I saw what they'd all said.

And not one thing was negative.

"You people have to give us some credit," Tammy said when I was done. "We might post some dumb shit on there, but we aren't gonna expect everyone to be perfect. We take everyone as they are. Henry, you're a part of us, at your worst *and* your best."

I numbly handed the phone back to Tammy. I wasn't sure what I felt. Relief? Joy? Gratefulness?

Maybe it was all of it.

"T-thank you," I said. "You have no idea how much it helps to hear that."

"You've really been going around thinking we would judge you? Good lord, we've seen Hugh's whole ass!"

"I prefer *not* to think of that."

"Oh *God*," Wren said. "Seriously?"

"Yep. Last year. It was both hilarious and scarring. Henry, you're good. Whether you're crashing up or being the nice doctor we know and love."

"Crashing up?" I asked.

"Do you mean crashing *out*?" Wren asked.

"Is that the phrase? Kelsey used it last night to describe the state of her finances." She shrugged. "Crashing up would be better, though."

I laughed. I was finally able to name the emotion I felt. It made a smile break out onto my face. It made my chest light, and everything seem brighter.

It was love. Love for Wren. For Strawberry Springs. All along, I didn't think I would be accepted for who I was, and yet I had been this whole time.

"Henry wasn't the only one," Tammy told Wren. "I lost it too. Half the town *wanted* to, but Henry and I had it covered. Your egg donor is fucking *banned* from the town."

"Egg donor?" she asked.

"She ain't your mother. That's for sure."

"I suppose that's true." Wren's voice was quiet again. "I underestimated how good she is at making me feel like I'm not good enough." She looked out into the distance, and I wondered if her mom's words were playing on a loop in her mind.

"I hate that I wasn't there," I said.

"You needed rest after that," she replied. "And you can't deny it."

"You're right." I'd pushed myself and it had blown up in my face.

"This is where *I* come in," Tammy interjected. "Or Mollie. Or anyone. You have a lot of people who care about you, kid."

It hit me then. I could have worked with Tammy to make sure Wren was okay. If anything like this ever happened again, though I hoped to God it wouldn't, I could rely on the group of people around me. It didn't have to be all me.

Wren had a community, myself included. And together, we could handle everything.

Wren's eyes were watery, but she nodded. "You're right. I'm sorry. I shouldn't have faced her alone. She got really mean when I did."

"What did she say?" Tammy's voice was tight again.

"That I should have changed the way I dressed. I shouldn't, right?"

Tammy's hands tightened into fists.

My hands did the same. "No." The words were firm.

"And you won't hate me when I don't do what I'm supposed to do?"

"Did your egg donor say that to you?" Tammy asked.

"Yes. She did. She said I was too stubborn and should've let the show change my style."

"Fuck the show." The words didn't come from Tammy. They came from me.

"Is that another curse word from our resident doctor?"

"I do it from time to time," I replied.

"Well, you took the words right outta my mouth," Tammy replied. "Both before and now."

Wren sighed. "Madison already reached out to do a third season to conclude Jude's and my story. I haven't answered."

"And you shouldn't," Tammy said.

"No, definitely not. They didn't respect you."

"I know they didn't. And I wasn't going to anyway, but when Mom said all of that, it just opened me up. Just like Jude did the first time. Especially when she said I wasn't someone you'd want to . . ." She trailed off, cheeks going pink. "Never mind."

"Want to what?" I pressed.

"Want to marry me." The words were nearly whispered.

I had to force myself to look away. Not *wife* material? I'd share everything I had with her. I'd marry her any day, any time. She was more than just wife material, she was going to be my wife eventually. There was no one else for me.

"Do either of you know how to get away with murder?" Tammy asked. "I might need to soon."

"Wren, there isn't one way to be a wife, if that's what you want," I said, trying to make sure I was being there for her rather than focusing on my rage. "Your mother—"

"Egg donor," Tammy interrupted.

"Sorry, egg donor, has a narrow view on life. So narrow she couldn't see past it to be happy for all you've accomplished. You don't need to fit in with her. Or anyone else. You can do exactly what you want to."

"Deep down, I know. I just feel like that kid again, being judged by her."

"It won't happen again," Tammy said. "I promise."

"I'm sorry they had her come in," I said.

"And to think I really thought she was being nice." She sighed. "I should have known."

"You gave her a chance and *she* let you down," Tammy said. "That's on her."

Wren did the last thing I expected. She burst into tears.

"I'm *so* sorry for leaving. I should have tried to talk it out with you both, but I really thought—I let her get to me."

I pulled Wren in for a hug and Tammy joined in.

"It's okay, kid." It was the softest she'd sounded all day. "We all make mistakes, and we all learn from them."

"I'm so happy to be here. I hated being away."

"Then I'm glad we came to get you," I said as I pressed a kiss to her head. "We'd both do that and more."

Shortly after we finished our conversation, Mollie called and begged us to come to the farm. She had so many curse words for Wren's mom that Cain had to cover Eric's ears. Once she was done going off, both of them were crying again. Mollie hated that she'd been out of town when it happened, and Wren regretted not speaking up more.

In the end, Mollie made it clear she would be there for

Wren at any time, and Wren promised to tell her when something had happened.

It was late in the evening before we got back to my house. Wren showered and laid in the bed next to me. She was quiet, but I was happy she was here and in my arms. Things were right when she was here.

"Any time you need to be reminded how out of my league you are," I said, "tell me."

"I will," she said. "But since we got back, I feel . . . better. Like I'm not drowning in my own self-pity."

"It's what happens when you're around the right kind of people. The ones who build you up and not tear you down."

"You're right. Just like you usually are." Her arms tightened around me. "I just need my brain to stop talking sometimes."

"You do."

"At this point, just tie me down and make me forget everything." She burrowed deeper. "I'd probably do it if you told me to."

I had no idea if she meant it, but I could picture it. The first time we'd been together, I mentioned the very idea.

Even now, with all the stress of the day, it injected my body with liquid heat.

"Henry?" she asked. "Did I say something wrong?"

"No," I replied. "We can talk about it later."

Wren lifted herself up on her elbow, her hair falling down her back. "No, not later. Now. You know I'll worry about it."

"You said nothing bad." I pressed my lips to hers. "I was thinking of something else and got lost in thought."

She raised an eyebrow. "Care to share?"

"It was about me tying you up. And making you forget everything else."

Now Wren's eyes were wide. "Really? Even after today?"

"Yes, but this isn't the time for that. You need rest—"

"Fuck that. Are you being serious?"

"I don't joke about what I wanna do to you." My voice grew huskier, and I ran my hand up and down her back. "And this is included."

Wren's eyes met mine for all of one second before she was off the bed. I blinked, wondering what she was doing.

Then she threw my ties at me.

"Why are you going through my closet?" I asked.

"Because you have so many things we can use." She pulled out a red one. "Think this one is good for my arms?"

"You want to—*now*?"

"I want my brain to shut off, and you can make me do whatever you want." She turned to me. "You've earned it after coming after me."

Jesus.

This woman. She was going to kill me.

I wrestled with it for half a second as I gazed at her, trying to see if there was any hint of doubt in her voice. But her eyes were steady. Hopeful, even.

"Get on the bed," I said.

Wren wasted no time.

I'd never been happier that I'd chosen a metal bed frame. I wrapped the red tie around her wrists before attaching it to the headboard. When I was done, she was already breathing heavy.

"Still want this?"

"I didn't say the safe word," she whispered. "I'm just so *excited.*"

I huffed out a laugh before kissing her cheek and moving down to her legs. I left them splayed open as I used the other ties she'd grabbed and attached them to the frame.

Wren tugged on them lightly. "I really can't move."

"Good," I said. "Now I can do what I want."

Her breath hitched as I kissed a freckle on her shoulder

before covering her mouth with mine. I'd missed her even though we'd been apart for only one night, and all I wanted was for her to be unable to run. She was stuck with me in more ways than one.

Wren was already writhing, trying to angle her hips up. It was fruitless.

There was no rush. We had forever together. Despite what she thought, there was no growing tired of her. No future where I'd waste this chance she was giving me. I had her. I wasn't losing her. And I'd chase her to the ends of the earth to prove that.

Or tie her up and *show* her exactly how much I wanted her.

"You're gonna go slow, aren't you?" she asked when I pulled away.

I only nodded.

"*Fuck.*" She tried to get out of her restraints. "I don't know if I can wait."

"You will," I whispered into the place where her jaw and neck met. Then I bit down.

Wren let out a moan, going slack for a second. I moved onto the next freckle, giving it a gentle kiss before scraping her delicate skin with my teeth.

She was out of breath by the time I got to her breasts. I tugged up her T-shirt, watching as her peaks hardened in the cool air. I straddled her to keep her down before covering them with my mouth.

"*Christ,*" she muttered. "I can't . . . I need . . ."

"I know what you need. And you'll have to wait."

"Henry, I—*fuck.*"

Whatever she was thinking was cut off as my teeth lightly grazed her nipple. Her body tensed and her mouth fell open in pleasure.

She was quiet as I moved downward. I nipped at different parts of her on the way, stopping at her hips.

Wren had only come to bed in a T-shirt and her underwear after her shower. At the time, I didn't dream of suggesting this after the day she'd had. Now I was glad for one less layer to remove. With both of her feet bound, there was only one way to remove the last barrier between me and what I wanted so badly. I gripped the side of her panties and ripped the seam apart in one smooth motion.

She gasped. "Henry!" Her entire body flushed despite the sharp edge to her voice. "I liked that pair."

"I'll buy you more." My finger teased her pussy everywhere except where I knew she wanted me. "You're soaked for me, aren't you?"

"Yes," she whispered. "I need you. *Please.*"

My mouth watered at the thought of tasting her. I had great self-control, but I couldn't wait forever. I brought my mouth down onto her wet pussy, fucking her with my tongue.

"Yes," she said, bucking her hips against my mouth. "Just like that."

I spent time on her core and then moved up to her clit. After I circled it with my tongue, I went back down to her opening, making sure to give them both attention. She was whining on the bed, hands still bound by my tie. I kept her on the verge of coming by moving back and forth, and I could tell she was growing desperate.

"Please," she said. "I need to—"

"You can handle a little more."

"I *can't.*"

"Let me decide that."

She gasped as I took a break to admire the way she was laid out for me. Her body was tinted pink, highlighting every single one of her freckles.

Fuck it. I needed her to come.

I renewed my movements, focusing my mouth on her clit and pressing one finger inside of her. She jerked her hips as she muttered my name.

I felt it all when she came. The way she shuddered. The way she tightened on my fingers.

And I knew I couldn't wait any longer.

Taking off my shirt, I reached for a condom.

"Finally," she said.

I knelt between her legs once more as I slowly worked my way in. It had only been a few days since I'd fucked her, but every time felt like the first. Otherworldly and perfect.

Wren gasped for breath when I was fully seated inside of her. The heat of her pussy alone was almost too much, but I also had to contend with the fact that she was completely under my control.

She was always gorgeous, but the sight of her tied up for me, tugging at her restraints while I made my way inside of her, was too much. I bit the side of my cheek to keep from coming.

For a moment, I stayed still, reveling in the way we were joined. All I could feel was her, both underneath me and wrapped around my cock.

Then I felt her tighten around me.

"H-Henry," she begged. "Please. I'm begging you to move."

My mouth covered hers before I pushed deeper into her. I felt her sharp intake of air as I pulled all the way out and plunged inside again.

Normally, she would wrap her perfect legs around me and make me stay close to her, but this time, she couldn't. She was completely at my mercy.

I wanted this to last forever, but this was too good. Watching her continue to tug at her restraints, and the way she moaned my name as I fucked her, pushed me to the edge. I wanted to hold out and make this go on for longer. But I also wanted to come, and the very next night, I'd tie her up and make her do it all again.

We had forever, after all.

My thrusts were erratic and she must have already been at the edge. She arched into me and I felt every part of her tighten as she came once more.

And that did it for me too. Heat exploded from my cock, spilling into the condom as I pressed into her one last time.

It took both of us a long time to catch our breath.

"What was I thinking, giving this up?" she asked.

"There was no way I'd let you," I said as I caught my breath. "You're too perfect."

"And so are you." She smiled up at me. I had her here with me, in my arms and in my life.

And I'd never let her go.

Wren broke out into a massive yawn right after.

"Tired?"

"Yes," she said, shaking her head. "Actually, I don't think I've ever been this tired in my life."

I rubbed up and down her arms. "Let's see. You fixed up a mansion. Stressed for the one week you had off before starting on a whole library, and then had to deal with your awful mother and the subsequent emotional release that caused. Did I miss anything?"

"I also tried to go immediately back into work."

"You should rest."

"I don't know if this is the kind of tired one night of sleep can fix."

"Then take as long as you need."

I expected her to fight me on it, but she yawned once more and said, "You know what? I think I will."

WREN

RWL Superfan Discussion Central

Carly Ware: The season two finale is OUT! What are your thoughts?

Comments:

Alicia Parrish: The library looked SO good, though I was shocked by her mom coming back. That felt a little weird.

Kerry Winsor: It was weird, actually. Wren wasn't made aware and it actually was really bad for her.

Alicia Parrish: Really? That's terrible.

Jamie McCullough: I don't believe baseless rumors. Jude and Wren are meant to be together.

Kerry Winsor: You know what? I joined this group to talk about the show, but you guys only care about the spectacle. Wren is a real person and deserves more than this. I'm happy there won't be a season three!

Neve Bullock: NO SEASON THREE? HOW DO YOU KNOW THAT?!

Jamie McCullough: YOU HAVE TO BE KIDDING ME!!

I finally got my week off from working, even if it took me finishing up season two to get it.

Instead of searching for my next project, I barely left the house. The fixing up, running, and then being chased by Henry unlocked an exhaustion that I'd never felt before, and for the first time in my life, I did *nothing*.

Technically, I did Henry. But that was beside the point.

He'd needed the recovery too. After his meltdown, he'd closed the clinic and posted in the group that he needed a break. The outpouring of support had made him tear up.

Still, he recovered faster than I did. When Wednesday came around, he was ready to get back to his routine, though he told me multiple times to take as much time as I needed.

By the seventh day, I was feeling more like myself. Who knew eating three square meals a day, getting eight hours of sleep, and having an actual routine could make a huge difference?

Not me.

Mollie and Tammy checked in. Kelsey had already friend-requested me on Facebook and sent a long message about how she wasn't here to take her mom from me and how she was super excited to get to know me. I'd promised to make an effort once I felt up to it, but for the longest time, I was happy to stay in my pajamas and sleep whenever I needed to.

Until today.

Usually, Henry would be coming inside from watering all the plants. When I came downstairs, I expected him to be in the kitchen, but he was nowhere to be found.

I went out the back door. The smell of blooming late-summer flowers hit me the second I went outside, and I heard voices near the back fence.

"So, with that, I think we could rely on pansies and violas for the pots. But vary the color to brighten up the space, you know?"

"That's what I usually do, though the pansies are easier to find. Everyone goes for those."

Henry was talking to Kerry. His hands were in his pockets, and he was nodding along to what she was saying. She had been coming by to talk about all the plans she had for the square ever since she found out he was the one taking care of it.

"Well I don't wanna do what *everyone* does. What do you think of a native flower?"

"I'm always interested in that."

"Oh, Wren!" Kerry's face broke out into a smile when she saw me. "I haven't seen you in forever!"

Henry whirled around, blinking when he saw me.

"You're dressed."

Kerry gasped. "What does *that* mean?"

Henry's eyes went wide. "Oh, *no*. I-I meant—"

"I spent the week in pajamas," I explained with a laugh. "Though now, it's time for my being a recluse to come to an end."

"We've all missed you!" Kerry said. "Henry's been very clear about letting you rest."

"I appreciate it." I put a hand on Henry's shoulder. "And I don't mean to cut the flower talk short, but if this one doesn't get breakfast soon, he'll be thrown off."

"No problem," Kerry said with a wave. "I now have to find native plants that are good in pots."

"I have a few ideas," Henry began. "You could just—"

"No, no. I wanna learn! It gives me something to do. I'll catch you tomorrow." She waved and walked back toward the square.

"You're gonna have to add chatting with her to the schedule," I said.

"I think so," he replied. "But she's excited. And it's nice to have someone to talk to about the square. Even if she's the one doing most of the talking."

"I'll also help," I replied. "I'm back in business now."

Henry grabbed my hand and led me inside. "Please tell me it's because you want to and not because of anyone else."

"I want to," I said. "I miss my work pants. And seeing the sky. Plus, I wanna meet Kelsey when I'm not having a mental breakdown. She's been waiting patiently."

"Sounds like a plan," he said. "Are you heading to the diner now?"

"I think so. You should do your usual, but I'll grab something there."

He checked his watch. "You know, I was thinking that we should have a day where we usually go. You and I can check in with Tammy and Kelsey. It's a Monday, so it shouldn't be too busy."

"It's been a week, and you're wanting to change the routine?"

"Update it a little," he corrected. "I'm always open to good changes. And Tammy's been calling the clinic line and checking in."

"Does she not have your number?"

"She does. She thinks it's fun that my office has a landline."

"That sounds like her." I laughed. "Should we head out now?"

"We have time," Henry said, holding out his hand.

The weather was finally cooling as fall rolled in, though the heat would linger for longer than anyone would have liked. Henry had been busy updating the annual plants in the pots at the square, something I wanted to help him with as time went on. Some of the leaves on the trees were starting to change, promising beautiful hues in the coming weeks.

Before, I didn't stop to notice the season changes. This year, I would.

"Finally!" Tammy said when we walked in. "She's outta the house! This has made my day." Henry cleared his throat and Tammy's eyes widened. "I mean, I'm happy you got the break you needed."

"It's okay," I said. "I don't feel bad for lounging for a week. No matter what anyone says."

"That's my girl," she said as she pulled me into a hug. "Are you two stopping in for breakfast? I have a new omelet topping for you, Wren."

"What is it?"

"Love." Her smile was as wide as it had been on camera.

I blinked. "Really?"

"No, it's olives. Did I get you?"

"I'm sure love *does* go into your food, but I'm not used to you being so . . . sweet."

She sighed. "Kelsey told me I should be sweet as well as snarky. I'm trying." She waved her hand.

I would take her any way she wanted to be. "Where is Kelsey, by the way?"

A distant, muffled scream echoed through the diner.

Tammy winced. "She's having a moment in the cooler. She must still believe that the cooler's soundproof. Ron used to tell her that as a joke."

"Is she dying in there?" Henry asked with horror.

"No. She gave Hugh the wrong order, and he said she should dye her hair blonde to match her brains. I told her to let out her frustration at that in the back and not at him. Usually, I find a towel to scream into. She must have needed more than that."

I looked for Hugh. He'd been at the opening for the library, but I hadn't met him directly yet.

He was in a corner, grumbling under his breath. He angrily sipped his coffee before catching me looking. I gave a wave, but his eyes cut to Henry.

"It's decaf, Doc!"

"It's not," Tammy said under her breath.

"Do I give him this?" Henry muttered. "Or do I tell him he has to take his health seriously?"

"If you wanna open that can of worms, be my guest." Tammy shrugged. "He's already in a bad mood, so I bet he'd be real fun today."

"On second thought," Henry said before nodding at Hugh, "have a great breakfast."

Hugh nodded and went back to his grumbling.

"Want the corner table?" Tammy asked. "Seems to be your favorite."

"I'd love that one," Henry said.

"It can be your usual." She led us over to our table. "Though, you'll have to make a habit of coming in."

"We plan on it," I said.

Henry was the picture of ease, and so was I. This was the complete opposite of how things had felt when I'd gotten here.

"I'm gonna let Kelsey take care of you," Tammy said. "Please be gentle. She's trying her best. After I make sure Hugh isn't still pissy about the order mix-up, I'll be back to chat more."

I took a breath. "Time to get to know Kelsey," I said.

"Are you nervous?"

"A little, but she seems nice."

"She is. Tammy's always had good things to say about her."

Minutes later, Kelsey walked toward us. She wasn't smiling, though I knew it had more to do with the grumpy old man who'd ruined her day and not us.

"Hi," she said. "It's so good to finally meet you more than just in passing, Wren. Sorry that I'm not in the best mood. Did Mom tell you what happened?"

"She did. And I heard your screams."

She blinked. "I thought the cooler was soundproof."

I slowly shook my head. "Sorry, it's not."

"Oh my *God*," she groaned.

"If it helps, it was funny."

"I'm sure I'll laugh about it later when Hugh's *not* in the building." She turned and looked at Tammy, who was still smoothing things over. "It was an honest mistake."

"He's like that with a lot of people," Henry said. "Especially doctors."

"I'm just adjusting to waitressing," Kelsey said. "I have a degree in communications, so this should be easy."

"I don't think there's anything easy about being a waitress," I said. "All the things you have to remember? No thanks."

"That's nice of you to say." Kelsey let out a breath and smiled. "How are you feeling?"

"Like a human again," I replied. "I needed that break."

"I saw a few episodes of the show you're on and am wondering how you're functioning at all. Seriously, you did not stop."

"She really didn't," Henry said.

"What's next?" Kelsey asked.

"I have no idea." I shrugged. "Today, I'll probably catch up with a few people. See if Mollie needs help with anything. But other than that, I have nothing. It's . . . weird. But I'm sure there's something out there."

"There're all those old storefronts," Kelsey said. "Maybe they could be something."

"Wait a second," Henry said. "I think Theo had something for you."

I blinked. "Who's Theo?"

"A guy who lives here," Henry replied. "He's been here longer than me, but he's not from here, as far as I know. Now that I think about it, there's not much I know about him at all."

"But he has a project?" I asked.

"I don't know anything about it. He's pretty tight-lipped about things."

"Mom!" Kelsey called. "Come here a sec!"

Tammy had just finished up with Hugh and was next to Kelsey in a heartbeat.

"I was coming back over here anyway. What do you need?"

"It's not for me," Kelsey said. "What do you know about Theo?"

"Quiet guy. Mid-thirties. Tattoos. He came in here once and got pancakes."

"He apparently might have a project for me," I added. "Do you know his number?"

"I know how to contact him. Everyone does. He works on a lot of odd jobs for the town. Plumbing. Yard work. Whatever. He fixed a tile here once."

"In theory," I began, "I could lure him out with a job and then get to know him, ask him about the project—"

"Or you could step outside." Tammy pointed at the window. "He's right there."

I turned. True to her word, there was a tall man with tattoos walking down the sidewalk.

"I'm catching him now!" I turned to Henry. "Can you get me a—"

"I know your whole order, buttercup. Go talk to Theo."

"Thanks. Love you."

"Love you too," he said as I nearly ran out the door.

"Good luck!" Kelsey called.

"Hey," I said as I stepped into Theo's line of sight. "Theo, right?"

"Uh, yeah. Wren, right?"

I nodded. "Henry told me you asked if I was staying, and I am. And that you might have something for me to work on."

"Oh," he said. "Yeah, I might have something. It'll take me a few months to get everything sorted, but it would be here on the square."

"In one of the super dusty abandoned shops, right?"

"Yeah. Hopefully it's not a problem."

I laughed. "Oh no. Trust me, I love old things. And if I get to stay in the town I love? It's even better. Why don't we go into the diner and you can tell me all about it?"

"I have a job to get to. Something about installing a lock on the supply closet in the bar. Can I talk to you after?"

"Yep. I can find plenty to do here in Strawberry Springs in the meantime." I thought of Mollie, who would need help with planning out a nursery. Or Cain, who could probably use help with the farm. Or I could help Henry with the town square. All of them sounded fun, but if no one needed anything, I could spend the day enjoying the library I worked on. "Here's my card. Call me when you're ready."

He nodded, eyes flicking to one of the storefronts and then to me. I turned to go back inside and enjoy the rest of my breakfast with my favorite people.

WREN

Two Months Later

Strawberry Springs Neighborhood Watch

Kerry Winsor: She's finally here! EVERYONE BETTER SAY WELCOME TO **@Wren Hackett** AND YOU BETTER NOT SAY SOMETHING WEIRD.

Comments:
Tammy Jane: Finally, something I can agree with Kerry on.
Kerry Winsor: We can't run her off this soon!
Marjorie Brown: Something weird.
Kerry Winsor: I hate you.
Hu Gh: Wait a second, isn't that the girl the library was named after? I thought she was dead.
Kerry Winsor: Hugh, we told you that was a secret. PLEASE get it together. Just this once! I'm deleting your comment before you ruin it.

"I know you wanted payback for covering your eyes when the library opened," I muttered. "And I'm sorry, but this is terrifying."

I had no idea where Mollie was taking me, and she wasn't the best guide.

"Sorry, sorry." She laughed. "This is hard to do while pregnant."

"I could cover my own eyes—"

"Nope," she said. "Don't you dare."

I sealed my mouth shut as we crossed the street. Finally, we came to a stop. "Can I see the surprise now?"

"That was terrifying to watch," a very familiar voice said.

"Henry? You're here?"

"I had to finish up the last bit of it, but yes. Obviously, I should have done the guiding."

Mollie laughed. "What's a surprise without a little bit of chaos?"

"Please save me," I said as I reached for Henry. His hand curled around mine.

"All right, I think she's suffered enough."

"You love to watch me suffer," I muttered in his direction.

"Only when it's me in control." His voice was low, but Mollie definitely heard it.

"All right, well, I know way too much, but also not enough." She laughed. "Now, without further ado . . . Here it is!"

Light rushed in. We were in front of the library, and my eyes traced over the brick for a second. "What am I looking at? Did something break?"

"No," Mollie said with another laugh. "Look down."

She gently guided my head to a newly installed sign. It was in warm wood tones, similar to the one in front of the town.

Underneath it was a garden of all different kinds of flowers. At first, I thought it was a cute way to show off the library, but then I read it.

"Mollie, what the—"

She bounced on her feet. "Surprise! I've been holding this in for *weeks*! I can't believe I made it!"

I turned back to the sign, tears springing into my eyes.

It didn't have much on it. Just the newly minted name of the building.

Wren Hackett Library.

"How did you two do this?" I managed.

"It wasn't all us," Henry said with a smile.

"There's technically a party tomorrow, but I figured you'd start crying." Mollie laughed as I wiped a tear. "And you'd want to spend tomorrow being happy."

"Still. *How?*"

"After your mom came, the whole town wanted you to know you're a part of things here. What better way than to name the library you fought for?"

"I—you could have gotten me a thank-you card."

Henry's lips pressed to my cheek. "We're a fan of bigger gestures here."

They were. I'd never been welcomed somewhere faster. After I returned, most people made sure to say hello to me every single morning or ask me how I was doing. There was no talk about the show or about my mom or Jude.

Only me.

"Guys," I said, "how am I supposed to work now? I'm gonna keep looking over here!"

"Should we have saved it for tomorrow?" Mollie asked.

I wiped at my eyes. "No."

"We'll still need to cover it," Henry reminded. "No one else knows we did this. You'll have to act surprised."

"Oh, great. Put my acting skills to the test." I would still be surprised every single day. Probably all of the days. "But thank you. This is . . . this is more than a thank you can even cover."

Mollie pulled me into a tight hug. "You deserve it."

When she pulled away, Henry checked his watch. "We should get this covered up. It's our usual diner time. Wanna join?"

"Unfortunately, I can't." She let out a sigh. "Doctor's appointment. Cain won't let me miss it."

"Didn't you just go?" I asked.

"I'm now on an every-other-week basis. The last trimester *sucks.*"

"Good luck," I said. "Tell Cain to chill."

She rolled her eyes. "He won't. He's such a panicked dad, but I can't fault him for it. He didn't get to see all of this with Eric."

"He better calm down for the next one," I said.

"I'll make him if he doesn't." She gave me a final hug before making her way to her car. "Have a nice breakfast!"

After Mollie was gone, we walked over to Center Point. This was our usual schedule, and my stomach rumbled already. Henry and I had worked out how to make a routine that worked for us both, and now I was so used to it that I didn't want to deviate, even if it was a special morning for multiple reasons.

"There you are," Tammy said with a smile. "You ready to knock some things down?"

My first Strawberry Springs project started today, and even though I was still emotional from the library, I was ready to do something else for the town.

"You know I am," I said.

"I already told her to wear a mask," Henry added. "I can't even imagine what all would be in there." He shuddered.

"It hasn't been closed for too much longer than the library. Only ten years longer, in fact."

"*Only* ten years?" Tammy asked with a raised brow. "Who knows what all's in there!"

"The older the better," I said with a smile. Tammy took us to our usual table, but didn't get to stay long since the diner was busy. Since the show finished airing, people flocked to the library, even though they weren't residents. Marjorie and Henrietta were planning multiple events that would benefit the other smaller towns in the region. Tammy had help, though she preferred to try to do anything else.

Kelsey trudged to our booth. Henry and I had a habit of sitting on the same side so we could be close, so she was able to flop on the old leather dramatically.

"*Why* does Mom have such a huge fucking menu?" she muttered.

In the two months since Kelsey had come to town, she and I had become good friends. Mollie even got along with her too, and we'd had some card game nights at the farmhouse that went late into the night. Mollie would always be my best friend, but it was nice to have my group expand. I even chatted with Grace and Jade whenever I went shopping. I felt like a part of something here, and I was.

"It's great for the customers."

"I'm just so bad at being a server. I forget things all the time, and Kerry already went to the Facebook group about it."

"We did all tell her that petty stuff was fine," Henry said. "Sorry, Kelsey."

"I just need to find something else," she said. "But I hate reading and planning things, and no one else is hiring right now."

"Give it a few months," I said. "I bet something'll come up."

She let out a sigh before sitting up abruptly. "I forgot to refill Hugh's coffee! Shit!"

She was gone before we could say anything else.

With Tammy running the show, our order came out smoothly. I wasn't trying to get in the middle of their drama, but I'd heard both sides of the story. Tammy was being far more patient than most moms, but it was clear Kelsey wasn't cut out for this.

I'd privately told Tammy to hold out as long as she could. Kelsey wasn't bad at face-to-face interactions. She could charm anyone. The issue was when she got overwhelmed, she would forget to refill drinks or grab a side of ranch.

She would be far better behind a counter, not providing full service.

We ate quickly since today was Henry's day to restock the clinic coffee from Food 'n' Things. We walked together up until I broke off at one of the older empty lots on the square.

Theo was waiting in front of it, tattooed arms crossed. He was looking over the space. I knew we wanted to get this done on as small of a budget as possible, so it would mostly be him, me, and one other person working on it.

"Ready?" I asked.

"Nope," he replied, "though I don't think I'll ever be."

"All we need is for—" I paused when another truck pulled in.

Dean Briggs was one of my best contractors when I worked in Nashville. I was happy he was willing to work with me after not being invited to work on the show.

And I'd heard he'd done great work on Violet and Charlie's house.

"Mornin'," he said as he stepped out of the truck with a coffee cup in his hand. Dean was a good man, but he also loved women. He was a playboy in every sense of the word, though I wouldn't lie and say I hadn't considered it many times before I met Henry. Once on a project in East Nashville, he'd gotten together with the owner. She was heartbroken when he didn't want anything else, yet still said the sex was the best she'd ever had.

Even back then, I didn't want to complicate things.

"Hi," Theo said. At first, I was worried about how few words he spoke, but according to everyone, he never had a lot to say.

"By the end of this, I'll be getting coffee from you." He tilted his cup. "This is from your sister store, isn't it?"

Theo eyed the cup. "It is, though I have a different name in mind. The manager I spoke to said she didn't have a problem with it."

"I bet it's gonna be the hot spot of the town," Dean said. I saw Theo's shoulders relax a bit. He'd been nervous about this since we first met to talk about this renovation, but Dean's easygoing nature seemed to calm most people. "Should we get started?"

"I have one thing before we do. You're staying in one of the hotels for a month, right?" I asked.

"It's a bit of a far drive, so yeah. Why?"

"You're from a small town, so you know how this works, right? Gossip, Facebook groups, and all that?"

"I don't care what people say about me. I'm only here for a month."

I groaned.

"He hasn't met the people here, has he?" Theo asked. "They'll *make* you care. Even if you don't want to."

"I doubt that."

"Okay," I said, getting in Dean's line of sight. "Ground rules. Can you follow them?"

"You sound like my mom."

"*Dean*. I live here. I want people to continue to trust me and those who I trust."

He let out a sigh. "Fine. What are the rules?"

I read them off each finger. "Don't add to the population. Don't subtract from the population. Stay out of the hospital, the newspaper, and most importantly, the Facebook group." I paused when I realized he wasn't looking at me. He was looking *behind me*. I turned, only to see Grace walking down the street. "You've gotta be kidding me."

Dean didn't budge until I snapped my fingers in front of him. "What?" he asked, blinking back into himself.

"New rule. Stay away from Grace."

"Why?"

"She's *not* a one-night stand type." I turned to Theo for confirmation. "Right?"

He shrugged. "How would I know? I don't date anyone."

"Ever?"

"Sounds like my kind of man," Dean added.

"Or have one-night stands."

Dean's eyes widened. "Then what do you do all the time?"

"Work." He said it like it was obvious.

"Okay, then I'm gonna make an assumption based on what I've seen. Grace is kind and sweet and doesn't need you breaking her heart."

"I don't break hearts," Dean said. "I make it clear from day one—"

"And yet they get mad when you leave. Just don't do that to Grace, okay?"

He let out a sigh, but nodded. "Fine. Now, can we get to work?"

"Yes, but Theo should get first dibs."

Dean blinked. "Wow. You've matured. Usually you're first in line."

"Theo's spent less time listening to us and more time looking at the door. I'm not heartless." I turned to Theo. "Go ahead. Crack it open."

"Technically, I've already seen it," he said. "But I appreciate the gesture."

"So have I," I replied. "It's the symbolism. Get with the program!" I pulled on my mask as Theo put up his hands in mock defense before going to the door. He took a second to put on his, and Dean did the same before the door opened.

Dust was *everywhere*, as well as old brick. What I could smell was thick and stale. "We'll definitely need to air it out," I said. "But this could really be something."

"Hopefully," Theo said.

"I see a wall that could come out." I grabbed a sledgehammer. "I call dibs!"

I ran over to it. Dean got to work on the electrical, groaning about how poorly it was done. As I swung the sledgehammer, I thought of all the other things I could work on in Strawberry Springs to make it beautiful. The STM grant seemed to be willing to pay it out. I could even renovate the apartment upstairs for Theo if he wanted to live here, or for someone else to rent.

I had plenty of work to do, but because I didn't need to fix myself, I was happy to do it.

It wasn't that I needed to distract myself with projects anymore. I didn't need to break things to fix them. I didn't need to do that to hide from what had hurt me. That was the thing about emotional wounds. There was no fixing it. I had to take them as they were and find *people* who helped me with them.

Not just old buildings.

THANK YOU

I've written a lot of these by now (I think I'm up to twelve?) yet every time I sit down to write one, I realize just how many people help me bring these novels together. As a child who grew up alone and lonely, it's hard for me to comprehend the life I've built for myself. I have so many incredible friends and family who make this possible, almost too many to name.

There was once a time where a story like this would have been impossible for me to write. Wren's struggle is my own in so many ways. And until now, I couldn't write a character who had been left by their mother like I had. It hurt far too much to. And now I have. So, for that, I have to thank my found mothers, Tina and Anne, who stepped in when they didn't have to. Who welcomed me with open arms without the need for a biological connection.

Who did what the woman who gave birth to me couldn't.

This novel is for you. Thank you for slowly teaching me that I could find love somewhere else. In so many ways, Tammy is based on you guys.

And as always, I have to thank the team that worked on this

with me. To Mae, the superstar PA and editor. To Kasey, who always is a rockstar copy editor, and to Summer, who creates the most beautiful covers I've ever seen. I can't do this without each and every one of you.

WANT MORE?

Get a bonus chapter about Henry and Wren here!

INTERESTED IN VIOLET AND CHARLIE'S STORY?

Read *To Make Matters Worse* here!

ABOUT THE AUTHOR

Elle Rivers writes fun romance books filled with real-world problems wrapped in beautiful, heartwarming happy endings. When not writing, she can be found speed-reading other authors' amazing romance novels, curling up next to any warm object she can find, or singing obnoxiously loud to Taylor Swift.

Elle was born and raised in Nashville, Tennessee, and she considers herself one of the few native Nashvillians who does not like country music. She has eight cats who fight for the spot on her lap and eight chickens who couldn't care less about her unless she is bringing them food. She lives with her romance hero of a husband who endlessly supports her writing endeavors, and her son, who is the biggest, but most adorable, distraction.